Best me

Harri

Inside The
Cuckoo's Nest

Harri Atkins

About the Author

Harri Atkins spent many years working in corporate training and development, before qualifying as a psychotherapist and setting up her practice. It was during a workshop as a trainee that she rediscovered her love of creative writing.

Harri lives in Surrey with her husband and two children. Inside the Cuckoo's Nest is her first novel, she is currently working on her second.

Acknowledgements

THE COMPLETION OF this book is the result of much kindness and support. Without it, it would have remained tucked away in the dusty corners of my imagination.

I am hugely grateful to Sarah Heyden, whose unwavering belief in this story and my writing was a much needed constant. Thank you for always giving me the words I needed to hear. For Gina Carribine, whose insistence meant quitting was never an option. The Posh Totty book club, your honesty and encouragement meant this book is certainly better for your critiques. For Debbie Dallas, you are the best of sounding boards! To Katie Stephens, your advice as an established author is much valued. For Rachael Peters, who tirelessly picked over the bones of the first drafts and helped create the form it now takes. My Editor Lauren Simpson, thank you for all your nips, tucks and advice, and for helping to keep the integrity of the story. Andy Fergus-Smith, your creative eye and determination really has captured the story so skilfully in the art work, thank you for all your hard work. Also a massive thank you to all the early readers of this book whose feedback made this all start to feel real.

Lastly, for my family, for readily accommodating the size this book has become in our lives. I love you all endlessly.

Dedication

To Darren, for always being brave enough to grab the tiger by the tail.

Part One: The Past

CHAPTER 1

Eight years ago

THE GYPSIES' CARAVANS were scattered across the arid land, glinting in the hazy summer sun while children burst with noise and energy, kicking dust up as they ran, their faces streaked with dirt and joy, playing hard and free. They ran swiftly between great lengths of washing hanging between the trucks and the caravans. They moved quickly, weaving in and out, just skimming the white sheets billowing in the warm air as it flowed across the common.

'When did they turn up?' Brendan O'Rourke asked as he drove by with his father and his brother Liam.

'Trash,' Brendan's father, Lester, grumbled.

'Vermin,' added his younger brother.

Brendan looked away to the road ahead, already beginning to feel irritated about returning to the family home, Lowlands, for the summer holidays. The only way he'd been able to get his parents to agree to support him through university was to work at the family's breaker's yard during his holidays. He hated it. The tedium of his summer days spent ripping cars apart. Long, dirty hours of hard work, hauling metal across a filthy yard, the grease and oil mixing with his sweat. After only a few days, Brendan was unable to shift the black oil from his hands, and his body had absorbed the acrid smell of engine fuel. This time around, at the end of his second year, he was even more resentful about coming back.

Several evenings later, his mother Lyla announced that their dogs needed walking. The dogs had lazed around all day, fighting over patches of shade, their tongues lolling and flanks heaving in an attempt to stay cool. Even though Brendan ached from his day's work, he was desperate for some space and he welcomed the opportunity to get out of the house; the thought of spending the evening with his family made him feel as though something was curdling in his stomach. As he left the house, his eldest brother Sean rushed to catch him up, and Brendan felt his heart sink. Ignoring him, he carried on walking through the woods towards the common. They carried on like this for a while, Sean appearing comfortable with the silence; eventually, a taste of the easiness that had once existed between them before Brendan moved away soon returned.

When they reached the common, the dogs raced off into the wide expanse of heather, scouring the undergrowth to pick up the scent of wild rabbits and foxes. The two brothers continued along the soft silvery sand of the wide track, which snaked out in front of them, marking the common's undulating terrain. Firs and birches still scorched from the previous summer's fires lined the path, their blackness stark against the bleached-out colours of the surrounding land. The dull moan of traffic on a far away road was all the brothers could hear as they walked along with no particular purpose.

Sean pulled his t-shirt off, wiped it across his forehead and tucked it into the back of his jeans. 'We should've taken the dogs to the lake. They could've done with a swim to cool down,' he said, as one of the dogs started to bark, frantically pawing the ground, which encouraged the other two dogs to bury their muzzles deep into the heather. 'They've found something!' he shouted, running towards them and calling them away. Brendan watched Sean grab a long stick and dig at the earth. When he held it high, a long dark shape, like a piece of old rope, hung twitching and jerking from it.

Sean carefully carried it towards Brendan, who now realised it was a snake. The symmetrical zigzag pattern that ran down its body, and the golden inverted 'V' across its neck, confirmed it was an adder. Its tongue flickered in and out as it tried to make sense of the unexpected danger. 'She's beautiful, look at how large she is,' Sean exclaimed, mesmerised.

Brendan was keen to keep his distance. 'How do you know it's a female?'

'Her markings,' Sean replied, 'they're so dark.'

'What do I do if it bites you Sean?' Brendan half joked.

'Suck out the poison and get me to hospital!' Sean laughed, waving the stick towards Brendan, who flinched.

Carefully, his eyes not wavering from the snake, Sean lowered the stick, and both brothers watched the creature slide towards the safety of the shrubs, until all that remained of its presence was the gentle sweeping curves it left in the sandy track. They stared after it for a short while, the dogs whimpering with the disappointment of losing their catch.

Turning to continue their walk, they were met with an unrecognisable sight, blurred by a heat shimmer, coming over the brow of the hill. As it grew nearer they could make out the rhythmic roll of a jet-black horse, ridden by a teenage girl, bareback, with a makeshift rope bridle. Her long dark hair swayed with the movement of the animal and her bare white arms and legs looked almost metallic against the evening sun. Just behind her they could see another rider, a young man, riding a piebald gelding and pulling along two reluctant horses. The piebald appeared frisky and, sensing this, the O'Rourke dogs barked defensively.

'Pikeys,' Sean mumbled. 'They're looking for somewhere for their horses to graze.'

The young man and his horse grew agitated. 'Call your dogs off, will ya?' he shouted. 'They're upsetting our horses' His skin was as pale as the girl's, and his hair as dark, his coal black eyes darting nervously between the horses and the dogs.

Brendan shouted for the dogs to calm and grabbing two of them, attached their leads. Reluctantly, Sean followed with his own dog. 'This is common land. You don't own it,' Sean shouted back, staring firmly at the young man. Brendan felt his heart sink; he could almost taste the tension between them. The girl leaned forward, whispering gently into her horse's ears as she stroked its neck. All the time she whispered, she kept her eyes fixed on Brendan.

'Neither do you,' retorted the young man angrily.

Brendan stepped forward. 'Excuse us, we're not used to coming across horses when we are out walking our dogs,' he interjected, diplomatically.

The young man eyed him suspiciously. Brendan secured his grip, pulling two of the dogs aside and gesturing for the riders to pass. The young man sized Brendan up before turning his attention to Sean. 'See, your man here talks some sense,' he told him.

Sean glanced sideways at Brendan, and reluctantly moved himself and his dog out of the way. The young man, kicking his horse on, urged them quickly past.

As the girl rode by, she glanced momentarily down at Brendan. The young man called out, 'Cassie, get a move on!' His voice rang with fresh irritation.

Brendan's eyes danced over the girl's impish face and her willowy frame, before finally resting on her long white legs and the upturned toes of her bare feet. There was something familiar about her, but he couldn't place what, or whether they had actually met before. Encouraging her horse to walk and making a sharp clicking noise with her tongue, she shimmied slowly past, leaving Brendan staring after her.

'Told you we should've gone to the lake,' Sean grumbled petulantly, as they released the dogs from their leads. Brendan ignored the comment and set off up the hill, but he couldn't resist turning around to take a last look at the gypsies. Catching sight of the Gypsy girl's long dark hair swaying hypnotically down her back and her long legs hanging freely, he willed her to turn around, one last time, and look at him – but she did not. Aware of Sean watching him, he called out his dog's name to mask his interest in the girl, and feigned a look of relief when Kaiser bounced across the heather towards him. He carried on purposefully, fixing his attention on the horseshoe prints left on the track, the only clue that his and the Gypsies' paths had crossed.

CHAPTER 2

Eight months ago

THE LAST THING Brendan wanted was to meet up with his friend James and his fiancée Tanya, across the other side of town on a hot, humid Friday night. His week had been full of back-to-back meetings, in which he'd outwardly placated angry clients, while inwardly cursing their greed and impatience with the lack of global economic stability. He had watched as his boss, Lance, capitulated to their demands and he was tired from dealing with the bloated, bruised egos of his colleagues. Fortunately, Brendan had managed to keep some distance and observed, with some amusement, the aftermath of these meetings – the sniping and snarling of his co-workers blaming each other and tying themselves up in their own vitriolic knots. He liked his bird's eye view and, at the end of what had grown into yet another tiresome day, appreciated Lance's comment: 'Christ, I think you're the only one keeping this department afloat.' Brendan had smiled his slow, cool smile, tugging gently at his cuffs as he left Lance's office. He also knew the comment was part loaded; Lance would love him to work over the weekend, trawling through the figures, weaving his algebraic magic to set the financial trends back on the right path, to save grace and face.

--»»═◎ ◎═««--

He had first met Lance seven years ago, in a pub; the type of establishment that managed to survive in the side streets of EC1 on the back of bankers' thirst for expensive reds and nostalgia – City boys loved indulging in a slice of East End atmosphere along with their overpriced Barolo and wild boar sausage and mash. Lance had been drunk – a glassy-eyed, swollen-lipped and claret-stained tooth kind of drunk – and his words knocked carelessly into one another when he spoke. But Brendan had kept quiet, letting the other graduates jostle for position, watching them fidget, eager with anticipation. He'd learnt from an early age that it was only worth speaking when he had something worth saying, and it was a strategy that had served him well; over the months, ten graduates became eight, then five until, finally, only two remained. Brendan had no intention of competing directly with his opponent and was quietly confident that Lance, who eyed him suspiciously but always sought his opinion, would make the right choice. Then, one morning, Brendan arrived to find his opponent gone and a bottle of Bollinger wrapped in cellophane and gold ribbon parked on his desk with the message: 'Well done, now let's get some fucking work done' written in neat cursive script.

--»»═◎ ◎═««--

An hour-and-a-half after leaving the ultra-modern, air-conditioned home of Bluestein PLC, the bank where Brendan worked, he managed to get across town, having waded through the rush hour's heavy tide and against the impending storm which, over the last couple of days, had begun slowly sucking the air from London's inhabitants. Its bruised clouds, pregnant with rain, pushed relentlessly downwards towards the horizon. He arrived at the pub to find it packed – drinkers had spilled messily across the pavement and into the road, and cyclists cursed as they swerved to miss them, causing the drivers of oncoming vehicles to sound their horns angrily. However, despite the crowds, Brendan had no trouble spotting James and Tanya. James's shot of floppy raven-black hair, and the way he repeatedly pushed it lazily from his eyes, made him stand out as the ex-public schoolboy he was; and Tanya – tall, elegant, beautiful Tanya – he could notice from a mile away, and when she spotted him she embraced him in a cloud of lemon scent and cool smooth skin.

James handed him a cold bottle of beer and Brendan waited for the buzz as it made its way to his empty stomach. He let James and Tanya do the talking, tuning in and out of their tight surroundings. Bodies were pressed unnaturally together and sharp words tossed over shoulders cut through his friends' conversation. Moving to hear better, he leaned towards Tanya and took another swig of beer. However, his attention rested some distance away, on a pretty face with large eyes, which flickered nervously. For a moment they settled moth-like upon him and he smiled, noticing the young woman smile shyly back before her eyes self-consciously took flight. He was amused by the effect he had had on her. He deliberately kept her in his sightline, along with the group of increasingly rowdy drinkers stood nearby.

Jemima Cavendish hated crowds. She hated how she always felt so insignificant surrounded by other people, as if her identity suddenly became invalidated, rendering her unrecognisable and uninteresting. Standing with her back jammed against the pub's full-length window, she hoped her friends would soon suggest moving on to somewhere else. She struggled to breathe in the heavy air of the tightly packed bar and she could hear a nearby group of men becoming increasingly raucous with alcohol-fuelled machismo, the type of behaviour that always backfires. Trying to locate the trouble, her eyes picked carefully through the thick lines of people. In doing so, she spotted a pair of cobalt blue eyes, which appeared to be pinned to her. Startled, she stared back and watched a well-rehearsed smile stretch across the man's face, leaving her stunned, unsure how to react, before her own eyes darted away like those of a frightened animal, back into the throng of hot bodies. She hadn't known how to respond – she never knew how to respond.

The noise from the group of men next to Brendan grew louder. One of them staggered backwards, knocking into him. Brendan glared hard into the drunk's bloodshot eyes. The group he was with jeered, and Brendan's finely-tuned instincts for trouble scanned them, taking in their intoxicated confidence. He could see their tempers straining to escape, struggling against the tightness of the crowd and the oppressive air. Brendan backed down.

Fights like these were behind him these days. Instead, he slowly released his scowl, turning his attention back to his own friends. He knew that the trouble would continue to rumble on, like the threatening storm above them. His own family had taught him that once anger was stirred, its release was always explosive. It was just a matter of time, he concluded, until this group found another mob to spar with or started fighting amongst themselves. Either way, he wasn't getting involved.

Jemima didn't hear the shouting at first or, rather, she heard it but made sense of it too late, just as the bodies slammed into her, squashing her further against the window before moving away, pushing aggressively back towards the trouble that had erupted. In this momentary lull, some of the drinkers dispersed before the crowd swept violently back in her direction.

The smash was deafening and the impact of the crowd piling on top of Jemima winded her. She felt herself fall, her world tipping upside down, as the window of the pub shattered under the pressure. She hit the floor with a thud and wanted to scream for help, but she needed air for this, and the last of it had just been forced from her lungs by the weight of bodies on top of her. She was trapped beneath them as they squirmed and snarled, like one massive beast, grinding against her bones, breathing their bitter breath into her face. She could hear other people's shouts, chairs scraping against the stone floor, and her friends screaming her name. She sensed there was something wrong with her forearm but as she tried to look, she felt something pulling firmly at her other arm. Turning in the direction of the pull, she saw a bright flash of blue, and then the face she had seen earlier came into view. The pull was quick and strong, and she found herself unsteadily back on her feet, before being yanked away.

Witnessing the violent scene, Brendan had reached out and grabbed Jemima, forcefully kicking someone out of the way as he did so. As soon as Jemima was on her feet, Brendan moved quickly, dragging her behind him. He felt her stumble but tightened his grip and forged on, determined to put some distance between them and the carnage that was spewing out of the pub, where shouts and screams mixed jarringly with the sound of an approaching siren. When they eventually stopped, his blue eyes turned to her, noticeably pausing on her arm before shifting to her face. She looked down and saw a large piece of glass jutting from her forearm. A steady trickle of blood flowed along her wrist, snaking towards her fingers and momentarily hanging from her fingertip before dropping to the pavement. Then the burning started, and rushing air filled her ears. She looked back at the blue eyes to find them gradually becoming shrouded in darkness, their brightness burning wildly at first, but receding into small sparks.

Later, inside the hospital, they'd waited ages to be seen. Jemima's friends kept telling Brendan it was okay to go, but when he looked at her he didn't seem so sure, so he stayed. He tried to keep some distance and sat sending texts. Only occasionally did he glance up at her, catching her eye and watching her cheeks flush with embarrassment at being caught looking at him. The triage nurse's voice was terse, causing Jemima to jump to attention when her name was called. He watched Jemima disappear towards the consulting room and suppressed a small smile when he noticed her glance back at him, her cheeks turning apple red once again.

In the early hours of Saturday morning she finally reappeared, smelling of iodine, with her arm stitched and bandaged, her eye swollen and the scratches on her face having been cleaned. She smiled apologetically, and he smiled back, before leading the way out of the hospital, hailing a cab and insisting on accompanying her and her friends home. When the cab pulled up, she hadn't wanted Brendan to leave; she hadn't wanted to say goodbye, but it was the only word that filled her mouth, and she stared at him not wanting the word to escape. While her friend Minnie hunted for their keys, Jemima dawdled on the front steps, looking back at him and, as the front door swung open, she gave him a small wave which he returned before the taxi indicated and drove away. Jemima realised that she desperately wanted to see Brendan again. However, in her experience, girls like her stood on the periphery of someone like Brendan's life. She was shy and often found herself looking on as more confident girls dazzled whoever had caught her eye, leaving them so blinded they never saw her patiently standing there. Girls like Jemima just didn't exist to men like Brendan O'Rourke.

So it was to her astonishment that she found him on her doorstep the next day, handing her a carrier bag containing a steak for her bruised eye. She took it graciously, looking a little bemused as she invited him into the kitchen, where Brendan placed the steak firmly over her brow bone and confidently announced, 'My Uncle Terry used to run a boxing club. He swore by steak to help with bruising.'

The steak was cold and clammy, and Jemima felt her stomach contract, but she sat rigidly, staring at the light blonde stubble on Brendan's chin and the gently pulsing skin on the side of his neck.

'I broke my arm when I was a kid,' he said, his voice coming from nowhere to fill the room. 'Fell out of a tree and ended up having it operated on. My brother got a right beating off my dad for it.' He smiled warmly, trying to get a better look at Jemima, to figure out what it was about her that had got under his skin so effectively. Memories from the previous evening still gnawed at him; images of holding her as she fainted, helplessly watching her slip away, and the taste of bitter, sharp, panic at the back of his throat. As she became heavier, his thoughts had quickened, something telling him he had to save her, that behind her serene expression she was being snatched away. These thoughts had refused to be soothed. He wanted to see her again and it went beyond checking she was all right.

Holding the steak firmly in place, and taking advantage of their closeness, he contemplated her elegant features – the slim straight nose, high cheek bones and oval face framed by long, light brown, wavy hair. She reminded him of the deer he sometimes caught a glimpse of in the woods at his family home, which darted gracefully between the trees, fearful of being caught.

Aware of his stare, Jemima coughed nervously. He removed the steak, wrapped it in the carrier bag, and told himself it was now or never. Leaning forward and without any warning he asked her out.

'Me?' she asked.

'You,' he replied, leaning closer, keeping his eyes fixed on hers.

She averted her gaze. *Don't just shrug*, she told herself, *look at him and say yes, just say it out loud.* What she did was compromise – she looked back at him and nodded.

Six days later Jemima found herself sat with Brendan in the garden of a fashionable bar, squeezed close together and verging on the edge of being too close for her. River cruise boats jostled noisily down the Thames as fellow drinkers kicked back against the pressures of the week and the sticky, sultry air of the impending storm which had still refused to break. Brendan did most of the talking, while Jemima sat mesmerised. Before long, she found herself caught up in the descriptions of his family; there were a lot of them, and she was keen to keep up, to grasp the details of his life.

'So you're the second eldest of six?' she asked.

'Yeah, there's Sean first, then me, then the twins Liam and Anne-Marie – they're three years younger than me – my kid brother Riley and, finally, Kelly, my little sister. I was ten when she was born.'

'I assume your family is Irish, judging from your names?'

He laughed. 'From way back. My gran's from Ireland, so my mum had a bit of a thing about us having Irish names – thought it fitted our surname better – but my dad's family are Londoners as far as I know.' He finished with a small sigh, then deliberately broadened his smile and turned his attention back to her. 'What about you?' he asked, enthusiastically.

Even in their short time together, Jemima had noticed how skilfully he could direct their conversation, and the direction it was now taking filled her with trepidation. 'Oh, I don't know,' she replied, looking down. She hated talking about herself, and her own small family seemed inadequate compared to the large one he had just described.

'What's your story Jemima Cavendish?' he continued, not put off by her bashfulness.

'I work as a PA at an art gallery in the West End,' she replied, 'and, well, there's not much else to tell really...'

'Your accent?' he probed. 'Where're you from?'

'Sussex and Hampshire. I went to school in Hampshire,' Jemima replied, and tentatively started telling him the story of her unusual upbringing; how she was raised by her two great-aunts after her mother had died when she was four years old. In the absence of a father or any other next of kin, her aunts had stepped in, dutifully providing an expensive education, a routine and a rare mix of love and sensibility. 'So you're lucky to have such a large family, I feel quite envious,' she finished, smiling shyly at him.

'I'd reserve your envy until you've met them,' he laughed tensely.

The comment landed awkwardly between them and Jemima stiffened. Uncertain of its meaning, and left unexplained, it protruded clumsily out of context. Brendan's eyes scanned her face, trying to read her reaction. She smiled diffidently, but his expression left her feeling scrutinised, and uncertain as to how their conversation had just dramatically evaporated. Jemima fixed her attention on a couple of fat spots of rain which had landed unannounced, wobbling slightly on top of the aluminium garden table. When a loud clap of thunder broke overhead she visibly jumped. As they stared up at the sky, large oily drops of rain landed on their faces. The brooding sky and bulging clouds were no longer able to carry the storm's burden and, at that moment, the clouds opened, as if a blade had sliced through their underbelly, causing them to dramatically spill their contents.

Jemima considered her bandaged arm and, as if reading her mind, Brendan leaned across the table and grabbed her hand. 'Quick!' he shouted pulling her upwards and they both started to run, along with the other drinkers, towards the door of the bar. Brendan glanced back at Jemima and caught her eyes wide with terror at being dragged toward the dense crowd. He searched for another way out, steering them both along a gravel path which led to the main road, filled with shops and bars, and other pedestrians running for cover.

As they ran, the rain forced them to squint, and soon they were soaked. For the second time that week, Jemima found herself being pulled behind Brendan as he turned sharply into a side road. Her shoes slipping on the wet pavement, she felt his grip tighten, making sure he still had hold of her, before darting into the doorway of an office block. Her hair hung like wet string around her face, and her chest heaved from the effort of trying to keep up with him. As she caught her breath, she watched him look out from beneath the doorway, and then quickly pull his head back under cover, shaking it free of rain.

'How's the arm?' he asked. Jemima touched the bandage; it appeared to be still intact. Involuntarily, she shivered. 'You cold?'

She nodded, wiping the wet hair from her face. Brendan folded his arms around her. His chin rested on the top of her head, forcing her face to nestle against his chest. The smell of his aftershave seemed to be revived by the rain and now, after days of heavy, close weather, she found she could breathe deeply again. He leaned back, his eyes scanning her face.

'This is going to last a while,' he said. Jemima turned her head to look at the rain; it fell in thick sheets, smashing noisily against the pavement. When she turned back, his face was closer to hers. 'Looks like we'll need to find something to do,' he added mischievously, lowering his face towards hers until their lips met. He felt warm and solid, and Jemima felt herself leaning into him as he pushed her backwards, until she was resting against the wall of the doorway. She felt a shift in him; there was an insistence about the way he was kissing her. She tried to pull back, but he had her wedged tightly between him and the wall. Raising her hands to his chest, she pushed against him, gently at first, then harder. He pulled his head back and looked at her quizzically.

'Sorry, it's my eye – it's sore,' she gasped, realising how pathetic her words sounded. Looking uncertain, he gently released her, leaned out of the doorway and flagged down a taxi.

CHAPTER 3

Eight years ago

BRENDAN LAY ON a scratchy woollen blanket, on the hard cold floor of an outbuilding in the woods of his family's home, naked and slowly smoking a cigarette. Cassie had her back to him. She was sat upright with her knees tucked under her chin and her arms wrapped tightly around her shins. Her back was bare, and she had pulled her long dark hair to one side so it tumbled over her shoulder. The pearlescent moonlight illuminated her milky white skin. Brendan reached across to her and ran a finger slowly over each protruding vertebrae.

'You've the sort of back that should be tattooed,' he said thoughtfully. 'Something Celtic, dark and brooding,' he continued, slowly releasing cigarette smoke.

Cassie turned to face him, her dark eyes taking him in before she swung herself around and sat astride him. He let his finger slowly glide down the side of her face and across her collarbone. She leaned forward, her hair spilling into his face. He carefully wiped it away.

'What about *"Brendan and Cassie Forever"* in a big love heart?' she asked, smiling playfully.

He smiled and continued to run his finger down her arm, across to her small left breast, and down the centre of her body, until he reached the place where her body joined his. His eyes followed his finger the whole way, taking in every detail of her, while he mulled over how to respond. He'd been meeting her each night in the rundown building in his family's woods, knowing that she would be waiting loyally for him at the end of each tedious day.

Since they had met on the common, it had seemed that everywhere he went he had caught glimpses of her until finally, one suffocatingly hot night, after the heat of the day had caused tempers to spark freely amongst him and his brothers, he had decided to escape the contentious atmosphere and take himself and his dog for a swim. It was there that she had appeared, nymph like, on the banks of the lake.

Moments before seeing her, he had dived into the lake. The cold water gripped his lungs, freezing them, making them feel as if they were curling in on themselves. He pushed up through the water, enjoying the sharp pain of its icy touch, hitting the barrier between pain and pleasure, then finally surging to the surface. His eyes were greeted with dappled light as he panted heavily, treading water and looking around for his dog. That was when he caught sight of the thin shape; his eyes took a while to adjust from the darkness to the shimmering light of the evening sun dancing across the lake's surface. He started to swim towards it and slowly made out the bare legs and feet, with patterns of light flickering up and down them. Her long dark hair fell over her shoulders to her waist. When he recognised the Gypsy girl, his interest sharpened. He swam closer until he could feel the bottom of the lake and stood, with the lake's surface reaching just below his hips. Droplets of water fell from his chin, and he could feel more inching down the side of his face.

'Hey,' he called. She looked startled, as if pulled suddenly from sleep. 'It's okay,' he called reassuringly, watching her face spread into a soft smile as she pushed her hair back to reveal her bony frame. 'Why don't you come in?' he continued, curious to see her reaction.

Her brow furrowed. Brendan held his breath, watching her closely as she gradually moved towards the edge of the lake, holding one foot over the edge to allow her pointed toes to just skim the water. He shivered, fighting the urge to wade over and pull her in. Instead, he continued to watch as she gracefully lowered herself into the water. The lake seemed to part as she glided through it, moving deliberately, her eyes never wavering from his stare. When she reached him, she let her hands rest on the surface of the lake while her hair floated around her like dark weeds. He looked down at her and resisted the urge to pull her to him and beneath the water where they could become entwined. Lightly, she ran her fingers across his chest, collecting the drops of water that clung to his skin and glistened like crystals in the evening light. He drew his breath in sharply, as her cold fingers traced the outline of his breastbone.

'You're as I saw you would be,' she marvelled.

He smiled back curiously, not sure what she meant and not really caring, but taking her touch as his cue to place his hands on her hips and pull her towards him. When their faces were just a few inches apart, they heard her name echoing around the lake. She jerked away from him. 'I have to go, they can't find me here with you,' she whispered, her voice tight with fear. As she turned to leave he grabbed her wrist.

'I want to see...' He never finished his sentence; she was pulling against his grip and speaking over him.

'I'll find you,' she stammered, freeing herself from him and disappearing into the woods.

⇢═◉ ◉═⇠

In a small town like Ashdowne, it was inevitable that the O'Rourkes and the Gypsies would soon run into each other. It happened outside the Queen's Arms Pub, where Brendan had been sat with his brothers in the garden when he spotted Cassie hanging around with a group of girls. They were wearing short skirts and tight tops, and teetered about in high heels which scraped crudely against the tarmac of the car park. A swish of dark hair caught his eye as Cassie turned around to face him. She stood motionless, her features darkened by the evening's shadows. Brendan studied her cautiously, wary of her reaction and desperately hoping that she wouldn't give away any clue about their involvement, which had grown quickly over the past few weeks. True to her word she had found him, appearing at the edge of the woods at Lowlands. And now, secretly, they met most nights, in the shabby outbuilding which housed the O'Rourke's broken furniture and other unwanted items.

Instinctively, Sean followed Brendan's gaze, letting his own eyes carefully study the group of girls, who were laughing raucously and busy chattering over one another.

'Fuck, that's all we need,' Sean murmured.

'What?' enquired Brendan.

'Trouble with that lot. The rest of them pikeys will be around somewhere,' Sean continued, sounding annoyed.

Liam and Riley turned to study the girls, holding their heads high and narrowing their eyes like pack dogs sniffing out their hunt. Liam turned back to face Brendan and Sean, looking put out that he had obviously missed something.

'We saw some pikeys the other night while we were walking the dogs. They got narked with us, started going on about our dogs frightening their horses,' Sean scoffed, while roughly grinding the stub of his cigarette into the ground with his heel.

Liam swung his head back to the girls again and scowled.

'Oi, don't make it any more obvious we're talking about them,' Sean whispered harshly.

'So what? They're scum,' Liam remarked.

'Oh great!' said Sean watching the group of Gypsies start to swell with young men. Bare-chested and proud, they gave off an air of trouble, pulling the atmosphere in the pub garden taut. The girls went silent as the young men made their way over to where the O'Rourkes sat. Brendan and his brothers got up, slowly and deliberately, refusing to be intimidated. From the corner of Brendan's eye, he caught Cassie's smile; it was a small and tantalising smile, acknowledging the connection between them. His eyes involuntarily flickered in her direction and he watched her momentarily, waiting to see if she was going to give anything away. Following Brendan's stare, Cassie's brother Jamie pushed himself in front of Brendan.

'Look who it is – it seems we keep meeting,' Jamie said sarcastically, not hiding the fact that he was enjoying the tension which crackled between them as he pushed out his chest, showing off his toned body. Brendan, however, held a height advantage and used this to stare the Gypsy down. 'I don't like the way yous were looking at me sister here,' Jamie continued, pointing towards Cassie. 'So, maybe we need to put a stop to bumping into yous,' Jamie continued.

Brendan looked back at Cassie; her brother was annoying him. He hated being told what to do and could feel himself wanting to fight, to release the tension in his muscles, to release the boredom of being back at Lowlands. Only a few years ago he thrived on situations like this, relishing the chance to fight alongside his brothers, to feel that oneness; bringing down gangs and watching them slink away into the night, with their shiny wounds and battered egos. However, time away from his family had nurtured a part of him that felt sickened by the damage they could cause, how mindless it all seemed.

While he contemplated this, his gaze ran down Cassie's body and he watched as she self-consciously wrapped her arms around herself. Realising the impact his stare was having on her, he turned back to Jamie, to find him staring furiously at him. Brendan now resigned himself to fighting. He glanced at Sean, who nodded sharply, acknowledging the inevitability; as with every dispute they found themselves in, it could only be settled with O'Rourke muscle.

'What the fuck is going on here?' Their father's coarse voice shattered the tension like a sledgehammer going through glass.

They all turned sharply to look at the tall, brawny man swaggering towards them, wielding a large spanner. When Lester got to them, he eyed his sons, suspiciously, before turning his attention to the Gypsies. 'You Jimmy's nephew?' Lester asked Jamie.

'I am... And you are?' Jamie replied, looking warily at Lester.

'Lester O'Rourke. Your uncle has got some business going on wiv me and me sons 'ere,' he said, gesturing to his boys, and watching as Jamie figured out what this meant to his family.

Jamie lowered his head belligerently. The Gypsies took this as a cue to back down and started to move aside. Leading the way, Sean and the O'Rourke brothers walked – pointedly – in single file through the centre of them. As he left, Brendan glanced at Cassie; she looked up at him nervously and a small, amused smile spread across his lips. Even though he could sense Jamie's rage reigniting, and his cool head telling him to walk away, he let his smile linger, leaving his adversary in no doubt that he was being mocked.

When Lester caught up with his sons, his lip curled viscously as he snarled, 'What the fuck was all that about?'

The brothers hung their heads in unison, as childhood memories of Lester's vicious temper resurfaced. Riley spoke up. 'They were just looking for trouble. We hadn't as much as said a word to 'em all night.'

'Yeah, they just started mouthing off at us about some girl,' Liam continued.

Lester looked suspiciously at Sean and Brendan, knowing that any trouble connected with girls would start with those two.

'We got no idea what they were talking about. We don't even know which one she is,' Sean said, shooting Liam a stern look.

Liam shuffled, reading the warning to keep quiet. Their father looked at each of them, trying to figure out if he could be bothered to dig around much more to find the truth; he knew they weren't being straight with him. He'd always believed that there's no smoke without fire – his own years of scrapping had taught him that. Finally, he leaned towards them and hissed: 'Them pikeys are delivering scrap to us in a few days and I don't want any fucking trouble with you lot and them. Understand?'

Under the heat of Lester's stare they each averted their eyes. Pleased with their compliance, Lester relaxed and laughed cruelly. 'After our business is done, you can do what the fuck you like with them!'

→►── ◄◄─

Straight after the trouble with the O'Rourke brothers at the Queen's Arms, Cassie's sister Nora followed Cassie into her trailer, shutting the door firmly behind her and peeking through the curtains to check that Jamie was not around.

'Was that him, the one you been dreaming of?' Nora asked, speaking in a harsh whisper and wishing now that, having met the O'Rourkes, Cassie had not shared the detail of these dreams with her. Cassie nodded and looked away. Nora grabbed her roughly by the shoulders, shaking her, so that Cassie was forced to look up into her older sister's worried eyes. 'You need to forget him,' she told her firmly.

'I can't,' replied Cassie meekly.

'Yes you can.'

'It's my gift Nora. Just like you have yours, this is mine. I know it's what's meant to happen,' Cassie said, shaking her sister free.

–⟴ ⟵–

At first, Cassie had found the dreams disturbing, leaving her with a heavy feeling that remained with her for the rest of the day. However, after so many of them, she was familiar with how they unfolded. She always found herself standing in the same garden, calling for someone. Calling a name that felt familiar and whole but which, like mist, quickly dispersed into the warm air. And later on, when she'd awoken, she could never remember it.

In her dream she looks around as she calls, noticing the garden in full bloom, a riot of colour, and bees buzzing industriously, their hum weaving through the lazy sounds of the summer day. Beneath her bare feet, the grass is soft and warm. Cassie is safe here; she knows that with an overriding sense, as strong as rock and as deep as the marrow in her bones. The shrubs rustle and then he appears, his white-blond hair ruffled, throwing her a broad smile. The unmistakable flash of his bright blue eyes, filled with delight at seeing her. The young child comes towards her, his arms outstretched, and she scoops him up, feeling his soft doughy arms encircling her as he buries his head into her neck. The smell of him is overwhelming – sugar and soap, sweet and clean. He giggles as she squeezes him, a soft tumbling laugh that he has only for her; because he is hers, all hers, and has been from the moment they shared the same heartbeat. He is the most precious thing in her life, and everything that has been good in it is wrapped up in him.

Her mood at this point always shifts. Her heart beats faster. She can feel another pair of eyes watching her, causing her skin to prickle. Turning towards the house, she sees the outline of a tall, slim man, but his features are hidden by the branches of the cherry tree. His shadow is cast across the lawn and, combined with the boughs of the cherry tree, his form takes on that of an angel, spreading its wings majestically, ready to encompass her and her child. Though his shape is unrecognisable, she realises she knows him; that they're connected in some way. She strains her eyes to catch a better look at him, the sun shining down on her and her child, illuminating them both, until a large black cloud blocks out the sun, stripping the garden of its glorious colour. When the sun returns, she knows he'll be gone. Because of these dreams, Cassie found herself nurturing every sign and putting the pieces together, quietly moulding her destiny. She found herself going about her daily chores but staring hard at the thin shadow jutting from her heels, waiting for his for wings to appear and unfold behind her; waiting to feel the arms she yearned for grab her and carry her high. At night when her head fell on her pillow, she imagined being caught by the angel sent to her. Feeling the soft warmth of his wings brush her skin, her stomach would lurch as he swept her away and took her somewhere she could finally be free; free to fly like the crows that encircled their camp.

⇢⫟ ⫟⇠

Nora could feel herself losing this argument. After all, how could she dissuade Cassie? These superstitions were ingrained in their psyche. Like their mother, Nora could foresee a person's death. Their mother had seen herself dying in childbirth but had welcomed the pregnancy right up until the end because that was how it was meant to be. Nora had then foreseen their father's death; the coroner's report said it was a heart attack but Nora knew he'd died from a broken heart. He just couldn't survive without their mother. 'It ain't always right Cass,' Nora told her, sounding desperate.

'When have you been wrong?' Cassie asked, and Nora looked away knowing that the timorous grip she had on the argument was indeed lost.

'You done the mirror?' Nora asked. Cassie nodded.

→═◉ ◉═←

Desperate to know who the man in her dreams would be to her, Cassie had taken to waiting until midnight to light a candle, holding it beneath her chin and staring into the small silver-framed mirror she had inherited from her mother. Then she waited for her reflection to change. She watched as her long dark hair melted away, her jaw became squarer, her nose slightly hooked. The features were still blurred but it was easy to see that they were changing into those of a man, and clear enough for her to know he wasn't one of them. At first the idea repulsed her but now, after nights of trying to see the face of the man in her dream, the anticipation washed away the distaste of his impurity at not being a Gypsy – a Roma. She would stare at the reflection as it continued to slowly morph, blond hair emerging, with long sweeping eyebrows, arched like a bird's wing. His long, sandy-coloured eyelashes parted, and from them spilled a bright blue, like a laser, filling the mirror.

⇥▭◯ ◯▭⇤

'But he's a Gorja!' Nora remarked, not hiding the disgust in her voice. 'Jamie will whip you for it,' she followed up desperately. But Cassie just stared back at her. She knew this was right. It felt right and all the signs she had been collecting about this meant it had to be right. 'I don't want to lose you,' Nora whispered, pulling Cassie close to her and holding her just a little too tightly.

⇥▭◯ ◯▭⇤

Lester's words, that the O'Rourke's could do what they wanted with the Gypsies once their business was finished, resonated with Brendan each time he met with Cassie, but he figured Lester hadn't meant what he was actually doing with her. He knew his family's prejudice against the Gypsies was only thinly veiled by its self-serving need to make a profit. By keeping her a secret, he wasn't just protecting her from them, he was also protecting himself.

Now, as he lay with Cassie in the outbuilding, he felt uncomfortable with the direction in which their conversation was heading. The idea of their names being immortalised in a tattoo made him uneasy; he'd been with enough women to know when they were getting in too deep, and too fast. 'Isn't there some nice Gypsy boy that should be in that tattoo heart?' he joked, referring to her suggestion of a tattoo and stubbing out his cigarette, hoping to deflect her attention from him.

'Not now, they won't want me. I won't be married to one of them now I've met you,' she stated defiantly.

'Married?' he exclaimed. 'You're a bit young to be talking about that aren't you?'

'I'm nearly fourteen!' she cried, indignantly.

Brendan sat up shocked, grasping her arms firmly. 'Nearly fourteen! Are you fucking serious?'

She looked down. 'I'm thirteen,' she mumbled.

'No, no! You're kidding me!' He pushed her away and staggered to his feet.

Staring up at him, his naked body towering above her, she struggled to read his expression, though it was clear from his stance that he wasn't happy. She stuck her impish chin out proudly, and stood to face him. 'I'm thirteen,' she said again, looking him straight in the eye.

Brendan ran his hands over his head; his face was contorted with shock – thirteen, only thirteen. The number ran through his mind, ricocheting around his skull. Cassie wrapped her thin arms around him, pulling her naked body tight against his. She leaned her head against his chest, pressing her ear against his heart. Slowly, he wrapped his arms around her; she was shivering, and he instinctively tightened his grip. He lowered his chin to the top of her head and breathed in her sweet, woody smell. It seemed as if only moments earlier he had been touching the firm, smooth flesh of a young woman, and now he was holding the fragile body of a child.

The following morning, the number thirteen was first thing that entered Brendan's mind, even before he had opened his eyes. He turned his thoughts over and over so that by lunchtime he was consumed by them. With his concentration so haunted by the night before, even the most basic of tasks he attempted went wrong. He could tell his brothers were getting irritated with him; Liam, as vocal as ever, couldn't hide his annoyance at having to sort out Brendan's mistakes. Sean was more gentle and jibed him, joking that he must be in love, at which point Brendan felt nauseous and left the workshop to get some fresh air.

Throwing himself down on a pile of tyres, he drew heavily on a cigarette, holding his head in his hands, trying to gather his thoughts. There was only one thing to do, he concluded. He stubbed out his cigarette and set off in search of his father to discuss leaving Lowlands early. He couldn't see a clean break happening with Cassie unless he left. He resolved, there and then, that whatever it was that they had between them, it had to stop right away.

But that evening, wherever he went in the house, he thought he saw her outside, darting from tree to tree, following him from inside the woods. He snuck into the dining room, took a bottle of vodka, and disappeared up to his room. Looking out of the window he swigged steadily from the bottle, staring hard into the darkness, until he thought he saw a flash of movement between two trees. He leaned closer to the window, not sure if he was somehow willing her presence to be near or wanting to repel it.

Deciding that it must have been his imagination, he drew the curtains roughly and went over to his bed. He placed the vodka down heavily on his bedside cabinet and rolled onto the mattress. Running his hands through his hair, he sighed deeply. He hated this feeling; a restlessness that bored into his spine and spread along his central nervous system, setting his nerves alight like a flame to a line of petrol. He had never felt so charged and exhausted at the same time.

'For fuck's sake,' he growled, taking another large swig of the vodka and waiting for the burn to subside. He lost count of how long he must have been lying there, with the stark electric light bearing down on him. He sat upright, swung his legs to the floor, and walked out of his bedroom, quickly and quietly heading downstairs.

An abundance of thoughts raged in his head, colliding, shouting for him to stop and turn around, but something inside him was driving him forward, in long deliberate strides. He crossed the backyard and headed out towards the woods. Consumed by a sense of urgency, he quickly lit a cigarette and dragged hard on it, disappearing into the black woods, roughly pushing branches out of his way. Nothing was going to stop him. *This is what madness is*, he thought to himself.

He got all the way to the outbuilding without any sighting of Cassie. He swung the door open forcefully and pulled out his lighter, the small flickering flame lighting up just far enough for him to see the makeshift bed neatly laid out. Next to it was the old tobacco tin he used for an ashtray and, next to that, a half-empty bottle of cheap whiskey, but no Cassie; *maybe that's a good thing* he told himself, extinguishing the flame. He turned to leave, not quite sure how he felt about her not being there, and started to walk back to the house.

'You decided to come after all then?' a soft voice sounded from the darkness. Brendan swung around, immediately recognising the thin, bony silhouette.

'Yes,' he replied.

In a few quick strides he was in front of her, holding her face with one hand, and pulling the door of the outbuilding open with the other. He kissed her roughly, his teeth grinding against hers, his mouth forcing her jaw to open as he pushed her backwards into the grubby building towards the grey makeshift bed. His moves were fast and deliberate; his hands ran through her hair and moved down her neck, his thumbs tightening menacingly against the gentle pulse at the base of her throat. He had an overwhelming urge to put an end to this life that had infected him and had drew him back here.

As she succumbed, his conscience battled to get the better of him. *You shouldn't be here. She is just a child.* Brendan felt a sense of shame so powerful that he thought it might crush him. But the forces that had driven him here were stronger than his conscience. This was all her fault, not his; she had been here, in the blackness of the night, weaving her spells, drawing him out.

His breathing became deeper and faster, and his hands ripped first at her clothes, then his. Angrily, he tugged her arms up above her head and looked down at her naked body, taking in her protruding pelvic bones, her concave stomach and her ribs, clearly visible through her paper-white skin. He looked at her small, neat thirteen-year-old breasts and never despised or wanted anything more in his life. Lastly, he looked into her eyes and saw the hunger in them. He pushed himself into her so hard he was sure she would break, and released a sound so loud and deep that it caused the crows resting in the woods outside to suddenly take flight. It was a sound of pure release; a release from his agony over how something so wrong could be so good.

CHAPTER 4

Eight months ago

LYING BACK AGAINST the checked rug, Jemima's body was warmed by the sun and the wine flowing through her veins. She was surrounded by noises – laughing, shouting, a group nearby playing Frisbee, and the background noise of traffic humming away. She lazily opened one eye and the sun flooded her vision before Brendan came into view. He was smiling his warm, confident smile. He lowered his head, kissed her gently and rested his forehead on hers.

'You taste good,' he whispered.

The effect of the wine and sun, mixed with Brendan and the ease with which he could shift back and forth from sincerity to mischief, left her feeling overwhelmed. She could so easily lose herself in him and was fearful that if she allowed herself to, she would never be able to return. As he loosened his tie – he was still in his work clothes – Jemima was reminded that she hadn't expected him to look like this; so smart and so handsome.

They had arranged for him to collect her from work and he'd casually walked into the gallery wearing an expensive tailored suit. She had gasped when she saw him; fortunately, she had been out of sight. Juliette, her boss Pablo's wife, had sidled up to her. 'You are one lucky girl,' she said, winking at Jemima who instantly blushed. Juliette smirked. 'Go on, finish early – I'll cover it with Pablo. Go.' She'd flapped her hands at Jemima, playfully shooing her away.

Jemima had grabbed her things, her shoes tapping loudly as she descended the metal stairs. Brendan swung around and his face had broken into a wide smile – he was unable to hide his pleasure at seeing her. She'd self-consciously smiled back and headed straight for the door. As they both reached it, a small cheer broke out around the gallery and they turned to see a small gathering of faces leaning over the balcony. Pablo's face was flushed with excitement. He'd thrown his arms into the air and passionately exclaimed: 'Enjoy this fabulous night, in this fabulous city. But most importantly enjoy this man, go make good love – we hear all about it tomorrow, eh?' His thick Brazilian accent had curled around the words, making them sound luxurious but, unfortunately for Jemima, perfectly coherent.

'Christ,' Jemima had mumbled under her breath.

'You take good care of her young man, you hear,' Pablo had continued. 'And, I mean in every way.' Pablo's face was serious, his stare fixed on Brendan. Jemima had thrown open the door and made a quick exit, wishing those last few moments could be erased from her life.

'I am so sorry,' Jemima had finally managed, walking briskly, not sure where she was heading, but wanting to get as far away from the gallery as possible. Brendan caught her arm.

'Hey, they care about you, that's all' he said. 'They wouldn't have done that, if they didn't.'

She had stared at her feet, struggling to fight back her tears, biting her lip hard to stop them spilling down her cheeks. It had been agonising waiting for him to call after their first date, and the countdown to this day had been unbearable. She hadn't been able to settle – every time the phone rang or someone had come into the gallery she'd nearly climbed out of her skin. She had badly wanted to see him and, now he was here, all she seemed capable of was dissolving into tears.

'I didn't know you were going to come into the gallery,' she said.

'I'm sorry. I didn't think it would be a problem.'

'No, no, it isn't. It's just that I hadn't prepared them, or you for that matter. And Pablo can be a bit... Pablo,' she replied, stumbling over her words. If truth be told, she had not been prepared for Brendan herself, in his dark suit, and the easy way he'd stood looking at the art. Determinedly, she fixed her eyes on a piece of gum stuck to the pavement. Brendan placed his hand on her chin and tilted her head up, gently forcing her to look at him.

'I will do exactly as Pablo says. I will take good care of you,' he told her. His words had slowly sunk in, including Pablo's connotations, and she'd struggled to smile, but she had let him hold her and lead her out into the evening.

⇢▬◉ ◉▬◟⇠

Now, lying on the soft rug with the spiky grass scratching the backs of her bare legs, she felt foolish for her earlier behaviour.

Brendan smelt clean and fresh as he bent over her and she could feel the warmth of his skin brushing against hers. He kept on kissing her, his hand sliding from where it rested on her hip, down her thigh to the edge of her skirt and slipping underneath. Becoming aware of his hand gliding back up her leg, she placed her hand on top of his to stop it. When she took her hand away, his hand moved again, edging higher. Again she stopped it and this time pulled her head back to look at him. His eyes were half open, that flash of blue, intensely bright, sizing her up. Eventually, he moved his lips to her neck. As soon as her hand slipped away from his, it moved quickly up her thigh and his fingers slid inside her knickers. Her hand immediately grasped his, and with her other hand she pushed against his chest. He broke away, staring at her, his eyes dancing with devilment. He unravelled his fingers and pulled his hand back down along her thigh to her knee. Raising his eyebrows to check she was happy with this he lowered his head back to her neck.

When he moved his mouth to hers and expelled a soft, low moan, she felt as if she had been pulled under water, dragged down by the sheer force of him. As she struggled to breathe, his hand had slid furtively back up her thigh and his long fingers gently hooked themselves around the edge of her knickers once more. Feeling them slowly sliding down her leg, she opened her mouth to complain but he kissed her harder. Gulping for air, she shoved hard against his shoulders. He released her, panting slightly, and his face fell into a confused frown when he spotted the panic in her eyes.

'Don't tell me you've never lost your knickers in the park before?' he joked. With that she hit him hard on his chest. He fell backwards with a thud, rasping and clutching his chest.

'Oh god. I'm sorry, are you okay?' She leaned over him, looking desperate. He pulled her onto him, holding her firmly around her waist, her mouth hung open with surprise, and he laughed. Shocked at being tricked, she felt angry and humiliated. 'I thought I had hurt you,' she hissed. 'Let me go.' She tried kicking her legs to help free herself.

'You did,' he exclaimed. 'That's quite a punch you've got there. Have you any idea how sexy that makes you?' he added, playfully.

'Let go of me. Now,' she growled.

His face changed, the playful smile disappeared. He released his hold, half expecting her to storm off. Instead, she sat with her back to him, pulling her knees up to her chin and staring straight ahead. They sat mulling over what had just happened, both sulking slightly. Finally, Brendan sat up and tentatively kissed her shoulder. She looked back at him and he cupped her face and breathed deeply, looking like he was trying hard to find the right words. Eventually, he moved his head back so he could take in her whole expression. 'Jem, every time I touch you, you seem so...' He looked at her intently. 'You seem scared of me. Is that it – do I scare you?'

'A bit,' she said, and saw his brow crease. 'It's just that I'm not used to this... to someone like you,' she ventured.

He looked hurt. 'Do you think this is all I'm after?' he asked.

'Isn't it?' she replied.

'No. Of course I want you, but I meant what I said earlier, about taking care of you,' he said and she looked away. He pulled her face back to him, guiding it with his finger. 'Jem, is it so bad to be wanted?' he asked.

She considered her one serious relationship and the handful of dates she had been on. 'I wouldn't know,' she replied innocently.

CHAPTER 5

Eight years ago

BRENDAN SOMEHOW MANAGED to convince his father to let him leave two weeks earlier than they had arranged, so he could fly out to meet some friends in Greece. Lester had complained and criticised him for being lazy and turning soft, but the insults were expected, and preferable to the increasing sense of madness Brendan had started to feel while at Lowlands. Relieved, he resolved not to meet with Cassie again, but still found himself creeping out to the woods to be with her. The insanity of their most recent encounter had now intensified, like an addiction. The more pliable Cassie became, desperate to hold onto him, the rougher he became with her. Since that night, his memories of her and the way he had treated her had turned into a tight ball of revulsion, calcifying inside him.

Finally, the time came for him to leave and when he told Cassie she didn't utter a word. Instead she rolled over, turning her back to him, and gazed out of the high windows as if absorbed by the moon. In a rare moment of tenderness between them, Brendan held her close, and buried his head into her neck. He could feel the dainty tapping of her heart beating against his arm as he lay there and he took in her rhythm for a while before slowly getting dressed in silence. When he got to the door he looked back at her, lying on her side, still staring at the moon. He lowered his head and left.

⇥▭ ▭⇤

Greece provided Brendan with some welcome respite from the events of summer. His friend James's parents owned the villa where they stayed. It was at the end of a gravel lane, surrounded by ancient, twisted olive groves and neat rows of lemon and walnut trees. Brilliant pink and scarlet bougainvillea tumbled down its walls, the slightest breeze catching the blossoms and tossing them into the large, kidney-shaped swimming pool. Its peaceful location provided some calm to Brendan's days, which contrasted with the buzz and thump of the nightlife a short distance away. His time soon fell into a routine of days spent lounging by the pool while recovering from a cocktail of alcohol and drugs from the night before. In the mornings, his head filled with blurred images of girls, singing and dancing, wrapping themselves around him. These images merged into ones of tangled bodies stumbling along cobbled streets, the opalescent moon lighting their way to the beach; the warm sand underfoot, carelessly discarded clothes, then the gentle lapping of the sea licking at his body, the ocean gently pulling him in, deeper and deeper, slowly cleansing him. The touch of new flesh pushed the memory of Cassie further out to sea.

On his return to Lowlands, he stayed away from the woods but he still felt Cassie's stare, burning into his back, noticing his every move, so it came as a great relief when it was time to return to university. Throwing the last of his belongings into the truck, he said his farewells and jumped in alongside Riley and Sean.

He made small talk as they drove to avoid glancing into the woods. Before long they were on the main road to the station and passing the Gypsy camp. Despite his efforts not to stare, he was drawn towards the signs they had put up in protest at being told to move on. The atmosphere had changed around the site since he'd been away; the sound of children's laughter had been replaced by dogs snapping at each other's heels, and the groups of gossiping women were nowhere to be seen.

'Looks like they'll be gone soon,' Sean commented casually.

Brendan ignored the comment, choosing to keep his eyes fixed firmly on the road and, before long, when he glanced in the wing mirror, the site had shrunk to a small speck in the distance and he felt a heaviness lift from him.

Cassie had watched him when he returned from his holiday, from behind the trees in the woods. The O'Rourke's dogs no longer barked at her, having become used to her presence. She moved deftly from tree to tree, catching glimpses of his tanned skin and sun-bleached hair. Brendan stood out clearly from the others. He was taller than Liam and slimmer than Sean; his shoulders we broader than Riley's and his swagger was less pronounced and more fluid than his father's. She even heard him a couple of times, calling his dog; Kaiser would stand looking in her direction, confused and torn between them, but in the end always loyally returning to Brendan.

She was there every night in the outbuilding, with the blankets straightened and his drink and cigarettes waiting for him, but he never came. She had watched him pack his things into the truck and saw him kiss his mother and sisters goodbye. He'd had a brief conversation with his father, given Liam a quick slap on the back and then jumped into the truck, seemingly carefree. As they rolled down the driveway she had stared intently at him and noticed how he never once glanced towards the woods, never once looked back. A lump gathered in her throat, creating a dull ache, and her eyes began to burn. *I will not cry*, she told herself over and over, *I will not cry*.

Nearing the end of his autumn term, Brendan's mother arrived at his flat in London, early and unexpected. He opened the door wearing just his loose, grey track pants, rubbing sleep from his eyes and rueing the amount he had drunk the night before. He had thought the buzzing on the intercom was James, having forgotten his keys again. So when he threw open the door in annoyance it took him a couple of seconds before he realised it was actually his mother, Lyla, standing there. 'Mum!' he exclaimed, stunned.

'You going to invite me in?' she asked flatly. He moved aside and she followed him in, her eyes darting around taking in the messy evidence of her son's bachelor life. In the kitchen she lit up a cigarette, placing the packet on the counter and indicating to Brendan to help himself.

'No thanks, not yet. Heavy night,' he smiled sheepishly while switching on the kettle.

She raised her eyebrows and breathed out her cigarette smoke. 'I'm here to talk to you about Cassie,' she said coolly.

'Cassie?'

'Don't you dare come the innocent with me Brendan O'Rourke,' she hissed.

'So you know.'

She stared accusingly at him, her blue eyes ice cold. He hated this look of hers.

'I'm sorry,' he mumbled.

'We found her, beaten up; she had run away from her family and was hiding in our outbuilding.' She paused, eyeing him up and down, noticing him grimace. 'She had been there for days. Riley had been trying to care for her, took her some food – your own kid brother, showing her more kindness than you did. It was Liam that brought her home. God, what a sight. Skin and bone, black and blue.' She paused, taking a long drag on her cigarette. 'A child Brendan, just a child. Jesus, what were you thinking?'

'I didn't...' He stopped himself. 'I don't know,' he muttered, looking away.

'Look at me!' she shouted and, compliantly, Brendan turned to face her. Lyla stared at him. Speaking more calmly she said: 'She was just a small, frightened little girl... carrying your baby.'

Brendan froze. 'What?! I didn't know, I swear to you I didn't know!'

'She lost it, the baby, a week ago. Poor thing never stood a chance. She was in no fit state to carry a baby full term so it's probably for the best,' Lyla said with a sigh.

'I didn't know she was pregnant, truly I didn't,' he implored, but his mother just raised her eyebrows in response. 'And I didn't know how young she was, not at first,' he continued. 'Then when

I found out, I lost my head over it all. She was always there, hanging around...' He trailed off, sensing a new outburst.

'Brendan, how old did you think she was, really? Surely you aren't telling me that you thought she was your age?'

'No, no, younger, of course. Seventeen, sixteen perhaps,' he replied. If he had been brave enough he might have added fifteen; he would have been okay with that. It still felt somehow acceptable. Fourteen, however, was moving into entirely different territory and thirteen seemed plain wrong. Perverse and dirty. With hindsight he could see that he should have realised how young she might be. He should have asked her the question before their very first kiss then walked away because, even if she had lied to him, he knew, really, deep down, that she was still a child. There was something Lolita-like about her, something telling in the way she gazed up at him, the lack of conversation between them and her eagerness to please. He had enjoyed it so much – the simplicity of her, the pedestal on which she had placed him. It had given him an overwhelming sense of power, something he never felt when surrounded by his family. And now? What a mess. A lost baby – his baby – a part of him gone forever before he had even had a chance to put things right. Guilt spread over him like a fungus, its spores feeling their way underneath his skin, working their way into his veins until it pulsed through him.

'I'm so sorry,' he finally managed, hanging his head in shame. His mother sighed loudly, leaving him stumbling on. 'I never beat her. I never hurt her that way, I swear to you,' he begged, still not able to look at her.

'Her family beat her. It was her brother most likely, though she won't say and they won't tell us. They got moved on, just after we found her, so we will never really know what happened. But it's their way Brendan. In their eyes she's ruined.'

Though his mother's tone had softened, the accusation stung. 'Where is she now?' he asked tentatively.

'We've taken her in. What choice did we have? It was the right thing to do, but make no mistake about it Brendan, they know it was one of us who disgraced her. Your father is raging with you – their businesses and ours are good for each other and he hates the gun being turned on him. We've had to earn their trust again, and it's been hard,' she said pointedly before letting out another long sigh. 'She's not so bad. Clean and tidy, helpful around the house… and Liam's taken quite a shine to her actually.' Now it was his mother's turn to look away.

'Liam?' Brendan exclaimed.

'Yeah, she makes him quite happy,' Lyla added, glancing sideways at him and stubbing out her cigarette. 'I know he doesn't have your looks or charm Brendan, but maybe they are more of a curse than a blessing eh?'

'What about Cassie, how is she now?' he asked, ignoring her jibe.

'Quiet, don't say a lot. She knows she can stay with us as long as she wants and I guess she ain't got no place to go, so it suits her.'

Brendan finished making their tea while he digested what his mother had told him. It felt like gulping down bitter medicine.

'It's all been such a fucking mess, so you best not come back for Christmas. Best put some space between you and all this. Let your father calm down, give Liam and Cassie a chance, eh? Liam will never forgive you if you turn her head again. You know how he is with you, always seen himself as second fiddle.'

'Yeah, fine, makes sense.'

'I know it'll be hard. What will you do?'

Will it be hard? He pondered. He actually felt relieved not to have to go back and face them all, knowing what a cruel mess he had made of things. He was the one with the intellect, the one who was going to make something of himself. Yet out of all of them he had got it so wrong while his family, for whom he felt so much contempt – with their narrow minds and ossified ways – had sorted all this out. While he had done what? Run away to Greece to drink and have fun, then back to London, putting distance between him and what had gone on with Cassie. 'I'll be fine Mum, I'll go to a friend's or something,' he replied, watching his mother weighing him up. She hugged him tightly.

'You have caused me nothing but grief from the moment I fell pregnant with you,' she laughed sadly.

CHAPTER 6

Thirty years ago

LESTER HAD NEEDED to lie low, get out of town and lose himself for a couple of months. He left London with a holdall stuffed with clothes and loose bank notes. The raid on Stevie Adams's garage had gone to plan, but he knew that he would be on Stevie's list to be checked out over it. So Lester and his accomplices had split the cash and hit the road. Bruno and Alec were heading for the ferry to France; Lester had originally planned to go with them, however, when they pulled over to fill up the old Ford Escort, Lester changed his mind. The idea of France – the language, the food, the foreignness of it all – turned his stomach. He also had enough sense to figure out that the five thousand pounds they had each fled with wasn't going to last them too long. So he climbed out of the car, grabbed his bag and started to walk towards the nearest town.

The November evening light quickly fell from the sky and Lester found himself in the centre of a village, his leather jacket and hair damp from the persistent drizzle and his stomach starting to complain from lack of food. The Queen's Arms public house stood in front of him, its windows glowing invitingly.

Lyla hadn't looked up when Lester entered, despite the pub falling silent and the other inhabitants eyeing the tall stranger suspiciously. She carried on reading her magazine, perched on a bar stool. As he neared, she felt his presence and, robotically, she slid off the stool, dropped her magazine on the bar and turned to serve him. They both stared at each other. Coldly, Lyla asked Lester what he wanted and he took his time replying. He spoke deliberately, letting the words hang between them, his eyes taking their time over her.

⊸▭▭ ▭▭⊷

Lyla could have any man she wanted in Ashdowne and its ten-mile radius, and she was well aware of the fact. The problem was she didn't want any of them. The indifference she held for them showed in the way she walked, her blonde hair with its large curls bouncing along behind her. Her back stiff with pride and her eyes full of contempt. She knew deep inside that she would know when the right man came along, and, as she looked into Lester's bright blue eyes, she knew the right man was now stood in front of her; not that she had any immediate plans to let him know that.

Lester liked the way Lyla stayed so cool around him, even after she had served him his meal and he'd asked if there were any rooms available in the pub to rent. By the fourth day of his stay he was becoming used to her one-word answers and the way that she stared at him blankly with her ice-blue eyes, and he decided to change the rules to this game they seemed to be playing.

As Lyla left the pub at the end of her shift, she felt two strong hands grab her waist and pull her backwards against the wall. The street light illuminated Lester's face, his strong jaw and sandy-blond hair. A slight smile played across his lips and his eyes flicked back and forth, trying to figure out her next move. She stared at him, not reacting, continuing instead this game of wills. He pushed himself against her and she watched his breath turn to white curls from the cold air as he breathed heavily. She allowed his hands to run over her, but when he tried to kiss her she turned her head away sharply and he stopped.

'My boyfriend's picking me up, so you better get your hands off me,' she stated coolly.

Lester scoffed. 'You ain't got a boyfriend.'

'Says who?'

'Where's he been then, these last few nights?'

'He's been away. He's in the army.'

'You're some squaddie's tart?'

'Better than some crook's tart,' she retorted and watched his face harden. 'I've been in your room, seen your bag and the cash. You ought to be more careful, with all those used notes lying around.'

'I cashed some bonds in,' he replied flatly.

She laughed. 'You turn up here, no place to stay, with a bag full of money – you're a lousy liar Lester O'Rourke.'

'So are you – there's no boyfriend. There's just you and me.'

Lyla's face broke into a wicked smile. 'Oh, and a bag full of cash.'

Lester stared at her hard before he kissed her; he wanted to get a really good look at the woman who dared speak to him like this. He felt as if she had thrust her hand through his chest and tightened her ice-cold fingers around his heart. It no longer beat under his command; it responded only to her grasp and he knew that she was well aware of this. He had never wanted anyone the way he wanted Lyla Shanly that night.

Getting Lester O'Rourke had been easy; far easier, in fact, than Lyla had imagined. Keeping him, though, was proving more difficult. She wasn't blind to the way other women looked at him – some threw shy glances from beneath their eyelashes, while others were more brazen, laughing loudly around him, touching him and leaving their hands resting on him that little bit too long.

Mandy Chinner was one of these women. Lyla stood behind the bar watching Mandy flirt with Lester, flicking her streaked blonde hair and shifting her weight from one leg to the other, gradually moving closer to him in the process. Lyla was also aware that Lester did nothing to discourage Mandy. However hard she glared at them both, they seemed able to dodge her stare; the more Mandy drank, the louder she became, throwing her head back and laughing throatily at something Lester had told her. Lyla saw Lester's hand slip around her waist; he looked amused with Mandy and she had his full attention. Lyla slammed the till shut and strode over, grabbing the empty glasses off the bar in front of them.

'Same again Lyla,' Lester said calmly.

'She's had enough, and so have you,' Lyla snapped. Lester eyed her carefully. Mandy protested but Lyla ignored her. Instead, she continued to look at Lester, daring him to respond.

'Come on, we'll get a drink some place else,' he said to Mandy, sliding off his bar stool and glaring at Lyla. A smug smile spread across Mandy's face as she grabbed her bag and looped her arm around him.

'You leave here with her and we're through,' Lyla hissed, trying to keep her voice steady and contain the tears which had started to sting the corners of her eyes.

Lester leaned towards her. Dropping his voice, he said, 'You don't tell me what to do.' Then left with Mandy, shooting Lyla one last self-satisfied look before disappearing through the door.

Mandy led Lester into an alleyway that ran from the shops to a car park. He looked at her, with her back pressed against the wall and her eyes filled with anticipation as she curled a long piece of hair around her index finger. As he stared, he noticed that everything about her – her skin tone, her hair colour, her nails – was false.

When Mandy pulled him towards her, he felt resigned to what would follow but let her hands investigate him anyway. There was a sense of insistence about her, a foregone conclusion. There had been so many women like Mandy – so many grunts against cold walls, the smell of cheap perfume curling into his nose, sticky lipstick smeared on his neck. They were all the same; like forced blooms, once opened, they faded too quickly. Lester knew his need to be with Mandy was like the need to scratch an itch and so he didn't think too deeply about what he was doing with her. He went through the motions, repulsed at her cries, shutting them out until his own relief came. He immediately pulled away, did his jeans up and lit a cigarette. Mandy, with her skirt still raised, reached for one of his cigarettes and placed it provocatively between her lips, eyeing him up and waiting for a light. He obliged and once the lighter was back in is coat pocket he turned to leave.

'What?' she gasped, 'You can't just go!' Lester looked back at her blankly, drawing on his cigarette and letting the smoke slowly escape into the cold night air. 'I might not be finished with you,' she added, dropping her voice low and touching his cheek, trying a different tactic to keep him there.

'We're finished,' was all he said, and he left her in the alleyway between the butcher's and the barber's.

Lester had shown up the next day at Lowlands, much to Lyla's family's relief as they had been on the receiving end of her temper all morning. Lyla had shouted at him, thrown things and then, finally, cried. He didn't speak through any of this. She hated how scared she had been at the idea of losing him. She hated how he didn't even try to deny any of what had happened. With every blow she rained down on him, he stood and took it and she hated him most for that. When she had eventually run dry of anger, the hurt she felt swamped her and he had held her tight. She refused to embrace him and kept her arms firmly against her sides but his arms around her were solid, pressing her head firmly against his chest. Then he spoke. He was careful not to make her any promises and he let her know that if she wanted him to be sorry, then he was. These were not the words she expected to hear and she looked up at him, her eyes still glassy from crying. His words left her feeling so drained that she wished she felt nothing; that she could be hollow in response to his promises. Despite this, she found herself agreeing to take him back.

As Lester held Lyla, he knew he had had a very narrow escape; he knew she was too smart to be lied to and he knew her temper ran deep. So he did the only thing he could think of – he took everything she threw at him, all the insults, venom and hate. Despite the fact that she hung lifelessly in his arms, he knew that if he held onto her long enough he could get her back.

It wasn't just Lyla he didn't want to lose; he liked what she was a part of and he saw himself fitting well into the family business. Jerry Shanly's breaker's yard was the type of work that suited him. He liked Lowlands, the family home, particularly its imposing size and how it was contained in the woods. Private and quiet. He liked Maggie Shanly's cooking and that, apart from Jerry, he was the only other male in the house. There was also a part of him that liked the fact that he was pitched twenty-five miles outside of London, virtually under Stevie Adams's nose, and he was getting away with it. He needed to find a way to make all this more permanent and, despite knowing he had shattered Lyla's trust in him, he was determined to find a way of doing so.

Within a month Lester had moved in with Lyla at Lowlands; two months after that, she was pregnant. The memory of Lester's behaviour that night at the pub still stung Lyla, but even though she hadn't received an apology she realised that Lester, in his own way, had worked hard to win her round. She also resigned herself to the fact that it would not be the last time he would break her heart and she hoped that, like a fractured bone, it would repair more solid.

Jerry Shanly did not like Lester. He distrusted the dark edge that hovered around him and he didn't believe his story about how he had come to Ashdowne. But most significantly he felt pushed out by him; by the way his wife Maggie enjoyed cooking for him, and how his daughters reacted around him. However, he was enough of a businessman to appreciate that Lester brought some much-needed brawn to help with the running of the breaker's yard; he also recognised that Lester could talk a good enough talk to make a profit. Of this reasoning he tried to convince his brother Joe, but Joe seemed warier of Lester, claiming that men like Lester were ten-a-penny in jail and that was perhaps where he really belonged.

Secretly, Jerry agreed with his brother's sentiments and when Lyla had galloped through the back door of Lowlands with Lester, pride shining in her face, he realised that he was no longer the only man in her life and his heart buckled. He resented having to share her, and he intensely disliked the moods Lester could put her in or pull her out of. It was bitter-sweet that Lyla was carrying his grandchild. Jerry was an old-fashioned man and he had insisted they get married before the child was born. His heart buckled further as he walked Lyla into the registry office and watched as she shrugged off her maiden name, knowing that one day his business too would lose the name Shanly and become O'Rourke.

→→▣ ▣←←

Lester and Lyla's child was born at the beginning of December; at last there was a Shanly boy in the family for Jerry. Sean Jerry

O'Rourke was a big baby with rolls of fat that creased his arms and legs. He was the most beautiful baby the Shanly family had ever seen – his head was crowned with soft white hair and his eyes were a deep blue. Jerry showered Sean with affection, which made up for the lack of it Lester displayed towards his child. Lester could see that Sean had taken on the Shanly's physical characteristics and he felt cheated.

Sean rarely cried, but when he did Lester complained loudly, sending Maggie into a panic in an attempt to calm the baby. Lyla stood watching on; she loved Sean and Lester in equal measure and was tired of trying to placate them both. Lester criticised the Shanly women for fussing over Sean, stating that they would turn him soft, but Lyla could see that Sean was already born that way and this worried her. Finally, she decided to have another child, to deflect the heat from Sean.

When Lyla fell pregnant with Brendan, Lester had moaned bitterly – he already felt trapped and resented having to share his wife with one child, let alone another. His mood was permanently sour and Lyla's pregnancy became more complicated by the month. Weak from morning sickness, she bled intermittently and her heart lurched at the spots of red on her sheets, convinced that she would lose this baby. Finally, she had been instructed to take to her bed and Lester had more or less taken to the pub each night. This baby seemed to be coming between everyone; everyone, that is, except Lyla and her father. They had grown close once again and Jerry would bring her tea each evening and place his giant hands on her stomach. This was the only time the baby settled and Lyla got some peace. Taking Sean's hand, Jerry would gently place it on Lyla's stomach and Sean's eyes would widen in amazement, his face breaking into a smile.

--⊨⊕ ⊙⊨⊷--

Brendan was born on a late January night; snow had threatened all day, with small flurries stinging the windows. A silence had fallen over the house, that dead silence that often accompanies snow. Lyla had woken to find her waters breaking. Turning the light on and realising she was alone, she pushed back the duvet and saw the large stain – her nightdress was sodden and she cried out in pain as the first contraction gripped her. Lyla's sister Bernie was sent to find Lester while her other sister, Kate, and Maggie took care of her and Jerry was sent to clear snow off the truck. When he came back into the house, he found Sean in the kitchen crying. 'What's up little man?' Jerry asked, scooping him up.

'Mummy,' Sean replied.

'The baby is coming, that's all. It hurts a little bit, like when you fall over.' Suddenly, a loud scream rang through the house, and both Sean and Jerry looked upwards, before Sean buried his head into his grandfather's neck.

'Quick Jerry, we are going to have to go!' Maggie shouted from the top of the stairs. Jerry carried Sean to the hallway and saw his wife's anxious face staring down at him. 'The contractions are fast, we haven't much time,' she continued hastily. 'Sean, you are going to stay with your Aunty Kate, okay? Jerry we need you to help get her into the truck, she's not good,' Maggie spoke quickly.

Sean had reluctantly gone to Kate and when Jerry saw Lyla, his heart buckled once more. Her usual creamy-coloured skin was tinged grey, she was panting hard and her hair was darkened with sweat.

'Is he here?' she asked, pushing the words out painfully. Both Jerry and Maggie looked away. A deep groan left Lyla and her head fell hard against the headboard, her chest rising and falling sharply. 'I can't do this without him,' she cried.

'Yes you can. This baby is coming tonight Lyla, whether he's here or not,' Maggie snapped, her voice uncharacteristically brittle. 'Is that bloody truck ready? If so, stop standing there and give me a hand!' Maggie barked at Jerry.

Gradually, they tried lifting Lyla; she was a dead weight and her legs gave way, pulling Maggie forward onto the bed and causing Lyla to let out an agonising scream.

'Should we not just get the midwife, Maggie? Only I don't think we are going to be able to do this,' Jerry said, and they both stared at each other, desperately wanting the other to come up with the answer.

'Kate, call the midwife. Let her know we might not be able to get her to hospital,' Maggie finally shouted.

When Bernie burst into the bedroom, her eyes were frantic. She shrugged and her mouth fell open in desperation. Maggie's lips tightened with anger and Jerry sighed heavily.

'Where is he?' Lyla moaned again.

'He's coming, he'll be here,' Maggie replied, looking at Jerry, who breathed in sharply and shook his head.

'Dad, please can you go and fetch him?' Lyla begged.

Jerry didn't want to fetch Lester – he would kill him if he found him and he wanted as much space as possible between them. He looked at Maggie desperately, and felt relieved when she shook her head.

Half an hour later, a midwife swept into the room and inspected Lyla, who hadn't moved from her position on the bed.

'Lyla, you need to start pushing, okay?' the midwife told her.

Maggie had got towels and hot water ready and Jerry was pleased when the midwife asked him to leave. During the next twenty minutes, Lyla thought she was going to die; she could feel all of her organs working hard, as each contraction gripped her. Feeling the child inside her push and turn, elbowing its way out of her, she felt as if she was being ripped apart, but her mother and the midwife were urging her on; to push harder, then breathe. She bit into the edge of the mattress and threw what strength she had left into getting this child out of her. As her muscles squeezed the infant out, she felt the child slither between her legs and she sunk into the bed, spent and torn as the sound of the newborn's cry, crisp and sharp, resounded through the house.

'Well done, you have a very strong and determined boy, Lyla,' the midwife said, smiling knowingly as she placed him on Lyla's breast. Lyla said nothing and simply stared at the bloodied baby lying there. Everyone would have understood Lyla's feelings towards the baby, given the difficult pregnancy and the shock of such a quick delivery. They would have understood her reluctance to hold him; after all, she had given birth to him with no pain relief and no husband to hold her hand. If Lyla had looked at the baby and rejected him, they would have understood why. However, when

Lyla looked at the child and saw the tiny muscles in his arms flex and saw him suck the air, searching her out, her heart melted. She realised that it had been just him and her in this together, and if she could survive this she could survive anything. She may have wanted Lester O'Rourke that night, but she hadn't needed him.

'A boy, another boy,' she murmured as everyone joined her.

Jerry leaned gently forward to peer at his new grandson, who was sleeping soundly, oblivious to the chaos he'd caused. Lyla turned towards Jerry and her eyes filled with tears. 'He missed it. How could he have missed it, Dad?'

Jerry was at a loss as to what to say, he couldn't look at her – it was too much to try and hold her disappointment.

Lester was surprised to see so many lights on in Lowlands as he staggered up the driveway, drunk and cursing as his footing kept slipping on the snow. He didn't recognise the dark car parked by the front door. It wasn't until he was stood in the doorway of his and Lyla's bedroom that he realised what he had missed. He noticed that none of them could look at him and, in particular, Lyla stared hard at the baby in her arms, refusing to acknowledge him.

'What is it?' Lester asked gruffly.

'It's a boy. You've another son Lester,' Maggie replied sharply and left the room. Bernie and Kate followed, Kate carrying Sean in her arms, who buried his head into her neck, too afraid to look at his father. Jerry felt rooted to the spot and he followed Lester's eyes as he stepped forward and stared at the baby. As both men stared at the child they recognised the same thing – the boy was undeniably Lester's. The outline of his jaw and arch of his brows were the same, his skin had the same tone and his forehead the same breadth. Lester sunk onto the bed, curling his arm around Lyla and towards the baby. Extending his index finger, he gently touched the boy's cheek, keeping his eyes fixed on the child's face.

'I like the name Brendan,' Lyla said. Lester slurred his approval and Jerry left the room. As he closed the door he knew his daughter would forgive Lester and his heart buckled yet again.

Three years later on a cold, frosty morning – one in which the sun shone brightly and filled the day with hope – Brendan and Sean were running around the kitchen laughing, weaving in and out of everyone's legs. Maggie scolded them softly, telling them to calm down as she placed Jerry's usual greasy cooked breakfast in front of him. As he ate, Lyla joined them; she looked pale and drawn. She sat heavily on the kitchen chair and poured herself some tea from the large brown teapot. Both boys ran to her and she half-heartedly clutched them. Jerry took in all this with one eye on his breakfast and one eye on her.

'You want some?' Maggie asked, offering Lyla some breakfast.

She shook her head. 'Can't face it.'

Jerry knew then that she was pregnant once more. He pushed his empty plate forward, got up, kissed Maggie and left the house. When he got outside, the cold morning air stung his cheeks. He took a deep breath, filling his lungs, and pulled back his arms as he turned his face to feel the winter sun. That was Jerry Shanly's last breath; he hit the floor hard and the ground shook with the weight of the big man. Jerry Shanly's heart had buckled for the last time.

CHAPTER 7

Six months ago

A CHEER BROKE out through the bar as Brendan walked towards his friends James, Gio and Matt.

'Hey stranger,' cried James and pushed Brendan's drink towards him. Brendan smiled, waiting for the questions he knew they were dying to fire at him. He took a gulp of his drink and stubbornly refused to enlighten them. He looked at James's enquiring eyes. Brendan had met James during their first week at university and was still surprised that they had hit it off so well.

⊶⊶ ⊷⊷

James was surrounded by girls with long, shiny hair and wearing expensive clothes when Brendan first saw him. He stood and watched as James revelled in their adoration, and concluded that he would likely despise him. James had a moneyed air about him, which gave the impression that he could afford not to take life too seriously, and Brendan had immediately felt intensely envious of him. James had looked in Brendan's direction and was rather bemused at the tall blond student in the sharp clothes leaning against a wall, scowling at him. He smiled – a self-assured, perfect, white-toothed smile – and sauntered over to Brendan, leaving the group of girls wide-eyed and open-mouthed behind him.

'Hi, I'm James Montgomery. I believe we are in the same hall of residence,' he said, holding out his hand.

Brendan eyed it suspiciously while stubbing out his cigarette with his heel. He decided not to shake James's hand. Instead, he responded with a simple 'Brendan O'Rourke.'

Undeterred, James threw his arm around Brendan's shoulders. 'What say we...?' he said, pointing towards the student union bar. 'I believe we have some time before our next lectures.' He winked and, as easily as that, their friendship was formed. And they formed a lethal combination – the handsome, smooth-talking public schoolboy contrasting with the good looking, but gritty, Brendan. The girls migrated towards them, like flocks of birds seeking a current of air. The other male students looked on in disbelief as the two of them swept through the girls at parties like foxes in a hen coop.

Soon, two others joined them: Gio, an Italian, whose family resided in Milan, and Matt, who was slightly more ruffled than the immaculately turned out Gio. A master practical joker, Matt brought humour to the group, taking the edge off their collective arrogance.

⇥▰ ▰⇤

Now, in the bar, Brendan was toying with their anticipation, hoping they would soon tire of the subject of Jemima.

'So, this girlfriend of yours, has she given you the night off then or has she got a puncture?' Matt enquired playfully.

Brendan scoffed. 'Who says I've got a girlfriend?' he asked, looking directly at James, who immediately turned his attention to his drink.

'What's she like?' Matt continued.

'Yeah, she's cool,' he replied vaguely.

'Ah, he's not talking about her, it must be serious,' added Gio.

Brendan stared back at them. What was he going to tell them? He could tell them the truth that, yes, it was serious – or at least it felt like it was – but despite six weeks of dating he hadn't done any more than kiss her. But they wouldn't buy it, knowing his track record, so he downed his drink and maintained the silence.

'Well, Zoe is very pleased you have a girlfriend now. She thinks you won't lead me astray anymore,' Gio contributed.

'Gio, you never needed any help from me mate,' Brendan replied, and while they were laughing he ordered more drinks and found a way to change the subject.

⇢▰ ▰⇠

Jemima stared at her friends' gobsmacked faces.

'You have got to be kidding!' exclaimed Abby.

Jemima flushed and looked down at her coffee. She had expected them to be surprised, but not this shocked.

'But he's gorgeous! How can you keep your hands off him?' Abby added.

Minnie shot her a harsh look. Realising her tactless remark, Abby slid off her stool and made her excuses to go to the bathroom, but before she disappeared, she gave Jemima a knowing look.

'She's right isn't she?' Jemima asked Minnie, watching Abby leave.

'She's just jealous,' Minnie replied. 'Hell, who am I kidding – we're both jealous!' She laughed then continued: 'What's up? Don't you fancy him?'

Jemima raised her eyebrows.

Minnie shook her head. 'Stupid question. Then what's the problem?'

'He's so… I don't know what the word is… worldly, I guess.'

'Hey, I know you haven't exactly been around the block but it's not as though you're a virgin, is it.'

Jemima sighed. 'It's not that I don't want to. I want to, really I do. It's just… I kind of panic each time. What if I'm not enough for him Minnie?' Jemima looked down, biting her lip nervously.

Minnie reached for her hand and smiled. 'Babe, how could you not be enough for him?'

⇢═ ═⇠

Jemima tried desperately to hold onto Minnie's words now that she was in Brendan's apartment. Looking around she concluded that it was a place he clearly never spent much time in. The living room was dominated by an L-shaped, black leather sofa and a large state-of-the-art television was mounted on one wall. On the opposite wall was a poster advertising a bullfight. The matador had his back arched tightly, forcing him onto his tiptoes, his muscled calves clearly defined under the strain of his movement. He was whipping his red cape into the air, narrowly missing the black beast, with its head down and shoulders taut, fury evident in the creature's eyes. Both were ready to fight to the end. Jemima stared intently at the picture; it was the only piece of art in the apartment, and it seemed felicitous that Brendan should own it.

'Drink?' Brendan asked, breaking Jemima's attention.

'Yes please,' she replied, jumping slightly.

She put her bag down on the sofa and wandered over to the large patio doors. Outside she could see the sprawl of the East End of London, the part that was newly refurbished and polished. Brendan wandered over and handed her a drink before sliding open the patio door and stepping onto the balcony. Jemima followed. The air was cool this high up and the breeze teased through her hair. She rested against the metal banister and gazed across the skyline.

'It's beautiful,' she said after a few moments. As if waiting for this cue, Brendan moved behind her, wrapping his right arm around her and using it to point out landmarks. With each one he described he moved closer, so that by the time he reached the Greenwich Observatory, shining from across the river, he was virtually whispering into her ear. Then he gently turned her to face him, took her drink and placed it on the small patio table. Jemima knew what was coming next. She was determined that tonight she would go through with it and she was desperate not to freeze; she wanted to feel her self-control disappear... she wanted to be lost in him.

For Brendan, it felt like a long thaw. He was anxious not to scare her and so he let his lips just touch her jaw and then trail down along her neck. Jemima's head fell back as she responded to him so he tightened his grip around her waist and pulled her closer. Her breathing grew deeper as his lips made their way back up her neck and touched the soft skin between her jawbone and earlobe. She gasped, a small, barely detectable sound, which caught Brendan like a spark, and he felt his whole body start to sear.

'Jem, I want you so much,' he whispered into her neck, bringing his mouth around to hers, pressing it hard, and letting his right hand travel down over her curves. Then he felt her stiffen and his stomach curled with a tight ache. He rested his forehead on hers and Jemima peered up at his pained expression. 'Please... don't turn me down tonight, Jem,' he pleaded.

'I'm not going to,' she whispered and watched his face break into a relieved smile.

The bed looked imposing in the sparsely furnished space and Jemima felt butterflies unfurl their wings in her stomach. Brendan watched her as she looked around. When she looked at him he smiled softly.

Holding her face in his hands he kissed her, the backs of his fingers lightly brushing her cheeks before his hands slid down her back, unzipping her dress. It fell to the ground in a soft rustle. He gazed down at her silk chemise, observing how it clung to her shape, and his lips curled with pleasure. Slipping the thin straps from her shoulders, the material fell gracefully away from her body. He stood back, taking the sight of her.

'God, Jem, you're beautiful.'

Taking her hands, he guided them, unbuttoning his shirt, her fingers trembling until the last button gave way, and he shrugged it off. She took a sharp breath as she saw his body for the first time. His muscles were clearly defined and, as he reached out towards her, she noticed them gently flex. Taking hold of her hands again, he coaxed them further down, letting her fingertips gently glide down his stomach to his jeans, where he led her fingers to undo the button. She glanced up at him and could see he was focusing hard; he looked as though he was just managing to hold onto a high ledge and could fall at any minute. He pushed her fingers towards his zip and slowly, together, they undid his jeans before he encouraged her hand inside.

He groaned softly, kissing her, holding her head firmly between his hands, all the while still keeping his eyes trained on her. She felt awkward, naked except for her knickers and shoes, her dress pooled around her feet as though she was standing in a puddle. His hands slid to her hips and, catching her unawares, he swiftly pulled her onto his lap and ran his index finger lightly over the scar on her arm, tracing the new pink flesh that marked the start of their relationship. She watched him; the sensation was strange, uncomfortable and intense, the newly formed nerve endings springing to life beneath his touch.

'You just don't realise how beautiful you are, do you?' he asked.

Her cheeks flushed. She wished she didn't feel so clumsy and dumbstruck around him; she wanted to be able to confidently match his every move but when he expertly shifted his position so that she lay beneath him, she knew that he was in control and setting the pace.

His fingers ran over her, lightly skimming her skin, keen to explore: 'You're trembling,' he said gently, looking concerned.

'I'm sorry,' she replied meekly, feeling embarrassed. She hadn't realised.

'You don't need to be sorry.'

Kneeling between her thighs he took one leg and lifted it high so he could remove her shoe. He repeated the manoeuvre with the other leg, gazing at her intently as he did so. Leaning forward and grabbing the edges of her knickers, he swiftly pulled them from her. She gasped as he threw them onto the floor and, still holding her leg, slowly brushed his lips over her ankle. Jemima squirmed with a combination of shock and delight.

He smiled wolfishly as he inched his mouth up the inside of her leg, knowing how he was making her feel. As she looked down she caught a glimpse of his bright blue eyes shining between her legs. Her pelvis tipped upwards reflexively and she felt her self-control finally slipping away, only to be replaced with a grinding desire to be touched. His lips washed over her, to her stomach, gently brushing her skin, and her hands found his shoulders. She could feel his muscles shifting as he moved slowly up her body until his lips found her breasts. Every movement was so subtle, slowly setting her alight.

He rested his forehead against hers and looked into her eyes. 'Now,' he said softly. Jemima stared back, not sure if this was a question. She had barely opened her mouth to acknowledge what he'd said, when his own locked with hers and he glided slowly into her.

He moved, gently, until her back arched and together they found their rhythm. She wrapped her legs around him, drawing him deeper and, as they moved together, a warmth grew through her. It spread fast, until she felt she would burst. Finally, the flames washed over her, leaving her smouldering beneath him and she realised, after all these weeks, what it was to be lost in him.

Chapter 8

Seven years ago

With trepidation, Brendan slowly pushed open the back door of Lowlands. It was the first time he had come home since his mother's visit six months previously. She had called him in the week and asked him to come back, her voice full of forgiveness. How could he not obey her? So he had changed his plans and caught the 16.40 train from Waterloo. As he walked in, everyone stopped what they were doing and stared at him.

'Hi,' he smiled nervously, scanning the room and making a quick mental note of his mother, father, Sean, Kelly, Anne-Marie, Liam, Riley and, there in the corner, stirring a large pot, Cassie. Their eyes briefly met and, as if burnt by each other's stare, they looked quickly away. After a few seconds of awkward silence, normal family life resumed – as if this was the same as any other time that Brendan returned home; as if the events of the past few months were wiped from the O'Rourke family history.

The next morning, he woke to the sounds of dogs barking and he had a strong desire to return to London, to the safety of the flat he shared with James and to be amongst his university friends. He dreaded the thought of spending the next twenty-four hours trying to avoid Cassie and Liam, and escaping his father's temper. Slowly, he climbed out of bed and lazily drew back the curtains. The room filled with weak sunlight. He'd spent the night in the spare room, his old room having been given to Liam and Cassie. When his mother announced this, he hadn't dared to complain. He looked around at the faded wallpaper, grubby carpet and cardboard boxes that were piled haphazardly, stuffed with his family's belongings. He wandered over to them and began to rummage around in one of the open boxes. He came across a yellowing envelope containing pictures of him and his siblings when they were babies; he flicked through them, not paying much attention. Then he came to a photograph of himself with his brothers. It had been taken about five years previously by a cousin who had stayed with them for the summer. They were by the lake a couple of miles away and they had been swimming; he could see that their hair was still damp. He remembered that afternoon which had slipped so easily into evening, then into night. Lester had finally driven out and rounded them up, angry at the inconvenience of having to fetch them back. He remembered how it felt when he'd jumped into the lake, swinging in from the branches of the willow tree that hung over its banks. The smack of the water stinging his body, then freezing cold against his sunburnt skin. He recalled the blackness of the lake itself, darker than the night as he disappeared from its surface, gripped with exhilaration as he fell deeper. He remembered his reflexes kicking in, forcing him upwards with urgent strokes, towards the mottled sunlight, his cheeks ballooned, lungs tight then – finally – breaking through the black skin of the lake, gasping for air.

⋅►══◉ ◉══◄⋅

He thought about the last time he had visited the lake; of Cassie wading out to him, her hair trailing behind her in the water as she slowly edged towards him. He had eagerly anticipated her then – where had all that want gone, that desire? He thought of her now and an iciness ran through him, forcing his mind back to the room. He looked around, slowly tapping the photo against the palm of his hand. All these boxes, filling the room like silt. *They don't let go of anything,* he thought.

After lunch when his brothers returned from the breaker's yard, Sean suggested they spend the afternoon with their air rifles and see what they could find to shoot. Brendan, rather resigned to filling in time while he was there, followed Sean and Riley out of the kitchen and into the backyard. Facing them was Liam and their father. The atmosphere changed. Brendan looked quickly between them and became aware of something going on that he had no idea about. He felt like he was surrounded by a pack of hungry dogs that was closing in on him. Sean took a firm grip of his arm and whispered: 'Don't fight back. It will be over quicker that way.'

Startled, Brendan stared at his father whose face was as difficult to read as ever. His eyes darted to Riley, who now had hold of his other arm and would not allow Brendan to catch his eye. Then he saw Liam coming towards him with a perverse smile stretched across his face, and before Brendan could figure out what was happening, Liam punched him.

Brendan felt the muscles in his neck tear as his head swung uncontrollably to the right. Before he had time to focus, he heard the dull smack of knuckles again, and his head swung violently to the left, the strength of this blow forcing his whole body away from Sean and Riley's grasp. He stumbled to the ground. Trying to look up and make sense of this, he saw Liam's foot swing into focus and connect with his chest, throwing him onto his back. Liam pulled him up by the scruff of his neck, then pushed him backwards until he hit the wall of the house. Brendan stared straight into Liam's eyes and, momentarily, saw the pleasure behind them, the years of rage and fury saved up for the older brother who stood in his way, who stopped him from getting what he wanted; then the pounding continued.

Cassie sat tensely at the kitchen table, poised on the edge of the chair. She looked at Kelly, who was colouring in a picture and had only briefly looked up when the scuffling sounds of the fight started. Anne-Marie flicked lazily through a magazine, lifting her head only to blow out cigarette smoke, and Lyla sat with her back to the yard, staring straight ahead, not an ounce of recognition registering on her face that her son was being violently beaten just a few feet away. Through the kitchen window Cassie saw Brendan with Liam in his face, pushing him roughly backwards. She jumped up and headed for the door to the yard. Quickly, Lyla sprang up and kicked the door shut, then swung around and grabbed Cassie roughly by the throat, bringing Cassie's face close to hers. Cassie could smell the stale aroma of menthol cigarettes on Lyla's breath, and stared at Lyla's stark blue eyes as she tightened her grip, digging the sharp edges of her nails into the girl's neck.

'You go to him and you'll find yourself out there getting a beating too and, I'll be true to my word, I'll rip your fucking heart out and feed it to the dogs,' Lyla snarled, still keeping her hold tight around Cassie's throat. Their eyes locked – Cassie's flashed with desperation and Lyla's burned with spite. Eventually, when Lyla saw the defeat in Cassie's eyes, she relaxed her grip and released her. Cassie turned to go upstairs but Lyla grabbed her arm. 'You stay here and you hear this, you little slut,' she spat at her.

Resigned, Cassie sank back into the kitchen chair and tried to block out the sounds coming from the yard; each blow felt like a knife being pushed into her, deeper and deeper.

Liam held Brendan tightly by his hair, and was banging his head repeatedly against the brick wall. His face inches away from him, Brendan could feel Liam's hot breath and sour spittle spray against his face. His mind raced as to why this was happening, and how to turn this fight around to his advantage. With each smack of his head against the wall, his train of thought jumped, like the needle on a record, and he felt as if he was repeatedly trying to fathom everything out from the start.

He had had many fights with Liam over the years; of all his siblings Liam was the easiest to goad, his buttons the easiest to press. As the years progressed, Brendan started to lose the advantage of age, although he held onto his edge with his athleticism and height, but Liam's stocky build, tenacity and rage made him a serious contender. Each fight became longer and more aggressive, often ending with heavy-handed punishments from their parents and long spells in their bedrooms, where their loathing for each other would ferment into revenge.

You know this, thought Brendan. *You know he keeps coming straight at you.* He pooled all his strength to lift his left leg and knee'd Liam hard in the stomach. Liam reeled backwards, doubled over, and stared up at Brendan with his face contorted with disbelief. Brendan staggered forward, trying to catch his breath and straighten up, but Liam's full rage was now unleashed. Letting out a low roar, he charged at Brendan, throwing his shoulder into his stomach and grabbing him round the waist. Winded, Brendan was surprised at how violently the surge of air was forced up out of his lungs, through his gullet and out of his mouth. Liam had gained the upper hand again, and Brendan fell hard against the dirty yard floor, face down, breathing in dust. As Liam kicked him again, he curled round involuntarily to grab his stomach, trying to deaden the pain. Liam then kicked him hard in the chest once more, causing him to flip over onto his back; another kick, harder, to his side. This time he heard a sickening crack near his ribs, then felt a kick to his jaw so hard that, for a split second, everything went black.

'Enough!' shouted his father, as if calling a dog to heel. The ferocious pace of kicks and punches stopped, and Brendan became aware of Liam standing over him, his chest heaving, gasping for air, his fists still clenched. Brendan could see his own blood smeared across Liam's knuckles as he tried to flex his hands, but his knuckles had started to swell, causing him to grimace. Their father walked over and looked down at Brendan slumped on the ground, his chest panting in swift, shallow movements; anything deeper sent a sharp pain through his chest. 'Well, at least you took that like a man,' Lester grunted.

It all made sense now. Brendan let his head fall back into the dust. This was about Cassie, his cowardice, and the shame his actions had brought on his family. It was about Liam letting him know that his place in the family had eclipsed Brendan's. He was now further up the food chain, pushing Brendan further out to the edges of the pack.

Liam stood away from Brendan, allowing him to roll slowly onto his side, away from the pain, as he struggled to stand. He knew that none of them would help him, and his pride was further shredded as he collapsed a couple of times trying to get up. He clambered onto all fours, sinking back onto his legs like a wounded beast, deeply aware of how humiliated this position made him feel. Blood had started to congeal in his mouth and he struggled to spit it out as it formed sticky strands of spittle which clung to his chin. He attempted to bring his hand up to wipe his mouth but the burning pain in his side tore through him again. Grimacing, he looked up at his brothers and father staring back at him, each in their own way. Liam took out his phone and, holding it up to Brendan, took a photo.

'What the fuck do you think you are doing?' Lester exclaimed.

'Sending them the proof,' replied Liam.

Lester grabbed the phone, threw it on the ground and stamped hard on it, smashing it to pieces, before leaning into Liam's face and snarling: 'You fucking imbecile. My word is my word, they don't need no fucking picture to prove we've done it. If I tell 'em it'll be done, it'll get fucking done. I've had enough to do with those pikeys over the years for them to know what I'm about. No one ever, ever gets to see O'Rourke blood.'

Liam hung his head, his bravado quickly evaporating. Lester pushed him backwards and walked back into the house; the others slowly followed. Brendan glared at Liam, who now would not hold his eye. Realising how fragile his father's respect was to hold onto, in relation to how hard it was to win, Liam dropped his shoulders and skulked into the house.

Brendan slowly crawled over to the wall and used it to help lever himself up. He struggled to stand straight; the pain in his side was too severe. He was still panting and blood kept refilling his mouth, hot and metallic tasting. He repeatedly spat it out, and it hit the ground like large globules of oil. Moving slowly, he managed to get to the back of the outbuilding, where he slid down the wall and spat out a tooth into his hand. 'Shit,' he murmured to himself, still gasping for air. His vision was becoming narrower in his left eye and when he touched the flesh around it, it was tender, causing him to wince. Kaiser crawled over to him and started to lick his wounds. Brendan grabbed large chunks of the dog's sable coat. 'Great guard dog you are,' he mocked and winced as the pain in his ribs caught again, sending another arrow of fire through him.

When the sun began to set and the commotion of truck doors slamming – announcing his brothers and father leaving for the pub – had died down, Brendan pulled himself up, his body stiff and sore, and slowly limped back to the house. Once in the kitchen, he ran the tap and filled a glass with water, gulping it down in fits, and as fast as the pain in his jaw and ribs would allow. He washed his hands, watching the dirt and blood swirl down the plughole, willing the pain to disappear along with it. Then he cautiously turned around to find Cassie standing in the doorway; they stared at each other, both looking horrified. Brendan watched as her eyes slowly moved over him, taking in his wounds, her lips and hands trembling. He would never have wanted her to see him like this, so broken and vulnerable, but he didn't have the energy to leave or the wherewithal to speak. Then, without warning, she turned and ran up the stairs.

Lyla appeared in the doorway, looking behind her, towards the staircase, and then at Brendan. She walked over to a kitchen cupboard and took out a bottle of antiseptic and some wads of cotton wool. 'Sit,' she commanded.

He did what she instructed. She sat opposite him, bathed the cotton wool in antiseptic and, holding onto his chin, held the pad to his left eyebrow. He flinched, drawing his breath in quickly, trying to override the pain in his ribs. He grasped his side firmly and looked his mother straight in the eye. *How could she have let this happen?* he thought, resentfully.

'Where else hurts?' she asked coldly.

Brendan stared back at her in disbelief, wondering how she could be so matter-of-fact about what had happened. Not only that, but she must have known. He had mulled this over outside for hours, trying to make sense of it all. She had called him deliberately to bring him home for this. She had known all along what they intended to do. He pushed his chair back and, with what was left of his dignity, he rose and slowly climbed the stairs.

He locked the bathroom door and turned on the shower. Kicking his trainers off, he struggled to get undressed, bracing himself before pulling his t-shirt over his head and stepping into the hot water, letting it run over him in twisting rivulets. Leaning against the cool tiles, he gradually began to feel his muscles ease from the fight. He reached gingerly for the soap, running the bar over his head and shoulders. It stung his wounds and his eyes, and his body jerked with slow sobs that came in waves but produced no tears. He stared at the plughole and watched the dirty, blood-stained water and soap scum run away from him. He realised that however long he stayed there, with the hot water pounding against his skin and the soap burning his wounds, he couldn't wash away his humiliation and the hate he felt for his family.

⇥▱ ▱⇤

On the other side of the wall, Cassie had heard Brendan slowly climb the stairs. She was still attuned to the sound of his step from the previous summer. She heard him lock the bathroom door and turn on the shower, the water splattering against the tiles. She heard his groans as he removed his clothes and she pressed her face against her bedroom wall, just inches from where Brendan stood on the other side. Holding her arms out wide, as if trying to embrace the space he was in, she pressed her ear harder against the wall, trying to pick up every sound from the bathroom – the water turning off, the sound of Brendan moving slowly around the room. Then, as he unlocked the door to go into his own room, Cassie slid along the adjacent wall until she came to the bedroom door. Her hands fell to the handle and she stared at them. She was trapped. She could not go to him and the tears which stung her eyes she refused to let fall.

CHAPTER 9

Six months ago

BRENDAN LAY DOZING with his right arm around Jemima, his left arm tucked under his head. The warm, late-summer sun seeped into his bedroom, washing over them both. Jemima hadn't taken her eyes off him since she had woken. She lay on her side drinking in every detail of him. There was a black tattoo on his chest, just above his heart, which had caught her eye; for a while she had been trying to figure it out. It looked like a ring of birds, positioned tail to beak, and was about the size of a large watch face. Eventually her curiosity got the better of her and she gently started to trace it with her index finger. Brendan's mouth flickered and she stopped, holding her breath, as if she had been caught doing something wrong. He slowly opened his eyes and tightened his grip around her.

'What's the tattoo of?' she asked softly.

'It's a circle of rooks. A play on our name – rook and Rourke. It was my brother's idea, we've all got one.' He shut his eyes again and continued to doze, leaving Jemima to ponder this while continuing to gently trace the circle of birds.

'Did it hurt?'

'A bit.' He opened his eyes again to look at her, wondering where this was going. She lay silent, running her finger around the birds in a continuous circle, looking pensive, her eyes narrowing to help her focus on what she was doing. He liked the feel of her touch, found it soothing; his eyelids became heavy again and he let them slide shut, feeling himself drift.

⊷⊨⊜ ⊜⊨⊶

Sean had been so insistent about them getting the same tattoo, to the point of being almost frantic with the idea. Brendan was seventeen and had just started to voice his university plans, which he knew rattled Sean. One particular evening Sean had burst into his room, which he often did in many failed attempts to sabotage Brendan's revision. This time though, he held a piece of paper bearing a design of a circle of four rooks, and talked of how great it would be for each of them to get one tattooed over their hearts. Seeing how important it appeared to Sean, Brendan agreed to go along with it.

The sharp smell of surgical spirit bit into their nostrils when they entered the tattoo studio. Its walls were adorned with hundreds of brightly coloured images, and the whole place felt forbidden. For the first time in his life, Sean had insisted on going first. He held his head high while the tattooist set about immortalising his design onto his chest. Sean radiated with pride, even when the tattooist had finished and wiped the last drops of blood away. They all looked at the dark mark, surrounded by inflamed skin. Then Sean looked straight at Brendan and announced: 'It's your turn now.' As Brendan climbed into the chair, he did not realise how ill-prepared he was for the pain. When the tattooist had finished, Liam had virtually pushed Brendan aside to get his done. When Brendan looked at Sean, relieved it was over and slightly shocked that they had gone through with it, Sean looked back at him proudly. A couple of years later, when Riley looked old enough, Sean had marched him down to the same studio, for the same tattoo.

Brendan now regarded his like some kind of branding, reminding him how estranged his relationship with Sean had become over the past few years, and regretted having the tattoo. Lost in his thoughts, he was unaware that he had placed his hand over Jemima's and stopped her touching it.

'I think that is lovely that you all have the same one. You must be so close,' Jemima said thoughtfully.

Brendan snapped out of his daydream. Uncomfortable with discussing this, he rolled on top of her, pushing her into the bed as if to squash her comment and looked into her eyes. 'What do you want to do today?' he asked, deliberately changing the subject. He knew he would need to answer her question some day, but in the warm glow of a late Sunday morning, with Jemima's smooth, naked body beneath him, he was aware that there were other things he would rather be doing.

Chapter 10

Seven years ago

SEAN OPENED THE guest room door and entered carrying a mug of tea and some painkillers. Brendan looked at him coldly, before pointedly turning to stare out of the window. Sean gently pushed the door shut with his foot and walked over to the bedside cabinet, placing the tea on it. 'I thought you might need some of these,' he said, waving the bottle of painkillers in the air.

Brendan struggled to tear his eyes away from the window; rage was churning inside him and the words he wanted to say stuck in his throat, bottlenecked and fighting to explode. There was a tense and awkward silence as Sean shoved his hands and the painkillers into his pockets and continued to stare at Brendan.

Brendan was reminded of the times they fell out as kids. Sean hated it and Brendan always managed to stay cool-headed, always winning Sean around to his way by using the silent treatment. Despite Sean's tough exterior, he hated to be in trouble with Brendan, so by playing it cool Brendan could start to work out his game plan with Sean, who was now sat on the end of the bed, still staring and waiting to take his cue from Brendan.

'Why?' Brendan asked, bitterly.

'Why what?' replied Sean, confused.

Brendan slowly shifted his eyes away from the window and scowled at him. Aware of Sean looking at his bruises, he deliberately faced him so he could see Liam's handiwork.

'You knew what they had planned. Why did you get involved? What does it have to do with you Sean?' he said after a few moments.

Sean blinked hard. 'You have no idea what you left behind do you? You weren't here Brendan; you don't know how it was,' Sean replied angrily, crossing over to the window and leaning against it. He stared out, across to the woods, deep in thought.

Sean's outburst surprised Brendan and he watched him in anticipation of another attack. He winced and grasped his side as he tried to move into a more defensive position and Sean glanced back at him. As if reminded of the part he had played yesterday, he softened his voice. 'I just don't know who you are any more,' he sighed, looking back out of the window. 'I never thought you could do something like that, just run out on us. You have no idea what it was like, the old man raging till he finally put all the pieces together. Then he just went mental, at all of us. Cassie was no help. She wouldn't talk, wouldn't drop you in it, and Riley got a right beating off the old man when he thought it was him who had been messing around with her. He didn't deserve to take that for you Brendan,' Sean finished, turning to face him.

With the early morning light behind Sean, his blond hair illuminated like a halo, he appeared inviolable. The look was accentuated by his large blue eyes and full lips. His upper lip protruded slightly over his lower one, giving him a pout, which caused his demeanour to be either sulky or innocent, depending on whether his eyes matched his mood. Despite his looks, like the rest of his brothers he had taken too many beatings from their father, which had spoiled Sean's gentleness and replaced it with an impenetrable hardness.

'You were always braver than me,' Sean continued wistfully. 'You always had more bottle. Remember that time on holiday when I got stuck on the high diving board? I just froze, so you climbed up, pushed past me, going first to show me that I could do it. You never lost your nerve, never. I wouldn't have done half the stuff I did as a kid if it weren't for you.' Brendan remained silent, watching him closely.

'I always knew, even when I was really small, that you wouldn't stay. You've always been restless – not like me, I'm happy here. But I always thought that even if you left, we'd still be us, that nothing would change. We were more than just brothers. Remember all the fights at school? No one would take the two of us on, it was always us against the rest of them, and you always made sure it got sorted.' Sean paused and breathed in deeply. 'But last summer when you came home, it was obvious you didn't want to be here. The thing that got me the most was that you didn't seem to want to be with me...' Sean's words trailed off; he'd reached an impasse, sensing he had shared too much.

'Is that why you let Liam beat me? You're pissed off I left and got on with my life?' asked Brendan harshly.

'What is it going to take to get you to understand what you left us with? We have two sisters for fuck's sake Brendan. The pikeys followed them... we were shitting ourselves every time

Kelly was late back from school or Anne-Marie went out,' Sean snapped.

Grasping the inference, a sickening feeling swelled in the pit of Brendan's stomach.

'I know you have your own life now,' Sean continued. 'You taking that beating had nothing to do with me being pissed off with you for moving on and leaving. This is my home – it's where I belong – and the business...? I don't know anything else and I don't mind the hard graft. I'm good at it. I couldn't do what you do; I've never had the brains. But I can't sit in the middle. You know our family – they make you take sides and what you did was wrong. You must know that it was wrong?'

They fell silent, leaving Brendan to figure out his reply and calmly manage the words which were the burning embers keeping all the rage inside of him alight.

'Yeah, what I did was wrong. I shouldn't have screwed a thirteen-year-old girl and got her pregnant and pissed off leaving you all to deal with it. I should've come back and sorted it out,' Brendan replied coolly. 'I should've stopped it but I didn't. It is my biggest regret Sean, but I can't change it and I did what I thought was the right thing; I got the hell out of here. When I left, I didn't know she was pregnant. I didn't know any of this because you lot chose to keep it from me – not one of you got in touch to let me know. I would've come back and dealt with it all, you know that Sean. I regret what I did, but I am not fucking ashamed of myself for it any more, and do you know why?' Sean opened his mouth to speak but Brendan didn't give him a chance. 'I'm not ashamed because what I did, I did in ignorance, without knowing what I had got myself involved in. It's no fucking excuse, what I did is still wrong, but it's a better fucking explanation than that cunt Liam has – he knows what she's been through, he's well aware of her age, and I... I get the fucking beating for it!' His fury snapped like static between them. 'I was never given the chance to put it right because, for some reason, Liam and Dad didn't want me to,' he finished, holding onto his side and grimacing with pain. When he started to get his breath back he continued more calmly. 'And you were quick to take their side... so save me all the fucking blood-brother shit.'

Brendan regretted his words as soon as they had left his mouth. Sean's face crumpled, clearly hurt but not articulate enough to respond to him quickly.

Eventually, Sean composed himself and casually threw the painkillers onto the bed. 'You'll need to get those ribs seen to, they're probably broken,' he said to Brendan coldly, before leaving.

CHAPTER 11

Twenty-two years ago

FOR A WHILE after Jerry's death, Lester took his responsibilities for his family and the running of the business more seriously. He drank less and stayed at home more. This appeased Lyla who, seven months later, gave birth to twins – a boy called Liam and a girl called Anne-Marie. While Lyla was busy with the twins and helping Lester manage the business, Maggie made sure that Sean and Brendan were fed and cared for, showering all the love she had had for their grandfather onto them. The two boys were a great source of comfort to her, especially Sean, who resembled Jerry in so many ways. Sometimes, when handing Sean his shoes or putting his tea down in front of him, Maggie would catch a glimpse of Jerry, which left her lightheaded with the longing she still had for him.

She could also see the large hole that Jerry had left in Sean's life. Well aware of the bond between them, she saw how Jerry's sudden departure had left Sean marooned, and she understood why he attached himself so firmly to his younger brother.

In contrast, Brendan reminded Maggie of Lester; not only in looks but also in his presence. She could see the early characteristics of Lester's arrogance in Brendan's wilfulness and in the way he led Sean into scrapes that Sean, eager to please, would participate in willingly. When she got cross with them, Sean's face would crumple but Brendan's expression was defiant. He would let her rant, then tell her what she wanted to hear. He'd tell her how sorry he was, with a mastered look of remorse, before smiling in a way that left her in no doubt about how he really felt. But as much as Lester's overbearing behaviour unsettled her, she found something more forgivable in Brendan, and she prayed regularly that their physical appearance was where the similarities would start and end.

The arrival of the twins meant that, secretly, Lyla was delighted with having a daughter, even if it did mean having to share her time with another baby boy. She spent ages playing with Anne-Marie's hair, white-blonde like her own, and growing into large curls. She adorned it with ribbons and dressed her in white lace dresses. Anne-Marie spent her early years resembling a china doll, and appearing so fragile that Lester was scared to pick her up for fear of breaking her.

Liam, however, was more robust and occasionally Lester would take him and his two brothers outside to play. Playing roughly, and encouraging them to fight, Lester and Liam would watch Sean and Brendan scrap. Sean would use his size to hold Brendan down but, undeterred, Brendan would wriggle and kick out until he was free. Lester also encouraged them to box. He would sit in the yard with his palms held up and get them to punch his hands. Sean's blows were hard and solid, and Lester's arms would swing back with the force of them. Brendan's punches didn't hold the same strength, but were faster and more accurate.

When Liam started walking at thirteen months, he stumbled across the yard to where Lester was sat with his palms raised in Sean and Brendan's direction. Liam pushed in front of them, drew his podgy arm back and swung it at Lester, his fist making contact with his father's large open palm. All three of them stared at Liam as he prepared to punch his father again. A satisfied smile spread across Lester's face and Sean and Brendan just looked at one another. Though they didn't always like having to fight each other, the time they spent in the backyard with Lester yielded the only positive attention they got from him. They both realised that now Liam had joined the group, things would never be quite the same.

Although distracted by the twins and the business, Lyla always tucked Sean and Brendan in at night. They shared a room that had belonged to their Aunt Bernie, who had moved out of Lowlands to live with her 'waste of space' boyfriend, as Lester referred to him. Lyla also made sure that Sean and Brendan were bathed at the end of each day and dressed in clean pyjamas; she pulled the duvets tight across them and stroked their hair before kissing them goodnight. When she looked at Sean, she would see her father, and her loss would swell quickly like a tide filling a cave. She would bury her face against the top of his head, breathing in his smell, and tell him to stay in his own bed. Then she would walk over to Brendan and stroke his forehead and he would stare up at her, smiling, his eyes shining brightly. 'Stay in your own bed,' she would tell him and his smile would broaden; and she knew that, by morning, she would find a large entwined bundle underneath one of the bed's duvets, and the other bed would be left empty.

Sometimes, they awoke before Lyla came to wake them. On these mornings, whoever woke first would fidget and sigh until the other stirred. They would be sweaty from each other's body heat, their hair sticking to their heads and their pyjama tops clinging to their backs. On these mornings, their day would start with a trip to the bathroom and a quick game of crossed swords in the toilet, followed by hushed steps downstairs to the kitchen. Emptying a mixture of cereal into two bowls that Sean would fill up to the brim with milk, they would sit eating in silence, swinging their legs, milk running down their chins, until their bowls were empty. Then they would put on their wellington boots and go out to the woods to play.

When Brendan was six and Sean was eight, the boys had taken to climbing an old yew tree about halfway down the drive from Lowlands; it was nestled amongst the pines and because of its breadth of shaggy, dark-green leaves, a small clearing had collected around it, making it perfect for hiding in as well as climbing. Its branches spread outwards, long and twisted, jutting out in the right places, making it easy to climb and explore from its main trunk. There were two particular branches that they enjoyed playing on; they were about four feet apart meaning that the boys could edge along one branch and hold on to the other. Once halfway out they would jump up and down, the lower branch bouncing beneath them, taking their weight, throwing them slightly in the air as its tension gave and it sprung back to meet the soles of their feet. This caused them to holler with excitement, their heads thrown back with laughter, and daring each other to look down at the ground far beneath them.

One particular morning, Brendan had raced out to the tree. He had shot up it, his feet quickly finding the familiar footholds, and he edged out along the branch shouting for Sean to catch up. When Sean reached the branches, Brendan was already halfway out and bouncing giddily up and down. There was something that held Sean back. He looked down at the branch and his eyes followed the length of it, looking at it carefully.

'Come on!' shouted Brendan impatiently, and Sean looked up to see Brendan's face brimming with excitement. As he reached across to grab the branch above him, they heard a loud creak; both boys stopped. Sean whipped his leg and arm back and held on tightly to the trunk.

Brendan looked shocked and, as their eyes met, he laughed nervously, holding on tightly to the branch above. 'Whoa, what was that?' he asked.

Sean was stunned and shook his head; they waited a few moments in silence. In the absence of any more noise, Brendan jumped high. As his feet hit the branch below the noise returned, a loud crack ripped through the air, and Sean watched in horror as the branch supporting Brendan broke and crashed heavily through the tree, with pieces of branch and leaves spraying out as it collided with the other branches, until it hit the ground with a loud deadened thump. Sean saw Brendan hanging onto the branch above him, his body and legs dangling in the air; one of his boots had fallen off and his pyjama bottoms were slowly sliding down.

'Bloody fuck,' cried Sean, watching Brendan swinging helplessly as he tried to pull himself up onto the branch. Sean started to climb along the branch towards him, inching himself forward. The branch was rough between his thighs and scratched his skin through his pyjamas. When he got about a foot from Brendan, he reached out his arm and shouted for his brother to grab him. Brendan looked back at him; his face was calm as he reached out a hand. Sean pushed his body forward with all his strength, reaching his arm out so far he thought he could feel his bones stretch. Their fingertips gently brushed against each other and Sean inched even closer, seeing that Brendan was now struggling to maintain his hold on the branch. He stared down into Brendan's face and shouted at him to hold on. Sean's eyes were wide with terror, his mouth was dry and his heart was pounding. Brendan looked back at him, serenely, with a knowing look in his eye. Sean knew that Brendan couldn't hold on any longer, and he also knew he couldn't reach him in time. Despite this, he lunged forward to grab him, his arm flailing in the air as he watched Brendan fall. A long shout left Sean. He would never be able to recall what it was he shouted, but he remembered the force of it, as it left his lungs and ripped through his throat; it formed the background noise to Brendan crashing through the branches, his route to the ground made more direct by the branch that had fallen before him.

When Brendan hit the ground he lay perfectly still, with his eyes open, staring upwards. Sean scrambled back along the branch shouting expletives that he'd heard his parents use; they left his mouth at random, fuelled by the adrenalin that pumped violently through his body. He jumped the last four feet of the tree and raced over to his brother's lifeless body, bending over him, tears streaming down his cheeks, not knowing what to do.

'Bloody fuck Brendan, don't be dead,' he cried, his eyes frantically searching his brother's body for signs of life. Then he saw Brendan's chest rise and fall and he was swamped with relief. He bowed his head and sobbed, letting large tears escape and drop onto Brendan's chest. All sorts of thoughts raced through his mind; stories from school assembly about people who had accidents and broke their backs and never walked again or who needed to spend the rest of their lives in wheelchairs. He had seen people like this in the town centre and on television. Disabled, they were called – he considered the meaning of the word and how life would be changed for them both.

'Bloody fuck Brendan, don't be disabled,' he sobbed and watched as Brendan's mouth spread into a smile.

'Whoa. Did you see that Sean?' Brendan said shakily, trying to sit up.

'You fucker!' Sean shouted, 'I thought you were dead or your back was busted.'

'My arm hurts,' Brendan replied, lying down again. Sean looked at Brendan's right arm, and saw a sharp white piece of bone jutting through his skin; blood had soaked into the ground around it, oozing from the tear in his pyjama top. Sean's eyes widened in shock and Brendan followed his brother's stare.

'I'm getting mum and dad,' Sean shouted, scrambling to his feet and starting to run. His voice was panicky, and his long legs strode out as quickly as he could push them across the woods and out onto the driveway towards the old house.

Brendan lay rigid. He felt queasy, and he couldn't tear his eyes from the bone jutting out of his forearm and the slow leak of blood that pooled around it. It hurt like nothing he had ever felt before. He lay there for what felt like hours before he heard the commotion of his parents running through the woods to him. His heart leaped when he heard Lyla calling his name, then sunk like a boulder when he heard his father's deeper tones behind her.

Lyla slid to the ground and pulled his head towards her; he just caught her look of horror when she saw his arm, before his head was buried into her breasts. They were soft and warm and she smelt of peppermints and cigarettes; it was familiar and comforting. He felt her breath push out of her chest as she screamed for Lester to help. Lester lifted him swiftly and Brendan felt himself rise smoothly through the air, as though falling in reverse. Lester held him tightly but Brendan kept his head down – he didn't want to see his father's face. The skin on Lester's neck shook as he swore furiously at Sean, and his swagger caused Brendan to roll about in his arms, making his pain worse, but he was too scared to complain.

When Lester placed him in the truck, he caught Brendan's eye. His face was filled with fury, his eyes glinted sharply and Brendan immediately looked away. He could feel his father staring at his wounded arm, and he wanted to pull it away from his gaze, but he couldn't move it. He also wanted to cry, to bury his head into his mother's chest again and scream out with the pain, to shout at her to take it away. He knew all the while his father was looking at him he couldn't show any of these feelings, so he looked down at his feet, one adorned with a red wellington and one grubby and bare. He curled his toes tightly and bit his bottom lip, then blinked hard to stop the tears.

Brendan's arm needed an operation to help set the bone. He arrived home a couple of days later with his arm in a sling and the proud owner of twenty-four stitches. He had quickly got used to the nurses fussing over him and telling him how brave he'd been. His chest had swelled with pride as he retold variations of his adventure, with the tree growing higher and his fall becoming further. Also, he quickly figured out the correlation between his telling of the story and how much ice cream he got with his dinner, meaning Brendan literally dined out on the episode for the duration of his stay. When it came time for him to leave, one of the nurses bent down to him and flashed him a broad smile, then handed him a sticker. He took it with a fixed grin on his face. Inside he felt disappointed. What use was a sticker to him? After all, he had nearly fallen to his death and the trophy seemed to fall very short. But he also realised that grown-ups didn't give away much for nothing, so he took it and planned to stick it over Liam's mouth the next time he annoyed him.

Sean received a beating from Lester for Brendan's fall. He had taken it silently and sloped off to be comforted by his grandmother. Maggie cradled him in her arms and rubbed his back, knowing his bottom would be too sore to touch from Lester's leather belt. Inside she fumed at Lester, and while watching Sean climb gingerly into bed and roll onto his side, she formed the words in her head that she wanted to say to him.

She had found Lester in the brick sheds in the yard, and spat her disgust at him for beating the boy. He looked at her blankly, before reminding her whose house it was now, and that she was free to go at any time. That evening, Maggie informed Lyla that she was going to spend some time with her family in Ireland. Lyla begged her not to leave, sharing with her the news that she was pregnant again and needed her in Lowlands. In the end, Maggie agreed to go for a couple of months and be back in time to help with the newborn baby. She begged Lyla to make this her last child, but Lyla fell silent, making her no promises.

When Lyla tucked Brendan and Sean in bed on the night Brendan came home from hospital, she stressed that they were to stay in their own beds.

'His arm is bad Sean. If you knock it he could end up back in hospital,' she said sternly. While Brendan was in hospital she had found Sean in Brendan's bed every morning. 'You miss him that much eh?' she had asked gently, as she ran her hand through his hair.

When Lyla left the room, Brendan called for Sean to join him. Sean propped himself up on one arm and hissed back that he couldn't. Brendan climbed out of bed, pulling his bedding onto the floor, and gestured for Sean to do the same. Compliantly, Sean copied and they lay huddled next to each other underneath their duvets.

'Does it hurt?' asked Sean, and Brendan nodded.

'Does yours?' asked Brendan, and Sean nodded.

'What did he use?' asked Brendan, watching Sean closely.

'His belt,' replied Sean.

'Bloody bastard,' mumbled Brendan, and Sean nodded in agreement then closed his eyes. Sean fell asleep quickly, with his arm around his younger brother, feeling his heat and his soft breath on his neck. Their legs were interlocked and he felt safe; now he had him back all was well with his world again.

CHAPTER 12

Seven years ago

WHEN BRENDAN RETURNED to London, he had tried to pass his injuries off as a pub fight that he and his brothers had got into. This seemed to satisfy most of his friends' questions. However, James looked at him strangely, as if feeling Brendan's embarrassment. Later on, when Brendan felt less sore and damaged, James discreetly arranged for both of them to stay in one evening.

'What really happened when you went home Brendan?' James enquired lightly, handing him a bottle of beer and sliding casually onto the couch opposite. Brendan stared at the bottle, picking at the label as he considered the question. Though his physical wounds were healing he still felt raw, and his memories of the fight and his conversation with Sean still jarred.

James had seen Brendan fight many times – he was fast and measured, he knew exactly what he was doing and, as a result, always walked away with barely a scratch. Like the time Brendan had intervened when a disgruntled rugby-playing boyfriend of one of James's many one night stands finally caught up with him. James had seen the rugby player clench his fist; he knew the thump was coming, and had shut his eyes in anticipation, but it never arrived. When he opened his eyes the rugby player was on the floor with Brendan standing over him.

This was why James was struggling with Brendan's story. From the little he had told James about his brothers, they seemed more than capable of sorting things out for themselves. Then there was the severity of Brendan's injuries – the fractured jaw and four broken ribs, his face, swollen and bruised, and his missing tooth. James just couldn't figure out how Brendan, fighting alongside his brothers, could have ended up in such a pitiful state. Also, Brendan had seemed dulled since he had returned, but not in the sense of being caught off-guard, outnumbered and outskilled; it was more like a light had gone out, something so terrible had happened that a part of him had switched itself off, permanently.

Brendan chose his words carefully, not sure who he was protecting; certainly not his family, but maybe James in some way. Perhaps from the horrors of knowing who his family really were. Maybe he was protecting himself – his pride, his secrets, the university life he had managed to keep separate from Lowlands.

'It was my brother, Liam. He beat me,' Brendan said cautiously.

'Why?' asked James.

Slowly, that evening, as the sun turned crimson and bled across the sky, Brendan unravelled the secrets he had managed to keep away from James and the others for past three years. He told James about the night he met Cassie: about the outbuilding and the thrill of sneaking out to meet her; the horror of finding out her age; the madness of not being able to stay away from her; and how he had run away from it all – from her and the lost baby.

As his words tumbled out, he found himself going further back in time, as if he had pulled on a loose thread, his past life untangling itself. He talked of how he hated his father and of the beatings he and his brothers took from him as kids; the struggle he'd had to get to university; his father hauling his maths teacher across the desk at the suggestion that Brendan should consider applying; about how he despised working in the yard, the dirt and mind-numbing boredom of stripping down car parts until nothing existed.

He told James about his guilt at leaving Sean, how he found Liam's behaviour disturbing and the rivalry that existed between them. He described Riley and explained how he had looked after him as a kid and had taught him to ride a bike and to swim. He recounted the time when he built Riley a tyre swing in the woods, and Liam had cut it down and burnt it, and how he had enjoyed beating Liam to the ground as a punishment. He expressed his fears for Riley, being trapped by his family and treated with as much respect as one of the O'Rourke dogs. He talked of his sisters: Anne-Marie, temperamental and harsh, always grooming herself and wasting her life bitching and moaning at them all, slowly turning into the mirror-image of their mother; and Kelly, the family's little princess – spoilt and bright and learning at a young age how to play them all. Brendan realised, with some distaste, that he actually held some respect for her for this. He talked about his mother and how they all tried so hard to please her but the gratification it gave them was as fragile and lasting as blossom in the wind. It chilled him to think of her, her cold, hard stare cutting as precisely as a steel blade, and her disapproval so apparent he could almost taste its harshness. Finally, he described the chaos of living at Lowlands – the large red brick Victorian house that no longer felt like home.

James remained silent when Brendan finally ran out of words; they sat still in the twilight and it was in this half light that James's words filled the room so poignantly. 'Why didn't you say something before?'

'My family's not like yours James. They sort everything out with their fists. Everything is a fight. They have always got their claws into someone or something. It's not an easy thing to explain and it's not easy to admit that it's... me.'

'It's not you,' James said kindly. 'That's not how you are.'

'I want to believe that, that's why it is so important that I am here. It's my only way out, my escape route away from them.' He closed his eyes and realised how exhausted he felt with them all.

'Come away with us then this summer. You can't go back there. You're not going back,' said James decisively.

Brendan had already made his mind up that he was not going back to Lowlands. He hadn't spoken to his father yet about this, but he knew in his heart that nothing could drag him back now. As James began telling him about the travel plans – the places they could visit, the sights they would see and the experiences they would share – the intriguing details of each city and country filled him with a sense of adventure. After all, he told himself, wasn't this the point of it all? Wasn't this the reason for his teacher's struggle to get him to embrace a new and exciting world and leave the old one behind? Didn't that make all the fights with his parents about leaving and not working for them, worth it? Didn't it take the sting out of the insults they hurled at him every time he went home? Being here among his friends was the antidote to the restlessness which nestled in his gut, and rose like bile when he thought of Lowlands.

He would have agreed to anything there and then, so grateful was he to James for not judging him, for not rejecting him. The relief, mixed with the beer, gave him a surge of confidence, and he found himself agreeing to everything James suggested.

After Brendan had returned to London, Sean had slunk out of Lowlands and was so lost in his thoughts about the harsh words that had come between them, that he never noticed Tess serve him or her furtive glances in his direction. The Fighting Cocks was a small pub on a quiet road on the edge of Ashdowne; it was the furthest pub from Lowlands, which made it the ideal place for him to lick his wounds. For five consecutive evenings he had pulled into the car park and drowned his sorrows in a cocktail of lager and whiskey. Sitting on the same stool, leaning against the bar, turning his lighter over and over in his hands, he spoke to no one, and the few customers in the pub knew enough about the O'Rourke family to leave him in peace.

One particular evening, Tess's curiosity got the better of her and after placing his drinks in front of him and getting no response she sidled over to Elsie, the landlady, and asked her who he was.

Elsie had stared at her hard before answering. 'Sean O'Rourke.'

'He looks so sad,' said Tess, wistfully.

Elsie was shocked. 'He looks like he is brooding for a fight if you ask me, and if that's the case I wish he'd clear off to The Queen's Arms.'

Tess continued to watch him. He glanced up, looking in her direction, and his hands fell still. Tess smiled, but he continued to look at her, not returning the gesture. Held in his stare for a while, she felt suspended, as if time had stopped. When he looked away he picked up his drink, downed it, and placed the empty glass on the bar. Tess made a move to go to serve him but found Elsie's hand, tight around her arm, pulling her back. 'You stay here. You're a nice girl and you need to stay that way,' Elsie told her.

She watched Elsie refill his glass, keeping the chat to a minimum and forcing one of her tight smiles as she took his money.

Elsie returned to Tess and whispered fiercely: 'You do not want to get yourself mixed up with that lot, Missy. I just hope he gets bored and finds somewhere else to drink soon, before the rest of them start coming down here.'

Tess remembered the name O'Rourke from school; she remembered there were twins, a year below her, a boy and a girl – Liam and Anne-Marie. She remembered now that Liam was always in trouble – his behaviour uncontrollable – and she had some recollection of him being expelled. However, Anne-Marie had been the scarier of the two. There was no girl in the school who would take her on, so Anne-Marie had ruled the girls' cloakrooms, picking out the weak, ruining their lives, and turning the even weaker ones into fellow bullies. Tess also remembered another brother, Brendan, who was older than Tess, and her friend's older sister had dated him. As much as Anne-Marie filled the girls with terror, Brendan had made them swoon.

Elsie tutted loudly when the telephone started ringing and she left the bar to answer it just as Old Mac staggered into the pub. His small frame was bent with age and struggled against the weight of the door. When he finally made it to the bar he grinned a toothless smile at Tess.

'My usual please, princess,' he asked her and Tess returned his smile fondly. 'I'd offer you one but I'm saving up to take you out dancing,' he continued, laughing at the same joke he made every time he came in.

Tess laughed good-naturedly and walked over to the till. When she turned around she found Sean staring at her. She smiled again and, this time, a small smile broke his lips as his eyes rolled smoothly over her.

'What time do you finish?' he asked.

'We don't usually have many customers after ten, so Elsie tends to let me go about then.'

He nodded. 'I'll wait for you. I'll drive you home.'

'Will you?' Tess asked, flicking her hair back and staring him straight in the eye.

'I reckon.' His smile spread with amusement. He wasn't sure how he had not really noticed her until tonight, with her strawberry blonde curls falling messily around her face, her light jade eyes and rounded cheeks, like rosy apples. It was her curves that had mostly grabbed his attention; the way her hips swayed as she moved around the bar, her tiny waist that blossomed out into her bosom. Her skin was fair and covered in little freckles, and she had a fresh look about her, clean and wholesome.

When Elsie returned to the bar, she found Old Mac with a look of gloom on his face. 'What's up Mac?' she asked.

'Looks like I lost my girl to a younger model,' Mac sighed, looking in the direction of Tess and Sean. Elsie looked on aghast at the two of them laughing, almost glued together.

'Do you think I can take him Elsie?' Mac asked.

'I hope so Mac, I hope so,' replied Elsie, her heart sinking.

CHAPTER 13

Four months ago

IN THE TAXI on the way home from James's birthday party, Jemima was quiet. It had been strange meeting one of Brendan's ex-girl-friends. She glanced sideways at him; he was staring out of the taxi window so she couldn't read his face, but she could feel his hand resting on her leg, his thumb slowly stroking it.

Each year Tanya threw a party for James's birthday, filling their small Victorian terrace with friends and family. Brendan and Jemima had squeezed through the guests to get to the kitchen where James greeted them both with a huge hug, already drunk and enjoying the audience that had gathered around him. Tanya came over, holding a martini glass high to avoid it getting knocked. The four of them had stood chatting and laughing at James as he lapped up all the attention. Jemima felt relaxed – the martini Tanya had handed her was loosening her muscles and the heat of the kitchen had meant she had finally been brave enough to shrug off her pashmina to reveal the little black dress that Brendan had pawed her in earlier.

⫸⫷ ⫸⫷

Jemima had met them properly for the first time one warm, sunny afternoon a couple of months after her accident. She was nervous. She knew from the way Brendan talked about them how important they were to him. She had found them both delightful and she couldn't help but like them – even when Tanya had engineered some time on her own with her. They had been clearing away the dishes in Tanya's kitchen, while James and Brendan were sat outside, both still drinking and smoking.

'You know they are talking about you?' said Tanya, softly. Jemima turned to face her, looking shocked. Tanya smiled warmly. She was taller than Jemima by a couple of inches, with an elegant and delicate frame, Jemima felt small next to her, and slightly clumsy. Tanya continued to smile at Jemima. 'He is absolutely blown away by you.'

Jemima looked down, feeling her cheeks flush.

'I have never seen him look at anyone the way he looks at you,' finished Tanya and Jemima struggled to look up at her. 'We're delighted he's met you – you'll be the making of him. He's needed to meet someone like you for a long time.'

'Someone like me?' Jemima repeated, unsure what Tanya meant.

'You're perfect for him,' Tanya responded, taking a large bowl of strawberries out to the garden.

⤙⟢ ⟣⤚

Now, a couple of months later, stood in the same kitchen, James's eyes appraised Jemima and her dress, and she caught him give an approving look at Brendan who looked pleased with his friend's response, and slid his arm around Jemima's waist. She always felt reassured by this, as if she could cope with anything life threw at her when she was near him. So when he announced he was going outside for a cigarette, she felt nervous at being left on her own and escaped to the safety of the bathroom. When she returned, she saw Brendan talking on the patio with a tall, thin blonde woman in a very short, slinky black dress and extremely high heels. Even from this distance Jemima could tell she worked out, her toned limbs accentuated by the patio lighting. She leaned towards him as he lit her cigarette and when she spoke to him he looked tense, while she looked relaxed, resting her hand on his shoulder.

James watched Jemima carefully, seeing her concerned expression. She looked fragile and he was reminded of his discussion with Brendan about her the first time they had come over. When Tanya and Jemima had disappeared into the kitchen, James and Brendan remained seated in the garden, sitting in silence for a while, staring at each other. James knew Brendan was waiting for him to comment on Jemima and Brendan knew that James would be considering his comments about her very seriously.

'She's very beautiful. In fact, she's exquisite,' James said, noticing the small smile flicker across Brendan's lips. 'You're serious about her?' he asked, somewhat rhetorically.

Brendan breathed out cigarette smoke. 'Yeah,' he replied, his voice assured and quiet, and James raised his eyebrows and nodded, smiling slowly.

'Who would have thought we would see the day, eh?'

Brendan smiled and the two of them fell silent again.

'She looks delicate, you know. You could easily damage her,' said James thoughtfully.

Brendan nodded his acknowledgement.

⟶▬◉ ◉▬⟵

'Trust him,' James told Jemima, sidling up to her.

'I do,' she stammered, surprised to find him by her side.

'But you don't trust her?' he asked, and Jemima looked back at the woman stood close to Brendan with her hip jutting out and her face turned to him inquisitively.

Jemima shook her head slightly as she replied and her voice was resigned. 'She's beautiful.'

'No, no she's not, not compared to you.' Jemima swung around to face him, looking at him with disbelief. 'Brendan and Kristen – it was always a very one-sided relationship, if you can call it that.'

As if he could sense that he was being watched, Brendan turned towards the house and gave Jemima a tired smile. She didn't know what to make of it, and she felt foolish to be caught staring at them both. She forced a smile in return as Brendan left the patio and made his way over to her and James.

'Alright?' he asked her, offering no explanation as to who he had been talking to, and Jemima nodded compliantly.

'Gio and Zoe are here,' he told her, loosely hooking his fingers through hers and leading her away. Jemima turned and saw Kristen still on the patio. She ran her eyes critically over Jemima, who immediately turned away, feeling awkward and exposed in her short dress.

When they got back to Brendan's apartment, he pulled her onto his bed and rolled on top of her, pinning her arms down. 'I'm not letting go until you tell me what's up,' he said, partly joking.

Jemima sighed. 'It was just weird seeing you with an ex-girlfriend.'

'She was never my girlfriend, Jem,' he replied, kissing her neck.

'James said you had a relationship with her,' Jemima said, determinedly continuing the conversation.

'Sex, that's all,' he replied flatly, letting go of her arms and gently pulling her upright before tugging her dress over her head.

'It's just strange seeing you with someone you've been with... I mean, her and I are nothing alike.'

'That's good. Believe me.' He ran his fingers down her back and felt her lean into him.

'How many?' she continued.

'What?'

'How many women have you slept with?'

He groaned and fell back onto the bed. 'Do we have to have this conversation now?' he asked, rolling his eyes in frustration.

Jemima dropped her head. 'I'm sorry,' she whispered. 'It's just playing on my mind.' She looked back at him, her eyes searching to see what reaction she would get. It was precisely the look that dissolved him; he felt his frustration dissipate, and he ran his forefinger down her arm.

I haven't kept count since I was about seventeen,' he said, watching her response carefully.

'You must have some idea.'

He shrugged and looked at her, trying to gauge how much to tell her.

'Okay, so last count when you were seventeen then,' she continued.

'Eighteen.' He watched her eyes widen and her mouth fall open.

'How old were you when you lost your virginity?'

'Fifteen,' he replied, cautiously.

'Oh, well I guess we're talking serious double figures then.'

He shrugged again, still watching her closely.

'Triple?' she cried.

'No, I don't think so.' He laughed and pulled her on top of him again. 'I mean, I don't know how many in double figures,' he said laughing softly. 'Jem, what does it matter?'

She looked up at him. 'I don't know why I want to know. It just feels important after tonight,' she murmured and they lay quietly for a while.

'How many for you?' he asked her, his curiosity now stirred.

She buried her head into his chest. 'Like you said, what does it matter?' she responded.

He frowned and tipped her head up to face him. 'That many?' he joked.

'No,' she replied, shocked and taking him seriously, before catching his smile. She lowered her head back to his chest and, realising she wasn't going to answer, he spoke quietly.

'Okay if you really need to know, about fifty,' he said, and she looked up at him. Her expression was difficult to read. 'Or perhaps sixty... sixty-five-ish,' he added and she continued to stare at him. 'Not much more than seventy,' he finished.

'Including me?'

'Yeah '

'Oh.' Her face fell. She looked at him uncomfortably before answering his question: 'Two,' she whispered.

He didn't reply, he simply nodded and laid his head back against the pillow, while she rested her head on his chest. Tipping his head back further against his pillow he tried to hide his smile. Jemima could feel him breathe in sharply and his stomach muscles flexing lightly beneath her. She looked up and peered into his face.

'Are you laughing at me?' she asked suspiciously.

Brendan pulled his face muscles taut and stared at her seriously. 'No,' he replied.

She lowered her head again and then caught the flicker of a smile. 'You are!' she cried, looking back into his face. He grabbed her head and buried it into his neck letting out a howl of laughter. She struggled as he held her tightly, continuing to laugh.

'I'm sorry, I'm sorry,' he spluttered, letting go of her and wiping tears from his eyes. She turned her back on him. 'I'm not laughing at you,' he tried to explain.

'Yes you are,' she snapped. He was trying to extinguish his laughter and he knew she was right.

'I kind of like it,' he said and she turned to look at him, her brow knitted with confusion. 'I like that there have only been... two,' he said trying to stifle a snigger before saying the number.

'It's not funny. Compared to you I am practically a virgin,' she said, sounding exasperated. He leaned forward and buried his head in his hands and she saw his shoulders shudder. 'Brendan!' she cried and he squeezed his eyes tight in amusement. She could see the effort it took to refrain from smiling and she glared at him.

Forcing himself to look at her he said, 'This is precisely why I was avoiding this conversation, Jem.' The amusement in his voice had changed to frustration now, as he fell back onto the bed and sighed heavily.

'You're a tart,' she said, looking out the corner of her eye at him.

'Thanks,' he replied flatly.

'Did you realise that I was so inexperienced,' she asked, turning towards him, and he could see her cheeks starting to flush.

'Only from what you said, not from how you are,' he replied, watching her carefully. She contemplated his answer before resting her head on him again and he ran his fingers gently through her hair. 'So,' she sighed. 'How many times have you actually been in love?'

'Once,' he replied, not offering any more detail.

Jemima thought back to Kristen, her slender body and glowing skin. 'Kristen?' she asked nervously, thinking back to them on the patio.

Brendan's face fell into a shocked frown and he shook his head. 'You,' he replied, surprised that she hadn't figured it out.

CHAPTER 14

Seven years ago

TESS FOUND HERSELF at the end of her road, with her heart jamming against her chest. She was clutching a bread knife, which she had just thrust against her stepfather's face in an attempt to get him to stop mauling her.

'Your mum's heard you've been hanging out with one of them O'Rourkes,' Jeff had sneered while she was washing up.

'His name is Sean, and if Mum doesn't like it she can talk to me about it,' she snapped, turning around to face him. He was half dressed and unshaven, the sight of him repulsed her and she felt uneasy. Something in his expression told her not to turn her back on him.

'Is it true what they say about 'em?' He asked, edging closer.

'What?' she sounded irritated.

'That they're all really well hung.'

His smile was goading and she closed her eyes in disgust. When she opened them he was in front of her pushing her back against the kitchen sink. She pushed against him, but he was too strong, and she could feel him winning out.

'I always knew you would get easy and if you're putting out for that scum you can put out for me,' he continued, thrusting his hips hard against her. She turned her head sharply away from his stale breath, continuing to try to push him away with one hand while the other hand searched around the sink, frantically trying to find the bread knife she had used earlier. As her fingers groped the dirty water, so his groped her, inching up her thigh and beneath her t-shirt. 'If you like a big cock, then mine can bang you into next week,' he said, breathing heavily into her neck.

She tried not to squirm as the serrated edge of the knife bit into her finger. Ignoring the pain, her fingers twisted to find the handle, but in the water the knife took on a life of its own.

'D'you know what the thought of you being wet does to me, eh?' He groaned, forcefully pushing his thigh between her legs.

Finally, she managed to grab the handle and she pushed the knife in front of his face.

'Get off me!' she screamed. Jeff froze. 'Get away from me you sick, dirty bastard!' she screamed again. He backed away, looking indignant. 'And stay away,' she barked, edging away from the kitchen, throwing open the front door and rushing out into the hot, sunny afternoon.

At the end of the lane she stopped; glancing down at the bread knife in her hand she shuddered, and threw it into one of the cottage gardens. She wondered where to go. Who could help her? Looking across the road to the Fighting Cocks she wanted to run to Elsie, but what could Elsie do? Realising this she set off running, taking the road towards Ashdowne – towards the O'Rourke's yard.

Sean was underneath a rusting Ford Transit when Tess turned up, standing by the high wrought iron gates looking about nervously as their dogs barked at her. Liam looked around the truck and Lester looked out of the office window, both wanting to see what all the commotion was about. When Liam saw her, he kicked the side of the van and Sean slid out looking annoyed with him.

'What?' Sean grunted. Liam nodded towards Tess and Sean followed his stare, quickly getting up, grabbing a rag and wiping his hands as he walked over to her.

When she saw him coming, she broke down, her body convulsed with sobs. Lester watched as Sean held the girl's shoulders, stooping down to face her. He could tell by the tension in his body that he wasn't happy with what she was telling him. When the girl had finished talking, Sean hugged her and stood rocking her gently for a while. Then he spoke to her again, holding her face in his hands before turning towards the office, his eyes thunderous.

Pushing the door to the office open with a hard shove, Sean was surprised to see Lester standing by the window. 'I need some time out,' he said.

'That your girlfriend?' Lester asked and Sean nodded. 'That's the girl you've been sneaking off with in the afternoons then is it?'

Sean lowered his head and mentally cursed Liam for grassing him up. 'I need to sort something out,' he continued.

Lester stared at him, coldly. 'And I'm owed hours Sean. I guess we don't always get what we want.'

'It's important, there's been some trouble with her stepfather.'

'Does this place look like a fucking charity?'

'Please, he's just tried it on with her – I need to sort it out.'

Lester's face hardened; he could see the anger brewing inside his son. Familiar with this feeling and the effort it took to contain it, he walked over to his desk, opened a drawer, picked up the keys to the black truck and threw them at Sean. He caught them swiftly. 'You need any help?' Lester asked,

'No, I've got this,' said Sean, and turned to leave.

When he got to the doorway, Lester called out: 'Don't leave anything left of him son.'

Sean looked back, but his father had already sat back down at his desk, his attention turned to the computer.

Sean drove steadily but fast, with Tess sat beside him anxiously chewing her thumbs. When he walked in through the front door of her family's cottage he immediately saw Jeff, who was sat facing away from him watching daytime television. Walking up behind him, Sean grabbed his shoulders with both hands and pulled him over the back of the sofa, letting him fall heavily onto the floor. Then he picked Jeff up by the scruff of the neck before dragging him outside, while Jeff hollered at him to let go. Ignoring Jeff's cries, Sean hit him and watched as he fell backwards, losing his balance and landing hard on the pea shingle in front of the cottages. Sean strode over and, pulling him up, curled his large, thick fingers into a ball, making sure his opponent could see the size of the fist about to come his way, before punching him again. Jeff staggered and fell once more, the shingle cutting into his hands and knees. When he heard the crunching of gravel getting closer he cowered.

Grabbing Jeff by the throat, Sean snarled into his face: 'Touch her again and you're fucking dead.' With that, Sean kneed him hard in the stomach and let him drop to the ground before heading back to Tess.

Jeff curled into a ball, gasping for air, and huskily retorted: 'I never touched her, she came onto me. I'm always fighting her off – didn't your little slut tell you that?'

Sean closed his eyes and breathed deeply before turning and striding back over to him. Lester's words resounded from earlier – *'Don't leave anything of him'* – familiar words from his childhood. He kicked Jeff hard in the ribs, hearing them crack, then he pulled him up and hit him again and again; as Jeff stumbled backwards, Sean's punches rained down on him relentlessly.

At that moment, Tess's mother arrived home with her young sons and began screaming at Tess to get Sean to stop. Tess's brothers were frightened and had buried their heads against their mother's legs. It wasn't long before they were joined by the neighbours, who had been drawn outside by the sound of the fight. They looked on, shocked, but did nothing to help.

When Sean finally stopped, Jeff lay on the ground, dirty, bloody and snivelling. Sean stood over him, panting hard and sweating, his hair having fallen into his eyes. Pushing it back roughly he said menacingly: 'Touch her or call her names again and I will hunt you down.'

Tess stared at Sean. His work overalls were pulled down to his waist, his black vest was taut against his chest, and dirt and blood covered his hands and face. She fixed her attention on the tattoo that ran in dark Celtic swirls along his shoulder and down to his bicep as he walked up to her and cupped her face in his hands.

'You're coming home with me,' he told her.

She stared up at him, taking in his blond hair and large blue eyes, his full lips and strong jaw. He appeared so angelic, his touch so light, and she marvelled at how – just moments ago – a beast had been unleashed from within him, and wondered where it had disappeared to now.

CHAPTER 15

Two months ago

BRENDAN WAS WATCHING Jemima sleep; she looked peaceful lying in his bed, turned partly on her side with one arm tucked underneath the pillow. Quietly, he walked around the bed and climbed in behind her. He curled his legs against hers and tenderly moved her hair away from her ear, running his hand tentatively along the side of her body and letting it rest lightly on her hip. His eyes followed his hand and he smiled contentedly. She started to stir; his lips just touched her ear as he whispered, 'Marry me.'

⟶▬◉ ◉▬⟵

They had spent Christmas and New Year apart and he'd hated it. Jemima had already arranged to spend Christmas with her aunts and New Year with Minnie, Abby and some old university friends before she'd met Brendan. So over the break he'd fitted in one fleeting visit to his family and spent the rest of his days working and his evenings with James and Tanya, turning down their invitation to join them skiing, insisting that he wanted to be around to collect Jemima from the airport. On his last evening with them, as James put another log on the open fire in their small lounge, he turned to Brendan and, seeing his sullen face, gave a sigh. 'What's up?' he asked, having a fair idea what it was likely to be.

Brendan sat staring at the flames licking the wood in the small cast iron grate, and shrugged, sighing heavily. James leaned across to him, refilling his brandy glass, catching Tanya's eye, and raising his eyebrows in exasperation. She smiled and put her book down.

'Have you spoken to Jem today?' she asked and Brendan responded with a small grunt.

'How is she?' Tanya continued, undeterred by his response.

He turned to her; his eyes looked pained. His chin was jutted forward and he had a look on his face that indicated trouble was brewing, a look that both James and Tanya recognised well.

'She's fine, she's having a good time.'

'That's good isn't it?' remarked James buoyantly.

'Is it?' replied Brendan, looking back at the fire. After a while he spoke again. 'Her ex-boyfriend is there – Will.' He almost spat the name out.

'So? You trust her don't you?' asked James, and Brendan grunted again.

'She would never cheat on you Brendan,' Tanya offered reassuringly.

'It's not her I'm worried about,' he continued, his face now set tightly in a scowl.

James stared at Brendan for a moment; then he laughed. 'Oh my god, you're jealous!'

Brendan's eyes whipped back to James and a look of horror crossed his face. 'No I'm not,' he snapped defensively.

'Yes you are,' James replied, hugely amused by the idea, and Brendan's scowl deepened. 'Oh I'm loving the irony,' James continued.

'I'm not jealous,' Brendan said gruffly.

James stopped smiling and looked seriously at him. 'What are you then?'

'I'm pissed off,' was the best he could come up with.

'You're pissed off that you are here while Jemima is in Scotland, tucked up in some romantic castle in the Highlands, probably doing the Gay Gordons with... Will, the ex?'

At the emphasis of the name, Brendan's eyes creased, he pushed his tongue into the side of his cheek and glared at James.

'You're jealous,' said James flatly.

'Stop teasing him,' Tanya intervened.

'Jealous,' James mouthed at Brendan, who was still glaring at him.

The room fell silent. Tanya returned to her book while James and Brendan continued to stare at each other. Eventually, Brendan broke the stare by looking down, 'What do I do?' he asked.

'What do you want to do?' Tanya asked.

'Take him out.'

Tanya and James rolled their eyes.

'Have you met him?' asked James.

'No.'

'Has Jemima said anything that might mean he's still interested in her?'

Brendan contemplated James's question for a short while. 'No,' he replied quietly, starting to feel foolish.

The next day at work, as Brendan sat at his desk beneath the strip lighting and amongst the rubber plants wrapped in tinsel, he scrolled through the contacts list in his mobile phone. With fingers moving deftly on the screen, he deleted nearly half the numbers in it that belonged to women; women who no longer had any relevance to him. When he left work, he meandered through an old-fashioned shopping arcade, in no particular hurry to get home. He gazed idly, from shop to shop, all of them small, exclusive and expensive. Tucked between two shops nestled a jewellers. As Brendan casually glanced in the window, a flash of bright blue caught his eye.

→══ ══←

Jemima thought she'd heard Brendan's voice, but she wasn't sure if she was still dreaming. His words were inaudible but his tone was serious and she started to float back to consciousness; his words skimmed her ear like a pebble across a pond, bouncing fast, just touching the surface.

He leaned in closer, tightening his arm around her waist. 'Marry me,' he whispered again. Jemima opened her eyes and turned her head towards him. He was smiling down at her, his eyes twitching with excitement. 'I want you to marry me,' he said, gently placing a small, powder-blue box into her grasp. When he released her hand, her eyes widened with surprise. The ring sat proudly inside the box, aquamarine and diamonds, nestled in oyster satin. Her eyes shot back to Brendan, and her mouth fell open.

'You're serious?' she exclaimed in a half-whisper and he nodded. Taking the ring from the box, he slid it onto her finger. She stared at it, her mouth still open and her eyes growing wider with disbelief. She flexed her ring finger, watching the light reflect off the stones. 'It's beautiful, just... beautiful,' she managed, before looking back at him.

He frowned; his voice was low when he spoke. 'Will you... marry me?' he asked.

She started with a slow nod, then a smile broke across her lips. 'Yes of course I will,' she said. How could she ever refuse him?

CHAPTER 16

Six years ago

LYLA HAD BEEN the first to greet Brendan when he walked into the kitchen. 'Hey, the wanderer's returned,' she exclaimed. 'Look at you, your hair is so long – look, it's going curly,' she continued, grabbing a piece of sun-bleached hair near his ear. He pulled his head gently away from her and smiled.

'How long were you gone?'

'Fifteen months.'

'All that sun, sea and sand, eh? Suits ya.' She reached out her hand and cupped his cheek. They held each other's stare for a while before Brendan broke the silence.

'I hear Sean got married.'

'Yeah, and I'm a grandmother now. They had a boy – another bloody boy in the family!' She rolled her eyes. 'Why don't you go up to see them, they're on the top floor. I've made up a bed for you in your old room.'

Brendan was uncertain about this. He wanted to be more prepared before he saw Sean. After all, he hadn't been invited to the wedding; he had found out about it while he was travelling via a blunt email containing a couple of wedding photos of Sean in an ill-fitting suit standing next to a heavily pregnant bride.

When he showed James the pictures he had scoffed: 'I guess you're all just moving on. He's got his life and you've got yours, and this shows how far apart they are. Good job really, otherwise that could be you in the photo, marrying some village girl, with a baby on the way.'

Brendan had agreed with him, but he still felt hurt by what they had done, and by the way they had let him know.

'We've got a party to go to tonight' said James, changing the subject. 'Some girls Gio and Matt met have invited us over.' He smiled as he pulled a dark cube wrapped in cling film from his shorts pocket, holding it up for Brendan to see. 'Local, very strong apparently. We just need some drink to go with it. What have we got left?' he asked, leaving the room.

Before they went out, Brendan replied to the email, and as he pressed the send button, he felt as if he had cheated them by lying. He wasn't sure he was happy for them at all; he didn't even know Sean's wife. How could he be happy for a complete stranger? It felt as if he and Sean were being stretched further apart.

⊷▻▭◉ ◉▭◅⊷

The first glance Tess got of Brendan was of him gazing around his room; she had been on the landing with Georgie. Brendan's door was open and she didn't know whether to introduce herself. He hadn't changed much since school; he seemed slightly taller and broader across the shoulders. His hair was lighter, the sun having turned it white-blond in places, and it was longer – it fell behind his ears and skimmed the base of his neck. As she stood looking at him, Georgie twisted in her arms and let out an impatient cry. Brendan turned to face them and she caught the shot of blue from his eyes. He stared straight at her, not smiling, his face hard. His look gouged through her sending her hurrying downstairs.

Tess was fitting Georgie into his highchair when Sean and Brendan entered the kitchen.

'Brendan's back for Christmas,' Lyla remarked, turning to face him. He forced a smile. Tess glanced around her, noticing his family's apparent indifference.

'This is Tess,' said Sean, and Tess smiled nervously while Brendan looked at her closely.

'Hi,' he said, his voice surprisingly friendly, a far cry from the hostile look she'd got from him earlier.

'And this is Georgie,' Lyla interjected, gesturing to the baby. 'Georgie Porgie, pudding and pie, kissed the girls and made them cry – just like his uncle, eh?' Lyla's voice was childlike as she recited the rhyme, whilst staring at Brendan. 'My first grandchild,' she said, and everyone jumped as Cassie dropped a serving spoon and it rattled harshly against the tiled floor.

→──◉ ◎──←

'Look at the colour of it. Surprised they let you back into the country,' Lester commented while they were all eating. Tess watched as Brendan avoided the comment and carried on with his meal. Raising his fork to his mouth Brendan caught Tess staring at him; he rolled his eyes at his father's comment and for the first time since she had met Lester O'Rourke he did not seem quite so terrifying.

'D'you go to Bangkok?' Liam asked Brendan, spurred on by his father's jibe.

'Yeah,' Brendan replied, turning to look at him.

'D'you see any lady-boys?' Liam asked, sounding juvenile.

'Yeah, I saw some.'

Liam's face broke into a wide smirk. 'I bet you did!' Everyone laughed, except Tess and Cassie. Cassie stared at her plate, looking as if she could take flight at any minute, while Tess looked on bemused.

'With his hair that long and that bunch of poofs he went with I bet he's well acquainted with them all,' his father added, to another round of laughter. 'He's come back quite the pretty boy,' Lester said, leaning his head back and staring straight at Brendan.

Brendan smiled through all the exchanges and steadily finished his meal. 'Why the curiosity Liam? You tempted?' he asked. At this, the table erupted in a roar of laughter.

'Fuck off,' Liam snarled.

Brendan surveyed Liam, noticing his red neck and face flushed with anger, and was pleased by his reaction. This was just the sort of occasion when he could have the upper hand with Liam, and it was too good an opportunity to miss, even though his better judgement was telling him to let it go. 'I think you've just answered that yourself,' he added.

Liam threw his knife and fork down. 'Who the fuck does he think he is coming back here and talking to me like that?' he spat.

'Liam, sit down,' his father instructed, already bored by the outburst. Then he turned his attention to Brendan and everyone fell silent. Inside Brendan a defiant spark had been lit from the exchange with Liam, forcing him to return his father's cold stare.

Georgie started to cry, abruptly bringing Tess out of her reverie; like the others at the table, she was absorbed by the tension growing between Brendan and Lester. When she lifted Georgie, he gripped her so tightly she could feel his small heart beating rapidly.

Many things were said between Brendan and his father during that silence – words not spoken but expressed through each other's measured stare – and the hate, the resentment and the defiance was palpable. Finally, Lester swigged the last of his beer, announced he was going to the pub, and left, making sure he nudged the back of Brendan's chair as he passed him. Suddenly thrust forward, Brendan tried not to smirk.

Once Lester had left, Lyla started to tidy away plates, and while doing so deliberately caught Brendan's eye and looked at him sternly. She had looked on helplessly as her buck and stag locked horns feeling torn, as she always did, between the two of them.

Cassie, keen to avoid Liam's temper, jumped up to help Lyla and Liam rose slowly, still glaring at Brendan menacingly. But Brendan looked back at him as if he couldn't care less. This was all starting to feel predictable and he sighed inwardly, leaving Liam to skulk out of the kitchen towards the brick sheds in the yard, which were now converted into his and Cassie's home.

'Well, it wouldn't be dinner if something didn't kick off eh?' joked Sean.

CHAPTER 17

One day ago

JEMIMA AND BRENDAN were stood in the large hallway at Clouds Reach, the home Jemima had grown up in. Her heart was pounding fast as she nervously awaited her aunts. Mrs Pickard, their housekeeper, had gone to fetch them; being nearly as old as her aunts, and given the size of the house, Jemima knew that it would take a while before they arrived.

Brendan looked about him, his eyebrows raised, a look of amazement on his face. At that moment Jemima envied his look; there was no trace of the apprehension she felt about turning up here married and breaking the news to her aunts. On their honeymoon she had started to feel the veil of excitement slip following the exhilaration of their extremely short engagement and small wedding. Brendan had been insistent that he didn't want to wait, and Jemima knew she could not face a large, formal wedding. Lying in the huge bed in their hotel suite, she had voiced her concerns. He had sighed and pulled her to him, assuring her that her aunts loved her and would be happy for her. She had desperately wanted to believe him. Now, here at Clouds Reach, his words of reassurance held little substance. She knew that they would be disappointed and, worse still, would probably try to hide it – at least Bridget would, though she reckoned on Martha having more to say on the matter.

Aunt Martha gracefully descended the sweeping staircase. She was a thin figure, tall and rather imposing, with straight grey hair cut into a sharp, jaw-length bob. Martha smiled when she saw Jemima but on seeing Brendan she appeared austere. Reaching the bottom step, Jemima approached her, kissing her lightly on both cheeks.

'Hello Aunty,' she said and then, noticing her aunt's attention wander to Brendan, she continued tentatively, 'Aunty, this is...'

Before she got a chance to finish, Bridget appeared from the back of the house, dressed in her gardening clothes. Her white hair, also clipped into a jaw-length bob, was ruffled. When she saw Jemima, her face lit up with delight.

'Oh my!' she gasped and held her arms out to her niece. She embraced Jemima warmly, holding her by her shoulders and exploring her face with busy eyes. 'What a lovely surprise,' Bridget gasped. Jemima smiled tightly and turned to Brendan, who smiled reassuringly at her.

'This is Brendan,' she said softly. Both aunts looked towards him. 'Brendan and I, well, we got married three weeks ago,' Jemima continued. The words she had practised in the car had sounded so reasonable but now, out in the open, they sounded ridiculous.

'Oh my!' exclaimed Bridget again, throwing her hands to her mouth.

Martha's reaction was imperceptible. Brendan smiled awkwardly then stepped forward holding his hand out to Bridget first, who shook it gracefully, looking up at him and smiling with amazement. He then turned to Martha and offered his hand. She took it politely, drawing her lips together; her grasp was firm and cold. The hallway fell silent. He stood back, placing his arm around Jemima's waist.

'Mrs Pickard, will you fetch us some tea? We'll take it in the drawing room,' said Martha in an authoritative voice. As she turned abruptly and headed through a large door off the hallway, Mrs Pickard, who had been hiding towards the back of the hall in order to not miss any potential gossip, scurried to the kitchen.

'Separate rooms?' Brendan questioned. They were stood in the bedroom that Martha had assigned Mrs Pickard to prepare for him.

'Sorry,' Jemima replied. He raised his eyebrows and folded his arms around her.

'But separate rooms? Come on, we're married.'

'It's only for one night,' replied Jemima, trying to placate him.

Brendan looked at her, partly in amusement and partly in disbelief.

'Brendan, they don't know you; they're shocked. They have their way of doing things. Please, just for one night,' she pleaded and stood on her tiptoes to kiss him.

'Where will you be?' he asked.

'Across the landing, see?' She pointed towards her old bedroom and he picked up her bag and walked towards it. The room couldn't have changed since Jemima was a little girl. She walked in behind him and watched as he looked around, his eyes settling on the antique rocking horse, a dapple grey made of real pony skin on dark oak runners, with a shiny red leather bridle and saddle.

'Wow, this was your room,' he finally managed. 'It's huge.'

'Come on, I'll give you a tour,' Jemima said excitedly and grabbed his hand, gently pulling him from her room.

As they went from room to room, Jemima offered explanations as to their purpose and history, and he followed behind in wonder. When they got to the kitchen he spotted the servants' bells. 'Do they work?' he asked.

'Yes, that's how they let Mrs Pickard know when they need her for something.'

Brendan raised his eyebrows in sympathy for the old lady. 'Jesus, even James's family home doesn't have servants' bells,' he laughed.

'There's a button in your room to push, by the fireplace,' continued Jemima and he smiled wickedly, looking closely at the little brass bells lined up neatly with a copper plate underneath each one with a room name etched on it.

'Which is it?' he asked.

'Your room is named "Master Bertram". He was my aunts' eldest brother. He was shot down in the Second World War, over France; my great grandfather never got over it, apparently.'

Jemima forced Brendan a smile and turned to leave the kitchen. Brendan followed, still looking about him at the large, shiny cooking range and the marble-topped kitchen table. The place was like a museum – a well-preserved slice of history.

The back door of the kitchen led to the garden. It was walled by thick ochre brick, which absorbed the sun and warmed the climbers that meandered along it. As they turned a corner, plumes of thick blossom blocked their way. They both ducked underneath the low-hanging branches and frothy pink canopy. As they emerged into the garden the impact of the Edwardian house was striking. Every storey was clearly defined by a change in the pattern of the brickwork, and the top storey was hung with decorative red tiles. An ancient wisteria, its trunk gnarled and twisted, had spread itself along the south wall and the house exuded an air of bygone eras. It belonged to a different time, one of fighting spirit and old-fashioned values.

'My great, great grandfather had the house built when he came back from India. He always missed the English coast apparently, which is why he settled here. He wanted bracing winds and cold air after the heat of Bombay, though there were bits he missed about India – that's why he had the veranda built."

'What did he do in India?'

'He owned an export business – spices, silk, tea, ivory, that sort of thing.'

Brendan looked back at the house and breathed in. 'Wow, Jem, it's amazing. You are so lucky to have grown up here.' As soon as the words had left his mouth he saw her face fall and he recalled the portrait of the young woman hanging on the stairs, with honey blonde curls and light brown eyes, her smile and gaze following him up the stairway. The picture was of Lilly, Jemima's mother. 'I'm sorry, I didn't mean...'

'I know,' she replied quietly and took his hand.

CHAPTER 18

Six years ago

BRENDAN HAD TROUBLE sleeping in his old room; he was unnerved. The last time he was here it had belonged to Cassie and Liam, and somehow their presence still lingered. He got up and quietly slipped downstairs. Passing the sitting room, he saw the outline of Tess huddled on a sofa, the phosphorescent moonlight spilling through the French windows and illuminating her silhouette.

Tess always woke in the small hours when Georgie became a bit restless, and she spent a couple of minutes settling him so as to not wake Sean. Though Georgie fell back into a deep slumber, Tess often found herself unable to get back to sleep so she would go downstairs. Sometimes she read, falling asleep on the sagging sofa and waking with the first stirrings of the house; sometimes she just stared out of the large windows to the back garden, and thought about how differently her life had turned out compared to the plans she had made. After a couple of hours, she would sigh deeply and return to her warm bed. This night though, she had found Brendan's phone on the coffee table and curiosity had got the better of her. Finding the photo album icon, she tapped on it and was soon gazing at white sandy beaches and deep blue seas.

The photos took her through towns and cities – some angular and modern, others crumbling and old. From vibrantly coloured street markets to underwater images of Brendan surrounded by shoals of fish, his hair floating around his head like a halo, his blue eyes shining brightly through his snorkel mask. There were pictures taken at night of groups of young men and women, spread out lazily on a beach by a bonfire. Then there was a picture of him with a blonde-haired woman, her eyes almost violet, his arms around her waist. There was an intimacy between them that the picture had captured and Tess stared intently at it, drawn in by the way he was looking at the girl.

'Do you want some tea?' Brendan asked Tess from the doorway, startling her.

'Oh god, I'm sorry, I was looking at the pictures of your trip. They're amazing.'

'That's okay.' He smiled kindly and walked towards her, handing her a mug. Tess handed him his phone. When he looked down at the photo of himself with the girl, the smile disappeared and he shot Tess a sharp look.

'Some of the places look so beautiful. You are so lucky,' she said, feeling the need to change the subject fast.

He scrolled forward to a picture of a beach and his smile returned. 'That's where I was staying when I got the news about you and Sean,' he said, showing her the picture. Tess looked at the beach; with its palm trees leaning lazily towards the white sand and deep turquoise sea, it felt so far away – particularly from Lowlands.

He handed the phone back to her and sat down. Tess followed his lead, continuing to look at the pictures, while he leaned back into the sofa and lit a joint. Out of the corner of her eye she could see him drag deeply and was aware of him watching her as he slowly released the pungent smoke from his mouth. They sat like that for a while, Tess poring over his pictures and finding the confidence to ask him where places were and Brendan happily pointing out landmarks. When she got to the end, she handed his phone back and he smiled appreciatively, offering her the joint.

'No, thank you,' she said sounding uncertain.

'Takes the edge off this place. It's quite intense living here isn't it?'

Tess nodded and found herself taking the joint, drawing a small amount into her mouth, and then carefully releasing the smoke, painfully aware of him still watching her closely. His eyes were fixed on the slight opening in her lips. He looked predatory. In an attempt to discreetly cover her bare thighs, she tugged at the edges of her nightshirt, conscious of the faded Minnie Mouse picture on the front and aware of how childish it looked.

'I remember you from school. You were three years above me,' she remarked, handing him his joint and trying to turn his attention away from her.

'I thought you looked familiar,' he replied, before deliberately releasing another mouthful of smoke, which edged its way towards her.

'All the girls in my year fancied you,' she gabbled.

'All of them?' he asked slyly, smiling.

She instantly blushed and, as the smoke cleared between them, he offered her the joint again. Obediently, she took it and this time she dragged harder, spluttering as it stung her eyes and throat. She immediately handed it back to him.

'You probably knew that though – the girls at our school weren't exactly subtle.'

He laughed, quietly. 'What about you?'

'I think I was too subtle. I just tried being really aloof and pretended to ignore you. It was a very flawed strategy – I can honestly say you didn't know I existed,' she laughed nervously.

His eyes narrowed, as he tried to remember her. 'Shame you didn't try a bit harder.'

Embarrassment radiated from her. She was afraid to look at him as he leaned casually against the sofa, taking her in, playing cat and mouse with her. Now he had her firmly cornered.

'Oh, well that was a long time ago. I'm a very different person now. I never would've believed at fourteen that I would be sat in the dark with you now, smoking that thing,' she said laughing lightly, trying to lighten the mood.

'Or that you would be married and be a teenage mum?' he added.

The smile dropped from her face. 'No, that wasn't part of the plan,' she replied quietly.

Brendan leaned forward and hooked a large curl of hair behind her ear, and gently lifted her face towards his with his forefinger. 'You are the only one here who has shown any genuine interest in my travels, Tess. You want more than this and it won't go away – that want – it will eat away at you from the inside. I know how that feels.'

He had just put into one short sentence the torment she had been feeling these past few months, though she hadn't recognised it as that. She had seen it as a deep-rooted restlessness, blaming it on lack of sleep, the relentless responsibility she had for her son and Sean's demanding ways. Every morning, with the promise of a new day, she had told herself how much she loved them both. By nightfall, she had fallen into bed too weary to weep, the day having sucked her dry. The words left her so quietly she hardly heard them herself.

'I can't do this anymore,' she whispered.

Brendan stubbed out the joint. Tess stopped trying to pull her girlish nightshirt down and let her hands fall free. She felt his warmth as he moved closer to her, letting him pull the edges of the nightshirt up until it was over her head. She watched him look her up and down, feeling the danger in his stare as his eyes glided over her. She felt his warm hands encircle her waist and neck, felt his breath on her skin, felt her legs part. After months of numbness, she felt every part of him that night, but most significantly she felt something close to living.

They lay together for a long time; Tess running her fingers through his hair, while he ran the palm of his hand along her thigh. They touched each other lightly, not wanting to leave a mark, no evidence as to what they had just done. As the radiators started to creek and Lowlands began its slow stir to life, Brendan turned to look at her.

'You ok?' he asked.

Tess nodded but she wasn't entirely sure. She knew she needed to get back upstairs, before Georgie woke; before she was missed, before they were both found on the sofa lying naked together. 'I need to get back,' she replied.

He nodded but made no move to release her. Instead, he kissed her, forcing her lips apart. She felt his breathing change pace as she began to move with him. When he'd finished, he smiled, a small smile that ran across his mouth in a wave, then he slowly moved so she could get up. Standing with her back to him, she picked up her nightshirt and quickly slid it on. She could feel his eyes on her and she felt exposed, not knowing what to say to him or how to leave things. She smiled awkwardly at him. He smiled back, with an expression that gave nothing away, and she turned hastily and left the room.

Climbing carefully into bed, Sean turned over and reached for her, burying his face in her hair and breathing deeply. He did what he always did when she came back to bed, though he could never recall it in the morning. Wrapping his arm around her, he had the distinct feeling that something was amiss. The scent from her hair was wrong – too heavy – and it pulled him through the layers of sleep until he found himself wide awake trying to figure it out, watching her chest rise and fall slowly through his narrowed eyes. The smell, he finally recognised, was dope – thick and sweet. But there was another smell, a pronounced undertone, which emanated from her skin. This smell was sharp and clear; it filled his nostrils and took him back to his childhood. Then it came to him, what she smelt of – Brendan.

Chapter 19

One day ago

THE TWO PEKINGESE dogs charged into the dining room, yapping and scurrying around. Martha shot Bridget a stern look and, instantly, Bridget jumped up from the table and started to usher them back to the kitchen.

Sitting in silence in the imposing dining room, listening to the dogs' sharp barks echo through the house, Brendan and Jemima sat side by side, tense, and stealing quick glances at one another. When Bridget returned, her cheeks were reddened and she was trying to smooth down her soft wisps of hair.

'Oh dear, Mrs Pickard had not shut the door properly. They had escaped,' she tried to explain, avoiding Martha's disapproval. She sat down and they all continued eating their first course, their knives and forks tapping against the bone china plates and, for a while, it was the only noise that filled the room, until Martha broke the silence.

'What is it you do Mr O'Rourke?' she asked inquisitively. Brendan considered the question; he felt guarded from the way she had asked it.

'It's Brendan, and I work in banking,' he replied carefully. 'I'm a financial analyst for an investment bank.'

Martha raised her eyebrows. Brendan was unsure whether this was in approval, interest or scepticism. 'Which bank?' she asked, sounding curious.

'Bluestein – they're in the City.'

'Brendan's degrees are in economics and mathematics,' Jemima chipped in enthusiastically.

'Your family are in banking?' Martha asked pointedly.

'No, they run a breaker's business – scrap metal, that sort of thing,' Brendan replied, holding Martha's stare.

'Quite a contrast. Where were you schooled?'

He looked at her firmly and felt his jaw tighten. 'Heathfields Comprehensive School,' he replied and watched as Martha's eyebrows inched further up her forehead; her eyes shone with confirmation that she had expected his answer and was playing with him.

'I was always under the impression that banking – particularly the field you work in – is quite a closed profession. Apart from needing the right qualifications, isn't it still rather an old school network?'

Brendan smiled sharply before responding. 'I was fortunate. I had a good contact, a friend's father. I started at a junior level and the rest of it was down to hard work,' he replied, sounding irritated.

The table fell quiet again as Mrs Pickard cleared away their first course and replaced it with their second. Brendan slowly turned his knife over in his hand. His dislike for Martha was growing, but he was determined to get through their stay without altercation. Returning a serving dish of vegetables carefully to the table, Martha looked at Brendan and Jemima.

'Why the urgency to get married?' she asked.

Jemima looked down and bit her lip; noticing her discomfort, Brendan turned to Martha to reply for both of them.

'Once we had decided, we didn't see the point in waiting,' he said. He could see Martha deliberating over his comment, trying carefully to interpret his words.

She sighed slowly before she spoke. 'Where fools rush in.'

Her words floated into the air harmlessly enough, but the disdain in which they were dressed did not pass Brendan by. He looked at her indignantly.

'You think Jemima and I have been foolish?'

'No,' interjected Bridget, now flustered by Martha's statement. 'No not at all.'

'I believe Jemima has been, yes,' said Martha deliberately ignoring her sister. 'You, however, Mr O'Rourke, have been very canny. Very canny indeed.'

Brendan looked bewildered. 'How so?'

Martha smiled slowly. 'I am sure Jemima has explained our family's situation to you, and that you are aware she will inherit a substantial estate. She has been well provided for in terms of trust funds, the potential of which your financial background must give you great insight.'

'You think we got married because of Jemima's money?' he responded, flabbergasted.

'I think you married Jemima for her money. I think she married you... well, there is a certain roguish charm about you and I am sure that she has never met anyone quite like you before, making her easy pickings, I should imagine.'

149

Brendan dropped his cutlery and, resting his forearms on the dining table, clenched his fists tight. 'You're unbelievable!' he exclaimed. 'I married Jemima because I love her very much, and because I want to spend the rest of my life with her.'

'See Martha. They married for love and because they want to spend their lives together, that's all,' said Bridget, in a vain attempt again to calm the conversation.

'And a comfortable life it will be,' Martha replied, sardonically.

Brendan scoffed in disbelief. 'I couldn't give a damn about her money. I would have married her regardless.'

'Always an easy statement to claim, when the opposite is not actually the case,' Martha retorted sharply.

Brendan shook his head slowly and dropped his voice in an attempt to contain his anger. 'I appreciate you must be hurt that we didn't invite you to the wedding. We were selfish and I get why you are angry with us but…'

'Selfishness I understand Mr O'Rourke. The self-serving motivation is logical; there is rationality to it. But foolishness I cannot tolerate and, Jemima, you have been a fool.' Martha's voice was caustic, her self-control had disintegrated and they all got a glimpse of the fury that boiled inside her.

'Aunty please!' cried Jemima. 'Please, I just want us all to get along.'

Martha raised her eyebrow again in disbelief. 'You bring some stranger into our house Jemima, a man you have only known for a matter of months and announce you are married to him, and we are all just to get along? Really Jemima? Your foolishness is bordering on stupidity.'

'I don't give a toss about what you think of me,' Brendan snapped at her, 'but I won't put up with you insulting my wife.' Jemima flinched at his harsh tone.

'Are you threatening me, Mr O'Rourke?' Martha's voice was quiet but firm and Brendan sensed that she was leading him somewhere dangerous.

'No. I am just explaining to you what my intentions are,' he replied, his own voice more controlled now.

'Well, I guess only time will show us,' Martha responded, thoughtfully, keeping a close eye on his reaction.

CHAPTER 20

Six years ago

TESS BUSIED HERSELF over the next couple of days, in an attempt to avoid Brendan and to deliberately avoid dealing with the tangle of feelings that came when she thought about him. However, when she was on her own, her remorse attached itself to her like an ugly stain. She was angry with herself for letting him seduce her so easily, for putting everything in her life in jeopardy. She felt tainted and couldn't shake the feeling of being condemned, as if a giant axe swung precariously above her head.

Brendan had slipped into a lazy routine, rising late and taking the dogs for a walk, afterwards retreating to his bedroom to read and smoke his neatly rolled joints, until his head was as foggy as his smoke-filled room. Sometimes he joined his brothers in the evenings at one of the local pubs; sometimes he vegetated in front of the television, staring at the screen, not taking anything in. Passing time until he returned to London. He realised that Lowlands had not changed in his absence; it was still filled with the same tired furniture and his family were still as predictable.

Lying on his bed, doped and content, Tess would wander in and out of his thoughts. Since the other night she was clearly avoiding him. Which made it easier for him, less complicated; the last thing he had wanted was for her to believe that he was her escape route. This thought had fleetingly crossed his mind when he had let her nightshirt fall to the floor, realising that as soon as he touched her, the vulnerability that drew him to her could quickly develop into dependency, their secret binding them together through the fear of being found out. But what they had done had felt dangerous, and to feel anything other than boredom and discord at Lowlands felt good.

Brendan was lying on the bed reading when Sean entered his room. Sean behaved oddly at first – avoiding Brendan's eye, leaning awkwardly against the chest of drawers and looking a little lost. Brendan shut his book and sat up, offering him the joint he was smoking. He watched Sean for a while as he dragged hard before exhaling.

'I'm scared of losing her,' Sean finally said, staring at the floor and sinking into his own thoughts.

Brendan's conscience brushed roughly against him, like steel wire.

'Why do you think you're going to lose her?'

'Cos I tricked her into being with me,' Sean replied, looking up at Brendan expectantly.

'I don't understand,' said Brendan, uneasy with this confession.

'We had an accident one night, she doesn't know. At the time I didn't know what to say. I wanted to make her mine so much and I couldn't bear the thought of her being with anyone else, so I said nothing. And when she told me she was pregnant, I couldn't have been happier. But she's changed.'

Brendan stared at him blankly. He knew Sean was telling him because he wanted something from him. 'How?' he asked.

'She looks at me like I've trapped her.' Sean took another long drag. A poignant silence followed, ramming hard against Brendan. 'I love her, but it's not enough for her is it?' Sean finished.

'Why are you asking me?'

'Because you know, you know how she feels. You and her both have that same restless look.'

Brendan looked away, relieved now that Sean had taken the conversation away from where he feared it was heading.

'You should tell her about the accident. She should have had a choice Sean,' Brendan told him firmly.

'I can't. I'll lose her. She and Georgie are my world now you've gone. I can't lose them as well as you.'

Brendan's stomach jolted as he saw the young boy inside of Sean resurface. Years of taking care of his brother compelled Brendan to reassure him. Brendan slid off his bed and went over to him, resting his hand against the back of Sean's head, pulling him closer.

'You've not lost me,' he said staring hard into Sean's eyes.

Sean looked back, a sad smile growing across his lips. Brendan was trying to smooth over what Sean was really saying to him. They both knew the depths of betrayal that had taken place between them; that they had pushed each other too far away to ever be close again. They were now permanently disjointed and things would always sit ajar. They could no longer completely block out the light together.

While Georgie was napping, Tess was in her living room folding washing when she became aware of someone behind her. She looked down and recognised Brendan's smart trainers and expensive jeans and she deliberately ignored him, turning her attention back to the washing.

'We need to talk,' he told her.

'There's nothing to say,' she replied, refusing to stop what she was doing. But when the basket was full, she was forced to turn around and face him. He stepped forward and she felt herself stiffen. 'Excuse me,' she said curtly, trying to pass him, but he blocked her way and the two of them ended up in an awkward dance for a moment. Exasperated, she stood still.

'It's important,' he told her.

'No it's not. It meant nothing,' she hissed back and saw his jaw tighten. He looked hurt. 'Let it go Brendan please.'

Glancing at the basket of washing she was holding, he pulled out a nightshirt and unfolded it, taking in the Mickey Mouse picture on the front.

'You have a matching pair then?' he joked lightly, smiling mischievously, pleased to see her relax slightly.

'What do you want?' she sighed.

'There's something you need to know.'

She stared at him with her jade eyes, wild curls framing her face and ginger freckles scattered across her nose and cheeks. Her mouth was parted slightly and he could see the white tip of her front teeth. He wanted to grab her, hold her and make her his again. He understood exactly what Sean saw in her.

'There's something I need to tell you before I leave,' he continued, looking around at the top floor of Lowlands, the space which Sean and Tess had converted into their home. He visualised

Sean enjoying the hard work and Tess enjoying the nesting – both of them working together, sharing their ideas – and a small streak of envy flashed through him.

Tess's throat felt dry and the washing was heavy in her arms. She put it down and rested her back against a small table, watching him looking about, taking in her and Sean's things. *God, he's good looking,* she thought involuntarily, and the weight of that axe swung precariously over her head once again. She was excited and nervous – she didn't want to feel like this around him.

'What d'you want to tell me?' she forced herself to ask and he buried his hands in his jeans pockets and sighed.

'You shouldn't feel bad about what happened between us,' he stated.

'That's it?' she asked with disbelief.

'No... what happened was you reacting to being here, to finding yourself in a situation that you didn't envisage for yourself.'

Tess stared at him blankly, feeling confused. He stepped forward, pulling his hands out of his pockets.

'Thing is Sean knew there was a chance you could have got pregnant and he chose not to tell you.'

'What?'

'There was an accident with...'

'What do you mean he didn't tell me? You're lying, he would've told me,' her voice sounded thin. She felt winded.

He breathed deeply. 'Tess, he didn't tell you because he didn't want to lose you.'

'Did he tell you this?'

'Yes. He realises he has trapped you.'

'He told you that? They were his words?'

'Yes.'

'Why are you telling me this?'

'Because I think you have the right to know. You should've been able to make a choice Tess.'

'I had a choice and I chose him and Georgie. I didn't get rid of him did I?'

'And would you? Would you have got rid of your baby, if you had known for sure?'

She looked away again, clamping her teeth around her bottom lip.

'Sean knew you wouldn't, that's why he let things run their course. Things just happened to go in his favour.'

She glared at him. 'You shouldn't have told me this,' she whispered angrily.

'You should know the truth. Sean should never have tricked you into this situation. It's wrong,' he told her. 'That's why you shouldn't regret what happened between us.'

He fell silent and turned to leave; when he got to the door she spoke.

'He wanted you there, at our wedding. He wanted you to be his best man but your dad wouldn't let him contact you. He let you know the only way he knew how; he has never stopped missing you.'

Hidden in the shadows on the landing, Cassie watched Brendan descend the stairs from Sean and Tess's attic rooms. She'd been secretly following him since his return, hopeful for anything from him which acknowledged what had been between them. When she had discovered him and Tess entwined on the sofa early one morning, she had started to understand why nothing had been forthcoming. After all, her dreams about him had stopped, had been snuffed out when she had lost her baby. However much she longed to return to that garden, to feel the sun on her skin, her child in her arms and his attention on her, that dream had abandoned her and now, each night, instead of dreaming she was left in darkness.

He caught sight of her and stopped a few stairs from the bottom. It was hard to decipher his expression in the half-light. As he slowly descended the remaining stairs, the landing light illuminated his features. He looked unsettled, almost wary of her. Cassie stepped before him and looked up towards Sean and Tess's rooms, aware he was following her gaze. She let her eyes linger at the top of the stairs long enough to let him know what she suspected, before she looked back at him and found him staring at her as if to say 'What did you really expect from me?'

CHAPTER 21

One day ago

AT CLOUDS REACH, the meal with Jemima's aunts dragged on painfully. After desert Martha stated she had some affairs to attend to and retired to her study, while Jemima went to her room with a headache, leaving Brendan and Bridget alone together in the dining room. Brendan was still trying to calm down and Bridget was trying to figure out a way to restore some harmony.

'Do you smoke, Mr O'Rourke?' she asked him lightly.

He sighed and looked at her. She looked nervous, and he couldn't help but smile gently at her. 'Bridget, please, it's Brendan, and yes I do.'

'Well then Brendan, how about we retire to the drawing room?' she smiled back.

In the drawing room Bridget drew the heavy drapes, took a silver box from a large antique bureau and offered him a cigarette. Taking one, he eyed it curiously before leaning forward to let her light it. Then Bridget invited him to take a seat, and he sank into a deep sofa, feeling swallowed up by the pile of brocade cushions.

'Cognac,' she said brightly, handing him a drink. He took it from her and watched as she settled herself next to him; she looked agitated and coughed lightly before she spoke.

'I am sorry about Martha. It's just, well, Jemima is very precious to us and I guess we probably appear over protective.'

'She is precious to me too, Bridget.'

'Yes, I can see that but Martha, well, she has never been one for romance and affairs of the heart.'

He flicked his ash into an ornate silver ashtray and looked back at her – despite her explanation, he was still annoyed with Martha. 'She made some very strong accusations about me tonight.'

Bridget stared timorously at her drink. When she looked up, she reached for a framed photograph of Jemima's mother, Lilly. Lilly looked about Jemima's age in the picture. She was smiling and her hair was caught in the wind; she had raised a hand to wipe it from her face and the gesture gave the impression that she was waving goodbye.

'I don't know how much Jemima has told you about her mother?' Bridget said, hesitantly.

'I know she died when Jem was about four, in a car accident,' he ventured. 'She was very attractive,' he said, looking back at Bridget.

'Yes, yes she was. Lilly's mother was our sister Prudence. She married an RAF captain.' Bridget stopped and breathed deeply before continuing. 'They were killed by a bomb in Nicosia, Cyprus – Turk nationalists claimed responsibility for the attack. Martha and I were Lilly's next of kin, so we raised her. She was just a baby when she came to us,' Bridget told him, her voice faltering.

'I didn't know.'

'Did you know that Jemima's parents were not married?' she asked and Brendan shook his head. 'Rather, her father was, but not to Lilly. He was Lilly's boss and he told her he was trapped in a childless and loveless marriage. Lilly was very much in love with him. Jemima... well, we will never know for sure. Perhaps Lilly planned her, perhaps not. When he found out she was pregnant he promised to leave his wife, but of course he never did. Martha wanted Lilly to...' Bridget broke off and stared at the picture. 'Martha knew he was never going to leave his wife but, thankfully, Lilly chose to have Jemima. Though there were a lot of fights, Lilly was quite headstrong.' She stopped again and Brendan could see, just for a moment, Bridget's memory came alive with recollections of this beautiful young woman.

'Anyway, Lilly seemed to hang on his promises and once a month he took them out for the day. Probably told his wife he was on the golf course or had gone sailing. I doubt she had any idea about Lilly and Jemima, until the accident. One Saturday they brought Jemima back, they had been down to the beach and were both going back out for a drink.'

Bridget stopped speaking and Brendan watched her carefully replaying the events in her mind.

'She never came back. We got the call late that night; they had collided with a minibus on the hairpin bend up on the coastal road. He was driving some small sports car and they didn't stand a chance, neither of them.' She looked down at the photograph again and then up at Brendan, her eyes pooled with tears. 'So you see, Brendan, Jemima is also all we have left of Lilly.'

'Yes, I see that,' he told her softly.

'Oh my, I didn't mean to be so morbid,' Bridget said suddenly, a little too breezily. 'You and Martha never married?' Brendan enquired, changing the subject.

'No. Well, Martha was very much married to her career – she worked for the Home Office. She is terribly bright. I think there was a lot of interest in her – she was quite a stunner in her day – but, well, she is headstrong and was very determined about what she wanted. I nearly got married – to a GI. Drew his name was. He was based on a camp up on the cliffs here. Oh, we used to dance up at the base, to all sorts of music we hadn't heard before; Martha was horrified of course.'

She leaned closer to him and raised her fingers towards his face. He sat motionless, carefully watching her fingers as they brushed his cheek. When he looked back at her he could see that the person she was staring at wasn't him.

He took her hand, gently squeezing it. 'Bridget, it's been a long day,' he said quietly.

'Oh, my,' she sighed, coming to her senses, 'it certainly has.'

The next morning Jemima waved at her aunts while Brendan, forcing a smile so tight his jaw ached, reversed his car out of the driveway of Clouds Reach. He watched them wave back, Bridget reacting enthusiastically, while Martha's gesture was tightly controlled.

Despite Brendan's apology to Martha that morning, made in an attempt to smooth out the harsh words between them the night before, he couldn't help but wonder if he had made matters worse. 'She hates me,' he mumbled to Jemima, carefully keeping his smile locked firmly across his face.

'Nonsense,' she replied, continuing to smile and wave.

When he turned the car onto the road and they headed off, he was relieved to be able to drop his heavy smile.

'Are you sure we shouldn't call your family first, to let them know we are on our way?' she asked. Jemima had seen how shocked and hurt her aunts had been and now wished that she had let them know beforehand, instead of turning up unannounced and springing their news on them.

Brendan, however, wanted the element of surprise. He needed a strategy to help him and Jemima get through this, something that would help satisfy her curiosity about his family and also prevent them from being too overbearing. Hoping they would be shocked and, therefore, stunned, was the best he could hope for. He was keen to get their visit over with so they could get on with their married lives. Brendan drew in his breath and responded to Jemima's question with a sigh.

'What do you think they'll say?' she asked.

'Don't know. Look, Jem, my family are feral, particularly in comparison to yours. I just want you to be prepared for that. I don't want you to take what they say or do too personally okay?'

CHAPTER 22

Six years ago

BRENDAN FELT HER stare. Her breath was cool and soft against his face and, without opening his eyes, he wrapped his arm tighter around her, pulling her underneath him, using his right thigh to separate her legs. Slowly he opened his eyes and saw two pools of jade, inches away from him, and her strawberry-blonde curls lying across the pillow. Her smile was wide and amused, and he felt her hips tip towards him, inviting him again.

A couple of weeks into January, arriving home from work, he had found Tess perched outside his front door. At first she looked worried, but once she had seen the puzzled look on his face, she was relieved he wasn't angry that she had turned up unannounced. She had walked towards him and that's when the tears filled her eyes again, the events of the last few weeks welling up inside her. As she blurted out why she was there, Brendan had held her, folded his arms around her like she was a small child. He'd invited her in and he'd been everything she had hoped for. When she told him that she had left Sean, he didn't judge; instead, he looked as if he understood why, as if he had always expected this day to happen – to find her on his doorstep like this. She explained that she needed some space, needed to go somewhere she could start to get her head together without Sean finding her. She'd arranged for Georgie to go to her mother's for the weekend, sent Sean a brief text and jumped on a train. When she had run out of things to say, he had cooked a meal and opened a bottle of wine.

James had hung around in the background, throwing Brendan warning glances. When James finally went out for the night, Tess felt herself relax. Later, as she washed up, Brendan came up behind her, resting his hands gently on her hips.

'You can take my bed,' he said softly. Tess breathed in and her heart skipped a beat. Delicately, he pushed her hair away from her neck and whispered, 'I'll take the sofa... If that's what you want?'

She turned to him and saw that same look on his face as the night in Lowlands; it made her feel as if she was freefalling. She shut her eyes, her heart pounding. 'Tell me what you want?' she asked.

'You need to ask?' he replied.

That was all that needed to be said. Within moments, she was on his bed and he was stood over her, looking at her curiously as he pulled his shirt over his head. She closed her eyes again and gasped when he touched her. When he eased himself slowly into her and murmured her name she wrapped her arms around his neck and pulled him tightly to her, delighting in the quickening pace of his breathing and the deep roll of his hips. This is what she had come in search of; this is what she craved – to feel wanted.

Now they lay together, their limbs locked, listening to the wind and burying themselves further beneath his duvet. Both still sleepy, they were enjoying each other's warmth when there was a tap on Brendan's bedroom door. James entered, looking concerned, and Brendan instinctively sat up.

'Your brother's here,' James told him. 'Sean,' he continued hesitantly.

Brendan quickly glanced back at Tess, who looked scared.

'It's okay,' Brendan said, pulling on his jeans. 'Stay here, and keep quiet,' he instructed her. When he got to his bedroom door he ran his hands over his head and breathed deeply, before stepping out into the hallway.

Sean was standing by the open-plan kitchen, stony faced, and with his coat still on. James was in the kitchen, pretending to look busy but, instead, glanced nervously between the two brothers.

'Alright? What's up?' Brendan asked casually.

'I'm looking for Tess.'

Brendan didn't reply. Instead he looked quizzically at his brother, who was annoyed with his response.

'Is she here?' Sean stated flatly.

Brendan knew he wasn't going to lie, but he was trying to figure out how to respond. Eventually he settled on a quiet, 'Yeah.'

A small contemptuous smile flickered across Sean's mouth. 'Tess, get out here I'm taking you home,' he shouted.

Brendan stiffened as he heard his bedroom door slowly open. Tess emerged wearing his white cotton work shirt, which skimmed her thighs and fell open at her cleavage. At the sight of Tess in Brendan's shirt, with her ruffled hair and flushed cheeks, Sean looked visibly hurt. His eyes narrowed as he focused his attention back to Brendan.

'You know, if you wanted her, you only had to ask,' he said coldly.

Brendan scoffed, astonished by Sean's reaction. 'With your permission? Where would the fun have been in that, Sean?' he replied sarcastically.

The blow hit him as soon as the last word left his mouth. Sean's fist connected hard against his jaw, catching his bottom lip. Brendan staggered from the punch and instinctively drew his arm back to retaliate.

'Brendan, you deserved that!' James bellowed.

Brendan froze.

'I told you this was not going to end well,' James continued, sternly, as Brendan wiped his mouth with the back of his hand and studiously sucked his swelling lip to stop the bleeding.

'Get dressed, we're going home,' Sean barked at Tess.

'I'm not coming back, Sean.' Her voice was firm.

'You really think he wants you, and a baby?'

Sean's words hung heavily in the air, and Brendan looked back at Tess. 'Do as he says Tess.' He watched her mouth fall slack from his betrayal.

'See,' Sean told her defiantly.

Tess felt tears sting her eyes. She turned away abruptly before any of them saw and headed back to Brendan's bedroom.

'How did you know she was here?' asked Brendan.

'I figured out something was going on at Christmas. That's why I came to you, told you how much she meant to me. I was asking you to leave her alone.'

'What made you think something was going on?'

'I saw the way you watched her – I know that look of yours too well. Then one night she came to bed and she smelled of you. Your scent was all over her.'

Brendan looked away guiltily, just catching James shaking his head.

'You must really hate me,' Sean remarked.

'No, no I don't.'

'Then why?'

Brendan shoved his hands in his pockets and rocked gently, while thinking how to reply. 'I was angry with you. When you let Liam beat me up, it was like you'd betrayed me. But I don't hate you, I don't think I could.'

'Is that what this is about? Revenge?'

'In part, but she had her whole life ahead of her and you deliberately misled her. You should have told her, Sean.'

Sean shook his head. 'Don't turn your mess back onto me.'

'There'd be no mess if you had told her Sean'

'I can't now, can I? Because you already have.' He waited for Brendan's response, but Brendan remained silent. 'Or perhaps I should've run, left her pregnant. Funny how you see fit to interfere in my life when you can't even deal with your own.'

'That's unfair and you know it,' replied Brendan sharply. Sean's remark had hurt and he let him see it before he returned to his room. Tess was sat on his bed, still wearing his shirt, staring out of the window. Her cheeks were stained with tears, and her bag was perched beside her, empty.

'I'm not going back to him,' she said, her voice thick from crying.

'No one is asking that of you Tess, but you need to go and get this sorted out. You've Georgie to think of and your own interests to fight for.'

'He's right about you, isn't he?' She turned to face him. 'What was all this about for you Brendan?'

'I didn't ask you to come here, Tess.'

Tess laughed. 'Oh my god, I have been such an idiot.'

'I never made you any promises,' he continued, defensively.

'No, no you didn't, you just walked into our lives and smashed them to pieces. Why?' She stood and faced him and watched him consider her question. 'Was it jealousy, at what he had? That you weren't the centre of his world anymore?' she asked.

'We were both angry with him, that's how this happened, Tess,' he said sighing. 'I'm sorry, I never wanted to hurt you.'

Tess forcefully wiped the tears from her cheeks. 'I think you've hurt yourself more than me. Nothing is ever going to be the same for you now, you do realise that don't you?' she said, her eyes fixed on his face watching him realise the significance of her words.

Part Two: The Present

Chapter 23

OVER THE PAST couple of months, Cassie's dream had returned, often jolting her awake. She was calling that name again, holding the small boy with his soft blond hair, standing in the large garden with the sun shining down on her. Then the feeling of being watched, knowing he was there beneath the heavy boughs of the cherry trees, her skin prickling with anticipation.

Luckily for her, Liam never stirred, allowing her to catch her breath. The disturbing dreams had once again dredged up memories of the child she had lost and how she could never escape this life, never realise her dream. She was stuck here now, with Liam and his bad temper, jamming his fists into her thighs so the others couldn't see the bruising. There were other women – she knew that, and cared even less. It gave her a break. Sometimes weeks would go past until he would pin her down and force himself inside her, not even looking at her afterwards. With every grunt and push she felt a small piece of herself disintegrate. She'd shut her eyes and try to float away, but he took her distraction for disinterest; this he used against her, pushing harder until she cried out with pain and not the pleasure his bruised ego allowed himself to believe.

On this particular night, she rolled onto her side and stared at the mottled moon. She pulled the pillow tightly under her head and lay wondering what the return of these dreams meant. They left her feeling desperate and hollow. Her heart pulled at the chains that kept her in Liam's bed. She wanted so much to lay her hands on the man she loved, to breathe his scent and feel his warm skin. He was so close to her now. The dreams were telling her that.

→▦◌ ◌▦←

As Brendan swung his car into the driveway, Lowlands came into view. The redbrick Victorian house looked incongruently placed against the woods surrounding it. The silhouettes of the match-stick thin firs, jarred against the solidity of the building. It was as if the earth had cracked unwillingly and Lowlands had pushed itself out in hard thrusts, twisting left then right, ripping through the layers of sediment, finally reaching its rightful position. It sat at an imposing angle. The entrances were not obvious and its windows seemed somehow opaque, as if they could only be used for looking out and not in. The space around the house was dark and mossy; a patchy lawn ran around the left-hand side and to the right of the house lay the woods, dense, cold and brooding no matter how much sun there was. Brendan parked next to a dirty, red flatbed truck, and he and Jemima sat in silence.

'Ready?' he asked after several moments and Jemima who, having looked up at the house nervously, turned and tried to force smile.

Lyla was startled to see them both in the kitchen doorway. 'Well, what a surprise! You couldn't call ahead?' she said.

Brendan smiled as she came over, her eyes darting between them both as if she couldn't decide whether to look at the son she missed or at the stranger stood next to him.

'Mum, this is my wife, Jemima.'

Lyla's eyes narrowed, her pretend smile pulled her face tight and stretched the skin across her high cheekbones. 'Your wife?' she replied, her voice sounding measured.

Jemima held out her hand. 'It's a pleasure to meet you,' she said, enthusiastically, but when Lyla's eyes fell on her, she felt as if her core had frozen. Despite the smile, Lyla eyed her suspiciously and Jemima was aware that her hand, still outstretched, might be ignored. Eventually, Lyla took it, wrapping her cold fingers around it and squeezing it hard before dropping it and turning back to Brendan.

'When did you get married?'

'A couple of weeks ago.'

'We didn't know.' She sounded sharp and Jemima noticed Brendan's jaw clench.

'We really didn't want any fuss,' he replied, tensely.

Lyla nodded her head as if she understood but her smile had dropped slightly. The three of them stood awkwardly in silence, their words having dried up, until the back door crashed open and the noisy presence of Brendan's brothers spilled from the utility room into the kitchen.

'What you doing here?' Sean asked gruffly.

'Brendan's called round to tell us he's got married,' Lyla told them. The kitchen fell still and Jemima felt herself prickle with discomfort as their attention fell to her. 'Riley, go fetch your sisters. Looks like we've got some catching up to do,' Lyla continued.

Some whiskey was opened and the brothers drank greedily, their voices growing louder and their laughter becoming more raucous. The kitchen, full of O'Rourkes, was chaotic. To Jemima it was like trying to take in the view from a high-speed train; their voices ran into one another and their faces blurred. So lost had she become in them, that she was unaware of the doorway darkening and the room falling silent as Lester stepped into the kitchen. When she noticed him, it was as though she had travelled forward in time. The man had Brendan's face – the same slightly hooked nose and bright blue eyes – but it was etched with deep lines around the mouth and across the forehead. His hair was slicked back into a widow's peak and his jaw was softer, the passage of time having slackened the skin. When Brendan introduced her to his father, she noticed him hesitate under Lester's hard stare. Moving closer to Brendan, her fingers searched for his hand, and she loosely hooked them around his. Brendan remained motionless, watching closely at his father staring at them both. The others were quiet and shifted uneasily, not daring to look at him; even the dogs had fallen silent. Finally, Lester let out a deep grunt, a small but significant sound, which gave permission for them all to start talking again.

Jemima found herself trying to ignore Lester's stare which he had doggedly attached to her; and the harder she tried, the more she ended up fighting the urge to look his way. She was so involved in this tug-of-war that she didn't hear Brendan at first.

'Jem?' Brendan said, 'Mum's just asked if we are staying over. I said we'd stay until tomorrow morning. Is that ok?'

Jemima stammered her agreement, tripping clumsily over the words.

'I'll fetch the bags then,' he said, looking at her curiously, before leaving the kitchen.

Once he'd gone, his family stared at her in silence. She felt awkward, like a chess piece in the wrong position. 'I need to get something from the car,' she said quickly, rushing out to catch up with Brendan.

She caught up with him just as he was shutting the boot, their bags by his feet; he looked surprised to see her. 'What's up?'

'Nothing. Well...'

He spoke softly. 'We don't have to stay.'

'Yes we do, this is important. It's your family.' Jemima tried smiling but he could see her doubt and pulled her closer to him.

'You don't have to do this. This is not an easy place to be and they are not easy people to be around.'

Jemima desperately didn't want to back out of the situation and she didn't want him to make things easy for her either; she knew that if they didn't stay now, then the next time would only be harder. Despite the gestures of goodwill, she had sensed Lyla's unhappiness with their news. She'd watched it settle across her face and Jemima knew that she needed to stay to stop it turning into bitterness. If they left, she knew Lyla would see it as a further rejection and she didn't want to start her married life having to carve her way through her mother-in-law's resentment every time they met.

'If you survived my aunts, I can do this,' she told him. He laughed softly and kissed her, his eyes filled with her reflection. She returned his kiss and wanted desperately to bury herself in his embrace where she felt safe.

As Brendan turned to go back into the house, his expression changed. Behind them was a woman wearing shorts and a t-shirt, her long, sinewy legs sticking out of oversized wellingtons. There was a shotgun slung across her shoulders and tied at her waist were two rabbits, hanging limp. Her thick black hair hung around her face and she glowered intently at Brendan. Her eyes burned, as if trying to incinerate him.

'Cassie,' Brendan said, throwing her a sharp nod.

Jemima looked nervously between them.

'This is my wife Jemima. We just got married.'

Cassie flinched, almost imperceptibly, but he had registered it. Then she slowly averted her eyes to Jemima and Jemima felt herself shrink. Cassie looked back to Brendan; it was a hard stare, and Jemima could see Brendan trying to hold his nerve in the face of Cassie's hostility. Finally, Cassie turned to Lowlands taking her stare with her but not before letting her eyes scale over Jemima one last time. Jemima shrank further back against Brendan who held her hips in an attempt to steady her and they both watched, transfixed, as Cassie walked away.

Once Cassie was out of earshot, Jemima whispered, 'Who was that?'

'Cassie. She's Liam's girlfriend,' he replied.

Jemima tried to recall Liam – his stocky build, thick neck and solid head – and place the two of them together. A disturbing image came to mind and she shook it away.

'Come on,' Brendan urged, giving her a tight smile. He was rattled; he knew that coming back meant they would have to face Cassie, but she had caught him unawares. He was disturbed at how long she must have been watching them – watching him. And that look: carving him hollow, scraping him out with a knife and leaving just an empty shell. He took Jemima's hand firmly, quelling his need to flee and strode back to the house.

Later on, while Jemima was unpacking, Brendan stared out of the bedroom window at Cassie, who was sat on the steps of the brick sheds. She was barefoot and her hair hung loose, he could see the determined look on her face as she pulled the skins from the rabbits. He was fixated on what she was doing, as she tugged and twisted the carcasses, her hands covered in blood. As the last skin came away she looked up towards him, holding the skinned rabbit in one hand – its eyes bulbous, its naked body shiny and raw – and its soft tawny fur in the other. He knew she could see him looking at her. He could tell by the way she stayed perfectly still, her head tilted in his direction, as if able to read his thoughts. He closed his eyes and thought of nothing until, finally, she threw the rabbit in a bowl and returned to the brick shed that was now her home.

CHAPTER 24

LYLA STOOD BACK from her bedroom window. Drawing on her cigarette and steadily releasing the smoke, she was contemplating Brendan and Jemima carefully. They were at the edge of the woods, playing with the tyre swing that Brendan had rebuilt for Riley a few years ago. She watched as Brendan helped Jemima climb into it, pulling her legs through the other side; they both laughed as he pretended to pull her too hard and she nearly toppled backwards. He was now pushing her and as she glided through the air she clung tightly to the rope, her legs straight out ahead and her hair flowing behind. Lyla was trying to recall when she had last seen him look this happy. She was also trying to fathom why they had got married so quickly.

Lester walked into the bedroom, casually throwing his t-shirt on the floor. Noticing Lyla, he wandered over to where she was stood.

'What you looking at?' he asked.

'What do you think he sees in her?' Lyla replied thoughtfully.

Lester stared at Jemima for a moment and grunted, then continued getting changed. Lyla turned and looked at him impatiently, expecting an answer.

'She's quite pretty, I suppose,' he mumbled, choosing his words carefully. He could see how perturbed Lyla was and wanted to avoid a long, drawn out discussion about this.

Lyla turned back to the window. Stubbing out her cigarette, her eyes narrowed. 'Why did they get married so quickly?' she asked and Lester let the question go unanswered.

'And why has he bought her here?' she mused, turning to Lester for an answer again.

'You know what he's like. He only ever comes back when he's got something to show off – new car, new job. This is his new trophy. He likes to rub our noses in it, jumped up little...'

'No,' Lyla cut him short, 'that isn't it. This is something else.'

'Oh come on Lyla, you know what he's like with women. He'll move on in a year.'

'Maybe he will,' replied Lyla wistfully.

Lester watched her look back out of the window for a while; he could see her thinking hard.

'She was raised by her aunts, her great-aunts actually; she went to boarding school from the age of seven. She's got no family to speak of and I get the impression that her aunts are absolutely minted.'

'Didn't take you long to find that lot out,' Lester joked.

'You think I don't have the right to know who my son has married?' Lyla bit back and Lester held his tongue.

'So, you think he married her for money?' he said after a while.

'Partly, but I think he really married her to make amends.' Lyla said, and when she turned back to Lester, her mouth spread into a calculated grin.

'Make amends for what?' he asked, frowning.

'For turning his back on us, for the mess he left us in with Cassie. I think this is his way of saying sorry. I knew he'd come back eventually Les.'

Lester looked at Lyla carefully; the mention of money had piqued his interest but he was unsure of Lyla's motivations. He considered Jemima and concluded that, though she was no stunner, she was pretty enough, and he could cope with waking up next to her each morning. He contemplated Lyla's idea of Brendan bringing her to them as an apology; that somehow he planned to share her wealth with them. He always thought of Brendan as selfish and couldn't see him sharing anything, let alone any inheritance that Jemima may be entitled to. As for whether he was sorry, Lester had never got any inclination from Brendan that he was regretful. Lester reckoned that his theory about Brendan coming back to show off and rub their noses in it was much more likely. So he dismissed Lyla's ideas, all except the one about the money; maybe she had hit on something, clouded though it was by her feelings for Brendan. Lester rolled this idea over in his mind for a bit while watching Brendan and Jemima playing on the swing. They appeared so carefree, so unburdened by life – so unaware of the plot that was starting to form.

CHAPTER 25

A COUPLE OF weeks later Brendan and Jemima were back at Lowlands and Brendan found himself walking through the woods to his Uncle Joe's house. He deliberately hung back from the others, dragging hard on his cigarette, feeling uncomfortable that they were visiting him mob handed. Brendan was disturbed by the age-old dispute between his father and uncle over his uncle's land. For as long as he could remember, Lester had coveted it for his business and relentlessly badgered Joe about selling it to him. Their grandfather, Jerry, perhaps foreseeing Lester's intention, purposely left the bungalow and land to his brother to ensure that Lester didn't turf him out. When Lester had stormed into the kitchen at Lowlands raging at Joe for snubbing the invitation to the party they were throwing for Brendan and Jemima, Brendan realised that matters had grown much worse over the years. So it was with a heavy heart that he followed Liam, Sean and his father into the woods, anticipating the conflict that lay ahead and which he knew would rumble on into the future, flaring up occasionally like an ulcerated gut. *What was the point?* he thought.

Aside from this, he was also uncomfortable about leaving Jemima with his mother and sisters. She had looked happy enough when he left – the drink was flowing; the party his mother had insisted on throwing to celebrate their wedding now in full swing. So much drink had already been consumed that Riley had been sent out for more, but something about the way his mother had looked at him made his distrust for her resurface. When Lester told Brendan that he had to come with them, Brendan knew better than to argue; he resigned himself to get on with it, offer the odd placatory word and get back as soon as possible.

Liam swung the back door of Joe's bungalow wide open and they walked in unannounced. Joe was sat at the kitchen table. He jumped up, looking sour and annoyed. The bungalow reeked of mildew and fried food; a heavy, fetid smell that weaved its way into Brendan's nostrils and stuck to the back of his throat. The place was filthy. Dirty pots lay in the sink, half submerged in dark, oily water. Every surface of the kitchen was covered in a slick film of grease, clogged with months of dust.

'What d'you want Les?' Joe grumbled.

'I want to get this sorted out once and for all Joe,' replied Lester coldly.

Joe hung his head. He was weary of this fight; he was a man that looked a lot older than his sixty-something years. His frame was scrawny and he wore a permanent scowl, a result of his distrust and hate for a life which he felt had treated him cruelly. No one actually knew Joe's entire story – a spell in the army, some time in prison and an ex-wife who had left him childless. He had eventually cocooned himself against the world in this small, dirty bungalow.

Despite his few fond memories of his grandfather Jerry, Brendan had none of Joe. He recalled the occasional times he'd spent as a child with Joe as being desperate – the old man whinging, grassing him and his brothers up and making up spiteful tales about them, knowing Lester would knock them into next week for whatever Joe had told him they'd done. Now, Brendan felt sorry for him. He seemed so pitiful sat in torn trousers and a dirty vest, his chin covered in patchy grey stubble, his greasy hair stuck to his narrow skull like white wisps of smoke. He could see Joe's anxiety – his pulse thumping in his temple, his jutted-out chin and narrowed eyes.

Joe crossed his scrawny arms defensively. 'I've told you Les, I'm not giving it up. It's my land and I will do what I want with it, d'you hear me? You lot don't scare me, now fuck off,' he shouted, his watery eyes darting between them.

'It doesn't have to be this way, Joe, you know that. You could do well out of this if you weren't so bloody stubborn,' said Lester, his voice rough with frustration.

'You think I haven't realised that you lot will do best out of it? You're trying to rip me off, and you know it, and now you realise that I can't be swindled out of it you've come round to intimidate me. As I said, you lot don't scare me. You're nothing but a bunch of bullies – always have been, always will be – and the lot of you haven't got the balls to do anything. You're all fucking mouth and no trousers, that's what your father-in-law used to say, Lester. All mouth,' Joe snarled.

Lester's face hardened. 'You're making this so hard for yourself old man,' he spat back at him.

Joe backed away and looked around his kitchen. In the dull orange light, he struggled to recognise Brendan at first. 'Brendan, what are you doing getting yourself all caught up in this for, son?' he said more gently.

Brendan stepped forward with his hands raised. 'Look Joe, this isn't my fight,' he told him.

'Too bloody right it isn't. Jesus, you must be getting desperate, Les, if you're dragging the lad into it.'

Lester stared at him coldly, while Brendan, Sean and Liam stood quietly, staring at the old man standing centre stage saying his piece. Finally, Lester stepped towards him.

'Last chance. You either sell the land or we'll take it.'

'Fuck off!' shouted Joe, spittle flying through the air as he spoke. 'Over my dead body, you greedy fuckers,' he barked, baring his rotten yellow teeth and trying to pull himself up to Lester's height.

Lester flicked his eyes towards Liam and Liam pulled out a hammer from beneath his hoodie. Following Lester's stare, Joe's eyes fell on what Liam was holding. Slowly, Joe turned his head back to Lester.

'You haven't got the balls,' he sneered at him.

Joe's expression quickly switched to horror as he saw Lester nod at Liam. The hammer was brought down heavily against the old man's skull with a sickening crack as the bone split. Joe sunk to his knees, still alive, but in his last moments of consciousness realised that he had overplayed his hand, had called Lester's bluff – and that the game was now over. Liam raised the hammer again and pounded it against his head, over and over, grunting with the effort he invested in the blows. Joe's skull broke open, the bone shattering into small shards, followed by thin streams of blood, splattering everything in its way. As the hammer found its mark again there was an audible squelch; a sticky, oozing sound as it was forced further into the old man's cranium and made contact with his brain. Joe fell to the floor, his eyes wide open with terror, the back of his head decimated, with blood flowing in waves from the gaping hole. Liam paused; he was panting hard as he looked at Lester, whose expression remained unreadable.

'Check he's dead,' Lester barked at Liam.

Liam bent down, looking for a pulse. 'I think so.'

'Brendan, double check,' Lester told him.

Brendan had stopped breathing. His mouth hung open, his face stung where tiny, sharp fragments of skull had scraped it and he was covered in blood spray.

'What the fuck have you just done?' he cried. 'My God, you're mad, you've killed him, you've fucking killed him!' he raved, confused as to why they were all looking at him so calmly while he stared back aghast. 'Have you any idea what you have just fucking done?' he asked again, exasperated.

'Get him out of here and calm him down,' Lester instructed Sean, who compliantly pulled Brendan by his arm; but Brendan was rooted to the spot, staring uncomprehendingly at the lifeless body in front of him.

'Come on,' gestured Sean firmly.

Finally, Brendan allowed himself to be led from the bunga-low. When the fresh air hit him, his stomach lurched violently and he threw up. The bile burned, leaving his teeth feeling stripped. Panting, and covered in sweat, he carefully rose to face Sean.

'You have to realise this is wrong, Sean?' he questioned, but Sean looked back at him blankly.

'He had it coming, bitter old tosser,' he replied.

'He didn't deserve that Sean, nobody deserves that. Are you out of your fucking mind?'

'Keep your voice down,' Sean hissed.

'Liam has just killed Joe. Our mum's uncle. Put a hammer through the back of his fucking head. We are all covered in his blood and bone and pieces of his fucking brain. Does that not have some fucking effect on you Sean?' Brendan moved closer to him as he spoke. 'What has happened to you? When did you cross the line?'

Sean didn't respond, but carried on watching Brendan.

'What are you going to do, when one day there is something they want of yours, and you don't want them to have it, eh? What are you going to do when one day it's Liam stood behind you with a hammer in his hand? Because they have just proved how fuck-ing twisted they are capable of being and I want nothing to do with it. I'm out of here, for good.'

As Brendan turned to go, Lester came out of the bunga-low. 'Where the fuck do you think you're going?' he barked. There was something threatening in his expression and tone that Brendan found unsettling, and he lost the nerve to reply. 'Get the shovels from the outbuilding,' Lester continued. 'We'll bury him down there. And Sean, keep a fucking eye on him,' he said, pointing at Brendan. 'He's not going anywhere.'

→══ ═══←

'Why aren't you digging?' Lester snapped at Brendan. Brendan stared at him blankly, and shrugged, still numbed by what had just happened. He felt as if he were detached from his body, as if he was one of the crows in the branches of the fir trees towering around them, looking down at the macabre scene below, made all the more sinister by the torches they were using to help them see. 'Bit late to be scared of getting your hands dirty. Well, what you waiting for? He's not going to bury himself,' his father taunted, throwing him a shovel.

Brendan caught it awkwardly, the metal spade scraping his shin. 'Shit,' he mumbled under his breath and Sean looked at him, studying him closely. Brendan tried to avoid his eye; he didn't want to acknowledge the enormity of what they were doing. It felt easier to stay like the crows, distanced from it all.

The digging was hard work and Brendan struggled to keep up with Liam and Sean's rhythm. He was hot and his sweat ran in a steady trickle down his spine. Stopping to take off his shirt, he pulled his arm across his forehead, taking a moment to catch his breath. They had dug down as deep as their knees and, as he looked about him, his father spoke.

'Couple more hours should do it, you tiring already?' he said, the comment aimed firmly at Brendan. Brendan knew there was no point in answering; he knew his father was looking for another fight.

'That's the trouble with office work. Turns you soft,' Lester scorned, shrugging off his leather jacket and pulling his t-shirt over his head. He snatched the shovel off Brendan, pushing him out of the way, then started digging, quickly, forcing the pace forward, so that Liam and Sean, already starting to fatigue, struggled to keep up. The muscles on his father's arms and back were clearly defined; for his age he was still well toned and physically strong, not looking out of place amongst his sons. Brendan watched him, remembering what the power contained within those muscles felt like.

⋯⋯

When Brendan was twelve, his father had knocked him across the kitchen floor with a single blow. Brendan had expected it, invited it almost. 'So who gets the pleasure of your company tonight?' he'd asked, looking sideways towards his mother, letting her know he knew about Lester's infidelities and letting Lester know he knew what he was up to when he disappeared from the pub with some woman he'd met at the bar.

He used to watch as his father filled their heads with florid comments and listen as he made empty promises to the women he'd bedded and to his sons left standing outside the pub waiting patiently for him to finish. Brendan's guts twisted with the vulgarity of it. Until one night it had got too much for him to stifle; he had opened his mouth and, with one comment, he had ended up with a split lip and a reminder of where the power truly lay in the household.

His mother, who had been washing up, stood between Lester and Brendan, who was lying on the floor. She pushed a carving knife against Lester's chest and hissed, 'You strike him again, O'Rourke, and I will stick this knife so far into your chest that you will know exactly how painful it is to have your heart broken.'

Lester had backed down and left the house, disgruntled at having to hold back his fury for the time being. It was the only time Brendan's mother had defended any of them against Lester. As Brendan washed the blood away from his face, his mother started drying the dishes. Looking out of the window, her eyes seemed glassy, but her face was hard; she refused to acknowledge that she had understood his intention, that they both knew about Lester's affairs and that Brendan was trying to defend her against them. Trying to let her know she didn't have to suffer in silence.

When she finally spoke, her voice was brittle. 'Anyone asks about that cut at school, tell 'em you had a fight with one of your brothers. Just make sure you get your stories straight with each other first.'

→▭◌ ◌▭←

When the grave was dug, all four of them stood looking into it, their bodies covered in a sheen of sweat and filth and their faces streaked with dirt.

'Let's get him in,' said Lester, turning towards Joe's body, which was wrapped in an old rug and tied up with rope. Brendan and his brothers struggled to lift Joe. Between them they were uncoordinated and clumsy handling the dead weight of his body and, despite their efforts to throw him squarely into the grave, he landed at an angle so that one end of him lay pointing up against the side of the hole. Liam jumped in and roughly pulled the corpse straight; as soon as he jumped out, Sean picked up his shovel and they started to push the earth in rough clumps back into the hole. Brendan joined them, even though his arms and shoulders burned with exertion; he felt exhausted and a thirst gripped his throat leaving it raw.

When the grave was filled, Brendan, Sean and Liam put down their shovels and stood quietly, staring at the large patch of freshly turned-over earth. Lester pushed past them carrying some long fir branches and placed them precariously around and over the grave. Then they all circled Joe's grave, while Lester raised a half bottle of whiskey to the air. 'To Old Joe... he was fucking miserable when he was alive and may he continue to be fucking miserable now he's dead,' he laughed callously, taking a large swig.

He passed the whiskey bottle to Liam, who raised it like his father had and said, 'To old Joe,' before taking a long gulp and passing it onto Sean, who repeated the ritual before passing the bottle onto Brendan, who found himself copying robotically and passing the bottle back to Lester.

'Oh, and we mustn't forget Jemima, Brendan's lovely new wife, the delightful Jemima,' Lester said lewdly, taking care over the words, making sure each one punched through Brendan. As Lester raised the bottle to the air, Liam smiled perversely, causing Brendan to tighten his jaw and scowl at his father, who had passed the bottle to Liam so the ritual could begin again.

'To Jemima,' Liam cried, swigging hard and passing the bottle onto Sean, who eyed Brendan carefully.

'To Jemima,' Sean said firmly and took a swig before handing it to Brendan.

Brendan felt sickened. He glared at each of them, breathing heavily. 'Go fuck yourselves,' he spat at them, throwing the bottle to the ground and snatching up his shirt. He took large strides back to the house, his temper boiling, and his fists were clenched so tight his short nails dug painfully into the palms of his hands.

'Get a grip Brendan,' Sean said, catching up with him.

Ignoring him, Brendan carried on towards the house until, eventually, Sean grabbed his arm, swung him around and stared hard into Brendan's face, their foreheads almost touching.

'You need to get a grip, or you will end up losing it,' Sean continued. 'They're messing with you, trying to get you to react. You're pissed off and they were out of order back there, so hit me, take it out on me, but get it out of your system before you walk back into the house and drop us all in it.'

Brendan looked back at him. He wanted to hit out, to release the rage that was tying him in knots, but he was scared of how powerful it felt. If he started to hit Sean he wouldn't be able to stop, and he had had enough violence; there had been too much blood spilt and he was tired, tired of all of them, and of Lowlands. He desperately wanted to get back to Jemima, to crawl into bed with her and have her hold him. He lowered his head so that his forehead rested on Sean's chin. Surprisingly, Sean folded his arms around his shoulders and pulled him closer, taking his younger brother's weight.

Chapter 26

Brendan didn't sleep. He'd washed and climbed into bed and lay staring at Jemima, watching her features becoming clearer as the sunlight seeped in through the window. He took in every detail of her face in an attempt to block out the horror of Joe's death, until she eventually stirred, opened her eyes and smiled as she wrapped her arms around him.

'What time did you get back?' she asked sleepily.

Brendan was struck dumb, the words would not form; she pulled her head back and stared at him.

'You look terrible!' she exclaimed and he swallowed hard, trying to look back into her eyes. 'How much did you drink? I'll go and make you some tea,' she said slipping from his grasp. Wrapping her dressing gown around herself, she turned to him and her smile shone, lighting up her face. He forced a tight smile and after she disappeared he noticed his hands were shaking. He rubbed them over his head and then looked back at them; they still shook, so he shoved them under the duvet.

'Alright?' Sean asked Brendan. He was leaning in the doorway watching him carefully.

'Not really. It keeps going around and around in my head, I can't get the images of him out of my mind.'

'You crack and you'll take us all with you.'

'You think I give a fuck?' Brendan said fiercely.

'And that includes Jemima,' Sean added.

Brendan shook his head. 'I didn't ask to be part of this and she certainly has nothing to do with it. You knew though didn't you? You knew what Dad and Liam had planned. Again, you let me walk right into it.'

Sean stared at Brendan, his eyes hardened, but Brendan could still read him well. He could see all the past events that had happened between them, churned up and swirling like a vortex, and yet Sean calmly held onto them, as if using his physical strength to hold them in place.

'The old man wants to see you before you go,' Sean said.

'I've got nothing to say to him.'

'I'd see him before you go, if I were you,' warned Sean before turning to leave.

Brendan found Lester in the office at the breaker's yard. He didn't look up until Brendan had walked right up to his desk, and even then he only acknowledged him with a grunt.

'Sean said you wanted to see me,' said Brendan to get his father's attention.

Lester looked at him for some time before he spoke. 'About last night,' he said slowly.

'Nothing to do with me. As far as I'm concerned I wasn't even there.'

'But you were, you're an accessory to murder – you make out you had no part in it, that just confirms your guilt.'

'You want me to go to the police?' Brendan retorted sharply.

'What will Jemima make of that then?' Lester asked, sardonically.

'She'd want me to do the right thing,' he replied firmly.

Lester's bright blue eyes flickered like flames. 'You do that and you'll lose everything. Everything you've worked for – your fancy job, your fancy friends, your flash car and her. Think she'd stick by you? Can't quite see her in the line-up on visiting day, getting frisked by some horny prison guard.'

Brendan stared at the floor and struggled to swallow. His throat felt tight now he realised his father had him trapped. 'What do you want?' he asked.

'There's a lot of clearing up to do. I want the land to extend the breaker's yard and the bungalow needs clearing out and knocking down. You'll be needed to help at the weekends. The business is too busy in the week for us to make much progress.'

'How do you think you'll get away with this?'

'As far as everyone will know, Joe has finally sold up and gone to Spain. He was a fucking recluse. No one gave a toss about him – only your mother and her sisters – and they suffered him out of duty.'

'What you going to tell them? What you going to tell Mum? How you going to tell her you murdered her uncle?'

'You leave your mother to me. Just get yourself back here next weekend and bring that pretty little wife of yours,' snapped Lester. Then he turned his back on Brendan and busied himself with some paperwork, making it clear it was time for Brendan to leave.

Brendan shut the office door firmly behind him. He still felt shaky and nauseous, and when he saw Jemima look up and smile, a cold streak of fear shot through him. Everything he had worked so hard for now rested on a knife's edge and he was furious that his father had so easily been able to put him in this position. He opened the car door, and slumped into the seat.

'What's up?' Jemima asked, running her fingers soothingly down the side of his cheek. He took her hand and held it firmly, staring back at her, realising how much he could lose if she knew.

'Nothing,' he replied, shaking his head. 'Let's go home.'

→⇒ ⇐←

It was another nightmare, just a bad dream, Brendan lay in bed telling himself. But it was the fourth night with the same dream – his uncle's face looming towards him, then blood, lots of blood, and the sharp crack of breaking bone before his father and brothers gathered around him growing great arcs of dark wings and taking flight, leaving him cradling Joe, desperately trying to fit the pieces of his broken skull together. When he awoke he was clammy and shaken, and felt an overwhelming sensation of being buried alive.

The first night they had got back from Lowlands was the worst. Brendan had woken with a shout, coming to with Jemima shaking him and him staring into her face with no recognition of who she was. She had held him until his breathing steadied, but he had been unable to return to sleep, too fearful of what may visit him again. Over breakfast Jemima chatted lightly, while he sat on the periphery of her conversation.

'You look so tired,' she said and he looked up at her and frowned. 'I'll get you some of those herbal tablets to help you sleep,' she continued, picking up her bag and kissing him. 'You going to be alright?' she asked.

'Yeah, I've just got some pretty big deals going on. It gets to me every now and again, I'll be fine,' he said to reassure her. She smiled, but it didn't reach her worried eyes.

He didn't want to sleep and he didn't want her to get tablets to help him sleep. Sleep was the problem and he didn't know how to tell her without explaining the real reason why. So each night he became locked in a battle of wills with himself, trying to control his dreams and, in turn, his dreams controlling him. At work he had found an empty meeting room and caught up on twenty minutes' sleep. He could have slept longer, but his phone had buzzed, waking him. It was a text from his father, reminding him that he was to come back at the weekend to help clear out Joe's house. On mentioning it to Jemima that evening she had smiled cordially, agreeing to go with him, telling him she didn't mind.

The rain fell heavily at Lowlands. On late Saturday afternoon, having spent the day pretty much by herself, Jemima found a quiet space in a room at the front of the house. She wandered into it, looking about her, taking in the large dark wooden desk littered with papers, and its scuffed bottle-green leather inlay stained with time and lack of care. She meandered over to a small couch, its tapestry pattern faded, and carelessly ran her fingers along the back of it. Despite two large bay windows, the light in the room was gloomy. Wandering over to the window that faced out to the front of the house, Jemima looked up at the large mass of grey sky. Lowlands felt damp and the room was cold. She tightened her cardigan around herself and, sighing heavily, followed a raindrop with her forefinger as it slid down the window pane. That was how everything felt today, she thought – heavy. The greyness of the sky, the weight of the rain, the slow passing of time. Her fingers lightly touched the window seat, gliding over the dark red velvet and the jagged edges of the cigarette burns which were dotted across it. She sat down, pulling her legs up underneath her chin, and continued to look out of the window, waiting for Brendan to return.

Finally, she heard the rumble of the trucks and spotted Sean's first, bouncing slowly up the driveway. He parked it beside the window and she watched Sean, Brendan and Riley climb out and head to the back of the vehicle. As they emptied it of tools, Sean spotted her staring at them and his eyes locked onto hers coldly before he glanced back at Brendan, who smiled weakly in her direction.

Once in their room, Jemima pulled Brendan's t-shirt up over his head, while he undid his jeans; wet from the rain, they stubbornly stuck to his thighs as he tried to remove them.

'I missed you,' she whispered, wrapping herself around him. Holding her forearms, he smiled appreciatively, but his eyes were heavy with fatigue and the muscles in his back and arms were stiffening in protest at the strain he had put them through.

'I need a shower,' he replied, wearily.

She smiled and pressed closer, running the bridge of her nose along his jaw. He felt gritty and smelt salty. 'Yes you do, but I'll wait,' she answered playfully.

He raised his eyebrows. 'I don't think I am actually going to be much use to you,' he laughed.

While Brendan was showering Jemima was disturbed by a loud shout. She walked over to the window where she could see Liam calling Cassie to come out of their home. Gingerly, Cassie approached the doorway and, in an instant, Liam grabbed her arm and dragged her outside, like a reluctant calf to the slaughter. Liam tugged her roughly towards him, grabbing her other arm, pulling her close and shouting in her face. Cassie managed to turn her head away and Jemima watched as he yanked her chin and pulled her face back to him.

'What's up?' Brendan asked. Jemima had been so caught up in what she was watching, she hadn't noticed that he'd finished showering. He joined her at the window and looked out to see Cassie sinking to her knees. Liam still had a firm grasp on her arms and was bent over her, still shouting.

'Brendan, you have to do something!' Jemima cried.

He watched closely as Liam swung his fist into Cassie's face. She fell to the ground and Jemima's hands flew to her mouth to stifle a scream.

'Please Brendan, you have to stop him!'

Riley ran into the yard and attempted to talk to Liam, but Liam immediately turned on him, causing Riley to back off, hands raised in surrender. Sean appeared. There was some heated discussion and all three of the brothers looked at Cassie. She had managed to stand and was holding her head in her hands, her hair having been shaken forcefully from its ponytail. Sean gestured to Riley to take Cassie inside and turned to face Liam.

'It's okay, Sean and Riley have got it,' said Brendan, walking away.

But Jemima continued to watch, fixated by the scene below. Sean was standing very close to Liam, jabbing him hard in the chest, while Liam glared back at him. She watched him try to push Sean backwards and saw Sean waver, then raise his fist. She had no idea what Sean then said, but Liam's head fell and he skulked away to the house. Sean watched as Liam walked off and when he had disappeared, he looked up at Jemima, his eyes more thunderous than usual. She backed away, awkwardly, from the window, tripping over her own feet.

'What?' asked Brendan.

'It's Sean, he's staring at me,' she stammered.

Brendan came back to the window and saw Sean staring up at their room. As their eyes met, Sean raised his head and gave an abrupt nod, like he was quickly casting off a threat. Brendan stood motionless, holding his stare, deliberately keeping his face blank. The two brothers stared at each other like this for a while with Brendan the first to turn away.

'He's not there now,' Brendan lied, and continued getting dressed.

Sean carried on staring up at their room, watching Brendan turn his back on him and pull on a shirt. Sean pushed down the anger that growled inside him. He breathed deeply, flexing his fists, and then headed out to the woods. When he got to the edge of the trees he turned back and could see Brendan, still dressing. Brendan glanced back over his shoulder; Sean could just make out his eyes searching the space where he had been standing and he smiled, enjoying seeing Brendan so on edge.

CHAPTER 27

TWO WEEKS AFTER the incident with Cassie, Brendan was sat in Sean's truck, his fingers rapping against the dashboard in annoyance; he wanted to get back to Lowlands for a shower so he could wash the dust from his skin and hair and get rid of the stench of Uncle Joe's home. Sean had insisted on refuelling his truck, despite the tank being a quarter full. Sean and Riley had dawdled at the dump dropping off Joe's old carpets and, with no sense of urgency, they had meandered back towards Ashdowne. Brendan watched as Sean left the petrol kiosk, stopped and studied the receipt. Brendan groaned and Riley looked up from his newspaper; as Brendan tried to catch Riley's eye, Riley quickly looked back to his paper, studying the page hard. When Sean finally got into the truck Brendan snapped at him.

'What took you so long? Jemima thought I was going to be back an hour ago.'

'Alright, we're leaving now,' Sean replied defensively and slowly pulled out of the forecourt, leaving Brendan rolling his eyes and sighing with frustration.

Jemima hated waiting around for Brendan. She had run out of things to busy herself with and the conversation between herself, Lyla and Brendan's sisters had dried up a couple of hours ago. She had smiled at Cassie earlier, in the hope that she may finally get more than a grunt out of her, but she had thrown Jemima her usual scowl and disappeared with a basket full of washing. She heard a truck pull up, but her heart sank when Liam and Lester had strolled casually into the kitchen.

'Where's Brendan?' she asked. Lester eyed her suspiciously, before ignoring her – which she now realised was his usual way of responding – but Liam looked at her with more interest.

'They've taken some stuff down the dump. Always busy this time of day so he might be a while.'

Jemima felt too unsettled around Liam to pursue the conversation any further. She had seen how Brendan and Liam's hackles rose when they were near each other. It wasn't just this tension that caused her to feel nervous around Liam though; it was the way he looked at her, as if he was always one step ahead of her next move.

'Have the dogs been walked yet?' Liam called out, his eyes fixed firmly on Jemima.

'No, I haven't had time,' Anne-Marie called back from another room.

'What's Cassie been doing all day?'

'God knows, I haven't seen her,' Anne-Marie replied, sounding irritated.

'Lazy bitch,' he muttered, leaving it unclear as to whom he was referring.

'I don't mind taking them,' Jemima said, happy to find something to do. Liam narrowed his eyes and pondered her request.

'Take Kaiser. Cassie can walk the others,' he said bluntly.

When Brendan arrived back at Lowlands he went from room to room looking for Jemima. He had already been in the kitchen once but returned to it only to find Riley still with his head buried in his newspaper, while Sean was cleaning a shotgun.

'Have you seen Jemima anywhere?' Brendan asked.

They looked up at him briefly before turning their attention back to what they were doing. There was something in the way Riley had looked back at his paper so quickly that made Brendan suspicious.

'Do you know where she is?' he asked more firmly.

Neither of them looked up this time but Riley frowned and stared harder at the paper. Brendan could tell he wasn't reading it; his eyes had stopped scanning.

'Riley, where is she?'

Riley looked helplessly at him. Brendan looked around, mentally searching the house. When he spoke, he was trying hard to keep the panic out of his voice. 'Where's Liam?'

Sean stopped cleaning his gun.

'If he touches her I will kill him Sean, so where is she?' shouted Brendan leaning across the kitchen table towards him.

Sean eyed him for a couple of seconds then pushed his chair back and, without saying a word, headed for the back door. Taking his cue, Brendan and Riley followed. They headed towards the outbuilding and when Brendan saw the door was ajar, he started to run, passing Sean and swinging the door wide open. There she was, leaning against a workbench, looking startled, with Kaiser lying at her feet. Opposite her, leaning casually against a stack of broken furniture, was Liam, who looked delighted to see Brendan, and broke into a wide satisfied smile.

Brendan ignored him; he was more relieved to have found Jemima safe. He rushed over to her, pulling her to him and holding her tightly, but as he held her he could feel her rigidity. Carefully, he released her. Then he saw her expression, looking back at him like he was a stranger. He looked at Liam, then back at Jemima. Finally, she looked down and he knew that Liam had said something to her.

Liam studied Brendan while swinging an empty whiskey bottle over and over, catching it with his right hand. 'We've been getting to know each other better,' Liam told him sarcastically.

Ignoring him, Brendan took Jemima's hands. 'You okay?' he asked nervously. She pulled away and, when she looked at him, he could see how disappointed she was with him.

'We've been having a little chat, about the old days. About this place, about you and Cassie, and what you both used to get up to in here,' Liam continued.

'You had no right to tell her Liam!' Brendan barked. The edge to his voice made Liam stop swinging the bottle. Brendan turned back to Jemima, realising that his statement had just confirmed his guilt. He watched her close her eyes, as if she could no longer bear to look at him. 'It's not like he says, Jem, please believe me.'

'What was it like then, eh? Because I always understood that this...' Liam stated dramatically, throwing his arms out wide, 'is where you two used to meet, when she was just thirteen years old. Making you how old again? Oh that's right, twenty.' Liam laughed. 'Just the idea of it, eh Jemima? Those two sneaking out to meet up and do god knows what with each other... well... she ended up pregnant and he just fucked off!' he snarled.

'Shut your mouth Liam!' Brendan shouted. 'Jem, please believe me, it wasn't like he says. He's twisted this all out of context.' Brendan sounded desperate and when he tried to reach out to her, she flinched away from him. 'Jem, please,' he whispered, as she pushed past him and fled from the outbuilding. Her reaction acted like an on switch inside Brendan, his face hardening as he spun around. 'I'm going to fucking kill you!' he shouted, storming towards Liam. The smile quickly left Liam's face and he smashed the bottle against an old dining table, holding up the jagged end towards Brendan.

'Drop it Liam, fight me properly.'

'What like last time? I creamed you then and I'll do it again.'

Memories of seven years ago came back to Brendan, memories of him lying in the yard, covered in blood and dirt – retribution for Cassie.

'Not this time,' he replied and with one strong swipe, he released the rage that vibrated inside him and let his fist fill Liam's face. Liam dropped the bottle and staggered to keep his balance, and when he looked back at Brendan his expression was impenetrable. When Brendan hit him again, harder this time, he gave a low growl, and lunged at him.

At this, Sean rushed to intervene. Grabbing Brendan, he locked his arms tightly around his chest and pulled him away.

Brendan writhed forcefully, his feet dragging on the floor as he tried to wrestle himself free, while hollering threats and kicking out. Still Liam tried to come at him, despite Riley wedging himself between them and pushing hard against Liam's chest.

'Leave it!' bellowed Sean. 'Just fucking drop it!' he shouted at them both and, realising Sean's grasp on him was too strong, Brendan stopped thrashing and let his muscles slacken. He felt Sean slowly release his grip. The two brothers faced each other, both breathing heavily, both with clenched fists; Liam's nostrils flared and Brendan observed a trickle of blood from Liam's lip inch down his chin.

'Why? What did you tell her for?' Brendan asked. His voice was pulled so tight in his throat, it ached.

Liam stared at him for a long time before answering. 'I thought she should know who you really are,' he said, his voice rolling with contempt.

Brendan scoffed, letting his head fall back in disbelief. 'You don't even know who I really am... And what about you Liam? You think she should know who you are? Some backward hick who fucks his brother's cast-offs!'

Liam's face flinched and his eyes tightened.

'That's why you told her – you're jealous. She's way out of your league and she's mine, and you can't bear that!' He walked over until he was inches from Liam's face. 'You can't bear the idea of me and her together because you can never have her, and you'll never have her because you... are not me.'

Slowly, Brendan stepped back, smiling cruelly. Liam stared angrily back at him, struck dumb by Brendan's words. He watched as Brendan calmly turned away and strode purposefully towards Lowlands.

When Brendan got back to Lowlands he headed straight upstairs to their room and found Jemima sitting on the bed, with her back to him. Struggling to find the right words to explain his version, he settled for a simple, 'Hey' to test the water, but Jemima didn't respond. Instead, she carried on staring ahead.

'Jem, please let me explain,' he ventured tentatively.

'What's there to explain? That's why she hates me isn't it? From the moment I turned up here she's resented me. It's so obvious why now,' she said, her voice bloated from crying.

'She doesn't hate you, Jem. It's me she hates,' he replied softly.

Turning to face him, he could see her nose and eyes were red from crying. 'She was just a child, Brendan.' Jemima looked so ashamed with him; it left him feeling cauterised.

'I know,' he replied, in barely more than a whisper.

'You were the grown up, the adult. How could you?' she said, staring at him, her watery eyes wide with disbelief. 'Do you know how much I wanted him to be lying? When Liam was telling me, I kept thinking, *this isn't true, he would have told me.* Then when you turned up I wanted you to tell me it was all lies, not that you can... explain.' She looked away again.

Brendan slumped against the door. 'I am so sorry, Jem. Liam shouldn't have told you what he did.'

'Don't blame him Brendan, please. If Liam hadn't told me then I would never have known – you would never have told me.' She faced him again. 'You would never have told me that you got a thirteen-year-old girl pregnant and then abandoned her.'

'I never abandoned her, I left to go back to university. I left a few weeks early because it was the only way I could think of to end it. I never knew she was pregnant until after she had lost the baby and I didn't know how old she was until I was too deep into it all. Jem, she wasn't thirteen like you would have been at thirteen, she wasn't all plaits and knee-length socks,' he told her indignantly.

Jemima gasped, horrified at what he had just said and the tone with which he had said it. Seeing her reaction, he stumbled desperately on.

'I made a mistake and I have spent years wishing that I could undo it all. I wish I had never gone near her, I swear. I am so tired of being sorry for all of this; believe me, they have never let me forget what I did.'

They both fell silent. Holding his breath, Brendan watched her contemplate what he had just said.

'Is that why you never come back very often?' she asked, finally.

'A large part of it, yes.' He walked over to the bed, his eyes searching her face.

'Were you in love with her?'

'No.'

Jemima scoffed. 'So it was just sex then?'

'No, not entirely,' he replied, earnestly. 'It was about me getting to the end of the day and having something to look forward to. Being with someone who wasn't always on my back, judging me.

She was always there, she just accepted me. I didn't have to be on my guard all the time with her. I don't know, when I was with her it kind of blocked this place out. It blocked all of them out.'

Jemima blinked hard. She had anticipated excuses but not this much honesty.

'When I found out her age, I tried to stop seeing her. I knew it was wrong, every time I went back to her. I was selfish and I hurt her and I am so, so, sorry for what I did.'

Jemima rose and gently placed her hands on his hips and he carefully looked back at her. She smiled softly and he felt confused – she should hate him. She should still be angry and disgusted with him.

'Have you told her you're sorry?' she asked calmly.

He shook his head. 'I've kept away from her. I didn't want to make things worse.'

'You should tell her. She needs to know.'

Jemima hugged him and, relieved, he held her tightly, burying his head into her hair. 'I would have told you, Jem. I couldn't find the right time, but I would have told you.'

'Is there anything else I need to know Brendan?' she asked, looking at him seriously.

He frowned.

'I need to know if there is anything else because I couldn't take something like this happening again. It's important we are really honest with each other.'

His thoughts raced in all directions and his head filled with images of Joe falling to the floor, the warm and sticky blood spraying across his face and the sound of Joe's body hitting the floor of the makeshift grave. He wanted desperately to be free of these thoughts, free from the strain it took to contain them and from the speed with which they crashed into his mind. He desperately wanted to tell her and he knew that if he was going to, then this was the time. He smiled nervously.

'No. There's nothing else.'

She raised her eyebrows. 'You promise?'

'I promise,' he replied, pulling her tightly against him, while a large stone sunk to the bottom of his stomach, dread splashing up behind it.

CHAPTER 28

THERE WERE TWO apple trees at the back of Lowlands, standing at right angles to each other, lonesome and uncared for amongst the brambles and nettles where nobody could be bothered to cut the grass. In the spring the two trees foamed with white blossom and over the summer small fruits budded and swelled, slowly ripening until they fell, with a soft thud, to the ground where they stayed, slowly rotting.

Since Cassie had been at Lowlands she had painstakingly picked the fruit at the end of every summer, reaching on tiptoes and gently feeling the deep red apples, caressing them before placing them in her wide wicker basket and swatting away the wasps which buzzed, languidly, drunk from the bronzed, fermented fruit.

Riley watched her from the French windows. He saw her raise her head, tilt it thoughtfully and carefully select which apple to pick – as if somehow seeing its ripeness from within. He was mesmerised by the way she would hook her small pink tongue around the corner of her upper lip and narrow her eyes with painstaking concentration.

⋆⟞⟝ ⟞⟝⋆

All those years ago, when he had found her cowered in a corner of the outbuilding, she had turned away from him; but he had been patient, speaking to her quietly and holding his hands out, as if calming a wild animal. Gradually, over the next couple of days, she had turned to face him, allowing him to see the marbled blue and purple bruising on her face. He had breathed in sharply, shocked by the marks of such a brutal beating. But he had held eye contact with her, keeping his expression mild and his voice soft, and eventually she let him crawl over to her. Sitting with her in the dusty light, he wrapped his arm around her and pulled her rigid, cold body closer to him. He was calm and strong, while inwardly crumbling.

Then Liam had barged in on them, taking her from Riley and carrying her heroically into Lowlands. Riley had shrunk away; at thirteen years old he was no competition for Liam, four years his senior and built for fighting. Riley was willowy in comparison and though he would bend and flex against Liam's strong blows, he knew he was no match physically, and he also knew that a fight was the only way he would be able to claim Cassie for himself.

So Riley had looked on, tormented, burning inside with resentment as Liam pushed her around, shouting orders at her and filling her with fear. Impotent as he felt at being unable to protect her, their relationship developed through a mutual appreciation of each other's circumstances. As Lyla and his sisters ordered him around, his life mirrored that of Cassie's, and when the two of them were ever alone together, Cassie would smile, looking up at him with a warmth that he never saw her reveal to anyone else.

Every muscle in him felt as if it could explode as he returned her mesmerising smile.

⇥═◎ ◎═⇤

Cassie had reached up on tiptoes trying to reach a large glossy apple hanging tantalisingly out of reach. Walking up quietly behind her, Riley reached up to the branch, pulling it lower. Without turning around, she gently clasped the apple and twisted the stem until, with a small snap, it came away free in her hand. She studied it closely and eventually she looked away from the apple and down at the ground behind her. She could make out Riley's shadow, jutting out from his heels, long and thin. Behind him was the shadow of the other apple tree, its thick boughs uncurled behind him, emerging from his back in two large arcs; and the breeze catching the leaves, making them ruffle like feathers. For a brief moment, Cassie thought her long-awaited angel had landed behind her, slowly unfolding his wings in anticipation of catching her. She turned to face Riley and offered him the apple. The sun illuminated its skin, giving off a dark red glow, and he bit deep into it. The apple's sharpness hit the roof of his mouth in contrast with its soft white flesh, which fell to pieces easily as he chewed.

Cassie reached up to wipe away a thin line of juice running down his chin and he felt himself bowing towards her. He dropped the apple and folded his arms around her. His lips fell heavily on her mouth as he pulled her onto her tiptoes and kissed her. There was an urgency in his kiss, as if he was making up for the lost years. Running his hands over her shoulders, feeling the sun's heat on her skin, his fingers became tangled in her hair. His breath spilled from him unsteadily, forcing him to release her so he could take a gasp of air. Breathing deeply, he saw a large tear form in her eye. She was trembling. Her hand flew up to her lips, gently touching them as if she was tracing a memory across them. She looked up at him, into his bright blue eyes, the O'Rourke signature. His shaggy blond hair fell across his brow; he had the same gently curved nose as Brendan and his father, the same wide mouth, the same shaped eyebrows framing his eyes in sweeping arches.

'It was you,' she gasped. He looked confused. 'It was never him. It was meant to be you,' she whispered.

Pulling herself away she fled, her bare feet skimming the long grass, and her chest heaving with the pressure of what she was just starting to realise. She abandoned the apples in the wicker basket next to Riley, who stood helplessly as he watched her disappear.

Cassie slammed her door shut and leaned against it. She forced the images of her dream and the reflections from the mirror back into her mind, mentally turning them over and holding them at every angle, shaking them as if she was expecting some clue to fall out. Over the years Riley had changed. When she first met him, they were both just thirteen, their bodies stepping precariously from childhood to adulthood. As she recalled his face, she could see how it had developed from the gawky teenager she had first met, with harsh features and teeth too large for his mouth. Now his features had settled into the man's face that she had grown used to. Living alongside him she had not realised how much he now resembled Brendan. Finally, she realised she had got the wrong brother, the fallout from which had changed the course of all their lives.

Riley carefully placed the wicker basket by Cassie's front door. He knocked gently, not really expecting her to answer. He had chastised himself for kissing her and also for the force with which he had grabbed her and pulled her to him. He'd been desperate and now he felt foolish. All those years of wanting her had been jeopardised in a moment. His dreams of ever being with her were now over. Her parting words had been garbled and her expression was filled with regret. It was so clear and sharp – he couldn't mistake what her fleeing had meant.

Riley hadn't expected Cassie to turn up for dinner either, but she had, which made it worse for him as she avoided his eye. He forced his meal down, trying to tune into the banter around him, but he felt winded and the pain was unbearable. At the end of the meal, Sean pushed his plate out of the way, leaned back and stretched, then enquired if Riley was joining him and Liam for a game of pool. He smiled weakly, turning down their offer. The idea of spending time with Liam repulsed him; the fact that he so callously treated the one person Riley most desired was too much for him to bear.

Later that evening Lowlands had quickly emptied and Cassie picked her way through the empty house. She climbed the stairs slowly, placing a foot lightly on each step. When she got to the landing she could hear the water running in the shower, splashing against the tiles. She tried the bathroom handle, her heart skipping a beat when she discovered the door was unlocked. Slowly, she opened it, an eager cloud of vapour escaping as she entered. Shutting the door quietly behind her, she slid the bolt with her nimble fingers. The misty air fell on her skin in a fine spray as she slipped out of her own clothes and walked over to the cubicle. As she approached, Riley stood still, looking back over his shoulder; he could see her long black hair, like a shadow, surrounding her. When she reached for the shower door, he pushed it open and large, billowing clouds of steam enveloped her. She watched the drops of water running down his face, across his shoulders and down his chest. He watched her, transfixed, as she stepped into the shower and closed the door behind her. He was waiting for her to make the first move, afraid that she would run away again. Her forefinger followed a drop of water down his chest and along to his navel. When she looked up at him, droplets of water dripped from her dark eyelashes. She smiled, blinking away the water, looking shyly up at him.

'Are you sure?' he asked and, without replying, she stood on her tiptoes and kissed him.

Later, lying in bed together, their legs intertwined, he held her closely as she told him about her dreams, the mirror, and her mistaking him for Brendan. Regretfully, she explained what her mistake had cost them. They both knew that her involvement with Liam was their greatest obstacle. Riley tightened his grip, pulling her closer, and reassured her that they would find a way to be together.

She looked up at him sheepishly. 'But there will be no children,' she said, her voice wavering. The loss of Brendan's baby had left her young womb too scarred for pregnancy. She was told by the doctors that she would never conceive again and the fact that she hadn't fallen pregnant by Liam proved testament to their prognosis.

'I don't care,' he replied. 'It's you I want.'

CHAPTER 29

BRENDAN KNOCKED GENTLY against Cassie's open door and stepped in. The place appeared empty as he looked about him. Despite its shabby appearance, someone had tried to make the converted brick sheds into a home. Small stones and shells had been stuck together, attached to string and hung from the windows and, nestled on a window sill, sat an ornate silver-framed mirror. He carefully picked it up, but before he even got to look into it, it was snatched from his grasp. He turned to see Cassie holding it and scowling at him.

'Hi,' he said, watching her finger the silver roses on the frame nervously. 'Liam and the others, they're all up at the yard,' he added, trying to put her at ease, but his comment only made her appear more anxious. 'I've come to...' He ran out of words. When he had discussed apologising to her with Jemima it had seemed so straightforward but now, with Cassie finally in front of him, the words dried up and crumbled inside his throat. He coughed and tried to start again. 'I shouldn't have run out on you like that. I should have finished things between us properly. It wasn't fair of me to just leave you Cassie.' His hands were buried deep in his jeans pockets and he could feel himself stumbling over his words, acutely aware of her intense stare.

'I didn't know you were pregnant, until it was too late. I didn't find out until you'd lost your baby.'

'Our baby,' she told him, her voice sounding surprisingly firm.

Brendan stared back at her. He understood what she was saying but was struggling to make the connection. 'Our baby,' he repeated quietly, as if trying the expression on for size.

She slid out a photograph from the back of the mirror, holding it out for him to take. He stared at the picture of a newborn baby, pale skinned, its eyes tightly shut.

'They let me hold him for a while before they took him away. They told me to name him, said it would help.' Her scowl had disappeared, her gaze now falling onto the windows looking out to the backyard. 'I called him Storm. The wind really howled the night when I had him. Even though he was so small he looked like a proper baby, with tiny fingers and toes.' She looked back at Brendan. 'I could see you in him. He'd have grown up to be the spit of you. I wonder sometimes what sort of person he would have been.'

'Why didn't you get in touch with me? I'd never have let you go through that on your own. I'd have come back to help you Cassie.'

She looked back at him and tilted her head to the side, letting her eyes glide over him gently before she spoke. 'They told me not to. They told me you didn't care.'

'Who told you that?'

'Your mum and Liam.'

Brendan closed his eyes, clenched his fists and breathed deeply to calm himself. When he opened his eyes she was smiling warmly. She had the same look on her face as she'd had when she used to greet him at the outbuilding. He could see the same longing flickering behind her eyes. As he went to speak he noticed her stare was slightly off centre. In fact, she was not looking at him but past him, to the doorway. He turned and saw Riley watching him. When Riley changed his focus to Cassie, his face softened, and when Brendan looked back to her, he could tell that, as far as she was concerned, he wasn't even in the room.

Seeing them together had shocked Brendan; it had also shocked Jemima when he told her. She shook her head with disbelief when he had told her about his family refusing to let Cassie contact him.

'But that's so unfair. It was your baby too,' she pointed out. And for the second time that day he was uncomfortably reminded of what he had lost.

'How long has it been going on?' Brendan asked Riley later on that day. Riley was unaware that Brendan had entered his room. He had been rifling through his chest of drawers and stopped momentarily, before sliding one of the drawers shut and turning to face Brendan.

'How long Riley?' Brendan asked again, less patiently.

'What's it to you?' Riley said sharply.

'Liam will kill you, you know that. He'll kill you both.'

Riley lit a cigarette and sighed. 'I know what he's capable of,' he said.

'You're serious about her?' Brendan asked, but he had seen how Riley had looked at Cassie – it was the same way he looked at Jemima.

'Yeah, she means everything to me. She has ever since she came here.'

'You've been together since then?'

'No, only the last ten months. I'm trying to figure out a way we can be together, away from here.'

Brendan scoffed. 'Are you mad? He'll hunt you down, he'll never let her go. You know what a sick, demented bastard he is. He's not right in the head Riley.'

Riley shifted uncomfortably.

'D'you know what really happened to Uncle Joe?' Brendan asked cautiously.

Riley nodded.

'Then you know what he is capable of and he certainly won't lose her to you Riley.

You have no future together.'

Riley's face tightened. 'We'll find a way, Brendan.'

'You're only twenty-one. You can get whoever you want – anyone. Why her, why Cassie?' Brendan asked, exasperated.

Riley stubbed out his cigarette forcefully and turned to face him again. 'Yeah, why her Brendan?' he said pointedly.

Brendan shook his head in disbelief. 'It's nothing like what happened between me and her, nothing like it.'

'So it's more like you and Tess?' continued Riley sharply.

'Sean told you?' Brendan replied stunned that Riley knew.

'No. Cassie did. She saw you together. Sean has told no one. He's protecting you for some reason. Can you imagine if everyone found out the truth as to why they split up? You'd be the one who's dead.'

Brendan nodded, confused by the idea of Sean protecting him; it conflicted with the way he treated him.

'You going to say anything?' Riley asked him.

'Of course not. Jesus, why would you ask that? I just want you to realise what you're getting into because Riley she's not...'

'Don't tell me she's not worth it,' Riley cut across him. 'You don't know her Brendan. You don't know the first thing about her.'

The realisation of this was like a slap, there was no questioning how determined Riley was about her, and part of Brendan envied his conviction. 'You're right I don't,' he said and Riley's hard face softened and broke into a small frown. 'You need anything, you call me, yeah?' said Brendan, still feeling the pull to protect his younger brother.

Riley nodded and Brendan turned to go. When his hand rested on the door handle, he realised that he still hadn't apologised to Cassie. 'Can you tell her I'm sorry,' he said, keeping his back to Riley, not wanting to see his face. He knew he was taking the coward's way out and without waiting for an answer he left.

CHAPTER 30

'OH MY GOD, it is so good to see you!' exclaimed Minnie, throwing her arms around Jemima and squeezing her tightly. Jemima hugged her back; she was just as pleased to see her and Abby.

'Come in,' she said, pulling away and gesturing for them to enter the apartment.

'Well, this is very stylish,' said Abby, handing Jemima a chilled bottle of white wine.

'Umm, we're looking to move, actually. It's okay for one person but for two it's a squeeze. There's hardly any storage space.'

'Which is why most of your stuff is still in your old room?' added Minnie, winking at her.

'Sorry,' Jemima winced. 'I know, I haven't sorted it out yet, I just don't know where the time has gone!'

She knew exactly where the time had gone. Nearly every weekend since they were married, all their free time had been spent at Lowlands, with Jemima scuffing around the old house while Brendan spent his time with his brothers and father. She started to feel resentful so she quickly focused back on her friends.

'God, you are so lucky you are out of the rat race, Jem,' Minnie said, finishing off describing an encounter with a work colleague on a recent business trip.

'You caught a good one. Have you any idea how rare men like Brendan are?' added Abby, laughing along at Minnie's story. Jemima looked down momentarily and when she looked up two curious faces stared back at her.

'What?' Jemima asked.

'So, how is married life?' asked Minnie.

Jemima smiled tightly and rested her head against her hand, letting her fingers twirl through her hair. She managed a shrug.

'Please don't tell me the honeymoon period is over already,' said Abby light-heartedly.

Jemima bit her lip. She could feel tears beginning to prick her eyes. She tried to swallow, but a large lump had formed in her throat.

'Jem, what's up?' asked Minnie.

Jemima wiped her eyes. 'I don't know, I'm being silly. I've drunk too much and, seeing you both, it's just...' Her voice trailed off as her face fell. Minnie and Abby rushed over to her.

'You can tell us, we're still here for you,' Minnie said, and Jemima's body heaved; her tears escaped and the pressure of trying to pretend she was happy escaped with them. If she could just keep telling herself it would get easier, that they would get to a point when Brendan would be finished with Lowlands. Then they could start looking for a home together and she wouldn't have to face his family every weekend or deal with their sideways glances and loaded questions, always feeling like she was on the outside while at the same time feeling as though she was missing something going on right under her nose.

For her, Lowlands felt full of skeletons. In bed at night she was convinced she could hear their bones creaking as they moved uncomfortably around in their cupboards. Brendan was always jumpy when they were there, immediately falling into a dark mood when they returned. He had no involvement in their life together any more and any mention of moving house sparked a difficult discussion; on one occasion, Brendan even suggested that she go out and find somewhere to buy for them on her own. She had cried silently that night, hurt by his lack of interest.

His apartment was too cramped for the two of them. It also meant a long commute for Jemima and, more significantly, this had been his bachelor pad, a place he had brought other women back to. When she lay in bed with him, she knew that even though she was his wife, others had been there before her, and their presence hung in the atmosphere like stale perfume. She wanted somewhere new for them to live and since she had found out about Cassie – that they had nearly had a child together – her own desire to become a mother had started to stir. On the way home from work she would find herself lost in thoughts about their future. But when she got home, opened the front door and saw Brendan's face, his sullen expression fixed on the television and a glass of whiskey in his hand, her heart would sink. On the occasions she had shared her ideas with him, he'd scoffed – a small gesture that shattered her dreams like glass, cutting her deeply as she tried to put them back together.

'Perhaps we rushed into getting married,' she said, closing her eyes. A dull thud was starting behind them. Minnie squeezed her hand.

'Perhaps you did, but who really knows, eh? Marriage, relationships – aren't they all a gamble, no matter how long you've been together? Jem, what's going on between you both?'

'I don't really know. He's different. Ever since we went to see his family for that party, he's been... I can't explain.'

'I didn't think he was close to his family,' Minnie said.

'He's not. Well he wasn't. I don't know what's up between them. They seem to have some kind of hold over him; they certainly have more sway than I do.'

'What are they like?' Abby asked.

'Scary. Well, his dad is terrifying, if I'm honest. They all seem really scared of him.'

'God, I can't imagine Brendan being scared of anyone,' said Minnie.

'He's wary of him. His father is very intimidating.'

'What are his brothers like?' enquired Abby. Minnie rolled her eyes at her.

Jemima paused, and took a large gulp of wine before answering.

'It's weird. Before I met them he never talked about them much, but when he did I used to think how exciting it must be to be part of a big family. I was excited about meeting them; particularly Sean. I got the impression that when they were kids they were really close. I don't know what's happened, but there's some sort of atmosphere between them now. Though not as bad as the one between him and his brother Liam – they really hate each other.'

'Why?' asked Minnie.

'How long have you got?' Jemima sighed. The scraping of a key in the lock interrupted them. 'He's supposed to be staying with James tonight, that's why I invited you over,' Jemima told them, frowning.

Brendan walked in. Throwing his keys on the kitchen counter he nodded in their direction and walked straight into the bedroom.

'Excuse me,' said Jemima anxiously to her friends and followed him. Shutting the bedroom door behind her, she watched him take off his suit jacket and undo his tie and top button.

'I wasn't expecting you home,' she said, trying to read his mood. He stared at her coldly, then walked over to the wardrobe and pulled out their overnight bag.

'Change of plan,' he grunted.

'Minnie and Abby are staying over!'

'Get a taxi for them,' he replied gruffly, filling the bag with his old jeans and t-shirts.

'Why are you packing those things?'

'We're going to Lowlands first thing.'

'Brendan, I'm going shopping tomorrow with...'

'Get your things packed,' he cut over her and headed for the bathroom.

'No, no I won't,' she replied. He stopped still and turned to her.

'Get your fucking stuff packed now,' he told her, scowling, daring her to refuse him.

'Don't talk to me like that,' she replied firmly.

He walked over to her wardrobe and started to pull some of her clothes out, shoving them roughly into the bag before storming into the bathroom. Jemima looked on, stunned.

'You need this?' he asked, holding up a bottle of cleanser.

'I've made plans! I haven't seen my friends in over two months and you can't just change things like this!' she exclaimed.

He threw the cleanser into a toiletries bag, then in one smooth swipe cleared the contents of her shelf straight into the bag, zipped it up and threw it from the bathroom onto the bed.

'You are being so unreasonable,' she told him. 'Just one weekend. We have been there practically every weekend since we got married. This just isn't fair, I need some space from them all, away from that place.'

'You wanted to meet them,' he snapped.

'Yes meet them, not bloody well move in with them every bloody weekend!' she snapped back at him.

'The sooner I get this yard finished then the sooner we can get on with our lives, get your fucking house in suburbia and fill it with kids and dogs and God knows what other crap,' he hissed. 'Christ, Jemima, I am doing this for you,' he finished harshly.

'For me? What do I want a bloody breaker's yard for?'

He looked back at her and sighed deeply. 'You wouldn't understand. Just get your stuff together and tell them they've got to leave,' he said, turning his back on her. Jemima stared at him and tears started to roll down her face. When she opened the door Minnie and Abby were both ready to go.

'It's okay, you need to sort this out. Call us yeah?' said Minnie softly.

'Don't leave it so long next time,' Abby said kindly and Jemima nodded, choking more tears back as she saw her friends to the door.

When they left, she leaned against the door trying to stifle a huge sob by clasping her hands over her mouth. Brendan walked into the lounge and went to step towards her.

'How could you? How could you do this? You promised we could have this weekend to ourselves. You let me make plans to see my friends and I've booked houses for us to view on Sunday!' she cried. He stared back at her frowning. 'Remember, we talked about getting a new home or, as you just put it, *a fucking house in suburbia to fill with kids and dogs and crap.* Is that how you see the things that are important to me?' she asked him between sobs and his frown deepened. 'I didn't sign up for this Brendan. I would never have signed up to this life. You can't just push me around like this – Christ, it's just like Liam and Cassie!' she shouted. She saw him flinch and his eyes harden. He turned to walk back to the bedroom and stopped in the doorway.

'We need to leave by seven,' he said coldly, then kicked the bedroom door shut behind him.

Chapter 31

Brendan and Jemima had left their apartment without saying a word to each other and an angry silence festered between them as they drove out of London and followed the motorway down to Ashdowne. When the heathland came into view, Brendan turned off the motorway and glanced at Jemima through his sunglasses. Jemima was staring out of the passenger window; he could see that the muscles in her jaw were tense. As he approached Lowlands, he slowly pulled his car over and cut the engine. Jemima continued to stare out of the window, refusing to acknowledge him.

'Jem, please don't be like this,' he said softly, his voice cracking slightly under the weight of her name.

She ignored him, so he swivelled in his seat to face her, removing his sunglasses.

'I'm sorry,' he whispered, and she turned her head sharply to face him, staring at him critically. Unnerved by her expression, he resisted the urge to touch her. 'I'm sorry I changed our plans, I'm sorry I swore at you and I'm sorry your friends had to leave,' he said. He saw her swallow, the soft skin rippling against her throat, and he wondered if this was her cue to respond, but she remained silent. He moved in his seat, the leather creaking in resistance, announcing his discomfort. 'I'm sorry I said what I did about us getting a place together. You wouldn't fill it with crap – it would be our home and it's what I want.'

Jemima looked down and he saw her bottom lip quiver. He wanted to steady it, so he gently cupped her face in his hand and ran his thumb across it. Her lips parted and he could feel her drop the weight of her head slightly into his hand.

'I was out of order yesterday,' he continued, thinking back to the conversation he had had with his father earlier that day. Lester had used a threatening tone as he barked down the phone to tell him he was needed back again for the weekend. He'd ordered Brendan to change his plans and insisted that Jemima came to Lowlands with him.

Jemima looked up at Brendan; he was wearing the now too familiar frown. She moved towards him and his hand slid to the back of her neck.

'I need a break,' she spoke softly and he nodded. 'We can't spend every weekend here Brendan. Look what it's doing to us.'

'I know.'

'This place is changing you. You've seem so troubled ever since you've come back.'

Brendan looked away, uneasily.

'You promised you'd tell me if there was anything else,' she continued.

'I know. I will, Jem. Please. We only need to do this for a few more weeks, then I'm out of here.' Brendan's voice sounded desperate and he pulled her closer to him, twisting his fingers through her hair as he spoke. Jemima rested her hand on his chest and she looked into his eyes as if trying to find something.

'You promise?' she asked him.

He nodded back. 'Yes, I promise. A couple more weeks then we can move on.'

A small smile crossed her lips and he mirrored it; his heart was beating fast and he swallowed hard before he kissed her. Responding, she leaned into him, and he could feel her trust in that kiss and his own guilt rise to try to extinguish it. He gently let go of her and started the engine, replaced his sunglasses and drove the short distance to Lowlands.

At the end of the driveway, they could see Sean attaching a trailer to the back of his truck. He glanced up at them with his usual scowl. Once they had parked, Jemima and Brendan climbed out of their car and walked over to him.

'You're late. Dad told you we needed to be at Jack Slade's by nine to get that digger,' he snapped.

'Traffic was bad,' lied Brendan and Sean threw a quick look at Jemima, whose face registered how bad the lie was. He huffed then swung open the door to his truck. Brendan handed their bags to Jemima and kissed her goodbye, aware that Sean was watching. Ignoring him, he walked around to the other side of the truck and climbed in.

The two of them left Ashdowne and were travelling through villages that Brendan vaguely remembered from his childhood when Sean's mobile phone started to ring. Holding onto the steering wheel with one hand, Sean fished his phone out of his jeans pocket. Glancing at the screen, he gestured for Brendan to turn down the stereo. Sean was silently glowering about whatever he was being told. After a while he growled, 'On my way,' and threw the phone across to Brendan to catch before swinging the truck across to the other side of the road. Brendan fumbled with the phone, trying to turn it off, and ended up leaning against the passenger window from the force of the sudden U-turn.

'Where're we going now?' Brendan asked, puzzled.

'We need to get Kelly.'

'Was that her on the phone?'

'No, it was Anne-Marie,' replied Sean sharply, turning the stereo back on.

They found Kelly in bed with a man she had picked up in a nightclub. Finding no obvious way into the man's house, Sean had broken in, casually smashing a window in the back door like he had every right to, while Brendan looked on incredulously. As they climbed the stairs they had heard noises coming from the master bedroom. Brendan watched Sean's face harden and he knew that whatever happened next was going to be messy.

Kelly kicked and screamed as Sean dragged her off the bed and threw her at Brendan. Then he turned his attention to Kelly's lover, hitting him hard, stopping the man's protests short and leaving him dazed and bleeding, slumped between his bed and wardrobe. As Sean dragged Kelly away, Brendan looked back at the man.

'You might need to phone someone,' said Brendan, concerned for the man's state.

'Fuck you,' the man replied before shutting his eyes.

Outside, Sean was struggling to get Kelly strapped into the passenger seat of the truck. As Brendan climbed in, Sean let out a shout, pulling his hand away from her sharply.

'You bitch, look what you've done,' he snarled, showing her a red crescent-shaped bite mark on his hand. Kelly smiled snidely. 'You think this is clever? You think doing this is smart?' he said, grabbing her jaw firmly in his hand and using his spare hand to gesture back towards the house they had just left. Her eyes blazed into his, refusing to be shamed by him.

Jemima heard the commotion before she saw it. It spilled into the house in the form of shouts and expletives. She dog-eared the page of her book and walked out into the hallway where she was faced with Sean roughly manhandling Kelly, with Brendan behind them looking uneasy. Out of the corner of her eye, she caught Anne-Marie sauntering down the stairs smiling smugly. When Anne-Marie reached Kelly the commotion died down.

'You little whore,' Anne-Marie hissed at her.

Kelly's eyes widened then she smiled tightly. 'Least I'm getting some,' Kelly replied.

Anne-Marie's mouth fell open before she slapped Kelly hard around her face. Pulling her own hand back, and with twice the force, Kelly slapped Anne-Marie and then the two sisters lunged at each other. Sean waded in pulling Kelly backwards, while Liam, appearing from the kitchen, pulled Anne-Marie away, who ungratefully shook him off her.

'You, get up stairs now!' Sean shouted at Kelly. Turning to Brendan, he snapped, 'Watch her, make sure she goes nowhere.' He then turned to say something to Anne-Marie but was interrupted by his phone ringing. 'It's Dad,' he said. From Sean's expression it was clear that Lester was unhappy about the uncollected digger. 'My truck broke down and Liam had to give us a tow. We're just heading back out now to get it,' Sean lied, scowling at Kelly. When Sean finished the call he turned back to her again. 'I'll be home in a couple of hours. I'll deal with you then,' he told her firmly, before grunting at Liam to follow him.

Jemima looked up the staircase at Kelly who was glowering at Sean's back and then slowly uncurled her middle finger in his direction. Seeing she had the others attention, Kelly smirked before thumping up the stairs to her room.

Anne-Marie mumbled something derogatory under her breath and walked away, leaving Brendan and Jemima in the hallway.

'What happened?' asked Jemima,

'Don't ask,' replied Brendan sighing loudly. 'I need to go check on her. I'll catch up with you in a bit, okay?'

Brendan cautiously pushed Kelly's bedroom door open, unsure if he was going to get something hurled at him. Instead she slung him a quick look of disgust and kicked her shoes off across the room.

'Who was he?' Brendan asked, attempting to find some way to break the ice between them.

She shrugged. 'I don't know.' She smirked at his shocked response.

'Sean's right, it's not smart,' he stated coolly.

'Oh please, not a lecture from you, particularly about this, from you?' she said, her eyes widening with disbelief.

'You're worth more than that Kelly,' he replied, determined not to rise to her.

She stared back at him, weighing him up and slowly rolling her dress down. When it fell to the floor, leaving her naked, she jutted her hip out and looked at him defiantly. Brendan instinctively looked away, lowering his gaze but not before he had taken in her shape – her long legs and small waist, the clean cut of her hips in contrast to her full rounded breasts. He was amazed at how her body had morphed from the long-limbed scrawny one of her childhood.

He forced himself to look back, determined not to be intimidated by her, and deliberately focused on her eyes, trying to ignore how amused she appeared. Running her tongue seductively over her top lip, she delighted at watching him squirm.

'I've seen it all before Kelly,' he stated firmly, trying desperately to gain some control.

She raised her eyebrows, sending him the message that he hadn't seen her like this before. His breath rattled as he tried to avoid his own eyes being dragged down her body, taking in the exotic bloom of her womanhood. As a distraction he grabbed a short dressing gown from her bed and thrust it at her.

'For fuck's sake, I used to look after you when you were a baby,' he snapped.

Seeing him start to crack, she turned to put the dressing gown on, provocatively pulling her hair up and slowly letting it fall down her back.

'I'm not a baby now though,' she replied playfully.

His eyes flicked across her one more time before he forced himself to look out of her bedroom window. He thrust his hands deep into his jeans pockets and studied the tops of the pine trees waving gently in the early summer breeze. Holding his breath, he counted to ten – then to twenty – before he felt himself start to calm and was able to look at her again without wanting to slap her audacity out of her.

'You're my sister. Stop being so cheap.'

She instantly slumped onto her bed and studied her nails, staring intently at the luminous pink nail varnish. When she looked up her eyes were glassy with tears. All traces of the vixen had vanished; now she looked injured, leaving Brendan uneasy with this sudden change of character.

'I hate it here. I hate all of them. They're watching me all the time and I can't do anything or go anywhere. I want to come and stay with you,' she cried, blinking hard to release her tears.

'You can't Kelly, we haven't got room.'

'Please!' she begged. 'I can't bear it here anymore.' She got up and walked over to him, wrapping her arms around him and resting her head against his chest. He tentatively placed his hands on her shoulders and tried to read her face, to figure out what she was up to.

'We really don't have the room Kelly.'

Slowly she raised her head, her cheeks glistened from her tears and she dropped her voice to barely a whisper. 'If you won't have me, then maybe Uncle Joe will; I could get a flight to Spain, go see him.' She looked him straight in the eye. He stared back, his eyes narrowed, refusing to answer, instead deciding to wait and see what else she knew. 'Oh, but I can't can I? Because he's not in Spain. He's actually buried in our woods,' she whispered, raising an eyebrow and the corner of her mouth slid into a nefarious smile.

'I didn't kill him,' he snapped, pushing her away.

Her smile broadened.

'It was Liam. I had no idea that's what they had planned.'

'Whatever,' she replied offhandedly and walked over to her dressing table. Keeping her back to him she pulled a matching vest and knickers set out of a drawer and slid her dressing gown off, watching him in the mirror. He stared back at her with disbelief.

'Who does Jemima think it was?'

'If you know this much, you know she doesn't know. And it's going to stay that way Kelly,' he growled, watching her sliding her knickers slowly over her hips.

'Umm, well, this may be a very long stay with you then,' she replied.

'One week,' he snapped and saw her raise her eyebrows incredulously.

'Two weeks maximum,' he conceded. 'But you need to clear it with Sean.' He watched as she rolled the vest down over her body and flicked her hair back. The mention of Sean's name didn't seem to faze her and he felt disgruntled by his attempt to try and trump her by using their brother as a deterrent – sure that Sean would not entertain the idea — seeing that he had an enormous amount to say on what she did and with whom.

'That'll do for a start,' she mused, studying her reflection.

'No reruns of this morning. I'm not chasing your skinny arse all over London. If you come to stay, you behave yourself,' he said firmly.

Kelly looked back at him, her bright blue eyes burning into his. Then her lips broke into a half smile and she cocked her eyebrow at him.

'You're your father's daughter all right,' he snapped before leaving her room.

Brendan waited for Sean to be on his own before he went outside to see him about Kelly. As he approached, he saw the logo for the local gas works company on the side of the digger.

'On loan is it?' he asked.

'They don't use them at the weekends,' Sean laughed.

'It's going back on Monday then?'

'Yeah, first thing,' Sean replied with a wicked grin and, for a moment, when he looked at Brendan all his usual contempt was absent. Brendan smiled and Sean almost returned the gesture.

'That's why Dad was so keen to get it picked up then?' Brendan continued, encouraged by Sean's reaction.

'Yeah, we had to take all the back roads, case we got picked up. Took forever.'

'What will you do with it afterwards?'

'Probably scrap it.'

They both stood for a while staring at the stolen machine.

'How's Kelly?' Sean eventually enquired.

'Pissed off, you lot treat her like a kid, blah blah. She's come up with this idea of staying with me and Jem for a couple of weeks,' said Brendan, glancing sideways at Sean.

For a moment, Sean looked as though he was considering the request, then looked away from the digger to Brendan and non-committally raised his eyebrows. Brendan tried to decipher what this meant, keen to get Sean to agree.

'Well, she's eighteen now I guess, and she's certainly a grown woman.'

Sean smiled knowingly.

'Jesus Sean, what happened to our baby sister?' Brendan continued. Sean stared back at him coldly now. The usual tension between them had returned and a thunderous look rumbled behind his eyes.

'She grew up. You just weren't here to see it,' he replied gruffly, then walked into the house leaving Brendan feeling ambushed.

Despite their exchange, Sean agreed for Kelly to stay. When Brendan broke the news to Jemima, he had started by telling her they didn't need to come back to Lowlands for a couple of weekends. Her face lit up as she threw her arms around his neck. When she released her grasp, he casually dropped in the idea of Kelly staying with them.

'What?' she cried.

'It'll be fine.'

Jemima looked at him incredulously.

'She's cooped up here, with everyone breathing down her neck; maybe she needs to be treated like a grown up for a bit,' he justified.

Jemima sighed. 'I thought the idea was that we have some time together.'

'We can still go house hunting. We just carry on as normal, it's only for two weeks.' He sounded over-optimistic and, from the look on Jemima's face, he realised that this was going to be a harder sell than he'd realised. 'Jem, they asked me. What could I say? If you'd seen the guy we found her with and what she was doing, Jesus, it's frightening. If anything happens to her now, after they've asked me, I couldn't live with myself. She's my baby sister.'

Jemima nodded slowly. 'Okay,' she sighed. 'I always fancied the idea of a little sister,' she said smiling. Brendan smiled back, and turned away before raising his eyebrows, not sure whether Jemima would be feeling the same way at the end of the fortnight.

Within two days, Brendan and Kelly had had as many rows, one involving Kelly throwing her dinner at him, and one that resulted in him hurling her across the sofa.

'She a fucking slob,' growled Brendan, wiping spaghetti sauce off his face.

'We need to do something with her. She's bored, that's why she's acting out,' Jemima replied calmly.

'Is that what it's called?' he snapped back.

'Tomorrow evening there's an exhibition of an artist's work I'd like to go and see; it would be good if you brought her along. Change of scenery, experiences she won't get back in Ashdowne – isn't this what her visit was supposed to be about?'

'I don't know Jem,' he replied nervously.

'We can go grab a bite to eat afterwards; at least it gives some focus to her day.'

Reluctantly, Brendan found himself agreeing.

Jemima had gasped when they had swung into the viewing room and were faced by the large canvas of abstract shapes. They were now staring at the German artist's work, surrounded by hushed voices and shuffling feet. Jemima turned to them both, eagerly awaiting their reactions. Brendan smiled and raised his eyebrows; he was used to Jemima's passion for modern art. He personally didn't get it, though he wasn't prepared to let her know that – where Jemima saw struggle and anguish he saw pound signs. And, quickly checking the programme, he saw that this particular painting, made up of sludgy brown smudges, was worth seven hundred and fifty thousand of them.

'Impressive,' he announced, meaning the price tag, but letting Jemima think he was referring to the artist's work.

Pleased with his response Jemima turned to Kelly. 'So, what do you think?'

Staring at the painting, Kelly screwed up her small nose with concentration, narrowed her eyes and tilted her head to the side. She continued to chew noisily on her gum. Brendan and Jemima watched her closely, Jemima smiling with the anticipation of Kelly's critique and Brendan staring at her, nervously awaiting her response.

Finally, she flicked her long blonde hair back and raised her eyebrows before she turned to Jemima. 'I think it's bollocks,' she replied, her face holding a look of disdain. Jemima was gripped with shock.

Brendan slapped Kelly's arm. 'Don't be so fucking rude,' he hissed.

'Ouch. Don't fucking swear at me,' she snapped back, her voice loudly resonating around the room.

Jemima, aware of the disapproving glances from the other patrons, quickly interjected. 'Well, art is very subjective Kelly. If that's what you think, that's fine. How about we go and get a drink?' she said, leaving the room brusquely.

'What did you go and say that for?' Brendan said when Jemima was out of earshot. 'She's trying to be nice to you, show you different things and stuff,' he scolded, trying to keep his voice hushed.

'Brendan, look at it. It's shit. The artist – what's his name – hasn't even stayed in the lines.'

'He's a professional artist Kelly, he doesn't have to keep the paint in the lines. It's all part of his technique.'

'Ha, like you know anything about art,' Kelly replied, throwing her head back and rolling her eyes again.

Brendan looked back at the canvas. The blurred browns and greys made no sense to him. Jemima had used the word 'subversive' to describe his style and perhaps somewhere between Jemima's appraisal and Kelly's description lay the truth of the painting. He shook his head and sighed.

'Please can you just try to be nice?' he asked.

'I am. It's just that this is so boring. Anyway, I thought we were going for a drink?' she replied, heading off after Jemima.

Brendan and Jemima were emptying their dishwasher. Jemima could tell he was chewing something over; he looked perturbed and she hated it when he shut her out. She also hated how they couldn't discuss things freely while Kelly was staying with them. It felt as if they still had so much to talk about and sort out between them. Taking the opportunity of being alone while Kelly was showering, she spoke up. 'What's up?' she asked lightly.

He pushed the cutlery draw shut and sighed. 'I think we should give Gio's party a miss. Do something else with Kelly on her last weekend here.'

'What? But they're expecting us.'

'I don't want the hassle of taking her, she's too much to cope with – I'll be forever worrying what she is going to say or do. Anyhow, Gio has tons of parties. What does it matter if we miss this one?'

'It's his birthday – of course it matters if we miss this one,' Jemima snapped.

'Look, there will be more of us to keep an eye on her, which should make it easier for you – for both of us. We haven't seen Gio since our wedding day. Come on, if she gets too much then we can leave. Yes?' Jemima said more softly.

Brendan stared back at her, undecided.

'Perhaps, if we show her that we trust her, she will prove that she can be trustworthy,' continued Jemima. 'It's just a few hours at a party,' she finished, as Kelly entered the room.

'What party?' she enquired. Brendan shot Jemima a quick look and she forced a smile back at him before they both turned to Kelly feeling like they had just taken a step off a cliff.

Brendan stared at the mess that surrounded Kelly, who was sound asleep beneath the duvet on his sofa. Cups and plates lay scattered across the floor, along with dirty clothes and items of make-up that had fallen out of an overstuffed grubby cosmetics bag. Bending down to pick up the crockery, he gave her a sharp kick to wake her. The mound beneath the duvet groaned; by the time he'd got to the kitchen, her head had surfaced, with ruffled hair and red, eyes.

'What did you do that for?' she moaned groggily.

'It's nearly ten o'clock. You need to get up, I'm off to the gym soon.'

Kelly let out a long groan and pulled the duvet back over her head. Impatiently, Brendan walked over to her again, pulling the duvet off, and leaving her lying naked on the sofa. She glared up at him, pushing strands of hair out of her eyes, which shone bright blue against the dark rings of make-up smudged around them. He picked up her dressing gown, and the apartment's entry-system buzzed. He threw the dressing gown at her and walked over to the kitchen, picking up the intercom and pressing the buzzer roughly before he turned to face her.

'Get up, get showered and get dressed,' he barked, watching her pull on the dressing gown and tie it loosely at the waist. She yawned dramatically, ignoring Brendan's orders. Instead, she picked up the remote for the television and turned it on. As the screen burst into life, Brendan marched over and snatched it from her.

'Make yourself scarce,' he told her and she looked back at him, curiously. He stared at her, locked in yet another battle of wills. The knock on the apartment door broke their attention and, throwing the remote onto the sofa, Brendan went to answer it. Kelly slumped back down, pulling the duvet around her, grabbing the remote, and turning the television back on.

When James entered the apartment she glanced sideways at him and, as he came further into her view, she stayed determinedly fixed on the cartoon she had just turned on. James stopped his conversation when he saw Kelly and walked over, holding out his hand to her. 'You must be Kelly?' he asked, smiling full beam.

Slowly she slid her eyes from the television to his face, then slid them slowly down his body, raising her eyebrows as they explored him. When she met his eyes again, she saw his amusement. Coolly, she looked back to the television, sighed, and leaned her head to the side, away from him.

'I can't see, you're in my way,' she told him.

James shot Brendan a surprised look and was greeted with a deep frown and a shake of Brendan's head.

'Got any toast?' James asked. 'I'm starving; I didn't get any breakfast. Tanya had already left to go shopping with Jem by the time I got up,' James said, shaking off Kelly's rudeness. The question broke Brendan's scowl and he laughed as he set about making toast.

Keeping a discreet eye on her brother and his friend, Kelly leaned back on the sofa. 'I'll have some too,' she called out.

'Get your own when we've gone. You were getting dressed, remember?' Brendan snapped.

James looked over his shoulder to her, catching her eye. She shot him a quick smirk. When he looked back at Brendan he found him scowling again in her direction.

'Going well then?' he whispered.

Brendan shook his head. 'She goes home tomorrow. We just need to get through Gio's party tonight then she is out of my hands,' he replied, keeping his voice low and placing James's toast and a mug of tea in front of him.

James took a large mouthful of toast. 'Butter – God, Jem spoils you,' he sighed. 'Tanya has banned butter; she thinks I'm getting fat,' he laughed. 'I keep telling her it's contentment.'

Kelly, disgruntled with being on the outside of what was going on, casually sauntered over to them, picked up a slice of James's toast and took a large bite into it. Aware of her brother's glare, she leaned in closer to James and let her eyes drop down to his stomach. She then looked back up at him, placing the toast back on his plate and slowly licking her lips. James was fixated, watching the slow roll of her throat as she swallowed. Mesmerised, as her tongue glided over her oily lips, shiny and slick from the butter, he realised he had stopped breathing.

'You look all right to me,' she said, breaking into a lazy smile. Caught by the intense shine in her eyes and the soft fawn freckles that decorated her small nose, she rendered him speechless.

Brendan thumped his fist on the breakfast bar to get their attention.

'Get dressed,' he snarled at her.

She took her time to shift her gaze from James to her brother, before slinking away to the bedroom and pushing the door wide open. Once inside she undid her dressing gown and let it fall to the floor, aware that they were both still staring at her. She then looked over her shoulder at James, turning so he caught the outline of her breast, the inward curve of her stomach and her long, shapely legs, before rewarding him with an incorrigible smile and swinging the door shut.

James slowly turned back to Brendan, hoping to get his expression and breathing under control before he faced him.

'Don't even say it,' hissed Brendan.

James raised his eyebrows and hands in unison, and shook his head. 'Not even thinking it,' he replied.

CHAPTER 32

KELLY LOOKED AROUND the small, chic nightclub where Gio was holding his birthday party. It was quickly filling with guests and she marvelled at how beautiful everyone appeared. For the first time in her life she felt ordinary and she deduced that she was going to have to raise her game in order to get noticed.

Brendan reluctantly introduced her to his friends and their girlfriends, including the birthday boy, Gio. She had noticed how hard Gio had tried not to look her over, deliberately stifling his reaction, while his girlfriend Zoe had taken one sweeping look and immediately thrown her a warning look. Kelly was used to these looks from other women, and she treated Zoe's with her usual indifference.

As Brendan and his friends stood talking, Kelly noticed a tall man smiling in their direction. When he made his way over to them, her brother's friends playfully slapped him on the back and jibed him for being late. Kelly hung back, watching him closely, studying his good looks and charm as he effortlessly kissed the women around him on the cheeks, touching each of them gently at the base of their back. It was a small, intimate gesture that caused each of them to glow. Kelly craved that same touch, to feel him as close to her, and started to grow restless from his lack of attention.

After he'd kissed Jemima in greeting, his eyes flickered in Kelly's direction. He held them there a moment too long and Brendan, picking up on this, threw him a warning look, before reluctantly introducing him to Kelly by waving dismissively in her direction.

'Ah, your sister,' said Matt. 'Nice to meet you,' he added, raising his voice above the music.

Kelly swayed gently on her high heels, willing his eyes to roll over her; but they stubbornly refused. 'So, where's your girlfriend then?' she asked. His dark eyes glinted, her question amused him.

'I don't have one,' he replied.

'No one will put up with him,' interjected James, making light of what was going on between them. Kelly ignored James and, instead, raised her eyebrows and smiled, letting Matt know her full intentions.

Later on, Brendan caught up with Kelly, pulling her roughly into one of the black velvet booths. 'You're making a fool of yourself and you're wasting your time – my mates have been told to stay away from you,' he told her sternly.

Kelly's mouth hung open. She shot a look in Matt's direction, just catching a glimpse of his tall outline resting against the bar. 'Well you can just un-tell them then,' she hissed back. 'Or I might have to find myself telling Jemima some things,' she continued spitefully.

Even above the music, she heard him let out a low growl. She watched as his eyes twitched quickly, scanning her face, trying to determine how serious she was. He slowly let go of her arm and leaned in towards her. 'Go on then,' he said.

Looking about her for Jemima, she wore a smug smile, the same one she'd had on her face as she sat in the back of Brendan's car when they left Lowlands. She'd overheard Sean warning Brendan to make sure no one went near her; heard the threat that Sean would beat him if that happened. Brendan had sighed exasperatedly as he climbed into his car and then his eyes had met hers in the rear-view mirror. Both acknowledged the undercurrent, that Kelly had no intention of towing the line and, more significantly, no sense of loyalty to Brendan. She didn't care what happened to him, just so long as she got what she wanted.

He grabbed her arm, forcefully turning her attention back to him and stared hard at her. She could see his fear, and her smile grew. She was pleased at how she had so effectively squashed his short-lived victory. Shaking her arm free, she squeezed out of the other side of the booth and headed in Matt's direction.

Aware of someone close to him, Matt turned his head slowly and was greeted by Kelly's solicitous smile. He looked back at the barman and gestured for another shot of tequila.

'I'm trying to figure out the real reason why you haven't got a girlfriend, only, I reckon you'd be worth putting up with,' she told him.

Matt slid the shot of tequila over to her, smiled and shook his head. He could see Kelly had no plans to leave until she got an answer. 'I have a very demanding career,' he finally offered, turning to face her.

'What do you do?'

'If I told you I would have to kill you,' he joked back before downing his shot. His comment left her glowing with excitement; she had him fixed in her bright blue stare and he felt a rush rip through him.

'Sounds very 007,' she said, letting her head tip to the side. Her fringe fell across her eye, causing her to blink, and her long eyelashes peeled back to reveal the thoughts she was harbouring about him. Surreptitiously he looked her up and down. Her expression was making him nervous and Brendan's words rang through his head; a clear warning, leaving no room for interpretation or ambiguity – he wanted her left alone. He caught the barman's eye and ordered two more shots.

'Something like that,' he replied, shooting her a sideways smile, before downing his drink.

'You trained to kill then?' she fired back, downing her shot. He let out a small laugh and looked at her quizzically.

Their eyes locked and he felt his stomach muscles clench. He broke their stare, settling on the safer territory of his empty shot glass.

'Ah, it's all bullshit, I bet you're an accountant or something really boring like that,' she said, still smiling and swinging around so her back rested against the bar.

He laughed and stole another glance.

'I know you've been warned to stay away from me,' she said seriously and watched him sigh. 'Shame,' she whispered.

He nodded slowly. 'Yeah.'

Kelly rested her hand on his thigh. He stared at her hand as if it was scorching him. Finally, he took her hand and gently moved it away. 'Believe me, if things were different, then we wouldn't still be here,' he said.

She looked him up and down, deciding on her next move. Then, throwing him a coquettish smile, she turned and headed for the dance floor.

Brendan, James and Gio were staring down at the dancers from the mezzanine floor above. Kelly had worked her way to the centre of the dance floor and two men were moving in closer to her with every thump of bass. She swayed shamelessly in their direction, raising her arms high in the air and circling her hips. One of them came up behind her, pulling her tightly to him. She smiled invitingly at him over her shoulder before looking up at the balcony where she knew her brother would be watching.

'Who are they?' Brendan growled.

'Some business acquaintances of mine,' Gio replied, watching Brendan carefully.

Kelly continued to grind against the man and deliberately turned her attention to Jemima, staring at her, while Jemima, a few feet away from Brendan, was obliviously chatting away with Tanya and Zoe. After a few moments – long enough to let Brendan get the point – she looked at him, and grinned.

Matt wished he hadn't seen James try to catch his eye, or that he hadn't followed his signal. He rued spotting Kelly's long blonde hair splaying out around her as the man she was dancing with spun her around to face another man, who immediately grabbed her tightly. He hated how his stomach had curled with envy at the sight of this. He also wished he couldn't feel the pounding beat of the dance music nestling in his groin, or how that feeling intensified when he looked at her. Somehow, amid the music and surrounded by hot sweaty bodies, he had managed to placate the two men and manoeuvre her off the dance floor, although not before she had insisted he dance with her, pushing her body tightly against his and grinding against him, leaving his crotch aching and small beads of sweat prickling his temples. He held her hips firmly, pushing them away from him by a couple of inches; it was a couple of inches of distance that he desperately clung onto.

Away from the dancefloor he found himself at the back of the club with her and she was all wide smiles and bright eyes, the two soft mounds of her breasts quivering as she swayed provocatively in front of him.

'I didn't need rescuing,' she told him.

'Did you not see Brendan's face?' he asked, trying desperately to not to get drawn in by her.

'So?'

'You're lucky he hasn't kicked off. I've seen that look of his too often,' Matt replied.

'Was that who you were rescuing me from, my brother?'

Matt sighed. 'Do you take everything to the limit?'

'Pretty much,' she replied, folding her arms around his neck and turning him quickly so his back was against the wall, leaving him shocked at how skilfully she had manipulated him into this position. Kelly ran her lips lightly up his neck and along his jaw, watching him shut his eyes and swallow before he opened them again. Matt's resolve was slipping, he grabbed her arms and swung her around so her back hit the wall and leaned into her, pushing her arms down by her sides. His face was inches from hers, and she felt his warm breath on her lips when he spoke.

'I gave your brother my word.'

She smiled lasciviously. 'We could be gone and back before he's even missed us.'

He stared blankly at her.

She moved her face forward a fraction in an attempt to kiss him but he jolted his head backwards, continuing to stare hard into her face; their bodies were pushed hard against each other. She stared back, enjoying the power struggle.

'I don't want a quick one up against a wall somewhere,' he said fiercely.

'Then don't,' she replied coolly.

'Fuck it,' he growled.

Matt led Kelly out of the back of the club, flagged down a taxi and they headed for a hotel south of the river before he had time to change his mind. He ignored the scathing look he got from the hotel receptionist as they checked in but as he opened the door to their room, he felt guilty. Brendan would be furious with him, and rightly so – the least he could do was to let Brendan know she was okay he concluded. As Kelly looked around the room, trying to disguise her delight at what they were up to, he turned his phone on, ignoring the icon telling him he had several messages, and sent Brendan a blunt text. He would face him tomorrow; he would have something figured out by then he told himself.

When Brendan read the text, they were outside the nightclub, having given up searching for Matt and Kelly inside. He threw the phone against the wall and watched it smash to pieces. The others fell silent and looked at each other anxiously. Finally, Gio had offered to go and check Matt's apartment. They all knew the chances of Matt taking her back there were slim; they knew Matt was smart enough to stay out of reach.

Brendan and Jemima shared a cab with James and Tanya back to their apartment. None of them spoke during the journey. Once home, Brendan headed straight for the kitchen and poured himself a large vodka. Downing his drink, he sat rubbing his thumb over his bottom lip, lost in contemplation. The others looked on anxiously. Tentatively, James went over to him.

'Brendan, you've said as much yourself. Kelly is a real force to be reckoned with. Do you think Matt really stood a chance?'

'I couldn't have made it any clearer to him. He was told to leave her alone.'

'You asked him, Brendan, not told him. That is a whole different scenario,' added James, becoming irritated with Brendan's dogmatic reaction. It was hard for him – he felt his loyalty between his two friends was torn.

Brendan stood up suddenly and, standing close to James, his face hardening with anger said, 'He knew not to go near her, and he clearly doesn't respect me enough to do what I...asked.'

'She is your sister, he is your mate, and they are both adults. She could have gone off with anyone in that club. At least we know she's with Matt – she's safe, he'll treat her well, you know that,' James retorted sharply.

'I told him not to. So if you think that's okay, then it just proves I can't fucking trust any of you!' Brendan bellowed.

James dropped his head, hurt by Brendan's comment.

'Yeah, well, I remember your own brother begging you to stay away from his wife, but you didn't,' James replied and instantly the atmosphere in the room dropped a few degrees. Brendan instinctively glanced at Jemima, and saw her realise what James's comment meant.

'Sean and Tess,' she whispered. She looked directly at Brendan. He couldn't answer her, so he stormed over to the kitchen and grabbed the bottle of vodka, disappearing into the bedroom and slamming the door behind him.

Later, after James and Tanya had left, Jemima entered the bedroom, ignoring Brendan who was still drinking. He held his glass firmly in both hands and was staring out of the patio doors. She undressed, hung up her clothes, cleaned her face and brushed her teeth. She focused on the small details of her routine to help herself stay calm. Finally, she climbed into bed and turned her back on him. Hearing the clink of his glass on the bedside table, she felt the bed shift as he lay next to her.

'You've got no questions then?' he asked defensively.

'Why?' she replied, trying to keep her voice steady.

'Why what?'"

'Why did you do it? Isn't that what you want me to ask you?' she replied, flipping onto her back and pulling herself up. Brendan opened his mouth to reply, but Jemima quickly jumped in. 'I don't care why you did it. What I care about is you lying to me. You promised me there wasn't anything else – that you had told me everything. Everyone else knew, so what was your problem in telling me? Why do I have to find out all your sordid secrets from other people?' She stared at him fiercely, the skin on her throat marbling red with patches of anger. He stared back, stunned by her rage, not recognising this side to her.

Jemima shook her head and finally her tears she had fought to hold back started to flow. 'Have you any idea how humiliating it is to find these things out about you from other people? I am your wife Brendan. I should know everything about you, I don't care what it is; what I care about is you shutting me out. The deceit makes a mockery of our marriage,' she sobbed.

He grabbed her and, despite feeling her push against him, he pulled her closer, burying her head in his neck and forcefully holding it there. Finally, she gave up pushing against him and just let him cradle her; he could feel her tears hot against his chest, soaking through his shirt. 'I just don't know what to do to make this better, Jem.'

'Just tell me the truth, like you promised,' she whispered, pulling away.

He stared at her expectant face and realised how scared he was of losing her. She needed more, she needed to understand, and he was terrified of what telling the truth would mean for them. But at this juncture, he reckoned that she would be lost to him either by his confession or his silence. So, taking his time, he told her what had happened, starting with the beating he took from Liam, as that's where he felt things had really started to go wrong for him and Sean. His story ended with Sean punching him when he found Tess in London.

'I went back a few weeks after to apologise. Sean wouldn't have any of it and he wouldn't take her back; they were finished as far as he was concerned.'

'What about Tess?' enquired Jemima.

'Despite what she said, I don't think she actually wanted them to split up. She just wanted them to leave Lowlands, have a life of their own. She had plans before she got pregnant and Sean had made her promises to get her to marry him. Told her she could go to college; that they would find a way to make it work. After Georgie was born he changed his mind. That's Sean all over – everything has to be done his way. Jem, when I met her, she felt so trapped. I knew that feeling – that was how I felt around him.'

'So you slept with her because you felt sorry for her?'

'No, it just sort of happened,' he said bluntly. 'Perhaps I didn't stop it because I wanted to get back at him. It sounds odd but when Liam beat me I found myself on the outside of my family and as much as I don't like them – and, believe me, I despise them at times – it was much harder to bear than I could have imagined.'

Brendan paused, mulling over his words.

'I blamed Sean. I never thought he would ever choose them over me. It hurt, so my immediate reaction was to hurt him back.

It's funny, I always resented how he tried to prevent me from moving on and yet, when I went back that Christmas, he had clearly moved on... and I hated it. I hated the idea that he could do that without me.' Brendan sighed and rubbed his face. 'Jesus, I sound so fucked up.'

Jemima remained silent for a while, contemplating what he had told her.

'So this all comes back to you and Cassie then?' she said quietly. 'They would never have beaten you, if you and Cassie had never happened.'

He shut his eyes while he thought about her comment. He was exhausted and the thought of having to deal with Kelly again weighed heavily on his mind. He was also plagued by Sean's voice echoing in his head, reminding him of his threat: *Back in that yard for another beating.* Before the voice could grow in strength and remind him of Uncle Joe and everything else he was holding back from Jemima — and, more importantly, what he could lose — he pulled her to him. The smell of her made him want to weep; if he lost her, then he'd lost everything.

'I never thought of it that way,' he replied, wearily.

Matt's head hit the wall with a painful thud. The next thing he saw was the bright blue flash of Brendan's eyes before he heard the crack of cartilage and felt a searing pain. Then he felt the warm ooze of blood and realised his nose was probably broken.

'Brendan!' screamed Jemima.

Brendan leaned into Matt's face, his breathing jagged. 'I told you not to touch her,' he snarled before striking again. Matt fell to the right, got his footing and turned back on Brendan with a solid blow, knocking him backwards and splitting his lip open.

'Enough, Brendan,' he panted.

Running his tongue over his lip, Brendan could taste blood. He roughly wiped the back of his hand over his mouth and scowled at Matt, but didn't retaliate. Instead, he watched as Jemima handed Matt an ice pack. Matt held it to his nose, wincing and screwing his eyes up in pain. Sheepishly, Kelly went over to him and Matt wrapped his arm around her waist. Brendan watched the two of them carefully, surprised at how tender Kelly was towards his friend. Then he looked at Jemima's disappointed face, ran his hands through his hair and turned away from them all.

Jemima gestured to Kelly for them to leave Brendan and Matt to sort things out. Kelly looked nervously between them before reluctantly disappearing with Jemima into the bedroom. Matt walked slowly over to the couch and sat down, still nursing his nose, while Brendan purposefully ignored him and stared out of the window. Matt watched him for a while then, taking the ice away from his face, he decided to try and make peace.

'Do you remember that girl in Acapulco?'

Brendan turned towards him, his face still stony.

'We were so busy fighting over her that Gio went off with her in the end,' Matt laughed and saw Brendan's features soften. 'Sorry about your lip.'

Brendan touched it lightly and shrugged. 'Please tell me this was a one-off,' he said.

Matt looked guilty, and he knew it, and when he heard Brendan sigh he knew Brendan knew it too.

'If my brothers find out they will kill you. My father will enjoy watching and then they'll kill me. Believe me, they will really enjoy that,' Brendan said in a last ditch attempt to put Matt off, but Matt just remained silent.

'No disrespect,' Brendan continued 'but she made a massive play for James yesterday morning. She's not choosy. And she's revolting to live with.'

'I like her,' Matt responded defensively.

'I am telling you this as your mate, not as her brother. You really do not want to get mixed up with her and you certainly don't want my family breathing down your neck. I would never tell them, Matt, but I don't trust Kelly not to. She'd do it just to get a kick out of it.'

Matt frowned. Brendan could see he was wrestling with something.

'Are you saying that your family will try and stop her from seeing me?'

'Yeah. Although they won't be trying – they just won't allow it to happen.'

'So if she wants to see me, then she's going to need you as an alibi then?'

Brendan frowned.

'It's not in her interest to say anything to them is it, so she won't drop you in it.'

Brendan considered this and realised that as much as he disliked the idea of them being together, perhaps Matt had a point. Perhaps, without knowing it, Matt had helped Brendan realise that he held more power over Kelly than she realised.

Later on, when they delivered Kelly back to Lowlands, Sean had spotted Brendan's split lip. Jemima had turned away so as to not fall under Sean's interrogating stare as Brendan lied his way out of what had happened. On the drive home, they meandered through Ashdowne. Brendan was in no hurry to get back to London and face another drawn out discussion with Jemima about his past; all day she had maintained a frosty edge with him. So he took the long route back to the motorway and as they approached the common, he could see the caravans scattered haphazardly upon it. He slowed down, pulling the car into a lay-by. He studied the camp carefully, not sure what he was really looking for, but the familiarity of the trucks and washing billowing in the breeze told him the Gypsies were back.

CHAPTER 33

JEMIMA REFUSED TO spend the whole of the following weekend at Lowlands. Keen to encourage a thaw between them, Brendan agreed for her to travel down late Saturday afternoon, resigning himself to dealing with his family about it later.

When she pulled into Ashdowne station she called Brendan to come and collect her. At the time of the call he was hurling large chunks of concrete into a skip. His throat felt like sandpaper, dry from the dust and hot sun that had beaten down on him all day.

'I need to go and get Jemima,' he croaked at his father who was marking out lines on the land they had cleared.

'Liam can go get her,' his father said and all of them stopped what they were doing and waited for Brendan's response. His eyes had swung towards Liam in horror. Dropping his sledgehammer, Liam wiped his hands down the front of his jeans and smirked.

'No way,' Brendan retorted.

Sean was looking between them, as if observing a game of tennis. 'I'll get her. I have to collect Georgie soon anyhow,' he offered.

Lester huffed his approval and returned to his marking out. When Sean set off towards his truck, Brendan followed him. As Sean swung into his seat, Brendan grabbed his arm. 'She knows, about Tess,' he said, trying to hold his eye. Sean looked back at him blankly.

'So?'

'I thought you should know, in case she mentions it.'

'What do you want me to say?' Sean said curtly.

'The truth, that's all you can tell her isn't it?'

Sean continued to look at him while he pulled the truck door shut; then finally he raised his eyebrows, as if not entirely agreeing with Brendan's reasoning.

Jemima was surprised to see Sean. Hesitantly, she climbed up into the passenger seat of his truck, feeling awkward and not knowing what to say. When she grabbed her seat belt it jammed and the harder she tugged the harder it resisted. Finally, Sean leaned across her, grabbed it and yanked it free.

Bare-chested, his muscles rolled with the force of his pull and he was so close to her that she could smell the sweat and dust and sun which emanated from his tanned skin. He stared at her, his large, round blue eyes inches away from her face. She dropped her gaze and her eyes fell on the light blond stubble on his chin. They were then drawn to his mouth, his full lips, his pout – which always accompanied his disgruntled mood. She felt scrutinised, aware of every slight move she was making. She held her breath, tried to look away and, very slowly, he moved back to his own seat, started the truck and turned on the radio.

After a few minutes he grumbled something, startling her, uncertain as to what he had said. She stared at him, confused. He turned the radio down, knocking the dial roughly with his large thumb.

'I said I need to get Georgie.'

She smiled tightly, uncomfortable with the prospect of meeting Tess, and Sean slid her a sideways glance, noticing how uneasy she looked.

'He told you,' Sean stated gruffly.

'Not exactly. It came out accidentally, but Brendan has filled me in on his version of events,' she replied coldly, not wanting to discuss it further.

'His version of events, eh?' Sean replied sounding amused and she saw him smirk as he turned the radio back on.

The truck lunged up onto the pavement outside a neat modern terraced house. Sean lazily swung open his door as the front door of the house flew open and Georgie ran towards his father. Scooping him up, Sean spun him around; the late afternoon sunlight caught their faces, before Sean released him and gestured for him to join Jemima in the truck. As Georgie climbed in next to her, he gave her his usual broad grin and started babbling excitedly. Jemima found herself nodding and going along with what he was saying, while keeping an eye on the figure walking down the path towards Sean. Rich strawberry-blonde hair glowed in the sunlight, framing a pretty round face, and Jemima immediately saw Georgie in the young woman, who now stood having a heated discussion with Sean.

Tess turned to the truck and, seeing Jemima, whipped her head back to Sean and glowered at him. Undeterred, he observed her coldly before taking Georgie's bag and walking over to the truck. Tess followed him; she was angry with him for being nearly four hours late and she was tired of Sean's girlfriends thinking they could play mother to her son. She strode confidently behind Sean so she could get a better view of the slim-faced woman in the truck. Sean climbed in and lowered his window. Tess leaned in through it, reaching across Sean to touch Georgie's arm, telling him to be good. He beamed back at her and Jemima saw her bright jade eyes burn brightly with adoration. When she raised them to Jemima they hardened.

'I'm Tess, I'm Georgie's mum,' she announced.

Jemima felt off guard. 'Hi, I'm Jemima,' she offered, noticing Tess's full lips part with shock. 'Georgie has told me lots about you,' continued Jemima, trying to dislodge the awkwardness pushing between them.

'Yeah, Georgie's mentioned you too,' replied Tess, closing down the conversation before turning to Sean. She stared at him hard, her anger unyielding. 'You bastard,' she hissed before she turned and went back inside.

Back at Lowlands Sean strode into the kitchen and threw the bags onto the table. Jemima and Georgie followed obediently behind. When Jemima entered the room, Kaiser's tail thumped against the floor and he got up and sauntered over to her.

'That dog's soft on you,' Sean said.

Jemima let her hand run along the dog's back, her fingers splaying through his thick fur.

'Is that a problem?' she enquired, surprising herself by her sharp tone.

Sean frowned before shrugging, then threw open the fridge door, pulling out two cans of beer. Holding out a can towards her, he nodded sharply for her to take it. Jemima refused, and he eyed her carefully for a moment before putting her can back and pushing the fridge door shut with his foot.

Jemima continued to pet Kaiser, trying to ignore Sean; she felt unsettled by meeting Tess. It had left her agitated, particularly when she had noticed how much Sean was enjoying the scene he had obviously orchestrated between them. His smirk hadn't hidden his delight in making both women squirm. She had only been back in Lowlands for a matter of hours but already felt played; she always felt so under-prepared when she was here.

'I wouldn't get too attached. I'm not sure how much life is left in the old mutt,' Sean said, finishing his beer and stifling a belch. He waited for her reaction. Jemima continued to look down at Kaiser. Her head thumped with frustration at the things Sean was saying and, most significantly, with Brendan for not coming to collect her.

'I'm going to take him for a walk,' she announced firmly. Then she grabbed Kaiser's lead and marched purposefully out of the house.

The day's heat had pulled the resin through the trunks of the trees, turning it golden and syrupy. It leaked through cracks in the bark, oozing into small globules and releasing a heady veil of scent which cloaked Jemima and the dog. Crows perched high above them, tracking their movements with their shiny black eyes and twitching heads. Occasionally, one of the birds would throw out a mocking caw, which gradually petered away, letting the silence of the woods once again settle around them.

As Jemima walked further the trees became denser, the air started to cool and, after a short while, she stopped and let her head tilt backwards. Her face caught a stray ray of sunlight, which had managed to find its way through the labyrinth of boughs. It scanned her skin, dancing across her shoulders and down her bare arms, moving in time with the branches swaying in the slight breeze. Closing her eyes, she absorbed a peace she never believed she could find at Lowlands. She tuned into the quiet, the rustle of branches, the sound of Kaiser snuffling through the soft, pine-needled floor. Her earlier thoughts started to ease along with the tension she had felt in her neck and shoulders. *She could do this*, she thought, *she could be here and yet be removed from them all; she could make it through the weekend.*

Emerging from her thoughts, she realised Kaiser was nudging her; his head was tilted, his ears were pricked up and he stood rigid. The crows took flight, their black bodies skimming the sky like pieces of ragged cloth, their cries trailing behind them. Kaiser growled. Jemima reached for his collar to turn him around. With the crows gone, the woods were eerily quiet, and something wasn't right. She tugged at Kaiser, but the dog refused to move. He was determinedly standing his ground and suddenly let out a fierce bark. He barked again and this time she grabbed the scruff of his neck and yanked hard, but he still refused to move. Straining her eyes, she caught a quick glimpse of movement and heard the creak of wood followed by a brittle snapping sound.

She watched in horror as a man appeared to emerge from the bark of a large fir, uncurling, until he had almost blocked out what sun had managed to make it through the trees. His thick, dark beard ran into his long dark hair, making it hard to see his expression. Jemima quickly calculated that she had a short head start on him and she hoped it was a big enough to get her back to Lowlands. As she turned to run she realised that two other men had appeared behind her, blocking her way, and looking pleased with their find.

'You one of them O'Rourkes?' the large man asked and she swivelled round to face him again, not knowing how to respond, unsure whether being an O'Rourke would protect or incriminate her right now.

'You don't look like an O'Rourke. Are you the wife of one of 'em?' he continued, undeterred by her silence.

Jemima slowly nodded.

'Which one?'

'Brendan,' she replied, sure that this disclosure would seal her fate.

'He the one Cassie left us for?' the man asked, tilting his head back slightly so his thick dark hair fell away from his eyes. She could see his frown now, his dark eyes flickering brightly deep within their sockets.

'No,' she replied, a little too quickly.

The man stepped forward and Jemima was convinced he had seen through the lie. He looked at her distrustfully, opening his mouth and licking his bottom lip, dragging his tongue across his chapped skin. He towered above her and she watched his expression change, become firmer. He looked as if he was about to say something when a gunshot rang out. His head jerked upwards and his eyes swivelled around the woods before his face settled into a defiant scowl. Jemima followed his eye-line and saw Sean approaching with a shotgun held out in front of him and his dog marching by his side.

'You're on private property!' Sean bellowed, his voice as deep and as booming as the gunshot from moments earlier. Sean and the man eyed each other. Neither gave anything away, the shadows from the trees creating obscure shapes across their faces. Finally, putting his forefinger and thumb to his mouth, the man let out a piercing whistle and, with his shoulders hunched forwards, turned and headed away. The other two men followed compliantly and further away the ground shifted, boughs swayed, and more men emerged before falling in line and letting themselves be devoured by the darkness of the woods.

Jemima and Sean watched them leave. It wasn't until the last of the men had disappeared that Jemima became aware of the tremor starting to run through her, causing her teeth to chatter and her body to shudder.

'You okay?' Sean asked roughly and she looked down at the ground not knowing what she was most scared of – being in the woods with those strange men or him casually holding a gun. She tried to breathe deeply but ended up taking a large gulp of air which expelled itself as a muffled gasp. Sean pulled her to him. She felt his large hand cradle the back of her head and press it against his chest; his grip tightened as he folded his other arm around her shoulders. 'It's okay they've gone,' he whispered and she stopped resisting his pull and instead leaned against him. All his usual gruffness had disappeared. She seemed to have fallen through his impenetrable wall and found, on the other side, a warmth that, right now, she craved. He rubbed her shoulder lightly with his thumb and her trembling slowly calmed. When her breathing steadied, she realised that she had hold of him very tightly with both her arms wrapped around his waist.

'Sorry,' she mumbled, pulling away, unable to look up at him. He didn't reply, just picked up his gun and wrapped an arm around her, holding her firmly, and led her back towards Lowlands.

Brendan's jaw dropped when he saw Jemima and Sean emerge from the woods. Her face was ashen, Sean's arm was tight around her waist, and his gun was slung over his shoulder. Brendan ran towards them, instinctively grabbing Jemima, pulling her away from Sean.

'What happened?' Brendan asked.

'Pikeys. In our woods. They had her surrounded.'

Brendan clasped Jemima's head with his hands, tilting her face to look up at him. His eyes were frantically scanning her.

'What did they do Jem?' he asked, dreading the answer. Jemima stared back at him. 'Did they touch you?' he asked sternly, struggling to keep the panic from cutting though his words and Jemima managed a short shake of her head.

'Did you know they were in there?' Brendan snapped at Sean, whose face immediately hardened and his pout returned, letting Brendan know exactly how much the question angered him. Brendan leaned towards him. 'Did you let her go into those woods knowing they were in there, just like you let Liam find her and take her to the outbuilding?' he spat at him.

Sean indignantly raised his head. 'When I saw her head for the woods I went to fetch my gun and I followed her.'

'Because you knew they were in there!' Brendan retorted.

Sean looked sideways at Jemima and drew a deep breath before he spoke. 'I saw their trucks parked on the other side of the woods on our way back. I was suspicious.'

'And still you let her go in,' Brendan snarled.

'For fuck's sake, I went after her; I got her out of there,' Sean barked back.

'But you knew...'

'He was there, Brendan, you weren't!' Jemima suddenly screamed, pushing Brendan away.

'What?' he asked.

'You weren't there – he was, so just stop it,' she snapped, folding her arms tightly across her body. The full weight of her accusation hit him like a wrecking ball.

Lester watched the scene between the three of them and decided that something was going on that he needed to know about. As Lester approached, Brendan pulled Jemima close to him again. When Sean told Lester what had happened, Lester's eyes narrowed with contemplation. Finally, he bellowed across the yard for Liam and Cassie. As they emerged, Lester shouted for everyone to follow him into the house.

They were gathered around the kitchen table, all talking over one another, mild hysteria spreading with the speed of a virus. They had forced Jemima to repeat again and again exactly what had happened until Brendan had shouted at them to stop questioning her. Then their attention had turned to Cassie. Lyla was convinced Cassie knew what it was about and was refusing to tell them. Liam stood back and let Cassie take the full force of Lyla's interrogation. In the end, Riley suggested that he go and meet with them to find out what they wanted. Brendan stared at him with disbelief, before calling them to all hush.

'I'll go. Jemima said they asked if I was the one Cassie left them for. It could be me they're looking for, not her.'

'What will you do?' Lyla asked cautiously.

'Ask them what they want.'

'And if it is you?' she continued.

'Then, they'll have found me,' he replied flatly.

Lyla studied him before turning to Lester, who looked perturbed. Slowly he returned Lyla's look and nodded in agreement.

'Okay, but Sean goes with you,' Lyla instructed.

'We'll go in the morning, straight after I've dropped Georgie back,' Sean piped up. He looked at Brendan, his expression hollow, but his eyes held Brendan's for a moment, acknowledging the danger, before he turned and left the kitchen.

Chapter 34

Brendan lay awake, listening to the rhythmic call of a cuckoo in the nearby woods. He'd had a tense conversation with Jemima after he announced his plans to visit the Gypsies. Every reason he gave her for going she had skilfully batted back to him and, in the end, he had told her, emphatically, that he was going and ignoring her anguish as she conceded for the time being.

Now, as the night sky peeled back to reveal the silvery dawn light, he was wondering if her comments were, in fact, wise words; could he really trust Sean to cover his back? Jemima stirred; she was always cold in bed at Lowlands. She had a habit of nestling close to him to keep warm. It reminded him of how he and Sean used to sleep huddled together as children.

'Is that a cuckoo?' she asked sleepily.

'Yes.'

'Can't it go and steal a nest further away?' she groaned.

Brendan's attention wandered from his troubled thoughts about Sean and started to mull over how cuckoo's pushed eggs out of another bird's nest and plant one of their own inside it; the host bird then raising their chick. A picture in a book he'd once seen came to him, it was of a large, grotesque cuckoo chick, its underbelly lolling over the sides of the nest, while a much smaller bird was looking up at it, offering it a small worm that dangled from its beak. The cuckoo's mouth was open, demanding and greedy. The image reminded him of his father. The parallel struck him – how Lester had worked his way into Lowlands, taking over the family business after Jerry's death, pushing Joe out and taking over Lowlands until his grandmother and aunts had finally left. And now more recently, his father taking Joe's home and land, violently casting aside whatever stood in his way, just like the unhatched chicks of the host bird. Pushed out, just like he was after his affair with Cassie, until he had got married and brought Jemima to Lowlands.

'Please don't go,' she whispered after a couple of minutes.

He sighed loudly. 'Jem, we have gone over this a hundred times.'

'It should be Liam who goes – she's his girlfriend – or Riley.'

'How can Riley go? For God's sake Jem, think it through.'

Jemima was hurt by his harsh response and, pulling the covers tight around herself, turned her back on him.

'Jem, I have to do this. This is my chance to put an end to all that business with her. I can't carry it around with me any more – I feel swamped with it all. With everything.'

Jemima swivelled back around to face him; his change in tone had pricked her conscience. His face looked drawn.

'Does that include me?' she asked. A long pause followed her question. Brendan avoided looking at her while he figured out how to respond.

'I'm struggling to keep you safe,' he whispered.

'You make me sound like a burden.' Her voice wavered.

'I should never have brought you here,' he said softly.

'But then I would never have really got to know you,' she replied flatly.

He looked at her, stunned by her insinuation. 'I guess not,' he replied.

The following morning sitting in Sean's truck, Brendan tried pushing the bitter exchange with Jemima out of his mind. He was unaware that he was agitatedly tapping his foot until Sean pointed it out.

'You nervous?' asked Sean, staring at Brendan's jittering leg.

'A bit. You?' he enquired, shuffling his foot to still his leg.

Sean stayed silent for a while and looked across the road towards the camp. 'They're nothing I can't handle,' he said.

Brendan smiled to himself. 'I'm not nervous of them, Sean; I'm more concerned that I have you covering my back.'

Sean slid Brendan a look, slowly turning his head around to face him. 'You're still my brother,' Sean finally announced before throwing the truck door open and setting off in the direction of the camp.

It felt too still, too silent; the camp was absent of any signs of life. Brendan, however, could feel the Gypsies' presence, their invisible eyes staring at them behind the twitching curtains, and he could almost hear their whispers. He looked around at the empty deckchairs, the long lines of washing strung up, the rusting trucks and the carelessly discarded bicycles. Then he looked back at Sean, who was stood rigidly, his head held high. His eyes slowly scanned the camp for signs of trouble.

'What now?' Brendan asked.

'We wait,' replied Sean.

A small boy running across the camp caught their attention. A door to a trailer swung open then slammed shut, swallowing him up. The sound shook the crows from the trees, sending them flying, beating their wings hard against the air. Brendan watched them taking flight and a part of him wished he could follow. He flexed his fists and tried to gauge Sean's reaction. Instinctively, Sean looked at him, sensing Brendan needed the reassurance, before nodding over to where a large dark-haired man had filled the doorway of a caravan.

'You been looking for us?' asked Sean, watching the Gypsy deftly roll a cigarette with one hand while keeping a careful eye on them both.

'Have we?' the Gypsy finally replied.

'You were on our land yesterday, looking for the O'Rourkes,' Sean continued, seemingly undeterred by the Gypsy's aloofness.

The Gypsy lit his cigarette and drew deeply from it. 'You them?' he asked.

Sean and Brendan both looked around before answering, aware that they were now surrounded by several men, all of whom were watching them carefully, they both looked at each other before nodding their answer in unison.

'You still got Cassie staying with you?' he asked coldly.

'Who wants to know?' Sean asked.

'My missus, she's her sister. She's got a need to talk to her about something,' he replied and, turning his head towards the doorway of the caravan, he bellowed: 'Nora!'

Nora appeared at the side of the Gypsy; she had Cassie's long dark hair, and thin lips. She also had the same brooding look, but whereas Cassie's held traces of torment, Nora's was more menacing.

Walking insouciantly down the steps, she stopped in front of Brendan and Sean, pushing her hip out and folding her arms across her chest. She studied Sean first, who stared back incredulously. Unfazed by Sean, she turned her attention to Brendan, tipping her head back so the angle of her square jaw protruded defiantly towards him. He forced himself to hold his ground; he could sense Sean monitoring his response. She looked at him as if she had reached straight for his soul, grabbed it with both hands and violently shaken it. However, calm he was trying to appear she could see straight through him, see him struggling to win the battle this stare had become and he could feel Sean willing him not to concede. He drew a deep breath and locked his eyes back onto hers.

'You the one she left us for?' she asked.

'Yes,' he replied.

'But you're not with her now?'

'No, I'm not,'

'You got a message for her, we'll pass it on,' said Sean impatiently.

Nora eyed him coldly. 'There is something I need to tell her myself. I'm not trusting you two with it,' she replied curtly.

'We can bring her over to meet with you,' said Brendan and immediately felt both Sean and Nora turn their attention to him. Sean looked aghast while Nora looked anxious.

'No, she can't come here. She's not welcome, not after what she did. I'll come to you,' Nora told them. 'You still have that place in the woods where she used to meet you?'

Brendan nodded, surprised by what Nora knew.

'Tomorrow morning, first thing,' she continued.

'You come alone. Don't bring this lot with you,' Sean added, gesturing with a nod to the other Gypsies. Nora looked him slowly up and down and let a smile spread across her lips. It was goading and cocky, Sean's top lip curl into a snarl.

'You telling me I've got nothing to fear?' she said.

Before Sean could answer, Brendan jumped in. 'You're Cassie's sister, you're welcome to come and visit her.'

'Tomorrow, first thing then,' she said and slowly walked back to her trailer.

Brendan had heard Sean release a deep growl as he stormed back to his truck. When Brendan climbed in Sean turned on him. 'She's welcome? Have you any idea how mental the old man is going to be? They don't come on our land. They drop off at the breaker's yard, but they never come to Lowlands.'

'Sean, they are Cassie's family. Her sister needs to tell her something important. They haven't contacted her in all this time. Come on, if this was Anne-Marie or Kelly, you would've just stormed in all guns blazing.'

'Yeah well we're different from them.'

'Yeah, they are a lot more fucking civilised than our family.'

Sean's face twisted in shock but Brendan looked straight ahead, letting him know the matter was no longer up for discussion.

'No fucking way, she's not meeting her!' shouted Liam.

'It's not your call, Liam,' barked Brendan. He had anticipated Liam's resistance. He'd considered how to handle this on the way back and now, in the kitchen with the others, Liam was playing out true to form.

'Yeah, well it ain't yours either,' Liam barked back.

'You're right, it's actually Cassie's,' stated Brendan, as Cassie appeared in the doorway. He looked awkwardly at her. 'Your sister, Nora, said she's got something she needs to talk to you about. It's up to you whether you want to meet her or not.' He watched her look towards Liam then to Lyla then back to him.

'What if they try to take her!' Liam bellowed.

'They don't want her. They told us that she's not welcome back,' Sean butted in.

Brendan saw Cassie flinch at Sean's comment. He shot a stern glance back at him, but Sean just responded with a shrug.

'You want to meet her?' Brendan asked Cassie. Her eyes swept up to meet his and she gave a slight nod. 'Good, though I think it would be a good idea to take someone with you,' he added. 'Who would you like that to be?' He watched as her eyes flickered back and forth, while she grabbed the edges of her cardigan, pulling it tightly around herself. It was agonising watching her make the decision.

'I should be the one who goes,' Liam protested

'If you go, you'll cause a fight and it's not about you, it's about her,' said Brendan firmly.

'Who the fucking hell do you think you are?' Liam shouted.

'Whatever her sister has to tell her it's unlikely to be good news, so just for once can you cut her some slack,' Brendan told him.

Catching Liam's murderous look Lyla said, 'Brendan's right, they wouldn't have gone to all this trouble if it was good news. Brendan, you take her; they've met you, they seem okay with you. And take Riley with you too – just in case.' Then she added firmly, 'Liam you'll stay here, leave her alone you hear me? Sean, you make sure he does.'

Predictably, Liam stormed out of the kitchen. Sean raised his eyebrows, sighed and followed him, with Riley falling in line. Cassie, as usual, quietly disappeared, leaving Brendan and Lyla alone in the kitchen.

'You certainly sorted that out very efficiently. Powerful emotion guilt, eh?' she commented while lighting a cigarette and waiting for his reaction.

'I guess so,' he replied casually, deliberately avoiding any further discussion.

'Oh, by the way, Jemima has gone back to London. Riley dropped her at the station while you were out. Everything okay?' she asked.

'Yeah fine. She's got a lot of work on,' he replied coolly. He watched his mother nod and acknowledge the lie.

Jemima saw his name flash on her mobile phone screen. 'Hi,' she answered softly.

'You okay?' he asked.

'Kind of. You?'

'Kind of.'

'You in one piece?'

'Yeah, I'm in one piece,' he laughed gently, relieved she no longer appeared annoyed with him.

'What time will you be home?' she asked.

'I'm coming home tomorrow,' he said and waited anxiously for her response.

'Why?' Her voice was clipped.

'I met Cassie's sister today. She wants to meet with her, and I offered to be with her when she does.' A long silence followed which Brendan anxiously let run its course.

'Why?' Jemima finally asked.

'Because I am not entirely sure she will be that safe meeting her on her own and I can't trust the others not to turn it into some fight.'

'You're not struggling to keep her safe then?'

Brendan pushed the palm of his hand up his forehead, frustrated that she had turned his own words back on him. 'Please. Jemima. Stop it.'

'You're my husband Brendan, not hers.'

'Jesus, Jemima, listen to yourself. I have to do this; I have to be the one that goes with her – that's final. I'll see you when I get home tomorrow.' He ended the call and threw the phone onto his bed.

Brendan, Riley and Seth, Nora's husband, looked on at the two sisters hugging tightly. Brendan watched as Cassie and Nora chatted quickly. Their conversation was punctuated with unfamiliar words; Romany dialect he presumed. There was a part of the conversation which seemed to change direction. Nora's voice dropped low. She spoke softly and kept wiping the hair from her sister's face. When she finished, Cassie stared at the ground before she let out a high, hollow scream, and sank to her knees with her mouth wide open and her head tipped backwards. Nora slid down to the ground with her, trying to cradle her, rocking her awkwardly. Eventually, Riley gently pulled Cassie from her sister, folding himself around her until she had almost disappeared, and the noise finally dispersed.

Nora wiped tears from her own eyes and shook her head before standing up to face Brendan. 'Our brother Jamie, he's dead. Died a couple of months ago, in a fight,' she said.

'I'm sorry,' replied Brendan, recalling the dark-haired man he had faced in the pub garden years ago – his tight muscular frame and sharp tongue, goading the fight that Brendan and his brothers had started to rise for, until Lester had stormed in and broken things up.

'That was the only fight he ever lost,' said Seth, proudly. 'Bare knuckle fighter he were. Romany King, just like their father and grandfathers. We was real proud of him. He's a legend – was then and always will be.' His eyes were wet with tears that refused to fall.

'What happened?' Brendan asked.

'He was set up. Four of them set on him, our own as well. Turned on him like fucking dogs. No scruples and them's what gets us a bad name,' Seth said viciously.

Brendan's gaze wandered to Cassie who was still enveloped in Riley's arms, his cheek resting on her head. He was struck by this legend they described, the same undefeated legend that had supposedly beaten Cassie and abandoned her for getting involved with him – yet she was devastated by this news. He was contemplating this when Nora spoke.

'Is that who she's with now?' she asked, following the direction of his gaze towards Riley, and he wondered how he was going to explain the situation.

'It is who she would like to be with,' he replied.

Nora nodded, seemingly unsurprised. She found Cassie's hand and gently took her from Riley. 'Cass, Seth and I have talked about this. He has family on a camp up north. We can go there, break away. You can come too,' she told her gently, but Cassie stayed silent. 'Cass, we can be together, all of us,' Nora continued.

Cassie looked back towards Riley, who was trying not to intervene. She smiled warmly at him and he managed a small but concerned smile in response. She looked back at Nora who glanced quickly at Seth and, seeing the look of resolution on his face, she looked regretfully back at Cassie.

'We can't take a Gorja. They won't have us if we do and they'll tell straight away from the look of him that he ain't one of us.'

'I'm staying then,' Cassie replied firmly.

'Oh Cass, you can't stay,' Nora pleaded.

'Why?' asked Cassie.

Nora looked away awkwardly.

'What you seen?' Cassie continued. 'Tell me Nora.'

Nora deliberately composed herself before she spoke. 'I seen you three and another woman, thin, real delicate looking.' Brendan's head shot up. It had to be Jemima she was talking about.

'And blood Cass, lots of it, all over your hands.'

'Whose blood?' asked Cassie.

'I don't know. I don't see that part, but you think you'll never wash it off, that it will stain you for the rest of your life.'

Brendan and Riley glanced at one another, then Brendan shook his head, dismissing Nora's words as nonsense. Catching the gesture Nora continued.

'I seen it Cass, like I saw your baby grow inside you then stop. His little heart was weak. I saw it fluttering like a butterfly, it was never going to be strong enough for him to make it into this world.'

Cassie's hands reached for her stomach. 'You saw him, you saw Storm?' she asked, her eyes wide with wonder.

'Come with us Cass, that way you can be safe. You can come home,' implored Nora.

'I told you they would try to take her!' Liam's voice boomed as he waded over to Cassie and snatched her from Nora's grasp.

'She ain't going nowhere, so you two piss off!' he shouted.

'Liam, let her go, it's her choice to make!' Brendan shouted at him, walking over and trying to remove Liam's grip. Cassie was bent awkwardly, trying to pull away from him. 'You were told to stay away,' Brendan growled at him, finally breaking Liam's grasp and protectively pushing Cassie behind him. 'And you were supposed to be keeping him an eye on him!' Brendan shouted as Sean appeared, panting and resting his hands on his knees trying to catch his breath.

'He told me he needed to take a crap. I'm not following him everywhere!' Sean shouted back.

Brendan glanced back apologetically at Cassie and her family, to find them staring strangely at Liam. Nora's eyes had hardened; the hostility that Sean and Brendan had encountered the day before had returned.

'Get him out of here!' shouted Brendan to Sean.

'No,' said Nora, firmly striding over to Liam and slapping him hard across his cheek, leaving a red mark, before spitting hard into his face. His forearm swung up to his face, wiping it roughly and revealing the disgust he held for the Gypsies. Behind him Lester emerged, he'd been using the trees for cover.

Just inches from Liam's face, Nora started to chant. It tripped off her tongue rhythmically, piercing his face like needles, his eyes flicking shut with the delivery of each syllable.

'What did she say?!' Liam shrieked at Cassie. Cassie looked away, preferring to stare at the ground. 'What fucking curse has she put on me?!' he screamed at her again, but she just looked up at him blankly. 'Tell me!' he bellowed, starting to make his way towards her.

'She says you will rot alone for your evilness,' Cassie answered.

But Liam looked panicked; Cassie's translation seemed short in comparison to the length of the curse her sister had just delivered and he didn't have enough courage to test her for more detail, so he simply stared with his mouth gaping open.

'Ah for fuck's sake, it's just pikey mumbo jumbo,' chastised Lester, stepping from the trees and punching Liam on the shoulder, shaking him from his stupor.

Nora raised her head defiantly. 'He killed our brother, had him set upon because Jamie wouldn't fall. Our brother's reputation couldn't be bought,' she said proudly.

Lester stopped in his tracks; he stood almost motionless, with just his little finger gently tapping a piece of iron piping he held firmly in his hand, and looked contemplatively between Liam and Nora. 'Get lost! You've had enough time on my land, don't outstay your welcome,' he finally responded. But Nora wasn't letting this old Gorja tell her what to do or keep her from spilling out what had happened all those years ago to seal her sister's fate. So she took a deep breath and opened her mouth and set the truth free.

'He told on you.' She said, looking at Brendan. 'He told Jamie about you and Cassie, that you was meeting in secret. He'd been watching you both and told him everything in great detail – enjoyed it he did,' she said.

'She's lying!' cried Liam.

'I used to see him come over to our camp late at night, then I would hear them both – I'd hear him plotting against you. Winding Jamie up, saying terrible things about what you two was doing together.'

Brendan's jaw was pulled so tight his teeth grated. He looked away from Nora, letting his eyes find Liam and bore deeply into him. His fists were clenched and his vision narrowed; he wasn't aware of anything other than Liam and Nora's words.

Lester moved between them. Without acknowledging either son he dropped the metal pipe. It landed within equal distance between the two brothers, hitting the forest floor with a dull thud, then he walked away leaving them both to sort it out.

CHAPTER 35

BRENDAN WAS SAT on the sofa working, his laptop open on the coffee table in front of him. He was leaning forward and concentrating hard at the screen, when Jemima entered their apartment. He didn't acknowledge her. She noticed that next to the laptop was a half-drunk bottle of brandy and her heart sank. She walked over to him, watching for a moment as he tapped his keyboard, keeping his head low so she could only see the top of his head.

'Brendan, can we talk?' she ventured and was greeted with silence. 'This is ridiculous. We are never going to get anything sorted if we don't talk,' she continued, starting to feel the endless supply of tears well up inside her again. Slowly, he raised his head to face her and she gasped; her hands clasped her mouth. His right eye was swollen shut and ringed with red and purple bruising which ran down the side of his cheek and ended at his jaw. His lip was split with a deep cut. She saw that his right hand was swollen, his knuckles almost raw.

'What happened?' she cried.

'I got into a fight with a metal pipe,' he replied and tried to laugh, but all that came out of his mouth was a low rasp of air.

'Don't joke,' said Jemima, pushing the laptop out of the way and sitting down on the table to face him. 'Who did this to you?' she asked, softly touching his face with her fingertips.

'Liam,' he replied bitterly.

'Why, what happened?'

'When I met Cassie's sister I found out he'd grassed me up to Cassie's brother, about us seeing each other.' He sighed. 'I lost it with him, we ended up in a fight about it.'

'Why would he tell on you?'

He looked back at her incredulously; he marvelled at her naivety sometimes. 'Because he hates me, because he loves to cause trouble, because he's always wanted what was mine? Who knows? He's fucked up, and I don't really care why he did it. I care more about what happened because he did it,' he finished. Jemima remained quiet, looking perplexed.

'All these years I've felt guilty because of what happened and it was all his fault. Cassie's family need never have known.'

'She was pregnant Brendan.'

'She could have passed it off as one of theirs. Her family would never have thrown her out if it was one of theirs. Then she would never have ended up with Liam – her life would have been so different. That baby might have lived, Jem.'

'You don't know any of this for certain,' she replied, trying to console him, but he shook his head.

'She'd have had a better life. She'd be with her family, where she belongs.'

'She has Riley.'

'She has nothing with Riley. They can't even be together because of Liam; he has screwed her on every level.'

Jemima realised there was nothing she could say that Brendan would hear. Instead, she stayed quiet and reached out for his hands.

'D'you know what really pisses me off?'

Jemima shook her head.

'Not only does Liam grass me up and sell me out, he also beats me for it, and my family let him. Nothing I've ever done was bad enough to deserve that.' His head fell forward and Jemima gently stroked the back of it. Eventually he looked up at her. 'I don't want you anywhere near Lowlands. I mean it. I don't want you near Liam, or any of them.'

She nodded. 'Is that what you meant by trying to keep me safe?'

He nodded slowly, realising he was getting into dangerous territory again, that Uncle Joe's murder was close to resurfacing. 'I could do with a bath,' he said, changing the subject and trying to stand but his muscles had seized, as if they had rusted.

Leaning against Jemima they made it into the bedroom. She ran him a bath and helped him undress, gently pulling off his clothes to reveal more whorls of marbled bruising down his back and thighs. 'Do you need to go to the hospital?' she asked, horrified at what she was seeing.

'I know what's broken and what's bruised, there's nothing they're going to be able to do, Jem.'

'But your eye, it's worse than mine was.'

'I've been telling myself it's not,' he said trying another laugh and wincing.

'I'll get you some steak,' she replied, smiling up at him. He smiled back, resting his forehead on hers.

'I don't deserve you,' he told her and watched her shake her head, dismissing his words too easily.

After the fight, Liam limped home and laid low for the rest of the day. Sean had eventually broken it up, but only after Brendan had managed to get the pipe off Liam and start beating him with it, repeatedly pounding him, his hate and vengeance travelling the length of his arm with each blow. Lying on his bed, Liam mulled over the fight for the rest of the day. He concluded that the trouble with Brendan was he always expected a clean fight, which he was never going to get from Liam – no one would. He ruminated over Riley's involvement. When Brendan had managed to dislodge the pipe from his grasp, it had fallen and rolled away; he was sure Riley had kicked it towards Brendan. If so, Riley was going to get what he deserved and his thoughts turned to revenge until he felt hollow with hunger. He checked his watch, nearly six o'clock – dinner time at Lowlands – so he painfully made his way over to the house.

They all continued as normal, ignoring Liam's bruised face and his limping gait. He sat down heavily in his place and, after a fashion, managed to get all he wanted on his plate by shifting slowly and accommodating all his aches and pains. He had his first forkful raised just before his open mouth when his mother slapped a dog bowl down on the table in front of him. Grabbing his plate, she scraped the contents into the bowl. Everyone fell silent; they were all watching Lyla and her stormy face.

'You eat out there with the rest of the dogs. Grassing your own brother up, how fucking low could you get,' she hissed.

Beneath Liam's bruising his skin burnt with humiliation. He thought she couldn't be serious, but one quick glance at her expression told him how serious she was. He looked at his father who stared back unemotionally before nodding his head at him to leave. Slowly Liam rose; when he was steady on his feet he picked up the bowl and, trying to avoid their stares, left the kitchen, dragging his wounded leg and pride heavily behind him.

Once he was back in his own home, he scraped the contents of the bowl onto a clean plate and raked through it with a fork to discard the dog hairs and dried bits of biscuit from the dogs' dinners before he started to eat. With each mouthful he felt more isolated and he hated it. *After all he had done for them*, he festered, *how could they treat him like this?* He had to find a way to win them around, to get them back on side – for them to see that Brendan was the bad one.

CHAPTER 36

TEN DAYS LATER, Liam sat between his parents, waiting eagerly for their reaction. He watched his father lean back in the old armchair, narrow his eyes and hold Liam in contemplation, while his mother's stare never wavered from Lester. After the fight with Brendan, Liam had disappeared, staying only loosely in touch with his twin sister, Anne-Marie. Camping out in the back of the transit van and living off fast food and cans of cheap warm beer, he returned to Lowlands brimming with ideas of how to win his parents back around.

The large Edwardian house had been easy to break into, almost too easy. It had made him stop and contemplate that perhaps the two old ladies actually had a more sophisticated alarm system that would be triggered once he had stepped into their house. But with both feet placed sturdily over the back doorstep, he realised that this was an area where the residents just didn't anticipate this sort of bad luck. He crept around the house, knowing that he had twenty minutes before the old lady who arrived with the shopping bags would be here.

He had kept the house under close surveillance, turning the piece of paper with their address on it over and over in his hands, trying to fathom out his plan. He was familiar with the goings-on of the old women. He had concluded that, like most old people, they needed their routine, and this made his task a lot easier. As he had swept through the upper part of the house he had found some nice jewellery but he had determinedly put it back – this wasn't what he was there for. He needed to stay focused. It was on the first floor that he found a study and, on inspection of the desk and filing cabinet, he decided that this was the most likely room to hold what he was looking for.

He carefully moved papers around and quietly shut the filing cabinet, trying hard to contain his frustration at not quickly finding what he was seeking. Then the painting caught his eye – a large oil canvas, of an old man dressed in an old-fashioned safari suit, holding up a tiger skin, with what looked like the Taj Mahal in the background. Perhaps it was the fact that the portrait sat too far out from the wall – Liam wasn't sure what gave it away – but as he swung it gently to the side he found the safe nestled behind it. He tried the dial, just in case it should open as easily as the back door, but it didn't give, and he decided that given the absence of security everywhere else in the house, whatever was in this safe must really be worth protecting. He used his phone to take pictures of it, before placing the picture back and quickly leaving Martha and Bridget's home.

'What do you reckon is in the safe then?' Lester asked, careful to hide his enthusiasm.

'A copy of their will,' Liam replied, trying to hide his.

'How did you find Jemima's aunts?' Lyla enquired.

'Kelly got me their address when she was staying with Brendan.'

'Did she know why you wanted it?'

'Nah, she never asked. I made out I had gone up to check on her, when I went up there to drop the hammer off.'

'Yeah,' Lester cut across him, keen to save the gorier details of Joe's murder from Lyla.

'You've planted the murder weapon on Brendan?' Lyla asked, turning quickly on Liam.

'It's for our protection Lyla. If he talks, he will be the one that will come off badly because of it,' Lester informed her dogmatically. She pursed her lips and looked away, finding herself again torn between her second eldest son and her husband.

Liam struggled to contain his eagerness as he watched his father study pictures of the safe. 'It has to be in there and, if not, then we just take what is. The house is loaded with antiques and stuff – we can just help ourselves. It's like an Aladdin's cave,' he continued, fidgeting excitedly.

'How much would you say the whole place is worth?' Lester asked, his appetite whetted and his eye, as usual, on the bigger prize.

'Well over a million, it's huge. The back garden is about half an acre. It's prime location, right on the cliff tops, overlooking the sea. And that's just the property – the two aunts are proper minted, I saw their bank statements,' Liam replied, his eyes searching Lester's face, desperate to find signs of approval that he had done well.

'Are you sure Jemima will inherit all of this?' Lester enquired.

'Going on what she's said, her aunts only have her, so it don't look like there is anyone else to leave it to,' Lyla contributed.

'We need to find that will,' Lester mused, looking back at the picture of the safe again. Lyla knew what was coming next and could feel the dread building in her.

'I need to call Terry,' he said, raising his head defiantly and ignoring Lyla who had closed her eyes in response. 'He'll be able to get into it. Liam, go and fetch Sean. We need to work out how we're going to do this,' he finished.

CHAPTER 37

UNCLE TERRY HAD lived with the O'Rourkes shortly after Lyla had given birth to Riley. He had just served nine years in prison. He was Lester's younger brother and bore a strong family resemblance; the same curved nose, strong jaw line, dusty blond hair and, of course, the same bright blue eyes.

Terry had gone to prison aged nineteen, spent his time wisely, and convinced the prison officials of an early parole by appearing to take the group therapy sessions seriously and getting some qualifications. In short, Terry was bright enough to play the game, managing the precarious balance of impressing the authorities while pacifying the powers that really ran the prison.

⊷⊶

Lyla had suffered Terry in silence for a couple of weeks before complaining to Lester. Terry always seemed to be hanging around with no purpose, and as much as her kids loved his playfulness, he wound them up at the wrong times, resulting in missed meals and chaotic bed times. Huffing loudly, Lyla would try to settle the screams and shrieks that came from her children as they tore around the house, while Terry would spring from behind sofas, grabbing them roughly, and tickle them so hard their voices caught in their throats and, with their heads thrown back in exhilaration, high-pitched laughter ripped through Lowlands, rattling the glass in the window frames.

'He eats like a horse and pays nothing towards his keep,' Lyla moaned.

'If he goes back to London he'll be straight back inside; his only chance is to hang out here for a while,' Lester told her firmly and Lyla, regrettably, knew it was true.

The trouble was Terry didn't actually know how to live an honest life. Being born an O'Rourke, he didn't have access to much guidance to help him live one. Lyla knew little of Lester's family, having met his mother, Rose, only a handful of times. She was a large woman who complained bitterly about anything and everyone. There was little love lost between her and Lester and even less between her and Lyla. Lyla was aware of a collection of brothers and sisters, and some half relations, but the connections weren't clear. To confuse the mix further, from time to time cousins of Lester's got in touch and stayed for a month or two until it was safe for them to return home. Lyla had stopped asking Lester the details and accepted that any relation of his would eventually go home; however, Terry's departure didn't seem imminent and his habit of being under her feet was also getting under her skin.

As Lester's full-blooded brother, he had looked out for Terry in the absence of their father. Terry was a natural boxer and Lester had nurtured this talent, taking great pride in touring around the

London clubs with him. When Terry got sent down, Lester made sure that the right people on the inside were well compensated; some of this was financed through the breaker's yard and some of it on goodwill – with Lester's own contacts and reputation making up the balance. As a result, dirty money found its way to the O'Rourke breaker's yard and clean money made its way out. The open space at Lowlands was also a useful place to cool off, whether that was in the form of human cargo or guns. The breaker's yard was an easy way of disposing of vehicles too hot to sell on or to leave abandoned in a country lane, risking exposure of any damning evidence. In short, Lester was resourceful with how he used his gains since coming to Ashdowne, and this was not lost on Terry.

'Do you know what you miss most inside Les?' Terry had asked him over a pint in the Queen's Arms.

Lester had looked at him seriously.

'It's not the freedom, which is ironic. It's the sex. Nothing feels like a woman, you know? There is only so much you can do to relieve yourself, but nothing is like the real thing.'

Taking the hint, Lester lined Terry up with several women he knew; he also bought Terry new clothes and got him a truck to run around in. Terry tried to repay him by helping out in the yard, but he was easily distracted and lazy. In a desperate, last-ditch attempt to help keep Terry out of trouble, Lester got him involved with the local boxing club. It was, from the outside, a fairly run-down place and a far cry from the gyms Terry was used to, but the gym had snapped up Lester's offer and, once Terry got over being involved in such a backwater set up, he became a great asset to the club.

So, with some proper focus and a bit of money in his pocket, Terry started to look around for a girlfriend. Lester had warned him off Lyla's sisters but that only made them more appealing, though he found her older sister Bernie temperamental. He liked her younger sister Kate better; she had inherited her mother's co-louring, her dark curls and dark blue eyes as well as her instinct to nurture. Kate saw Terry as a lost cause, waiting to be rescued, and he did nothing to discourage this.

However, in secret, it was Lyla that Terry wanted, with her sparky temper, head-turning looks and neat curves. Despite Lester's generosity, he envied him – his marriage, his attractive wife and good-looking kids. He also envied his good fortune in inheriting the breaker's yard – a steady income and being his own boss. He wanted what Lester had, but the only means he knew of getting it were below the tide line and he knew Lester would outsmart any scheme he may have of taking it from him. So he settled on Kate as the next best thing, played with Lester's kids, put in a few hours at the gym and yard and tried to settle for ad-miring Lyla from afar.

It was a sunny morning when Terry woke and decided he needed to move on. The trouble with being settled, he mused, was its predictability. He ran his finger down Kate's bare back and watched as she stirred in the bed next to him. She raised her head slowly; her eyes were still heavy from sleep and her dark curls fell across her face.

'What time is it?' she groaned softly.

'Time to go,' he said, smacking her bottom and jumping out of bed. He dressed quickly and looked back at her before shoving a cigarette in his mouth. She turned onto her back, wiping the hair from her face. He smiled at her fondly. He liked her – he could even grow to like her a whole lot more – but as he had lain there that morning, he felt his legs jitter restlessly. He needed new challenges; life here was too soft for him. He threw her a wink before he turned to leave and saw how her smile broadened in response to it. She hung off his every action and that disturbed him. He knew she was too good for him and he hoped she would work that out once he was long gone from Ashdowne.

Lyla was making breakfast when he bounced into the kitchen. He leaned over her shoulder, too close as usual, to see what was sizzling in the frying pan. He felt her body tense, but instead of taking the cue like he usually did to move away, he stayed put, deliberately leaning in closer. 'Got any eggs to go with that?' he asked,

'It's not for you,' she snapped, keeping her back to him.

'Go on... let me have it, he won't notice,' he replied, taking hold of her hips with his large hands and burying his head into her neck. He felt her shoulders curl away from him.

'He'll be here any minute for his breakfast. What d'you think he'll do when he sees you?' she asked, keeping her eyes on the spitting pan.

Eventually he released her and stepped backwards. She turned to face him with a satisfied look. He shot her a smile to cover the jealousy he felt towards Lester, because Lester could touch her whenever he wanted.

'I'm only kidding with you Lyla,' he replied, trying to sound hurt.

Terry had cooked his own breakfast, which hadn't looked as good or smelt as good as Lester's. He sat through Lester giving him instructions for the day and agreed that he would take the boys to the boxing club after school. Lyla had stood to the side, nursing Riley and rocking him gently, keeping one eye on Lester and another on Terry.

Later that morning she had seen Terry load his bag into his truck. She knew he was leaving; he had a sudden purpose about him. She knew that Lester would expect her to call him, to alert him to the fact, but instead she carried Riley upstairs for his sleep, and she stayed up there until she heard Terry's truck rumble down the driveway.

She told the boys that Terry was too busy to take them to boxing so Lester would be taking them. They complained loudly. When Lester picked them up and walked through the kitchen looking disgruntled, Lyla feigned her surprise at Terry's departure, claiming that he asked her to step in as he had errands to run.

Eight months later Kate had just started to get over Terry. She had stopped crying herself to sleep at night and decided to move out; the memories of him at Lowlands were too much for her. Lyla had tried hard not to scold her younger sister for being so naive, but her patience had started to wear thin and she suspected this was more the reason Kate wanted to move out. Two weeks after Kate left, Lester got word that Terry was back inside and Lyla heaved a huge sigh of relief.

⊷⊶

During his last spell in prison, Terry shared a cell with a safe-breaker called Providence Adeoye. Providence was from Congo; he spoke fluent English and French and had worked across Europe unloading the safes of the rich and notorious. He was six foot five and his skin shone like polished bronze, but his hands were his greatest asset. His long fingers, which had gained their dexterity from untying his family's fishing nets back home, were precise and nimble, and it was precisely his fingers which had got him into trouble when Tony McBridie's secret stash went missing.

Providence had refused to mix in prison, preferring to keep himself to himself, but this unfortunately fuelled the paranoia of his inmates, to the point that Terry had found Providence face down on his bunk while Tony's men were threatening to break his fingers. Terry immediately saw this as an opportunity and talked Tony around. He explained to him how he could increase his circle of influence. Expanding into new areas of thievery always piqued Tony's entrepreneurial spirit and given that Providence only had six more months to serve, it also meant that it secured Providence's future career.

Terry also took this as his opportunity to re-skill, giving the prison courses a miss this time around. He spent the next six months learning everything Providence knew about breaking into safes. On the day Providence left prison he handed Terry a tightly wrapped bundle, a concoction of cigarettes, phone cards and rock cocaine. It was his way of saying thank you – it was also Tony's secret stash.

⋙ ⋘

All these years later, when Terry walked back into Lowlands, despite his cheerful smile and the bounce in his step, Lyla still felt her skin crawl.

'Alright Lyla?' he asked, bending forward to peck her on the cheek. She fixed him a frosty glare, reminding him she was still off limits. He shook his head in response, still unsure what he had ever really done to upset her. Lester had insisted his stay was necessary but assured her it would be short and Lyla looked up at the kitchen clock, starting the countdown to his departure.

They were gathered in the front room. Terry was swinging a glass of whiskey gently back and forth while he listened to Lester and Liam. As Lester talked, Terry realised that for the first time in his life his brother actually needed him – he had something that Lester wanted. He studied the pictures of the safe. It was old-fashioned, a job he could execute with his eyes shut, but he liked being the centre of their attention, so he deliberately delayed the answer and instead kept an eye on Cassie who had just brought in some sandwiches.

'So, this wife of his is minted then?' Terry asked.

'Yeah, right up herself an' all,' Liam scoffed.

'So where'd Brendan meet a girl like that then? Not round here?'

'Not sure. Can you do it? Can you get into the safe?' cut in Lester, tired of the small talk. Terry leaned back in his chair and drained his glass; he held it up, gesturing for a refill.

'Not for a couple of months, I've got a big job on in Amsterdam. I can't help before then,' he replied, watching Liam's face light up in awe and Lester's tighten with frustration.

Cassie had made it to the door of the room before Liam barked at her to fetch more whiskey. When she returned she tried to avoid Riley's eye. He was always on edge when Liam was near her and right now he was looking particularly perturbed – so much so he was the only one who didn't join in with the dirty laughter from the tail end of a joke that Terry just told.

'What's the matter Riley, didn't you get the joke?' Terry mocked. Liam scoffed

'Not much going on in there, he's as thick as two fucking short planks' Liam snorted, rapping Riley on the head with his knuckles.

Annoyed, Riley pushed his hand away and caught Liam's lip curl. Since Terry had arrived, Liam had strutted around with his chest puffed out and a broad self-satisfied grin plastered on his face. He clearly wanted to show Terry what a big shot he was.

In an attempt to distract Liam from picking on Riley she opened the bottle of whiskey and refilled Terry's glass, purposefully spilling some down his arm.

'Shit, watch what you're doing,' he barked.

Liam immediately jumped up and grabbed the bottle from her. 'You careless slag,' he growled.

'Whoa, Liam that's harsh,' Terry capitulated, shaking the spilled whiskey from his arm. Cassie had caught his interest now. 'So, who's this then?' he asked, grabbing her around the waist and pulling her onto his lap. She moved away quickly but, undeterred, he grabbed her wrist and pulled her back onto him. 'Not so fast, we haven't been introduced. I'm Terry,' he smiled, flashing his crooked teeth.

His breath – a fog of whiskey and cigarettes – hit her in the face. She could see Riley's agitation over how to respond to

Terry's manhandling of her. He looked like a tightly wound coil. She stared at him, willing him to stay silent. She could handle Terry – after all she'd been handling Liam for years.

'She's Liam's girlfriend,' said Sean, looking hard at Liam before walking over to Cassie and pulling her roughly off Terry. She scurried to the door and was quickly gone.

Terry apologised flamboyantly, typically overplaying his ignorance, and Liam just shrugged, not wanting to upset his uncle. Terry then turned to face Sean and caught the look of disgust on his face.

'You in on all of this?' Terry asked, his voice sounding hard. He was annoyed with Sean's stare – *who was he to judge him?*

'I guess,' Sean replied.

'Only, you and Brendan used to be so tight. What's he done to make you turn on him like this?'

Sean could feel his two brothers and his father waiting for the answer to his uncle's unwelcome but perceptive question. 'Just grew apart I suppose. We're not good enough for him, him having gone to university and all that. He ain't really one of us now,' he replied solemnly. He watched Liam and Lester nod in agreement and relax back in their chairs. He felt relieved that he had deflected the heat away from the real reason.

Riley made his excuses to leave, fobbing them off with some made-up story about Lyla needing him to collect something, and waited compliantly for Lester to give permission with his usual dismissive nod. As soon as he left he went in search of Cassie. He'd heard enough in that cloying smoked-filled room to know that perhaps he and Cassie had a chance after all.

CHAPTER 38

BRENDAN HAD TAKEN a call from his father telling him he was not required that particular weekend and Kelly had called to see if he would cover for her so she could stay with Matt. She also let it slip that Terry was staying for a while. Brendan agreed to Kelly's request, but was strangely put out at being excluded from Terry's visit – he had fond memories of his rogue uncle. However, faced with a break from Lowlands, he didn't dwell on this for too long. When he broke the news to Jemima he could see the relief spread across her face.

Terry's visit had also given Brendan a short respite away from Lowlands, and a chance for his wounds to heal before he was summoned back at the weekends and the tension between himself and Jemima resumed. His family now seemed less perturbed that he wasn't bringing her with him and, though he hated to admit it, not having her there was a relief.

However, the time they did spend together usually ended up with the two of them bickering, and it was usually over property. Jemima had set her heart on a townhouse somewhere leafy and near the river; he had taken one look at the details of a particular property she had fallen in love with and informed her they couldn't afford it. Jemima's argument was based on what else could she spend her trust money on if it wasn't a home for them both, and his argument was that if she spent her money on the house it would prove her Aunt Martha right – that he had, in fact, only married her for her money.

In the end they reached a stalemate and ended up viewing properties that neither of them liked. Jemima looked wistfully out of the windows, while Brendan became increasingly annoyed with her non-commitment. By the end of the viewings they weren't talking and eventually Brendan conceded. They took a look at the townhouse. He was an hour late for the viewing and, halfway round, the agent informed them that the vendors had just accepted another offer. Jemima had glowered at him all the way home on the tube and he had tried to ignore her by looking at his phone.

⊷⊨◎ ◎⊨⊶

So, despite the sticky heat and the oppressive grey sky that hung low over Lowlands, Brendan was in some way relieved to find himself back in Ashdowne and laying concrete for the huge base Lester wanted for his new premises. After several back-breaking hours, he dropped the shovel and looked at the grey sludge which was struggling to set in the humidity.

'We're fighting a losing battle. It's never going to set if we pour more on,' he sighed.

Riley, rubbing the back of his neck, stopped to survey their work, leaning against his shovel. Sean raised his eyebrows in agreement. They all looked like ghosts, their hair and skin ashen with concrete dust.

'Let's call it a day, go and get some drink in,' Sean announced. Riley made his excuses and left for the house, but Brendan followed Sean and climbed into his truck. Sean reversed it hard down the driveway and swung it out onto the road, setting off for Ashdowne's small supermarket.

Since the incident with the Gypsies, and his subsequent fight with Liam, Sean seemed to have softened towards Brendan and he liked that things seemed easier between them. He was surprised at how much he had missed their closeness and, with his constant bickering with Jemima, he felt less isolated.

Inside the supermarket, Brendan stood beneath the air conditioning to cool down, while Sean carefully studied the neat rows of beer. Sean always liked to deliberate over his important choices and Brendan felt his stomach growl impatiently. He was starving after the day's hard work, and he let Sean know he was off in search of food. Walking casually down the snack aisle, he grabbed a large packet of tortilla chips and when he turned towards the checkout, he spotted Tess. He found himself rooted to the spot until she turned to face him. They both appeared stunned as their eyes briefly connected. Hiding his uncertainty, he smiled and walked towards her. She looked nervously about her, her jade eyes moving back and forth between him and her basket of shopping.

'Hi,' he managed, smiling warmly.

'Hi,' she replied, letting her eyes rest on his face for a while.

'You look well,' he continued.

Her cheeks flushed. 'You look, um...' she replied, not sure what to say.

'Dusty?' he replied, laughing lightly. He liked how her mouth spread into a broad smile, that she was sharing his joke with him. 'I've been helping out my dad and brothers with some building work,' he explained.

'You have?'

'Mmm,' he agreed, raising his eyebrows in recognition of how unsuited he was to the work. He continued to look at her. She still had the same wild curly hair, its coppery tones glowing fiercely beneath the harsh strip lighting, and she was still wholesomely beautiful, with her clear skin and her eyes shining brightly back at him – he was enjoying looking at her.

'Mum, look, it's Dad!' Georgie cried, breaking the fragility of the moment between them, as he and Sean swung into their aisle. Georgie was hanging precariously, piggy-back style, on Sean's back, while Sean cradled cans of beer. Sean stopped abruptly, leaning to the side for Georgie to slide off. When he straightened up, he looked thunderous as he took in the sight of Tess and Brendan standing together.

'Err, this is awkward,' Brendan muttered, running his hand around the back of his neck and turning to face Sean.

'Uh huh,' she agreed quietly as they both stared at him.

Sean's face bore the same look as when he'd found Tess with Brendan in Brendan's flat six years ago.

'Mum, can I go and sleep at Dad's tonight? Can I, can I?' Georgie begged.

'No, Georgie, we have plans,' replied Tess sternly, picking up her shopping basket and starting to head for the checkout. Georgie followed, continuing to badger her. Sean glowered after her then slowly turned his explosive expression to Brendan.

'You finished?' Sean grunted and Brendan nodded meekly.

Sean deliberately queued behind Tess, continuing to fuel Georgie's pestering until Tess had had enough and turned around to face him.

'We have days you see him and days you don't, so why go and put the idea in his head that he could come over tonight?' she hissed.

Brendan moved to another till so he could stay out of the way.

'He's my son and I should be able to see him when I want,' replied Sean gruffly.

'We agreed this Sean. You are being so difficult,' she spat back, sounding close to tears.

The checkout girl serving Brendan was more interested in seeing what was going on between Tess and Sean than in serving him. When she handed him his change she raised her eyebrows, clearly enjoying the drama. He took his change, shoving it in his pocket, and marched out of the store, where he leaned against Sean's truck to wait for him.

When Tess and Sean left the store, she grabbed Georgie roughly by the wrist and pulled him, sobbing, away from the car park and headed home. Sean strode angrily over to his truck, flicking the remote to open it. He climbed in and sat down heavily, dumping the cans of beer next to him, and lit a cigarette. He breathed deeply, while staring into his wing mirror, watching Tess and Georgie walking across the village green towards home. Brendan climbed in carefully and sat next to him, watching him stare after them.

'It must be hard not being with them,' Brendan offered quietly.

Ignoring Brendan, Sean continued to stare, but his frown deepened. After a few moments of silence Brendan spoke again. 'You know, the only reason the two of you are not together is because of you,' he stated, looking down at the packet of tortilla chips in his lap.

Sean dragged heavily on his cigarette then turned his attention to Brendan. 'How d'you figure that one out?' he snapped.

'I know I played my part Sean, so did Tess and, you may not like it, but so did you. Difference is, you still are; it's only your anger and pride that's keeping you two apart,' he continued calmly, facing his brother who was staring back at him incredulously. 'She'd take you back,' he ventured.

'How do you know that?' asked Sean, his lip curled in disbelief.

'Because I don't think she ever wanted you two to split up. She just wanted things to be different.'

'Well, fucking you made a hell of a difference,' he barked, throwing his cigarette out of the window and starting the truck. Brendan lurched forward as Sean rammed the truck into reverse, swung the steering wheel around and jerked forward, slamming his foot on the accelerator. Now Brendan felt the real force of Sean's anger, felt it slam down between them like a steel shutter. The silence that sat between them was impenetrable and Brendan was back to square one with his big brother once again.

CHAPTER 39

BRENDAN'S THOUGHTS RATTLED around inside his head, in sync with his body rattling with the motion of the underground train. His manager Lance's words, innocuous enough at first, now started to permeate and fuel his paranoia. His team's bonuses were resting on the proposal Brendan had put forward and everyone in the team just couldn't see how he had got the numbers to stack up. Ralph had challenged him in their morning meeting and Brendan had grown instantly defensive, putting him down with the sneer he always reserved for him. After all, Brendan had told himself, this wasn't about the numbers; this was about Ralph trying to climb over him – his ambition was so strong you could almost smell it – surely everyone could see that. However, on this occasion they couldn't and Lance had called Brendan into his office later that morning to discuss his 'potential error'.

'Ordinarily, Brendan, I have complete faith in your decisions, but you don't seem quite yourself. You've lost some of that sharpness of late,' said Lance, sounding embarrassed.

Brendan had looked away. It hurt to see the disappointment on Lance's face, and he was intensely uncomfortable with the direction in which this conversation was going. Lance breathed deeply before he continued to speak. 'You know, after you get married, you hit a lull, when the honeymoon period, so to speak, wears off. Eloise and I had it, I believe it's very common. Normal life settles in and, well, we work long hours. Our salaries are intended to recompense our families for that, but sometimes it's not quite enough. Why don't you take the afternoon off, pick Jemima up from work early, go out for dinner, and spend some time together?'

Brendan had looked back at him, perplexed; it sounded like Lance was offering him some fatherly advice. He was trying to figure out whether he wanted to take it or not when Lance added: 'Ralph and Julia are going to take a look over the figures this afternoon. No offence Brendan, but too much is riding on this and I think it needs a fresh pair of eyes.'

Then he realised what Lance really meant. His team would be spending the afternoon in Lance's office and they didn't want Brendan on the outside looking in. He was being told to go home, to get out of the way. He nodded blankly and left Lance's office, picking up his keys, phone and jacket, aware that Julia was trying to study him discreetly. As he walked towards the lift, Ralph came out of the PA's booth, nearly bumping into him.

'Off early?' he enquired and Brendan glared at him, sending Ralph scurrying over to Julia's desk.

When he got off the tube and left the station, the buttery late-September sun hurt his eyes, momentarily stunning him, and the realisation that he was now losing his grip at work panicked him. It was hard enough dealing with his family, particularly Liam, who swaggered around the place like nothing had happened while the rest of them ignored what he had done. Then there was the constant see-sawing with Sean and having to walk on eggshells around Lester. Brendan had recently made the mistake of asking his father how long he may be required at Lowlands and Lester's tongue had lashed at him like the leather belt he used to beat his sons with when they were children. He was quickly reminded of his duty if he was to keep Jemima from knowing about Joe. And then there was Joe, his death still vivid in Brendan's mind, never letting his thoughts be still, reminding him how much he needed to keep his head down in order to protect Jemima.

The hustle and bustle of Oxford Circus engulfed him and, annoyed with trying to push through the slow-moving crowds, he dived down a side street and weaved his way through the back roads to Jemima's work.

Jemima was admiring Hector Mendez's collection – the way the colours picked up the light and subtly highlighted the female form. He painted women beautifully and Jemima often wondered if that was because he was gay; whether his perspective came from viewing them without any sexual undertone. Jemima and Hector were stood side by side when she turned to him and smiled, seeing the delight in his face.

'They are stunning, Hector,' she said and watched him nod in response very slowly. Hector was Jemima's favourite artist to work with; he was unpretentious and uncomplicated. Still staring at the collection, she became aware that Hector had shifted his attention; his face was studious and, as she turned to him, she was puzzled by the way he was looking at her.

'Would you sit for me?' he asked, looking like he was figuring something out.

'Me?' she replied, astounded. Hector's models were usually professional, such was his reputation, and recently he had started to gather some celebrity interest in posing for him.

He didn't respond, but tentatively reached out and held her chin, turning her face slowly to the golden light, which streamed in long shafts through the gallery windows. He released a soft 'Ah' as if he had just hit upon some inspiration. He peered at her face, looking closely into her eyes. Jemima could smell the oil paint on his hands; so intent was Hector's concentration, the only sound Jemima could hear was their breathing.

When Brendan got to the gallery, he saw Jemima stood close to a tall, thin Mediterranean-looking man. He watched how the man held Jemima's chin and leaned into her, looking deeply into her eyes. He also noticed that Jemima was letting him and this infuriated him. Furiously he swung open the gallery door.

'Get your hands off my wife,' he snarled and Hector jumped with surprise, staring at him in shock.

Before Jemima had a chance to explain, Brendan strode over to Hector and in one decisive move, pulled back his fist and hit Hector so hard he fell to the floor. Hector clutched his face and Jemima saw thin trails of blood start to trickle through his fingers. He looked up at Brendan who towered over him, breathing hard. Tugging at his arm and pleading with him, Jemima tried to pull him away, but Brendan shook her free, bent down and pulled

Hector up by his shirt collar. 'You don't touch her,' he said, his voice low, the words rolling slowly out of his mouth. When he straightened up he found himself faced by Jemima, Juliette and Pablo, all staring at him with disbelief.

Juliette pushed Jemima's bag into her hands and gestured to the door, snapping her fingers at her to leave. Pablo started to wail hysterically, his short arms flying around him. He was babbling in Brazilian, his gestures frantic.

'Leave, and get him out of here!' Juliette barked at Jemima.

'She's gone,' Brendan grunted back at Juliette, grabbing Jemima's arm and dragging her from the gallery. He didn't let go of her arm until they had walked several streets, leaving Jemima to jog by his side in order to keep up. He turned sharply into a pub, yanked the doors open and pushed her into a small booth before walking over to the bar. When he returned he found her still stunned by what had just happened. He drank quickly, watching her closely, his breathing still hard and his anger still rolling inside him.

'Drink,' he growled, nodding at her white wine. Her eyes darted towards it. She looked surprised – she hadn't even noticed him placing it in front of her. Downing his whiskey, he strode back to the bar.

'Why?' was all she said when he returned.

He looked at her for a while, his expression giving nothing away. 'Why do you think?' he finally replied, his voice hard.

'I have no idea,' she replied quietly and they both sat for a while staring at each other. 'Brendan, he's an artist. His collection is in the gallery and he had just asked me to pose for him. He was studying me as a potential model,' she continued softly.

Brendan took a large gulp of his drink.

'Hector is gay. He has a long-term partner. There is absolutely nothing going on between us. You would stand a better chance with him than I do,' she finished and noted Brendan's eyes flinch, before he rested his head against the back of the booth and continued to survey her. 'I am probably going to be fired for this. How can I ever face Pablo and Juliette again?' Jemima looked down and felt tears starting to well up; she swallowed hard to try to stop them, but a small tear escaped and trickled down the side of her face.

'You don't need to work, I make enough,' he replied coldly.

'That's not the point. I like to work. I like my job, it's important to me – the gallery is important to me,' she replied, forcing her voice to sound strong.

He scoffed, then downed his drink. 'More important than me?'

'No, of course not, but...' Jemima lost the words; she felt like she was being dragged into an argument she could never win, so instead she shut her eyes. When she opened them, Brendan was quickly downing her wine. He slammed the glass on the table and stood up.

'We're going home,' he told her gruffly, pulling her roughly along behind him.

Back at the apartment, Brendan opened a bottle of red wine and collapsed onto the sofa, kicking his shoes off and loosening his tie, while Jemima disappeared into the bedroom to call Juliette. He could hear her pleading on the phone and, in annoyance, he turned up the television and poured himself another glass of wine. Soon he had finished the bottle, so he fetched another and on his way back to the sofa he glanced at Jemima through the crack in the bedroom door. She was sitting on the bed, looking worried, biting her bottom lip. He sneered to himself and slouched onto the sofa again. Rebelliously, he lit a cigarette. He usually smoked outside as Jemima hated the smell, but this afternoon he couldn't give a damn and defiantly drew the smoke into his lungs, slowly releasing it in a steady stream through his mouth.

After a while, he heard Jemima padding around the bedroom. He got up, somewhat unsteadily from the alcohol and an empty stomach. Staggering over to the bedroom, he kicked open the door and leaned in the doorway, a glass of wine cradled precariously in his hands. She had just run a bath and had started to undress.

He let his eyes roll over her and his mouth turned into a languid smile; he placed his wine on the chest of drawers and stumbled towards her. Gently touching her shoulders, he hooked his fingers under the thin straps of her slip. The alcohol on his breath stung Jemima's nose, his eyes were glassy and there was a rough, black stain on his lips from the wine. Bending his head to kiss her, she whipped her face away.

'Brendan, you're drunk,' she hissed.

He swayed for a moment before grabbing her and slurring, 'Then that makes you the drunk's whore.' He held her tight with his left arm around her waist, while he ran his right hand roughly up and down her body, whispering fiercely into her ear: 'I bet he just loved you in this.'

Jemima pushed him firmly and in his drunken, uncoordinated state he broke free of her.

'For God's sake Brendan!' she cried, her voice sounding tired. He regained his balance and grabbed her firmly again, angry that she had pushed him away. Forcing her down onto the bed, her body stiffened and her hands pushed hard against his chest. Pulling her arms up above her head, he held her firmly in place with the weight of his hips, while he pushed her legs apart with his thigh. The slip was pulled tight against her legs and, as he pushed them further apart, the fine material finally gave way with a sharp rip. Jemima was shaking her head from side to side in disbelief at what he was trying to do. He raised his hips and she felt his hand reaching to undo his belt.

'No,' she implored, her voice weaker than the sound in her head. 'No,' she repeated, staring into his blank eyes. She heard his zip unfasten. She squirmed against him, trying to break free but he just pushed harder against her, trapping her. 'Brendan, please, no,' she begged. His free hand grabbed the side of her knickers and yanked hard until they tore. She felt him pull his hips back and lunge forward at her but he missed. Changing tack and lowering his head, she felt him fumble between her legs; then he turned his head and rested it against her breast, falling still.

Jemima lay there for a while, hearing his breathing rasp and watching the slow rise and fall of his shoulders. Gradually, she tried to slide out from beneath him, managing to get her right foot on the floor and her hips free. When he stirred she froze. He released her wrists and curled his arm around her waist, nestling his head against her breast once more and letting out a loud snore. She waited a few minutes more before slowly moving again. Once the lower part of her body was free, she gently took his arm and peeled it away from her, placing it on a pillow. Reflexively, he tightened his grip. She caught the start of a contented smile as she grabbed her clothes and handbag, and ran out of the apartment, frantically jabbing at the elevator buttons, while slipping into her dress and shoes. When the doors slid open, she was relieved it was empty. Once on the ground floor she raced out of the building but paused suddenly, bending double. She leaned over a potted palm and retched, her whole body shaking. When she was able to stand upright, she took a few deep breaths and then ran across the road, heading to the high street where she hoped to find a taxi.

The next morning, Brendan felt as if he had been hit with a hammer across the back of his head. Thoughts of Joe immediately came to mind and he groaned loudly. Peeling his eyes open hurt. He focused on the digital clock, squinting at the light from the red numbers, until he felt able to turn over. When he did, he let out another groan and fell heavily against the bed. He looked around the room; the curtains were still open, the bed hadn't been slept in and there was a pillow jammed uncomfortably beneath him. He saw the half-drunk glass of wine on the chest of drawers and frowned. He shuffled, feeling uncomfortable in his work clothes, and he looked down. His trousers hung open. His frown deepened. He checked his wrist and noticed he was still wearing his watch, concluding that he must have passed out from drink. He sat up gingerly, his head thumping. The apartment was quiet, with no sign of Jemima; he tried to fathom what day it was, wondering if she had gone to work. Then he remembered the events of the previous day – him hitting the artist, Juliette barking at them to get out of the gallery, then Jemima's tears in the pub. Everything after that was hazy, though he recalled Jemima on the phone in the bedroom. After that it was blank.

Jemima was sat with Minnie and Abby at their kitchen table when the doorbell rang. Minnie held her hand tightly, trying to contain Jemima's panic. She had turned up the previous evening, shaking uncontrollably. When they had finally got her settled, they managed to piece together what had happened. Jemima spent the night with them and the next day Minnie had worked from home, while Jemima had slept and wept intermittently. Minnie had called Jemima's work and spoken to Juliette, letting her know that Jemima was unwell. There was something in Juliette's tone, despite her sympathetic words, that didn't disguise the fact she didn't believe Minnie. The doorbell rang again and all three of them stared down the hall at the front door.

'What if it's him? I can't see him!' Jemima cried.

'It's okay, I'll get it,' Minnie said, trying to sound calm. She got up, shutting the kitchen door behind her. When she looked through the spy hole, she saw the distorted image of Brendan, the collar of his jacket pulled upwards and his hands stuffed deep into his pockets. He reached again for the bell, but before he got to it Minnie opened the door, leaning in the doorway, deliberately blocking his way in.

His eyes were dull, the bright blue had faded and his skin looked grey. Pulling his hands from his pockets, he held them upwards in a gesture of surrender.

'I just need to know she's safe,' he said, before Minnie had the chance to speak.

'She is now,' she replied,

'What?' he asked.

Minnie stepped onto the front step and pulled the door shut behind her. 'Look, how much did you drink last night?' she asked him, her voice softer now.

He shook his head before responding. 'A lot. Too much. Why?'

Minnie looked at him carefully; his expression seemed genuine and even though the idea of him forcing himself onto Jemima disgusted her, she had been surprised at what Jemima had told her. She was beginning to wonder if he had any idea of what he had tried to do. 'What do you remember about yesterday?'

'We had a fight. I opened some wine, Jem was on the phone to Juliette, that's about it. When I woke up this morning she was gone. She's not answering my calls and she didn't go to work. When you and Abby weren't answering them either, I thought I would call round; next stop I was going to the police.'

Minnie breathed out and looked at him seriously. 'You really don't remember what you did?'

'What did I do?' he asked, sounding panicked.

Minnie shifted her feet and folded her arms across her body. 'You tried to force yourself on her Brendan.'

'What?' he exclaimed, shaking his head. 'I'd never do that; I couldn't do that to her.'

Minnie sucked in her top lip before speaking again. 'Well, you passed out before you could actually do any real damage but she is very shaken up and, I'm sorry, but she doesn't want to see you.'

Brendan looked away. Everything Minnie had told him pieced together as he recalled the state of the apartment when he had awoken. He had some vague recollection of holding her and not wanting to let go, feeling the silk of her slip, hearing a rip.

'I understand,' he replied, sounding ashamed.

'Brendan, I don't know what is going on with you, and I'm not prying, but I'm aware that things have got tricky between the two of you lately. You need to sort yourself out, sort the drinking out and get your head straight, otherwise you're going to lose her.' Seeing she had his attention she continued. 'She loves you, but she can only take so much. You need to give her some time.'

He nodded. 'Tell her I'm sorry. I mean it, I really am.'

His reaction saddened Minnie. For the first time since she had met him he looked lost. Reluctantly she nodded and went back inside, closing the front door gently behind her. Brendan stood on the front door step for a couple of moments before turning and walking away. His shoulders were hunched and his step was heavy. Pulling his mobile phone from his pocket he called James. 'I've found her,' he told him.

'That's good news,' James replied. But Brendan remained silent – to him, she still felt lost.

CHAPTER 40

JEMIMA WAS SAT on a bench near the bandstand. She looked about nervously, pulling her coat tight against the autumn chill. The trees were advancing into their changing colours and their leaves shone like gems – deep crimsons, russets and golds burnished against the clear autumnal sky. On any other Sunday, Jemima and Brendan would have been meandering through this park, arm in arm, making plans for the week and enjoying each other's company. This Sunday, however, when Jemima had finally contacted him, Brendan had arranged to meet her here, so they could start the process of 'sorting things out'.

When Brendan turned up he looked tired. His face was drawn and he glanced at her sheepishly before sitting down, keeping his hands buried deep in his pockets and the collar of his black wool jacket turned up high.

'Hi,' he mumbled, staring ahead.

'Hi,' she replied softly, turning to face him.

His eyes flickered towards her before focusing on his chocolate-brown Chelsea boots that stuck out from his outstretched legs. He sighed deeply. 'I really am sorry, Jem.'

Jemima looked down and rested her hand on his arm. 'I want us to be how we used to be Brendan, like we were before we got married.'

He kept his eyes fixed on his boots while Jemima, trying to keep her anguish from the last couple of weeks under control, continued: 'We can be again, I know we can.'

Brendan frowned, and Jemima tightened her grip on his forearm. He stared at her hand.

'Brendan, please, we have to make this work. I don't want us to be apart any more.'

Slowly raising his head, he stared at the tiny shafts of amber that glowed in her eyes, then let his eyes fall apprehensively to her face. She slowly rubbed his arm; he felt confused.

'You want us to get back together?' he asked.

'Yes. What happened has happened, Brendan. I want us to put it behind us, start afresh. For things to be just how they used to be.'

'You've forgiven me?'

'Perhaps, I don't know. I just don't want this to come between us. I think we have something more than that one particular incident.'

'One particular incident – Jesus, Jemima, I tried to rape you!' he said, keeping his voice hushed and looking at her with disbelief.

'Don't say that.'

'But it's true! How can you even want to be near me? For Christ's sake, if I hadn't passed out...'

'Stop it,' she interjected. 'You didn't. It didn't happen and if I can live with it why can't you?' she begged.

'No, Jemima,' he replied.

'Brendan, please. I don't want us to be over.'

'Jemima, I can't believe you would take me back after what I did. Where is your self-respect? It's over, we're over,' he stated firmly. With that, he took an envelope out of his jacket pocket and handed it to her. Then got up and walked away.

Jemima sat on the bench and watched him walk away from her with long, purposeful strides. She hadn't anticipated his response; in fact, this was the outcome she had least expected. Her world had just dramatically tilted and everything in it had slid precariously, all at once coming to a final crash.

Brendan stood on the doorstep in the pouring rain, his jacket collar pulled up tight around his ears as he hammered on the dark green front door. Finally, lights came on inside the Victorian terraced house and he heard footsteps thudding down the stairs. He knew James must be at the other side of the door looking through the spy hole, as the house had fallen quiet again. Then the door swung open.

'Come in,' James exclaimed, pulling on Brendan's arm. Without speaking Brendan stepped into the warm house, rivulets of rain still running down his face, his boots, jeans and wool jacket soaked through.

'It's Brendan,' called James up the stairs and, almost immediately, Tanya appeared, wrapping a silk dressing gown around her. When she saw him, her hand flew to her mouth and her eyes welled up.

'Where have you been? We've been so worried about you,' James asked, peering into his face and holding his shoulders.

Brendan couldn't hold his gaze – he couldn't answer him. He had no specific idea where he had been or what he'd been doing. There were small snatches of memory, like faded photographs; images of him drinking in various bars across town, withdrawing money to buy cocaine and sitting in a club snorting it. It was while walking down an unfamiliar cobbled street, feeling the cold rain pounding against him, that he'd had a strong desire to be with James and Tanya.

'It doesn't matter,' James continued, manoeuvring him towards the kitchen. 'Just come through, let's get you dry.' James took Brendan's jacket and Brendan slumped hard onto a kitchen chair. After hanging the jacket over a radiator, James sat down opposite him. Brendan's face was full of stubble and his eyes were red-rimmed and distant. His cheeks had a hollowed-out look about them and his lips were chapped and split. There was a cut on his right hand, his knuckles were swollen and dirty, and he stank of alcohol and the sour smell of not having washed for several days.

'What happened to your hand?' James asked. Brendan looked blankly at his hands, turning them over slowly, looking at them as if for the first time in his life. 'Did you get in a fight?'

Brendan looked confused. He tried to recall a fight, a moment of flared tempers, but nothing came.

'It looks like you hit someone.'

'Why would I have done that?' Brendan replied, his voice cracked from dehydration and too many cigarettes.

'Because whoever it was probably pissed you off,' James stated flatly. He tried to contain himself – his earlier relief at seeing

Brendan was fast wearing off. Brendan had been missing for six days, ever since he'd met Jemima in the park. Now he'd turned up looking like a vagrant, oblivious to what they had all been through – the phone calls, the visits to his flat, constantly checking for messages with the dull hope that he would get in touch.

Brendan stared back at James, appearing as if he wouldn't – or couldn't – offer an explanation for his behaviour because he was so bombed. The cocoon of alcohol and drugs in which Brendan had wrapped himself while they were all frantic with worry angered James. He couldn't understand how Brendan could act so selfishly.

Brendan leaned back, reached into the pocket of his jeans, pulled out a bag of cocaine and started to prepare his next line. James sat in silence, watching Brendan's grubby hands as he pulled out a credit card and tipped what he had left of the fine white powder out onto the kitchen table. When Brendan held the rolled twenty pound note out to James, he shook his head imperturbably, daring Brendan to snort it. Tanya had stopped making tea and looked anxiously at them both. Brendan's eyes were half closed and he tilted his head back, viewing James cautiously, before he dipped his head and sniffed sharply. Then he let his head roll backwards as he felt the drug start to dissolve into his bloodstream, dulling the turmoil, taking away the aches in his tired muscles, and his mouth opened out into a broad grin. He could deal with them now; he could cope with James's disgust and Tanya's shock and he could talk himself out of this mess. He'd find the answers, the cocaine would help him – he could already feel it sharpening his brain, scraping the synapses like a file with bright sparks shooting off it. He was becoming fine-tuned and hard-wired and slowly he opened his eyes to look at James.

'I'm sorry. I should have let you know where I was,' he said confidently.

'And where were you?'

'Around. Different bars and clubs. I called in sick on Monday. I couldn't face going into work, not after I had seen Jemima on Sunday.' He could feel himself breaking now, recalling her face when he last saw her. 'It's over between us,' he continued. He knew he needed to give them more than this, but the words were painful to say out loud. Jemima had looked so hurt and confused and he had wanted to take her pain away, but that would have just put off the inevitable. They needed to part if he was to keep her safe. Safe from him, from what he was capable of doing to her, and safe from knowing everything about him. He couldn't cope with how devastated she'd be if she knew he had stood by and let his brother murder his uncle, help bury the body, then carry on as if nothing had happened. He needed to protect her from knowing he could be that person. He just couldn't face her knowing his secrets.

Then there was the matter of his family; his struggle to keep her safe around them had become too much and he was fearful as to what Liam might still try. All things considered, Jemima just couldn't be a part of his life any more.

Tanya placed a mug of tea in front of him and gently touched his shoulder. 'You look terrible,' she said, reaching out for his face and gently touching his cheek. He let the weight of his face fall into her hand and wrapped his arms around her waist, burying his head into her stomach. She stroked the back of his head and, as she did so, she looked at James and raised her eyebrows.

'You can stay here as long as you need to, but you need to stop drinking and taking the coke; you'll have to get yourself sorted,' James told him.

Brendan turned his head to face him and, holding Tanya tighter, he sighed deeply. His face was pained. 'I know – I need to get a grip,' were the only words he could manage, Sean's advice coming back to him in a fierce reminder of how this had all started to go wrong.

'Yeah, whatever it is we can sort it out, Brendan. Nothing is ever as bad as you imagine.'

Brendan gave a wry laugh and closed his eyes. He couldn't even begin to tell them – he'd shatter their world with what he was hiding. He knew it was his cross to bear and he hoped that, with time, the weight of it would lighten so that his bones creaked less and he could eventually stand straight someday.

'You need to sleep,' Tanya said softly, still stroking his head.

'I don't want to sleep.'

'Why not?' asked James.

Brendan ignored him. 'I need some vodka,' he croaked, keen to keep his feelings dampened down with a little bit of help.

Tanya tilted his head back, cupping his face. 'No, you need to sleep. Let's get you to bed.'

He woke late, unsure of the day and time, but with the smell of fresh coffee filling his nostrils. When he tried to move, his body ached; his muscles were burned out from the pace of the last few days. The toxins in his system were leaving his body painfully, but with considerable effort he managed to shower and shave. Some of James's clothes had been left at the end of his bed. When he dressed and looked at his reflection in the wardrobe mirror he realised he'd lost weight and could see the large black circles under his eyes. He looked as if all the life was being sucked out of him. He blinked back at himself then breathed deeply before going downstairs.

'Hey sleepy head, good sleep?' Tanya asked lightly.

'Yeah, what time is it?'

'Two-ish. James has just popped to the gym.'

'What day is it?' As soon as the question left his mouth, he realised how lame it sounded.

'Sunday.' Tanya's voice was too breezy, as if she was trying to play down the events of the last few days. Placing a mug of coffee and a bacon sandwich in front of him, she sat down. He smiled at her appreciatively before taking a huge bite.

'This is good,' he managed through the mouthful of food.

'How long since you last ate?'

'I don't know. I remember having a kebab,' he answered and she smiled, rolling her eyes. He was ravenous and, observing the speed with which he was devouring the sandwich, she got up to make him another.

'Thanks,' he replied, his mouth still full.

Sitting opposite him, she drank her coffee and watched patiently until he had finished, then she took his hands and twisted her fingers around his. 'What happened, Brendan?'

He didn't want this conversation.

'Jem told us you handed her divorce papers when you met. Why can't you sort this out? She's broken hearted, she's desperate not to lose you.'

He looked away, his throat constricting. 'Tanya, we can't be together. She isn't safe with me.'

'You were drunk, Brendan. It was a one-off...'

'No,' he cut over her. 'She isn't safe – the only way I can protect her is by not being with her.'

'Brendan this isn't like you. I've known you for years and this just isn't who you are.'

His eyes rested on the cut on his hand.

'That was the result of the drink and the drugs,' she said.

'That's excuses Tanya,' he replied sharply.

'You can see someone about the drinking Brendan. Jemima will support you through it. She loves you, we all do. We'll all support you and we'll do whatever we have to in order to help you get sorted out.' Her eyes had filled with tears and her grip on his fingers had tightened.

Words failed him and he slowly shook his head. 'It's over, Tanya,' he whispered.

Being around good people was painful; it felt like he was cheating them all. As disturbing as he found the thought, he'd been kidding himself all these years that he belonged in a different world. But the blood that pulsed through him had won out – his family had won. They'd got him back; they'd finally got what they wanted.

Brendan had driven out of London early and gone straight to Uncle Joe's house, or what was left of it. All that remained was a seemingly endless pile of rubble made up of broken bricks and slabs of concrete, which he climbed over and resumed breaking up. When it was in manageable pieces he tossed them into the skip. Despite the cold November morning, it hadn't taken long for him to start peeling his layers of clothes off, a thin stream of sweat running steadily down his back. Ignoring the rumble of an approaching truck, he continued to swing the sledgehammer over his shoulder, smacking the concrete with a dull thud and feeling the reverberation shudder up his forearms before he swung the hammer high into the air again and repeated the blow. Sean and Liam climbed out of the truck and eyed him warily, surprised he was already there, particularly after he hadn't shown for the last two weekends.

He stopped for a moment to watch them, trying to gauge their mood. Sean grunted and started to pull some tools out of the truck, while Liam simply glared at him. Ignoring him, Brendan fell back into his rhythm with the sledgehammer. The three of them carried on labouring over the concrete and bricks until Lester and Riley turned up. When Lester saw Brendan he checked his watch, looking at him quizzically.

'So, you decided to show then? What time d'you get here?' he asked.

Everyone stopped to look at Brendan. 'About eight-ish, just before,' he replied.

'Didn't see Jemima at the house,'

'No,' Brendan replied flatly.

'What time's she coming?' asked Lester, unwilling to let the subject drop.

'She's not,' said Brendan, letting the hammer strike the concrete and watching a sizeable chunk break away.

Lester was quiet for a moment. 'Why not, she's not been down here for a while?' Lester asked, sounding disgruntled.

Leaning on the handle of his hammer, Brendan leaned forward to pick up the pieces of concrete. He steadily threw each of them into a skip before turning to his father. 'Because she doesn't have to anymore. She's no longer my wife – we're getting divorced,' Brendan told him.

Lester threw his cigarette butt onto the ground, stubbed it out with his heel and shrugged. 'You never were the settling down type,' he said dismissively, and started back up the drive.

Brendan caught Sean looking curiously at him, trying to read the signs that Brendan was trying to keep hidden. Standing tall on the rubble, staring back at Sean, Brendan was determined to give nothing away, careful not to let Sean see how painful he was finding the split from Jemima; the last thing he wanted was Sean's pity. In the end, Sean just raised his eyebrows and turned away. Liam, however, was leaning against the truck, clearly displaying his pleasure at hearing Brendan's news.

'What?' Brendan finally snapped, losing his patience with Liam's mocking gaze.

'So, who was too good for who then?' Liam asked, in an attempt to goad his brother further.

Brendan inhaled deeply, attempting to calm himself, before he shrugged and nonchalantly picked up his sledgehammer again.

'Perhaps I should give her a call; make sure she's not too lonely now she's back on the market,' Liam sniggered.

Brendan held the sledgehammer still and turned his attention back to him. Both Riley and Sean stopped what they were doing, clouds of frosty breath escaping from their open mouths. Liam was now stood upright. Having hooked Brendan he carried on smiling, but experience told him to keep watching him closely.

Brendan was acutely aware of his brothers' attention; he knew they were waiting for him to make the next move and a part of him was ready to swing the hammer at Liam, take him out and release the tension that was building in his shoulders. Somewhere inside him was a small voice telling him that this was his chance to let Liam know that he was no longer prepared to be the underdog. It reminded him that if he let this comment go, his chance of ever being free of them went with it. If he didn't retaliate they would sense he was broken, and then it was game over. So he slowly started to walk to the edge of the rubble, holding the sledgehammer menacingly in his grasp. Liam's cocksure smile dropped and his eyes tightened. He shifted his stance and Brendan could see he was getting ready to fight. Sean had moved closer to Liam, still watching them both intently. Riley had stayed completely still, with his hands balled into fists.

When Brendan got to the edge of the mound, he let the height of the pile play to his advantage. He looked guilelessly down at Liam, letting a small smile curl up the edge of his mouth. 'So am I now – back on the market. That's why I came back here. There's usually someone available.' He spoke slowly, letting the words resonate. He could see Liam slowly making the connection and then watched him explode. He lunged towards him, his feet slipping on the gravel as he fell forward, and pushed his hands out in an attempt to reach Brendan, who was standing calmly above him, with the sledgehammer held casually in his hands. As Liam got closer to Brendan, Sean pulled him back. Held tightly by Sean, Liam ranted at Brendan, shouting at him to stay away from Cassie.

'She don't want you after what you did to her,' Liam spat.

'That what she tells you, Liam?' Brendan replied coolly.

Fuelled by this comment, Liam managed to shake himself free from Sean and lunged again. This time, Sean let him go and soon Liam had clambered up to Brendan and pushed his face into his. 'You touch her and I'll finish you for good!' he roared, a large throbbing vein standing proud and angry on his neck.

Brendan continued to smile.

'You think you can walk back in here and take whatever you want?' Liam shouted. 'Well, we're all different now. You ain't the fucking golden boy any more – you're nothing!'

Brendan calmly took the vengeance and fury that Liam rained down on him. Liam's eyes bulged and his nostrils flared, reminding him of the picture of the bullfight he had in his apartment; he half expected Liam to start pounding the ground with his foot, lower his head and charge at him.

'What the fuck is going on?' screamed Lyla, seeing Brendan and Liam locked in confrontation. Lester had returned to Lowlands with the news Brendan had just shared with him and then sent her out to try find out what had happened. Lester was anxious about the plans they had made and, while he was telling Lyla, she could see the tension building in him. Knowing his usual way of dealing with anxiety was to hit out at those around him, she had quickly left the house to go and find Brendan.

'You're like a bunch of fucking school boys,' she scolded them.

Liam's face dropped and Brendan half expected him to accuse him of starting it. He let a small chuckle escape with this thought, immediately drawing Lyla's attention to him.

She eyed him curiously before she spoke. 'Seeing as you two are at it already, Brendan, you can come with me. I need help moving some stuff upstairs.'

Brendan slid down the gravel mound and as he passed Liam he quietly told him: 'You're not that different by the way. None of you are.'

Brendan reached down from the loft to take a heavy cardboard box from Lyla and groaned as he took it.

'It's only paper,' she told him and he rolled his eyes as he slid it across the loft floor. Once the last box was up, Lyla joined him, standing with her hands on her hips, surveying the space. Brendan stood next to her, waiting for her next instruction.

'Over here, we can move this stuff back,' she told him and went over to a collection of boxes piled high in a corner. As they were moving the boxes around, Brendan became aware of his mother staring at him.

'What time's Jemima coming down?' she asked casually.

He sighed. 'She's not,' he replied.

'She working again?'

Brendan straightened up, stretching his back out. 'We've split up, Mum.'

'Oh,' replied Lyla, feigning shock, letting a furrow settle across her brow. She tilted her head in anticipation for the story, but he looked away.

'I don't want to talk about it; I'm done talking about it,' he murmured and turned back to the boxes. She leaned forward and placed her hand on his forearm, rubbing it slowly. His eyes slid sideways to her hand, then moved up to her face, trying to figure out what this meant.

'When you're ready, you know we're here for you,' she told him.

He sighed and he felt his shoulders drop; he was uncertain as to what he could share with her.

'It's definitely over?' she enquired, and he nodded, keeping his eyes fixed on the floor. 'You met someone else?' she continued,

'No,' he replied, aghast at the question.

'Why have you split up then?' Lyla persisted.

The loft was gloomy and cramped and his chest was starting to feel tight.

'Things just didn't work out; our worlds are too far apart!' he snapped and saw her flinch from his harsh tone. He sighed heavily. 'Mum, I just don't want to talk about it right now.' His voice sounded softer and he'd forced a tight smile. She smiled tightly back and stroked his hair, tucking an imaginary piece behind his ear before resting her hand on his cheek.

'You'll find someone else. You won't be on your own long – you're far too handsome. It's been the making of Sean, being single. He's had a steady stream of girlfriends since he ditched Tess.'

Brendan's stomach tightened from her comment and he made out he was trying to figure how to get the boxes into such a small space. He bent down and grabbed the end of a large canvas bag. It was heavy, and when he finally got it to move it made a loud clang. The bag had no zip and he used his foot to unfold the canvas to see what was in it. The dull glow of the loft light revealed an assortment of guns. He turned to Lyla for an explanation. She stared down at them and he could see her trying to fathom out how to explain them. Finally, she looked up at him, holding her voice and eyes steady.

'They're your Uncle Terry's. They're cooling off up here until it's okay for him to come and get them.'

Brendan stared back at them; they looked innocent enough lying haphazardly in the bag. He sighed. The discovery was just one more example of just how far apart his and Jemima's worlds were.

CHAPTER 41

TERRY, LIAM AND Sean had slipped into the large Edwardian house unnoticed; in fact, they were in and out in a record time for Terry. The safe was unsophisticated and easy to break into. He had enjoyed swinging the door open dramatically to reveal its contents. Liam had rushed forward, almost pushing Terry out of the way, grabbing at the contents greedily. He found an old cigar box containing some war medals, which he quickly discarded, then picked up three large brown envelopes. The first one Liam opened contained the title deeds to the house and was labelled Clouds Reach. The other two contained, as Liam suspected, the aunts' wills. As Liam scanned them, Terry and Sean watched a satisfied grin spread across his face.

'On the nail, Jemima gets the bloody lot,' he beamed at them.

When they left they jumped jubilantly into the transit van and, once at the end of the road, started celebrating their good luck with cans of lager. Liam, casually holding the steering wheel with one hand and swigging his drink with the other, didn't see Bridget and her two Pekingese dogs walking along the road. Bridget didn't hear the van. She was lost in the music coming from her personal stereo that she had finally got to grips with. She was listening to Mozart as she stepped off the pavement and into the path of the van. As it hit her, she saw a final flash of brilliant blue before everything turned black.

Bridget lay in the road. She knew she had been hit, despite the blackness that surrounded her, and she realised her music had stopped playing. She could faintly hear panicked voices and her two dogs yapping in distress. These noises then gradually faded away along with the blackness. It was replaced with the same blue she had seen moments before the van had hit her; a piercing blue, with the sharpness of crystal, and then she heard his voice, his lazy Texan drawl, calling her name. Somehow, she found herself back on her feet and Drew was in front of her, dressed in his army greens, his hair slicked back and those blue eyes glinting at her.

'Oh my. Drew?' she asked and was greeted with a warm smile.

'Well, don't you look just swell,' he replied, his voice as rich as gingerbread.

'I knew it! I knew you would come back!' she gasped before breaking into a laugh and he laughed too, holding his hands out to her.

'Time to go. The dance is in full swing, can you hear it?'

Bridget listened hard; she could make out the sound of trumpets blasting out some toe-tapping sound, then she recognised it – *Chattanooga Choo Choo* – and she jumped slightly in the air and clasped her hands together. 'My favourite!' she exclaimed and Drew's smile widened.

'They're playing it for you, especially.'

'But I can't go, I'm not dressed for dancing,' she cried and looked down at herself, gasping when she saw she was wearing the red suede shoes she had saved all her clothing rations for – her favourite dancing shoes.

'Everyone is waiting. You coming along now?' he asked patiently, extending his hand further.

'But what about the others? Martha will be so cross.'

'It's your time, Bridget, she will understand,' he replied, as he took her hand.

His fingers were warm and Bridget wrapped hers tightly around them. It felt good to be with him again after all these years – after all this waiting. She was drawn to his bright blue eyes, the colour of forget-me-not petals; his eyes were the reason she let the tiny flowers grow in mad abundance amongst the borders of the garden and she felt all her love for this man fill her up again. She released it, like a balloon, from the tiny space where she'd kept it locked away all this time and she felt as if she could soar through the sky with it. He turned her towards the sound of the music and, as it grew louder, she could see so many lights and the outlines of figures, dancing, swinging each other around, turning quickly then coming together again, limbs moving in sync with the music, everything blending in perfect harmony, with Drew finally by her side.

Liam, Terry and Sean stood silently in front of Lester, who was sitting at his office desk in the breaker's yard. The silence was ominous and felt particularly acute following Liam's earlier frantic explanation about what had happened. Lester stared at them firmly, making them sweat. Terry could see the effect it was having on Liam and Sean, particularly Liam, and he was having none of it – Lester didn't control him this way. Lester had needed him, and Terry had done what was asked, so he wanted his money and to get the hell out. It wasn't his fault that the stupid old woman had just stepped out in front of them.

'Look Les, like Liam said, none of us saw her coming. She just stepped out,' said Terry.

Lester swung his attention to his brother and scowled at him for a moment before turning to Sean. 'What did you see?' he growled.

Sean had seen the old lady look straight at him just before they hit her. He couldn't shake the image of her astonished face from his mind, her eyes wide with terror and her mouth forming a perfect O. 'It's like Liam said. She just stepped out; we couldn't stop in time,' he replied.

'And she is definitely one of the aunts?' Lester asked.

Liam nodded. Having watched them closely for days, he was certain. Plus, she had her dogs with her; annoying little creatures who had yapped and jumped around as he had reversed the van and driven it around Bridget and onto the pavement to get away.

'But we don't actually know if she's alive or dead, or whether she is able to identify any of you?' Lester asked, not hiding his irritation. 'What about the van?' he continued, after a long drawn out sigh.

'I changed the plates before we went down there, swapped them the other day before I crushed that old VW Golf,' Sean informed him.

'Well, at least one of you was thinking straight. You need to get rid of the van. That'll fucking cost you, I needed that van,' he said, turning on Liam. Then he swore and thumped the desk at Liam's idiocy and the others looked on sheepishly.

Brendan had just come out of a meeting and, turning his phone back on, saw Jemima's missed calls. Walking back to his desk he tried listening to her messages, but her signal had obviously been poor and he could hardly make out her voice. He was unsure whether to call her back – there had been no contact between them since he met her in the park a few weeks ago and he wasn't sure he wanted to discuss their divorce in the office, so he decided to call her later when he got home. Just as he made that decision, his phone rang again. Minnie's number flashed up. He stared at it for a moment before answering.

'Brendan, there's been an accident. Jemima is fine, but it's her Aunt Bridget; she's been knocked down. It doesn't look good.'

'What? When?' Brendan asked.

'She needs you, Brendan. Jemima needs you right now,' said Minnie. 'She's at the hospital in Eastbourne. Can you go?'

'Of course,' he replied, grabbing his keys off his desk.

Jemima and Martha sat in the long, soulless corridor of the hospital. They had just been told that, unfortunately, Bridget hadn't made it; she had been unconscious when she arrived at the hospital and, despite the surgeon's efforts to stop the internal bleeding, the damage was irreparable. They'd been assured, at least, that she had passed peacefully.

Jemima held Martha's hand loosely. They both stared straight ahead, at nothing in particular, trying to comprehend the suddenness at which their lives had just been so dramatically altered.

The sound of footsteps on the highly polished floor caught Jemima's attention. It must have been the rhythm of his walk that she recognised. On seeing Brendan taking the corridor in long strides, Jemima rose, letting Martha's hand slip away from hers. When he saw her stand he quickened his pace, his black wool coat floating behind him, and Jemima started to run. She didn't stop until she ran into him. 'She's gone,' she sobbed and felt his grip tighten around her. She wanted to crawl inside him and hide, let him make all this go away.

'I'm so sorry,' he said, speaking into her neck, holding her as tightly as he could.

'I didn't think you would come,' she rasped. He held her face. Some of her hair was stuck to her wet cheeks and he tried to wipe the tears away with his thumbs.

'Of course I'm here,' he whispered and, as if these were the words she was waiting for, her head fell against his chest and started her slow process of grieving.

When Martha, Jemima and Brendan returned to Clouds Reach it felt disjointed, as if all its contents had been moved out of position. With the absence of the dogs and Bridget's fussing, the place seemed uneasily quiet. Brendan helped Jemima upstairs. She insisted on going into Bridget's room, where she cried quietly as she looked at all the photos on Bridget's dresser before settling down on the bed, pulling her knees up to her chest and burying her head into the pillows. Brendan took the tartan blanket off the ottoman and placed it over her, then removed his shoes, loosened his tie and climbed in next to her, holding her tightly as she slept.

When the seagulls started their early morning cries, Brendan slipped downstairs to make some tea. He had slept as poorly as Jemima, having sat virtually upright to hold her securely. Now she was finally resting but he was unable to – he wasn't used to the different noises that came with living by the coast. On his way to the kitchen, he saw Martha sat in an armchair in her study. She was deep in thought and he didn't want to disturb her, so he continued downstairs to the kitchen where he made tea for them both, found some bread to toast and returned to Martha's study.

He carefully placed her tea and toast on the coffee table and picked up the blanket that had slipped from her lap, putting it gently back into place. She jumped as his touch interrupted her thoughts.

'Sorry, I didn't mean to startle you,' he said softly. He sat down in the chair opposite. 'Would you not be more comfortable in bed?' he asked.

'I can't sleep,' she replied.

'No, I don't suppose you can. I'm very sorry about Bridget,' he said earnestly and they both sat in silence for a while. 'I've made you some tea and toast if you fancy it,' he told her and watched as she slowly turned her head towards it. She sighed very heavily then looked back at him.

'I'm sorry, I don't have an appetite.'

'That's okay. Look, Martha, I'm going to arrange to be here for a few days – to help out in any way I can – okay?'

'Jemima needs you,' Martha replied looking him straight in the eye.

'I know,' he replied, looking back at her, not sure how much she was aware of.

She stayed silent and, feeling like he was intruding, he got up to leave.

'Brendan, I apologise. I think I may have judged you rather too harshly and unfairly. I'm sorry,' she said curtly. When he looked back at her, she held his stare for a fraction of a second, before looking away.

Brendan found Jemima holding a black and white photograph of an American serviceman.

'She loved him all her adult life; she never gave up on him. She always believed he would come back for her,' she said, sounding distant.

Brendan smiled, remembering the conversation he had had with Bridget about Drew in the study the first time they had met. Jemima put the photograph back on the dresser and continued to stare at it.

'If you are only here because you are being kind, then I want you to go,' she told him.

Brendan reached for her shoulders and felt her stiffen. 'Jem, you have just lost your aunt, I don't want to leave you.'

She swung around. 'I don't want your pity Brendan. When this is all over, I will sign the papers and you can have your divorce,' she snapped.

'Jem, please, let's not talk about this now,' he replied, gently running his hands down her arms. She pulled them away and her hands flew to her face. He wasn't sure what to do as he watched her shoulders shake with the effort of sobbing and he felt helpless. 'You're still in shock,' he finally managed.

She dropped her hands from her face, exposing her pain. He pulled her close and this time she didn't resist.

'Why does it hurt so much?' she cried.

'You need time to get your head around what's happened.'

'No, not that. You. Why does not having you hurt so much?' she continued. He could feel her ribs through the tightness of his grip. 'It doesn't get any easier, it just gets worse. I still love you,' she choked.

He knew what she meant – it felt almost unnatural to be around her but not with her. This invisible boundary he'd placed between them felt more like it was destroying them both rather than keeping her safe. He pulled her face up towards his, forcing her to look at him. 'I don't care about the papers. I don't care about the divorce,' he told her.

'Don't say this Brendan, not if you don't mean it,' she replied. Her eyes were damp with fresh tears.

'Jem, I love you. I love you so much,' he continued, pushing his mouth onto hers and feeling it give; feeling her lips part and the weight of her body lean into him.

They fell onto the bed clawing at each other's clothes until they were free of them and Jemima could feel his skin pressing against hers. She ran her fingers roughly down his back, feeling every muscle along the way, and then she spread her fingers out across his buttocks and gripped them tightly, digging her nails deeply into them and hearing him cry out. She pulled him towards her, letting him know what she craved and wrapped her legs tightly around his hips. She wanted to pull every part of him into her, as if she could devour him and contain him forever. Spurred on by his groans, she pulled him harder until she could feel sweat running down his back and she pushed her back into the bed, forcing him deeper inside. His breathing was fast and heavy. He pulled her arms up above her head and held them tightly, resting his head against her forehead. Their eyes connected. They both knew what was imminent and it arrived like a tidal wave, carrying them both high on its crest then letting them crash to the shore, gasping for breath as their backs arched, separating them both temporarily. She pulled her arms free, her fingers clawed down his chest leaving long, damning red marks and he cried out as his pleasure was sliced with this pain. He collapsed on top of her and they both lay still for a while before she opened her eyes and saw him staring at her, his face shiny with sweat and his hair damp.

'I can't do this without you,' he said. 'I'm being selfish, but I want you back. I want us back together again. I want it to stop hurting too,' he told her.

⇥⇤

Since Bridget's death, Martha had deliberately kept herself busy by throwing herself into organising the funeral and insisting that the wake be held at Clouds Reach, as well as dealing with the police about the accident. Despite their kind words, she realised that they were unlikely to catch whoever killed Bridget.

There was some issue over the number plate that Mr Rodgers had reported. At eighty-seven, he had to admit that his eyesight was starting to fail, and he could have mistaken the letters and numbers. Whatever the mix-up, the closest the police could find to the number plate was an old VW Golf that, according to the DVLA, had been scrapped and its log book returned to them. Within a couple of days it was clear that their lines of investigation were drying up fast, but Martha had listened carefully and thanked them for their time – even when they brought Bridget's two Pekingese dogs back home.

At Bridget's funeral, Brendan looked around at the small group of mourners huddled in a dark mass against the raw wind. He had his arm firmly around Jemima's waist, feeling like he needed to keep her upright. She had been subdued for a couple of days now, but this morning she had seemed wiped out. He'd ended up dressing her before passing her over to Minnie and Abby to help with her hair and make up. Now, strands of her hair had worked loose in the wind and whipped around her face as she stared blankly into the grave. Martha seemed more together and her attention was fixed firmly upon the vicar, whose melodic words were the only sound to be heard before the boom of a car stereo nudged its way into earshot. Some of the mourners turned towards the car park as three 4x4 vehicles swung into it. The drivers got out, slamming doors and bickering loudly amongst themselves.

Brendan, watched in disbelief, as his dad and brothers headed towards the funeral dressed in black suits, their hair slicked back and their necks held uncomfortably high in buttoned-up shirts and ties. His mother was carrying a large wreath of white carnations spelling out the word *Aunty*. His mouth dropped in horror. He looked at Jemima to see if she had noticed. She seemed unaware but Martha had been paying attention and she looked on, bemused, by this group of strangers. *What the bloody hell were they playing at?* he wondered and ignored them until the end of the service, when he then marched over to them.

'What are you lot doing here?' he snapped, looking aghast at the wreath Lyla was brandishing proudly.

'We've come to pay our respects,' his mother replied lightly, smiling pointedly at the other mourners.

'You didn't even know her aunt,' he said.

'She's Jemima's aunt and Jemima is family,' his mother replied sternly, then pushed past him and strode over to where Jemima and Martha were standing.

'Jesus,' Brendan mumbled, and turned to look at the others staring blankly back at him. His father looked him up and down before lighting a cigarette. Brendan shook his head and turned away from them. He headed back to Jemima and Martha, hoping to limit the damage his mother was about to cause.

'We are so sorry we were all late, but Brendan's directions were hopeless,' Lyla lied, grabbing Jemima's hand and looking at her wistfully.

Martha was stupefied. Brendan watched as her eyes dropped to the ostentatious wreath planted by Lyla's feet.

'Oh, God, how rude. Where do you want this? I'm gutted we missed the hearse with it. I thought it would look great next to the coffin,' gasped Lyla.

'That's very kind of you. Perhaps if you leave it by the grave to be sorted out with the other flowers...' Martha suggested.

'Of course, Martha. Last thing you need is all this fuss, all this bloody pomp and ceremony at a time like this,' said Lyla sweeping her hand around the graveyard, taking in the Cavendish family plot, with its large ivy-covered tombs containing Martha's relatives.

Martha raised an eyebrow and excused herself. Jemima followed and Brendan shot his mother a warning look.

Back at Clouds Reach, the house fell under the spell of hushed voices and the delicate clinking of bone china. Martha slowly made her way around the mourners, while Brendan stayed close to Jemima, his hand held against her back as if he was ready to catch her at any moment. He was painfully aware of his family, rooted in the corner, eating their way through the finger sandwiches and making serious inroads into the sherry. He was trying to ignore them and, instead, attempted to focus on Bridget's friends who were offering their condolences to Jemima.

Mrs Pickard brought out another platter of sandwiches and pushed roughly through the O'Rourkes to get to the table. She tutted at them, refusing to be intimidated by their dirty looks. While the O'Rourkes tucked in greedily, Sean made his way over to Brendan and Jemima.

'You weren't invited to the wake, so what are you all doing here?' Brendan hissed.

'Mum said we should come; that it was the right thing to do,' Sean replied. Brendan scowled in their direction. Ignoring

Brendan's hostility, Sean forged on. 'I'm sorry about your aunt. Did she go peacefully?'

Jemima looked at him, and stared blankly.

Brendan answered for her. 'She was unconscious when she got to the hospital. They don't think she felt anything.'

Sean looked down at the tea plate he was carrying, which looked undersized in his giant hands. 'Well that's something then,' he said, remorsefully. When he looked up, his face was more resolved. 'I'm sorry. I'm really sorry for your loss,' he said directly to Jemima.

Jemima stared at him for a moment then rubbed her forehead. 'I need to go and lie down,' she said.

'I've got her, you stay,' Minnie told Brendan, glancing over to his family, who were starting to look restless.

He saw Lyla approach Martha again and watched as she tried clumsily to do everything properly, but her skirt was too short, her heels too high and her voice too loud – the whole effect grated on him. He turned to his father who was standing at Lyla's side, ignoring his overzealous wife; instead, Lester's greedy eyes were working their way around the room, eyeing all the possessions it held.

Brendan wanted to throw them out, make it clear that they didn't belong at a place like Clouds Reach, that they weren't good enough to be there or amongst the friends of Bridget and Martha.

'They murder Joe and throw him in a makeshift grave to rot and yet they make all this fuss over someone they never even knew. It's twisted,' he whispered fiercely to Sean who looked at him carefully, choosing not to comment. 'They make me fucking sick,' he hissed and headed for the kitchen, where he knew Mrs Pickard kept her brandy.

He let the drink glug heartily into the glass, raised it and downed it, feeling it hit his throat then burn all the way down to his stomach. He refilled his glass and walked over to the kitchen window, lit a cigarette and blew the smoke slowly from his mouth. Cassie was standing on the lawn looking about her, slowly turning around in full circles, over and over again.

'What the fuck?' he wondered aloud.

'There she is!' gasped Riley, coming up behind him. 'She hates being inside for too long,' he said, as if this explained her unusual behaviour. They both stared at her for a short while. She looked as if she was trying to figure something out. As she swivelled towards the back of the house, her face lit up then fell with confusion.

'It's good to see you and Jemima back together,' he told Brendan. 'It didn't seem right when you told us you'd split.'

Brendan took a sip of his brandy then turned to Riley. Riley wore the same look he had as a small boy when he had broken something and was building up courage to tell someone. 'What are you not telling me Riley?'

'Not here,' Riley muttered. 'I can't tell you here.'

'What?' Brendan asked firmly.

'Not with them around,' Riley whispered and headed out of the back door and into the garden to fetch Cassie. Brendan watched as he gently guided her off the lawn, being careful not to touch her or raise any suspicions as to his real feelings for her.

As they disappeared out of view, Brendan downed the rest of his drink and resigned himself to going to save Martha.

Lyla's 'Oi' grabbed his attention as soon as he appeared; she waved an arm high in the air and called him over to her. He could see Martha's patience wearing thin.

'We're off now,' said Lyla.

'Good,' he said flatly.

Lyla looked annoyed and went to say something but Martha skilfully cut in. 'Well, thank you for coming,' she said, gesturing towards to the door.

Lyla deliberately ignored the gesture and turned back to Brendan. 'You coming down this weekend? You could bring Martha and Jemima. I'll do a big roast. Jem is looking like she needs feeding up – she's very gaunt, Brendan,' she chastised.

'We'll see. We still have a lot to sort out,' he replied curtly and Lyla flashed him a broad, but brittle smile.

'Of course, so much to do at a time like this,' she agreed, with her smile clamped firmly across her face.

CHAPTER 42

RILEY SAT IN Brendan's apartment and opened the conversation with how bad things had become between Cassie and Liam since her sister had visited. Liam had become more temperamental with her and Riley had seen the bruising on her arms and body; he knew how vicious Liam could be and Cassie's refusal to admit the situation distressed him.

'I have to get her out of there,' Riley said. 'She can't bear to be with him knowing what he did to her brother.'

'If it's money you need – to get away – then just say,' Brendan responded.

Riley's smile was resigned. 'It won't stop him though. Like you said before, he'll never let her go.'

'What are you going to do then?'

'He needs to be put away. To go to prison for what he did to Joe. That's the only chance we have.'

'Riley, think about this. It wasn't just Liam who was there – Sean was there, I was there. We are all implicated. Liam would just deny it, then the finger could be pointed at any of us, and given how they all feel about me, it will most likely point my way.' He watched

Riley study his hands, studiously rolling his thumbs together. 'If this got out, even if I didn't take the rap for it, I could still end up losing my job; this sort of stuff always makes the headlines. And Jemima can't know. Things have been hard enough for us as it is, we would never survive it – I'd lose everything. I'm sorry Riley. I can't help you with this,' he finished, looking down at his own hands.

'You owe her,' Riley replied bluntly.

Brendan closed his eyes and breathed deeply. 'I can't do it. I can't grass Liam up over Joe,' he fiercely replied.

'It's not just Joe he's killed,' said Riley slowly.

'Yeah, I know he was behind Cassie's brother's murder but that will be impossible to prove – you know that. You know Cassie's family will never go to the police.'

Riley fell silent again. He continued to look uneasily at Brendan, and Brendan studied him, sensing Riley's unsaid words bubbling away just beneath the surface.

'He's killed someone else?' Brendan asked cautiously. 'Who?'

'He was driving the van that hit Jemima's aunt.'

'He killed Bridget?'

Riley nodded.

'What was he doing down there?' Brendan asked and saw Riley tense with the enormity of what he had been keeping from him.

'They've got a plan. To kill Jemima's aunts so she will inherit everything and then they will blackmail the money from you both.'

'What?' Brendan exclaimed in disbelief. He sat motionless while he listened to Riley pour out the plans his father and brothers had made to kill Jemima's aunts, in order for Jemima to inherit their estate, and to blackmail it from her and Brendan, using Joe's death as the collateral to coerce Brendan. They knew that Brendan would never want Jemima to know the part he'd played in Joe's murder. They had figured it out early, how much she meant to him, and this was their leverage. Joe's death hadn't just been about Lester taking his land to expand the business, it had also been a way of getting Brendan back so they could bury him up to his neck in their antics and find out more about Jemima's situation.

Brendan heard how they had agreed to Kelly staying with him and Jemima, so that she could hide the murder weapon somewhere in his apartment and get the aunts' address for them – the fact that Liam had been the one to drop the hammer off and take her aunts' details didn't surprise him. He listened patiently while Riley explained his family's cover, their version being that Brendan had only married Jemima for her money, that his real affections still lay with Cassie and that they were having an affair, which is why Brendan had killed Joe – he had found out and threatened to tell Jemima. Cassie would testify to this; Liam had beaten her until she had agreed. Brendan and Jemima had witnessed the start of the fight that afternoon a couple of months back in the yard, when Riley and Sean had intervened. As far as his family were concerned, Brendan had bought the land off Joe and Joe had moved to Spain. They hadn't heard from him but, then, that was Joe – kept himself to himself. They believed that Brendan giving them Joe's land was just an act of his generosity; after all he was their fatted calf.

Then came the piece that was the final twist of the knife – if he didn't concede, they planned to dispose of Jemima. That way he would inherit the whole estate. They would make sure he was put away for the murder of Jemima, her aunts and Joe, unless he agreed to hand over everything. Again, they would use his affair with Cassie to provide the motive for Jemima's murder. After all, he wasn't happily married; he'd applied for a divorce and the fact that the papers remained unsigned showed she wasn't prepared to grant him one. Finally, Brendan breathed in deeply and ran his hands over his head.

'Bastards!' he exclaimed and then looked back at Riley. 'How do they plan to kill Martha?' he asked.

'Make it look like an armed burglary gone wrong, that somehow she disturbs them.'

Brendan leaned back. He stretched his arms out across the top of the sofa and let his head fall backwards as if to release the weight of what he had just been told. He thought of Martha alone in that large house, proudly going about her business. Then he thought of the guns in the loft at Lowlands and his mother's half-truth about what they were doing there. Up until now he had felt dulled by what Riley had told him. He had mechanically sat and listened, cataloguing Riley's words and systematically sorting through the information that was about to destroy his and Jemima's lives. He had held onto his panic when he heard of their plans to kill her, locked it away while he forced himself to absorb every detail, in order to somehow help keep her safe. But now, knowing his mother's involvement, knowing every calm question she had enquired of Jemima had been calculated, knowing that every smile covered up their deceit, he could barely contain his anger. He thought of the grotesque, oversized wreath she had taken to the funeral and how she had brazenly flaunted her self- importance. What he felt towards her ripped through him. Out of all of them, how could his own mother have betrayed him like this? The others he understood – he knew Sean's motive would be revenge for Tess, Liam's was jealousy, Anne-Marie loved the drama and Kelly was fickle; she'd bend towards the brightest light to suit her own ends. Lester, however, was driven by resentment for Brendan, the younger, brighter and more successful son, who served as a reminder that his control over his children was more fragile than he dared admit – after all, Brendan had broken away, become his own man – and the fact that Brendan looked so much like his father highlighted Lester's own fading youth and physical prowess. But what reasons did his mother have for stitching him up?

Brendan suddenly realised that the idea of sending Liam to prison now seemed a much more attractive option. 'Shit, they have thought through everything. What's their next move?' he asked.

'I think they are still planning to go ahead with the burglary.'

Brendan breathed out heavily. 'We have to let it happen, it's the only way we can stop them. We have to make sure they are caught, before anything happens to Martha, otherwise they will just turn it around to make out it was me. They have me completely screwed.'

Sean had started to get a bad feeling about the whole business that Liam and his father had planned. He couldn't put his finger on it but it nagged at him like a bellyache, nauseating and relentless, not allowing him to settle. The image of the aunt's face, the way she had looked straight into his eyes and the sickening thud of her body as it hit the front of the van still haunted him.

He was also mulling over Brendan's words about Tess – that she would take him back – but he never came to a reasonable conclusion as to why. Up until he had bumped into her in the supermarket that time with Brendan, he hadn't even wanted her back. Why would he? He couldn't trust her. However, now that he felt so unsettled, he found himself wanting to be with her again; that it was now or never, that his chances were fast running out.

Sat in his truck, Sean watched Tess across the road inside her house, turning lights on and drawing the curtains. She was oblivious to the fact that he was watching her, hidden away with just his cigarettes and thoughts for company.

Later on, Tess climbed out of the bath, quickly dried herself, grabbed her robe and, while tying it, checked on Georgie, who was sound asleep. All traces of his impish face were gone and, instead, he lay there looking blissfully angelic, with his full lips pulled into a pout, his rosy cheeks and blond hair. She thought he looked just like his father when he slept, then told herself that looks can be deceiving. She kissed him gently on the cheek and headed downstairs.

When she flicked the light on in the kitchen, she was greeted by a large figure leaning against her kitchen counter. She gasped, throwing her hands up to her mouth, her heart almost bursting out of her chest, before she realised it was Sean. 'Jesus Christ, Sean!' she shouted, her eyes wide with shock.

'You should keep your back door locked. Anyone could walk in.'

'Clearly,' she replied curtly and started to fill the kettle.

'Georgie's in bed asleep,' she said, trying to figure out what Sean was doing here.

'I didn't come to see him. I came to see you,' he told her, flatly.

She sighed and switched the kettle on. 'I don't want to fight Sean. I'm tired and I've had a hard day at work.'

'I don't want to fight either,' he replied.

She watched him cross the kitchen to her. The usual hardness was gone from his face and he smiled affectionately as he leaned towards her. When he got a few inches from her face, she realised his intention and pulled back, turning her face away from him. 'I don't think this is a good idea Sean. We're not together any more. You divorced me, remember?' she said and waited apprehensively for his reaction.

To her surprise, he gently tucked some of her loose curls behind her ear and rested his hand lightly on the back of her neck. 'I made a mistake,' he whispered, leaning forward again, reaching for her lips.

The slap was hard and it stung furiously. He rubbed his jaw and could see her rage ready to spill. 'After everything you put me and Georgie through these past years, how dare you stand there and tell me you made a mistake,' she spat, raising her hand to slap him again, but he caught her wrist and gripped it so hard he could feel her pulse jamming into the palm of his hand. 'Get out!' she screamed through gritted teeth, her eyes narrowed like a cat's, ready to attack.

'No,' he told her firmly and kissed her. She clawed his face with one hand while shoving his shoulder hard with her other one in an attempt to push him away, but she felt him tightening his grip around her waist. He grabbed her hand, yanking it from his face, but she quickly swapped hands, digging her nails into his cheek and watching him wince before he pulled it away. Forcefully, he held her hands firmly together behind her back and her wrist bones ground painfully against each other. With her hands momentarily out of his way, he secured both his arms around the tops of her thighs and lifted her high into the air. She pushed against him, managing to free her hands, which enabled her to claw his face again but, undeterred, he swung her around to the kitchen table, placed her down heavily, then pushed himself between her legs, forcing them apart and wedging them open with his thighs. Tess's breath was ragged from fighting him off and despite her efforts she could feel him overpowering her. Her fists were curled and hammered at his chest; she started to cry and told him to stop. But, instead, he grabbed her chin with one hand and firmly held the back of her head with the other, smothering her lips with his, feeling the outline of her teeth through them from the pressure he was applying. He could feel her trembling and he knew that if he got her past this point then he wouldn't be going home that night. He tightened his grip, spreading his hand wide to encompass the side of her face as he breathed her in, deeply, filling his chest with her scent.

Gradually he felt her soften. Her lips parted and the warmth of her mouth overwhelmed him, her tongue touching his. He slid his hand down her shoulder and ran it down the side of her body; she moved closer to him in response. Pushing her robe away he ran his hand along her thigh, then let his fingers run back up the inside of it, his touch just grazing her soft skin. Pulling open her robe, he looked down at her as he cupped her breast and felt her back arch in response. He saw her expression change; her eyes glowed with an appetite for him that he recognised from long ago. He felt her reach for him, her hand remembering how to hold him. He had got his family back. Brendan had been right all along.

Lying in bed, Tess stretched out and rested her head on Sean's chest. His arm cradled her back and his fingers moved slowly in small circles at the base of her spine. She was shocked by her capricious behaviour and the speed at which the events had happened. She could still taste him on the tip of her tongue, feel his mouth on her skin. Where had all the anger and bitterness of the past seven years gone? She thought she hated him and that he despised her, that what they were left with, aside from Georgie, was irreparable. And now this; whatever had just happened had felt so right between them. She ran her hand down his torso, slowly letting her fingers trace the outline of the tattoo on his sternum then follow the lines of the black snake curling around a dagger. She let her fingers glide over his stomach muscles and find the soft blond hair that ran downwards from his belly button. As her hand ventured lower he groaned and she felt his thighs tighten. She felt powerful lying here in his arms, knowing the effect she could have on him. Earlier, when his breath had caught in his throat and he had shuddered before calling her name, it had pleased her that she could affect this huge man in this way. In a moment of bravery, she smiled at him, tilting her head so her abundant strawberry-blonde curls fell away from her face.

'Am I forgiven then?' she asked, playfully.

He looked at her coldly, as the power shifted between them. Tess sharply pulled her hand back up his body and her own body tensed, anticipating the fallout from her question.

'No,' he replied flatly, and watched her shrink away from him. Her mind raced through all the possibilities as to why he was here and, just as she was settling on this being a further demonstration of his cruelty, he spoke. 'But I think I can learn to live with it.'

Jemima was surprised to see Riley when she got home. She smiled kindly at him but when she saw Brendan's face it stopped her in her tracks.

'What's up?' she asked nervously. Brendan came over to her, and took both of her hands in his. 'What's happened?' she asked.

'You know I love you,' he told her. 'You know I would never hurt you,' he continued.

Jemima closed her eyes. 'Oh God, what now?' she gasped and looked up at him, trying to ascertain from his expression how bad the news was going to be. She fell silent and let him talk.

He started with Joe's death, knowing that he was out of time now; he had to tell her everything in order to keep her alive. When he finished, she sat there staring at him, as if she hadn't heard a word. His jaw twitched nervously and the silence in the room engulfed them as she sat perfectly still, as if she was suspended in time. 'Jem, I'm so sorry,' he whispered, trying to reach out to her.

'Liam killed my aunt,' she stated flatly. 'He has to be punished. We have to go to the police.'

'We can't Jem, not yet. They will make out all of this was me,' he replied.

'But Martha is in danger – we all are.'

'I'm not going to let anyone come to any harm, I promise,' he told her forcefully, and watched her face fall before hardening again as she turned on him.

'You're already too late Brendan. If you'd told me about Joe then none of this would have happened. Your family would have had no hold on you. I begged you, Brendan, to tell me everything. I asked you over and over and you promised me you would. This is what happens when you keep secrets. This bloody mess is all your fault!' she screamed.

⊷⊨⊚ ⊚⊨⊷

'How can we trust Riley?' Jemima asked, switching on the bedside light.

'Uh?' replied Brendan. He was acutely aware that he and Jemima couldn't sleep. They had laid next to each other for a couple of hours now, not speaking, their breathing not slowing and their minds turning over and over what Riley had told them. He had anticipated more questions from her but not this one. 'What do you mean?'

'How do we know this isn't just some plan of his and Cassie's for us to help them get away from Lowlands?'

'What?'

'So, how do you know we can trust him?' she whispered, so as to not wake Riley sleeping in the next room.

'I trust him Jem, okay?' he replied, rubbing his hands over his face.

'Well I don't. I don't trust any of them. Actually, Brendan, we don't know who we can trust,' she told him, jumping out of bed and going over to their wardrobes. As she slid one of the doors open, Brendan pulled himself up in bed.

'What are you doing?' he asked in a loud whisper.

'Trying to find that hammer. How can you sleep knowing it's here?' she retorted, sharply.

'We'll call Kelly in the morning; she'll have some idea where he put it,' he answered, climbing out of bed and joining her.

'Oh, and we can trust her can we? She gave Liam my aunts' address! She led him right to their doorstep.' She stopped abruptly and, hearing her voice break, he folded his arms around her and rested his head gently on top of hers. He could feel her shoulders shudder; her grief was still raw. She pulled away from him and glared at his chest. 'And you can get rid of that,' she said, pointing to the ring of rooks on his chest.

Chapter 43

Martha listened patiently while Brendan told her about his family's plans and how, unfortunately, Bridget had already fallen victim to them. She gave little away, forcing him to continue, blindly, spilling out the ugly truth.

'You have to believe me, I don't care about Jemima's money. I appreciate that it's been in your family for generations and that, for Jemima, all of this holds great sentimentality, but I don't want a penny of it. I would gladly hand it all over to them to keep her safe,' he finished, looking at Jemima.

'And to keep yourself out of jail,' Martha replied coldly.

He looked back at her, stung by her tone. 'Yes, Martha, perhaps you didn't judge me so harshly after all,' he said.

She considered this remark for a while, watching him carefully. 'You are not responsible for your family. If you ever need an answer as to why you broke away from them, then this is it,' she told him and breathed in sharply. 'So, what is the plan? You must have a plan? Surely you don't intend to let them get away with this?' she asked, looking keenly at them both.

Lester was watching Riley from his office in the breaker's yard. Sean was sat on top of a low filing cabinet, with one of his legs swinging freely, nonchalantly smoking a cigarette. His thoughts had settled on the night he had just spent with Tess and the delight on Georgie's face when he had come into her room in the morning and found them together.

'Get him in here!' barked Lester to Sean and, slowly, Sean got up, leaned out of the office door and whistled sharply at Riley. Riley's head shot up; he was reversing an old Vauxhall which had no windscreen or doors. He jammed it into a small space then climbed out. Sean waved for him to come and join them, resumed his seat on the filing cabinet, stubbed out his cigarette and lit up another.

Riley walked anxiously over to the office; he rested a hand on the door frame and stuck his head in. 'What's up?' he asked lightly.

'Where were you last night?' Lester asked, accusingly.

'Out.' Riley answered.

'Who with?'

'Few of me mates.' he ventured.

'Liam never saw you last night and we was just wondering where you got to. D'you see him, Sean?'

Sean stared closely at Riley; he was working out how to answer. He didn't want them knowing about him and Tess. 'No,' said Sean finally.

'Your mum says your bed weren't slept in.'

Riley felt himself redden. 'Yeah, well, I met someone early on, went back to hers. Ain't a crime is it?' he replied defensively, hoping they hadn't found out he had been with Brendan and Jemima. Fortunately, Lester quickly lost interest and, telling Riley to come in and shut the door, got down to the real matter at hand.

Brendan and Jemima had just got home from visiting her aunt when his mobile rang.

'Riley,' he said, taking the call and catching Jemima's eye.

'It's happening a week on Thursday, in the evening. They want me to drive the car,' Riley blurted out.

'Shit, you can't Riley – you'll end up getting caught as well.'

While he was on the call their intercom buzzed. Kelly and Matt had come over, just as Brendan had asked them to. Jemima buzzed them in.

'What did Riley want?' Jemima asked as Brendan finished his call.

Brendan stared at her. She looked tired – there were dark circles around her eyes and he felt fearful of breaking the news to her.

'They're planning on next Thursday evening,' he said.

'Oh,' she replied delicately, then went to let Matt and Kelly in.

As Kelly petulantly breezed in, her irritation at being asked to come over was on full display. Jemima watched Brendan bristle as she flung herself onto the sofa.

'Where's the hammer, Kelly?' he asked her bluntly. She threw him a dirty look and shrugged.

'What are you talking about?' she replied.

He reached down and grabbed the fake fur collar of her coat and pulled her up to her feet so she was just inches from his face.

'When you were staying here, Liam dropped a package off; it was the hammer he used to beat our uncle's head in with.' He let her go, watching as she fell back onto the sofa, her face twisted with shock.

'Brendan,' Matt tried to intervene, raising his hand to him to calm down.

'I didn't know,' she replied weakly.

'What did he do with it?'

'He came in with a bag of stuff and asked me if I knew where he could hide something. I thought it was a gun, something to do with Terry, you know, like the stuff he gives Dad,' she broke off and looked at Matt, realising this was the first time he would be hearing this about her family.

'What did he do with it Kelly?' Brendan asked her firmly.

'I'd been looking through Jemima's clothes while she was out, so I suggested her wardrobe,' she replied, glancing guiltily at Jemima.

Brendan marched into their bedroom and slid open Jemima's wardrobe door; they had gone through this last night and had not found anything. Reaching around further, his hands patting every surface, he bent down, roughly shoving Jemima's shoes out of the way and patting the back of the wardrobe floor, going right into the corner. He felt something gritty. He drew his hand back to take a look. The tips of his fingers were covered with dust. Crawling into the space, he could just make out a patch of the stud wall that had been crudely cut away then plastered over. The wall concealed a gap between the bedroom and the bathroom which housed the internal plumbing. He grabbed one of Jemima's shoes and started hammering the heel into the back of her wardrobe. The plastered square of stud wall collapsed. Pushing it aside, he shoved his arm into the hole until he didn't think it could stretch any further, and felt around blindly, until his fingertips fell upon some rough material. He pushed himself further, his fingers feeling the outline of something solid wrapped in cloth. He grabbed at the bundle until he had enough material in his grasp to pull it out of the hole. Once he saw it he didn't need to unwrap it to know what it was but, tentatively, he peeled the material away to reveal the hammer with Joe's dried blood on the handle and head. He cradled it in his hands, staring with horror at his discovery. Up until now, he had been dealing with Riley's words; now, holding the hammer, he was dealing with evidence. Everything was now more certain, more concrete – this was really going to happen. He wrapped it quickly and went back to the living room.

'Well, he'd certainly gone to a lot of trouble to hide this Kelly. Are you really telling me you knew nothing about it?' he barked.

She looked away shamefully.

He held the hammer in front of her face. 'You take this back with you. You go to the outbuilding and you hide it there, put it inside one of the old desk drawers – but you need to let me know which one, okay?'

She shook her head. 'I can't,' she told him.

Brendan looked aghast. 'You little bitch! Jemima's aunt is dead because you let Liam know where they lived, and if you don't want her other aunt's death on your conscience you'll do what you're fucking told!'

'I didn't know about any of this, I didn't know it was the hammer, and I didn't know why Liam wanted her aunts' address. I'm sorry Jemima, I didn't ask, I just did what I was told, like you do when you are with them; Brendan, like we all do!' she shouted back at him. 'I'm scared. What if they find me?' she continued, fearfully.

Brendan stared at her, her words ringing in his ears. She was right – he did do exactly as he was told when he was around them. They all did. Refusal wasn't an option, but the hold his family had over everyone was never going to be broken through compliance.

'Kelly, this is your chance to get away, to be with Matt whenever you want. Live up here, do all the things you want to. It can happen, but you need to help me. If you don't, and I end up going to prison for murders I didn't commit, then it will be impossible for you to break away from them and there will be no more you and Matt.'

Kelly looked past Brendan to Matt, who nodded reassuringly.

'It's all I've ever known,' she said, the pitch of her voice rising with panic.

'It's all I had ever known once too,' he replied.

Riley was in the breaker's yard when Brendan called him. Taking the call, he turned his back on the others and tucked himself behind a stack of rusting cars.

'Right, you travel down with them,' Brendan said. 'Once they have left the car, you go to the end of the road, where I will be waiting for you. Then I'll call the police, let them know the break-in is taking place.'

'Okay, but why am I there with you?'

'I've asked you to stay at Martha's, to make her house more secure now she is on her own. I'll drop some stuff off so it looks like you have already started. Okay?'

'Okay,' replied Riley, carefully watching his brothers from between a crack in the vehicles.

'Tell Cassie she needs to be ready, and to bring only the stuff she can manage. She is leaving with Kelly. My mate will pick them up at the end of the driveway. Kelly's got the details, okay? Riley, if she won't leave then, Kelly will go without her; she needs to know that this is her only chance.'

'She knows that.'

'Good. So next Thursday then,' Brendan finished.

Just as Brendan was starting to feel more confident that the plans he and Riley had worked out were watertight, his mother called inviting him and Jemima for the weekend. She wanted to throw a family dinner to celebrate him and Jemima getting back together.

'I don't know Mum, Jem doesn't like much fuss,' he tried to explain.

'Brendan, what fuss? It's only dinner. But if you have other plans...' she tailed off.

He thought of what his other plans were. He didn't want them to get suspicious and his refusal would only antagonise them. So, keen to keep everything on an even keel, he agreed to the visit.

At first Jemima had resisted, nervous about facing them, but as he tried to convince her, an idea of her own started to grow. His family had their plans, he and Riley had made theirs, but she also felt like she needed to make some. She needed to protect her family – it wasn't just about his anymore.

→══◎ ◎══←

'Just carry on as if nothing has changed; we don't know anything, okay?' Brendan said as they climbed out of his car. He handed her his keys and kissed her forehead before turning to join his brothers. She watched them all disappear through the woods before she set off to find Cassie.

She found Cassie tucked round the back of Lowlands, hanging out washing. She appeared to be unaffected by the cold wind which was causing the sheets to flap around her. Jemima spotted her wellington-booted feet first, stretching up to tiptoe as she tugged the washing line towards her to attach another sheet. She noticed Cassie's red, chapped fingers but these didn't appear to bother her and she sang a happy-sounding verse which was unfamiliar to Jemima. 'Hi,' said Jemima and the singing and tugging stopped. Cassie remained on her tip toes, her fingers clasped between the top of a sheet and a peg.

'I'm glad I've found you. I wanted us to have a chance to talk,' Jemima continued.

Cassie finished pegging the sheet and peered at Jemima through a gap in the washing.

'There always seems to be an atmosphere between us and I would like things to change. I would like to think we could get on better; after all, neither of us want to be here,' she said. Cassie eyed her suspiciously.

'I know it can't have been easy for you, me coming here, seeing us together.' Jemima was stumbling. Cassie folded her arms and stared at Jemima. 'It may surprise you, but it hasn't been easy for me either,' she continued. 'You've had a huge impact on Brendan. He may not let you see it, but what happened between you both has affected him deeply.'

Cassie looked puzzled and, seeing she had her interest, Jemima ploughed on. 'I was so sorry to hear about your brother. But, I hate to admit it, I was also jealous. Brendan was so determined to help you with your sister, to put things right. I don't think he'll ever settle until he feels he has done that for you Cassie.'

Cassie looked away and they stood in silence while Jemima figured out which way to steer the discussion.

'I need to know how you feel about him,' Jemima asked furtively.

'It's you he married,' Cassie replied.

Jemima smiled slowly. 'I'm not sure what that really means – being married.' Cassie's face softened, she understood what it was like to believe in something but have it turn out differently. 'I thought I loved him, but I know what it is meant to feel like now,' she said.

'Riley?' Jemima whispered and Cassie nodded sharply before reaching down to grab another sheet to hang on the line.

Jemima watched her for a while. 'Would you do something for me?' Jemima asked.

Cassie straightened up and looked at her curiously.

'But please don't tell anyone – no one can know but us. Can I trust you?'

Later that day Cassie went up to Jemima and Brendan's room carrying a freshly laundered bale of towels. When Cassie came in, both women stared at each other momentarily before Jemima slid off the bed and went over to her.

'Yours are the top two,' Cassie told her and Jemima glanced at them nervously before carefully taking two towels from the top of the pile. She could feel the heavy weight of the handgun wedged between them.

'Thank you,' replied Jemima seeing Cassie's eyes soften.

'It's loaded, be careful,' Cassie warned.

Jemima looked back at the young woman and realised that Cassie had risked everything for her; if she had been caught in the loft getting the gun then she didn't even want to think about what the O'Rourkes would have done. She felt foolish now for being threatened by her, for envying the guilt Brendan harboured about their relationship, and for brooding about Cassie being there before her – knowing him in a different time, and a different way.

'I really appreciate this,' Jemima said, her choice of words seeming inadequate. She felt indebted to her now.

Cassie smiled. 'Things will be different from now on,' she assured her.

CHAPTER 44

WHEN THURSDAY CAME, Liam got the guns ready. He loved how they felt and liked the way they caused the adrenaline to pump around his body, making him feel wired. He laid the guns out on his kitchen table – three handguns and a sawn-off shotgun. He lifted each of them in turn, enjoying their weight, letting them bounce gently in his grasp and holding them out in front of him, locking his arm and taking imaginary shots at imaginary targets.

Sean spent the day quietly, picking Georgie up from school and eating a supper of boiled eggs with him. When Tess got in, he made sure Georgie was settled in front of the television and took her to bed. After they had made love she lay next to him, naked, with flushed cheeks and tousled hair. He smiled lazily at her; he loved how she glowed. If anything went wrong, this was exactly as he wanted to remember her.

Riley had spent the day nervously scurrying around and trying to keep his head low. He had quickly grabbed a handful of stuff together before his mother had bellowed up the stairs for him to run yet another errand. When his path crossed with Cassie's he had shot her meaningful looks, and as the time approached he had grabbed her, pulling her deftly into the outbuilding and stuffing his bag into her arms.

'You ready?'

She nodded. 'Is this really going to be it?' she asked.

'Yeah, but there's something I need you to fetch for me – I haven't been able get to my room all day. In my chest of drawers there's a small box. Get that, and at the back there's a roll of money. We need it Cass, then we're free."

Kelly slouched around her room. She had sent Matt several messages and each one he had replied to, confirming that he would be waiting at the end of the driveway for her. Then she let Brendan know where she had hidden the hammer.

Every noise in Lowlands made Cassie jump; so much so that, after she had dropped another pan, Lyla had shouted at her to leave the washing up and go vacuum the stairs and landings. She'd dragged the vacuum behind her, letting it bump up the stairs, and purposefully plugged it in inside Riley's room. Hurrying over to his chest of drawers, she had just got her hands on the handle when Anne-Marie walked in on her.

'What you doing in here?' she barked. Cassie froze, her heart pounding against her ribs. Anne-Marie looked about her, wrinkling her nose with disgust at the sight of Riley's unmade bed and clothes strewn on the floor. 'If you're looking for washing, my basket is full,' she announced and waited for Cassie to leave his room and obediently take up her instruction.

When the O'Rourkes sat down to dinner it was quieter than usual. Even the dogs seemed subdued. Lyla looked around at her family, then at Lester who glanced in her direction. She smiled at him, radiating with pride. She still loved knowing he was hers, even after all these years and all his indiscretions. She looked back at her family, all tucking into their dinners, and she realised that everything in this room defined who she was. Well, nearly everything; and that would soon be corrected. She would have Brendan back, for good this time, and everything would then be complete. Her pride and joy who had brought this great opportunity to them – she knew he could never leave her for good.

Lester, Liam, Sean and Riley piled into the getaway car. Sean had selected it from the yard, made sure it was reliable and had given it a respray, new plates and a change of chassis number.

After Lester and the brothers had left, Kelly and Cassie sneaked out of Lowlands. Kelly shut the back door quietly and then urged Cassie to start running. When they got halfway down the drive, Kelly stopped to readjust her large bag. Cassie stopped with her; she was travelling much lighter and there was little she had wanted to take with her from Lowlands. What she carried was mostly Riley's things. Both girls looked for a moment at the ramshackle Victorian house; it was all Kelly had ever known and it was the place where Cassie had stayed the longest.

Brendan sat in his car, parked discreetly between two others, just up from the corner of Martha's road. Earlier, Martha had appeared her usual collected self and Brendan had spent the day trying to appear confident for everyone else's sake. He wouldn't allow himself to think about what could go wrong. From his rear-view mirror he watched the car turn into the road and caught a glimpse of his father and brothers. Brendan checked his watch for what seemed like the tenth time that evening and forced himself to wait patiently.

Riley pulled the car up outside Clouds Reach, as Liam had instructed him to. The car fell silent and Lester looked out of the window at the large Edwardian house. He stared at the warm glow seeping through the edges of the heavily-draped windows and smiled. The old house just stood there, unaware of the events that were about to unfold within.

He felt himself shiver with excitement. Aside from the greed that pushed Lester along in life, this for him was also sport, a cruel game where he made up the rules as he went along. It was in moments like this that he felt most powerful and he wanted to savour this moment, this euphoric high; he felt so pumped up he wanted to roar. Instead, containing himself, he slowly turned to his sons who were all watching him, expectantly.

'Let's go,' he instructed them, pulling down his ski mask. The car doors flew open and the pack was released.

Martha was sat patiently in her study. She heard shattering glass and steadily took a sip of sherry, placing the schooner back on her desk and smoothing out the document lying in front of her. She had obediently followed Brendan's instructions, but she had some plans of her own that she was very much looking forward to putting into practice. Bridget's two beloved Pekingese dogs started to yap. Martha had locked them away in her bedroom to keep them safe. She had openly despised them when Bridget was alive but, since her death, she had taken great comfort in their funny little ways; they were the last link she had to her sister and she had allowed herself to become quite fond of them. After a few moments, their barks were drowned out by the sound of heavy footsteps.

Liam could see the light from Martha's study. He gestured to the others to fall back behind him as he inched over to the room and peered through the gap between the door and its frame. He saw Martha with her head down, studying some papers. He looked back to the others and gestured that they had found what they were looking for. At this signal, Lester boldly stepped forward, pushed the study door wide open and walked into the room, pointing his gun at her. Martha slowly raised her head and, on seeing him, cocked her eyebrow. For a moment Lester was confused – he hadn't anticipated this reaction. Sean and Liam joined him, and they all watched as Martha leaned back in her chair, slowly removed her reading glasses and offered the three of them a courteous smile.

'Ah, Mr O'Rourke. I think this may be of interest to you,' she said, holding out to him the latest copy of her will.

Brendan's eyes were stuck steadfastly to the rear-view mirror and when he caught a glimpse of Riley running towards him he sighed with relief. Riley pulled the passenger door open and fell into the car. They didn't speak, they just looked at each other momentarily. Then Brendan called 999.

Jemima was stood in the back garden at Clouds Reach, tucked behind the cherry trees, in the shadows where she knew Brendan's brothers and father wouldn't see her when they broke in. She held the gun Cassie had given her; it felt heavy and awkward. As the O'Rourkes passed by, she had held her breath. She didn't want to give them any clue she was there. Now she didn't feel so brave. She thought back to the conversation she and Brendan had had about this – he wouldn't hear of her joining him and he'd suggested that, instead, she meet Minnie for a drink after work. She'd agreed to his suggestion but had no intention of following it through. She felt guilty about deliberately tricking him but she couldn't leave Martha unprotected; she had already lost too much and she couldn't lose the final link to her own family.

Lester had pulled his ski mask up to read Martha's will. He couldn't believe his eyes – Jemima was no longer the sole beneficiary. The whole of the estate, including Bridget's share, was now bequeathed to Battersea Dogs Home. His roar resounded around the house, filling every corner of it.

'You see, Mr O'Rourke, I am worth nothing to you dead,' Martha informed him with a self-satisfied smile.

He grabbed her viciously and dragged her from behind the desk, forced her into an armchair and leaned into her face. 'You're worth nothing to me alive either,' he growled, before turning his fury on his sons and shouting at them for their carelessness – their betrayal.

'Stop it!' Jemima screamed.

The O'Rourkes turned to her, surprised to see her in the doorway. She had followed them in, while keeping her distance, and now she was facing them, holding the gun out in front of her.

'Don't hurt her. She's done nothing to deserve this, so leave her alone,' she continued, her voice surprisingly strong and clear.

She stared straight at Lester who was eyeing her coldly. 'You got her to change the will, to leave the lot to the dogs' home! You think you can have a fucking laugh at my expense, you cheeky fucking bitch?' he snarled.

When they had visited Martha a couple of days ago, Brendan had insisted she got her will changed immediately, in case anything was to happen to her; he was adamant that he didn't want to be included in the inheritance in any way. They had talked about Jemima still inheriting, but on the condition that he would receive none of the money. They had left it with Martha to discuss with Mr Harrington, her solicitor. So Jemima was as surprised by this as Lester was. Jemima glanced at her aunt, but Martha gave nothing away. She tried to pull herself upright in the chair and look solidly at Jemima but she looked fragile. For the first time in her life, Jemima saw that her aunt was frightened.

'It's up to my aunt who she leaves her money to. Please let her go,' Jemima said, still trying to hold the gun firm.

'Then stop covering for him. It's got your conniving husband written all over this,' Lester growled.

'If you really want to get to him, the best way is through me,' she continued and watched the cogs whirr in Lester's mind.

'Where is he?' growled Lester.

He doesn't know I'm here,' she replied weakly.

'Who knows you're here?' Lester asked. Jemima remained mute.

A tense, ominous silence fell on the room as all three of the O'Rourkes stared at her. Then Liam lunged towards her, taking her by surprise, grabbing her gun and yanking her towards him. He stared down at her, his eyes inching over her body, stripping her bare. He turned to the desk and started towards it, dragging Jemima with him. Lester looked on with amusement, leaning back against a cabinet and folding his arms across his chest.

Martha gasped and shouted at them, letting them know how disgusted she was. Before Liam got to the desk Sean spoke out.

'I should go first, I'm the eldest.'

Liam stared back at him, disgruntled.

'Technically, I am,' interjected Lester, while looking them both up and down. He walked over to Jemima and dragged a rough-skinned forefinger down the side of her face and across her collarbone, stopping at her shoulder. Then he swung her to face him, roughly removed her jacket, unzipped her jeans and force-fully pulled them open. He tucked his hands inside and grabbed at her bottom. The smell of stale cigarettes clung to his clothes which, mixed with his cheap aftershave, made her feel sick, caus-ing her to turn her head away from him. But she could feel him pulling her closer, all the while his rough hands continued to grope her, finding the edge of her knickers and carelessly pulling them down with her jeans.

Martha was quietly sobbing; her cries, pleading with them to stop, had gone unanswered, along with her insults about their barbaric behaviour. Lester leaned in close to Jemima's ear. His tongue extended and brushed against her lobe. Jemima heaved involuntarily.

Suddenly, he violently twisted her face back to him. She was greeted with a snarl, a look of indignation at her reaction.

'I'll go last, I don't want to be rushed,' he said menacingly, pulling her upwards by her face until she was standing on her tiptoes. Her hands were tightly wrapped around his wrist and her eyes were forced to meet his. She could see his perverse desire sparking behind them. He let go of her just as roughly and resumed leaning against the cabinet, lighting a cigarette and settling in for the show.

Sean moved between her and Liam; he faced her for a while, watching her breathe heavily as she wiped an escaped tear from her face. She couldn't look at him. She was biting her lip nervously.

'Please, I implore you not to do this young man. You can have whatever you want, but not this,' cried Martha, sensing his stalling as being an opportunity to renegotiate.

Lester picked his handgun up off the top of the cabinet and marched over to her. 'You can't be trusted you old bag!' he snapped, before jamming the handle of the gun into the side of her face. Martha's head swung violently and she fell quiet. Jemima screamed and tried to go to her, but Sean grabbed her around the waist and pulled her back to him.

'Get the fuck on with it will yer!' shouted Liam.

With one arm still firmly around her waist Sean used his other hand, still carrying the gun, to clear the desk. Pulling Jemima around to face him yet avoiding her eye, he manhandled her onto the desk and tugged her jeans further downwards, forcing her legs apart with his. Still holding her firmly with one arm, he placed his gun on the chair next to the desk. Aware of his father's and brothers' anticipation he pulled her shirt apart. Jemima looked down at the damage and gasped before she looked back at him. She was stunned that he would go through with this, this man who had held her so gently after he had saved her from the Gypsies. She tried to catch his eye, appeal to him to stop. He looked back at her, his pellucid blue eyes keeping his feelings locked away. Leaning into her, he cupped the back of her head; he could feel her heart pounding against his chest. She was shaking. He turned his head towards the side of her face, his lips brushed against her jaw and he felt her flinch with fright. She felt so delicate, her fine bones and soft hair held precariously in his firm grasp.

'You must really love him to go through with this,' he whispered and felt her turn her head slightly to him. Her eyes were now shut and there was a teardrop balancing on the end of her long lashes. 'Brendan doesn't deserve this loyalty,' he added, and saw her lips twitch in response to his name. She opened her eyes and looked at him. 'He doesn't deserve you.'

She pulled back from him, sharply. 'And you do?' she whispered fiercely, watching his response. He broke eye contact with her, momentarily too ashamed to look at her. When he did look back at her, his face had changed; his expression was functional.

He pushed her firmly back against the desk. She watched as he unbuckled his jeans and pushed them off his hips. She felt the coarse skin on his large hands against the insides of her thighs, felt them find their way upwards. She turned her head and gazed out of the large window that overlooked the back garden. It was dark outside, the window providing her with a black canvas as she forced her mind to recall childhood memories of playing out there amongst the flowers and bees; hazy sunny afternoons, running around barefoot, the sun warming her skin, her favourite floppy sunhat casting a halo-like shadow around her head. She was there now, the heady scent of the peonies and roses catching on the summer breeze and carrying her away from this nightmare.

Brendan's phone buzzed. Glancing at the screen he saw Minnie's number.

'Brendan, she hasn't shown. I called her work and she left at lunchtime. I'm at your apartment and no one is here, and she's not answering her phone,' Minnie told him, struggling to stay calm.

'Shit!'

'She isn't with you is she?' Minnie asked.

'Shit,' Brendan repeated. 'No,' he said, figuring out what Jemima must have done.

'Do you think she has gone to be with her aunt?'

'Yes, I've got to go,' he told her and hung up. Riley was looking at him, picking up the gist of the conversation.

'Why couldn't she bloody well stay put!' he shouted as started his car's engine.

When the doorbell rang at Lowlands Lyla carried on watching her soap opera, assuming that one of the others would get it. It rang again and, belligerently, Lyla got up.

'Where the bloody hell is Cassie?' she cursed.

She grabbed the dogs, who were barking aggressively, and shut them in the study before she tugged at the front door, which was stiff and swollen from lack of use.

She was greeted by a middle-aged woman and a tall man with a thin film of stubble clinging to his chin.

'Good evening. Would it be possible to speak with Lester O'Rourke?' asked the woman.

'He's not here,' replied Lyla curtly, her eyes narrowing with suspicion.

'Are you Mrs Lyla O'Rourke?' the woman continued firmly, undeterred.

Lyla threw her a quick nod and scowled as Anne-Marie appeared at her side.

'Mum, what's going on?'

Lyla ignored her and continued to stare at the strangers on the doorstep. 'I am Lyla O'Rourke. What d'you want?' she asked.

The woman revealed her police badge. 'We are investigating the disappearance of Joseph Shanly; we believe your husband may be able to help us with our inquiries.'

Lyla stared at her with disbelief. She needed Lester. She needed him to tell her what to do. She needed him right now.

Brendan ran into the house. His heart was pumping hard as he took the stairs two at a time, and raced towards Martha's study.

As he swung into the doorway the sight in front of him nearly knocked him flat. He grabbed the door frame in order to stay upright. His bellow, from deep within his rib cage, filled the room, drawing everyone's attention to him. 'Get away from her!'

Sean turned his head towards Brendan.

'Get away from her now!' he shouted again.

Liam stepped to the side of Sean and pointed his gun straight at Brendan's head.

'Do you really think that's going to stop me from getting to her?' Brendan told him, stepping into the room. He looked back at Sean.

'Get the fuck off her right now!' he shouted and watched as Sean raised his head, looking at him coldly but refusing to move, keeping his hands firmly clamped on Jemima's thighs. Brendan continued to stare at him. He couldn't afford to let his gaze fall to Jemima; he knew he wouldn't be able to stop himself if he saw her face, and he needed to think, needed to be clear about what he was doing.

'Drop the gun, Liam,' said Riley, coming up behind Brendan and brandishing a handgun Liam had given him earlier. Liam looked at him with disbelief.

'You! You were the fucking grass! I told you it weren't nothing to do with me!' he shouted at his father.

'Sean, listen to me, leave her be. You are better than this, better than those two,' Brendan said.

Sean looked back at him. He could see the fear in Brendan's face; he could see how desperate he was to save her, for her not to be damaged. He could also see Riley behind him, pointing his pistol straight at Liam. Sean then turned his attention to Jemima. He looked down at her; her face was turned to Brendan, her bottom lip quivering. A small laugh escaped him and he looked back at Brendan.

'Isn't this where you tell me that if I wanted her I only had to ask?' Sean said steadily.

Brendan exhaled sharply. 'Is that what all this has been about for you? Tess?'

Sean continued to stare at him, refusing to answer.

Becoming irritated with what was going on, Lester let out a low growl. 'Ah, for fuck's sake, I'm getting sick of this!' he snapped, grabbing his gun and pointing it at Brendan. Brendan looked at him and swallowed hard as the urgent cries of police sirens started to fill the room. As the sirens grew louder, the room became filled in swirls of blue light.

Lester looked around him then turned his attention to Brendan.

'You fucking bastard!' he barked and Brendan watched helplessly as Lester's grip tightened on his gun.

The explosion rang around the room, deafeningly loud, and Brendan waited to feel the burning pain of a bullet tearing through his body. He looked down at his legs, uncertain as to why he was still standing, when he noticed that his father had slumped to the ground, shouting in agony and clutching his leg. Then his attention was caught by the wisps of smoke coming from the gun Sean was holding. Sean was staring at his father writhing on the ground, still pointing his gun at him.

Slowly Brendan realised what Sean had done. He looked back at Sean and his mouth fell open; words jumped around in his head but struggled to form quickly enough before everything became chaotic. Clouds Reach filled with shouts as the police burst in, pouring through the house in a black wave. Sean could see that two armed policemen had him in their sights, so he let go of his gun, letting it fall heavily to the floor, and obediently held up his hands in surrender. Immediately, he was sprung upon by an officer, who pushed him face first into the wall before handcuffing him. Brendan rushed to Jemima and grabbed her tightly. She felt lifeless; as floppy as a rag doll. He held her to him, not wanting her to witness what was going on. He saw another officer bend down to Martha and heard him radio for an ambulance. He looked back at Sean and, with disbelief, watched as he was taken away.

Chapter 45

THE QUEUE FOR visiting moved slowly. Brendan had removed his shoes, been scanned and patted down, and now he was moving his tongue around his open mouth while a prison officer peered inside. It felt invasive and he caught himself scowling at the guard, who looked slyly at him before calling, 'Next.'

Brendan was then led with the other visitors through to a large, sterile hall filled with grey tables and plastic chairs, neatly laid out in rows. The other visitors appeared more familiar with the routine, quickly settling themselves in. Brendan self-consciously selected a table at the edge of the hall. His chair scraped on the polished floor as he pulled it in, and he looked around nervously. When everyone was seated, the prison seemed to jolt into motion. He could hear the distant slamming of metal doors and the deep echoing cries of instructions coming from the prison guards.

He saw a line of prisoners appear, each one standing still for their final search. Brendan spotted Sean lining up; he now doubted why he had come, and thoughts of leaving entered his mind as he watched Sean glare at the guards, who continued to jostle the prisoners along. But when Sean was released into the visiting area, he strode purposefully over to Brendan, and Brendan realised that it was too late now – he was going to have to face him. Sean roughly pulled out his seat and sat down opposite and the two brothers stared at each other blankly for a moment.

'I'm surprised you're here,' Sean said flatly.

'I nearly didn't come. After all, you did try to rape my wife,' Brendan bit back.

'I also saved your life.'

'One doesn't cancel out the other,' Brendan snapped and Sean looked down at his hands and studied them, while Brendan glowered at him. He hadn't anticipated feeling this angry towards him.

'How is Jemima?' Sean asked.

Brendan looked away before answering. 'She has good days and bad days. The bad days outweigh the good ones at the moment.'

'And her aunt?'

'She had a stroke. She's recovering but she can't walk. She's lost feeling down the right side of her body where Dad hit her.'

Sean sighed heavily. 'I'm sorry.'

'Jesus, Sean. Sorry?' Brendan's hands were shaking; he clenched his fists and pushed them into the table.

'Yeah I am,' replied Sean and looked back up at his brother. 'You probably won't believe me, but when Jemima turned up I knew you'd come for her. I thought that if I got to her first then I could play for time. I'd never have hurt her and I wouldn't have let Dad or Liam touch her. I would've stopped them.'

Brendan looked away; the idea of his father or Liam with Jemima repulsed him. He sat for a few moments staring at the random pattern in the grey flooring, trying to digest what Sean had told him. He wanted to hate Sean. He hated them all for what they did, but he particularly wanted to hate Sean.

'What she did was very brave, but I couldn't stand by and let that happen. I would've taken them out,' Sean told him.

Sean's comment dislodged Brendan's anger and he struggled to hold onto his hate. He looked back at him and shook his head.

'Would you?' he asked, his voice barely audible.

Sean nodded. 'No question.'

They both fell silent, continuing to stare at each other for a while.

'Why the fuck did you get involved? You had everything to live for. What about Georgie? Look at you, shut away in here. How long are you going to get?'

'My solicitor reckons fifteen to twenty, if I'm lucky.'

'For fuck's sake, Sean!' Brendan exclaimed.

'There's Joe's murder too. I'm getting done for being involved in that, as well as the aunt's hit and run, plus the break-in – and we were armed – they're shit hot on that.'

'Fuck,' Brendan sighed, rubbing the back of his neck.

'Still, you're in the right place. They didn't get you for Joe?' Sean asked.

'No, I had an alibi – I was with Cassie that night. Apparently we were having an affair. It was why Jemima and I weren't getting on too well, why I kept coming back at the weekends. I thought everyone knew that,' Brendan answered sarcastically, but Sean nodded and smiled slowly.

'You were always the smart one.'

'Not really. Sean, I asked you why?'

Sean pondered the question carefully. 'I had to take sides. That's what they're like – you have to take sides,' he finally explained.

'Why theirs?'

Sean sighed heavily. 'I wanted you to lose everything, to know what it was like. It didn't seem right, you being so happy and loved-up and stuff.'

Brendan remained silent; he wasn't entirely surprised by the answer.

'You had what I had once, before you took it away, and it didn't seem fair, watching the two of you together. And you'd met her and married her and I knew nothing about it, and I realised just how far apart we'd grown.'

'You did the same with Tess,' interjected Brendan sharply.

'I let you know.'

'Not till afterwards,' retorted Brendan, indignantly.

Sean hung his head. 'After Liam beat you all those years ago, everything seemed so bad between us. I never thought you would forgive me for letting that happen.'

Brendan looked away again, his jaw tensed with the memory of that fight.

'You said a while back that it was my pride and anger that was stopping me from moving on, with Tess and with you. You were right, but by the time I figured it out I was too far in, and going along with them was easier than making it up with you.'

'You could've let me know,'

'I made sure Riley knew. I talked Dad into letting him in on it, told him he could be useful. I knew Riley would tell you, he's always looked up to you. I also knew he wanted a way out for him and Cassie.'

'You knew about Cassie?' exclaimed Brendan.

'It's hard to keep secrets at Lowlands, you should know that,' Sean replied.

'Does Liam know?'

'He does now, but what can he do? He's in here.'

'Do you see much of him and Dad?'

'No, they've deliberately kept us separate. The old man's still raging at me for shooting him. I tried to get a message to him, to tell him that I figured out we were sunk and if he'd have shot you he'd never get out. But he's paranoid; thinks everyone's out to get him now.'

They both fell silent. Despite Brendan having so much he wanted to say to Sean, it was hard doing it surrounded by strangers, sitting in this hall, knowing the clock was ticking and that time would be called soon. 'Do you need anything?' Brendan asked cautiously.

'No, I'm okay. I'm in the right place. I've done some bad things.'

Brendan stared at him; he took in his large blue eyes and his strong features. He realised that Sean had really just swapped one institution for another. How different was life with his family to this? The daily drudgery, the bullying, the hierarchy – this was all Sean had ever known. Life at Lowlands had given him the strategies to cope well with prison.

'I miss Georgie and Tess. Can you make sure they're okay?' Sean's voice brought Brendan back from his thoughts.

'Tess?' asked Brendan, surprised.

'You were right, she took me back,' said Sean, breaking into a half smile.

'Has she been to see you?'

'Not yet.'

Brendan felt Sean's hand envelop his, wrapping itself around his curled up fist.

'We good?' Sean asked.

Brendan stared back at him; he was reminded of climbing trees and diving into freezing cold lakes on scorching hot days. Echoes of their childhood rang in his ears and he felt his throat tighten with the emotion that came attached to those memories.

'We're getting there,' he replied.

CHAPTER 46

TESS HANDED BRENDAN a mug of tea. She had been surprised to hear from him and even more surprised when he asked if he could come over. In her kitchen, Brendan made small talk while she made the tea and sent Georgie outside to play football. Too quickly, Brendan ran out of the easy things to say and they both ended up looking out of the kitchen window at Georgie.

'It's starting to snow, he won't be able to see the ball soon,' she half laughed.

'He seems happy enough,' replied Brendan light-heartedly. 'I've been to see Sean today,' he said tentatively, and saw her brow crease as she buried her face into her mug. Finally, she took a sip, carefully lowered the mug and turned to look at him. 'He told me you had got back together. He needs you Tess, he misses you both badly.'

She put her mug down and covered her face with her hands. Brendan noticed her shoulders were shaking and carefully he wrapped his arms around her, letting her cry softly into him.

'I'm pregnant,' she said, looking up to see his face stretch with the shock of what she had told him.

'It all happened so quickly. He just turned up, we weren't thinking. Why does he always do this to me?'

'Because he's Sean,' Brendan replied limply.

'How am I going to raise his baby without him here?' she cried, while he rubbed her shoulders gently.

'What are you going to do?' he asked.

'I don't know, I just don't know.'

He reached for her hand. She let him curl his fingers around hers and squeeze them softly. 'Whatever you decide will be the right choice Tess, and you're not on your own, not any more. Things have changed now.'

Tess smiled back at him. She wiped the tears from her face and sniffed. 'You don't have to keep rescuing everyone you know,' she told him.

When Brendan left Tess and Georgie, the snow had started to fall in large flakes, hitting the ground silently and dissolving the moment they made contact with the wet pavement. He set off in the direction of Lowlands, where he had arranged to meet Riley and Cassie with Jemima. Afterwards, they were going to head down to Martha's.

Riley and Cassie were going to move into Clouds Reach while Martha was still in hospital. They would stay on when she returned, to help look after her. Cassie had proved to be invaluable in helping to care for Jemima in the aftermath of events and the two of them had built up a strong rapport; so it was peace of mind for Jemima knowing that her aunt would be well looked-after too.

But as much as Brendan was looking forward to Cassie and Riley moving out of his and Jemima's small apartment, he was also apprehensive about being on his own with Jemima. Her silences unnerved him and he still felt responsible for what had happened.

As he pulled into the drive he could see the fresh tyre marks of Riley's truck in the thin layer of snow that had now settled. Brendan parked by the house; the place was practically silent except for the faint bark of the dogs in the background. He climbed out of his car as Riley climbed out of the truck. They briefly glanced at each other before Brendan went over to the truck and leaned in through the driver's window.

'We won't be long,' he told Jemima. 'We're just picking up some stuff Riley needs.'

He watched as she stared out of the windscreen. Nothing seemed to be registering. He looked to Cassie for encouragement but her attention had been drawn to the woods, towards the outbuilding, where the tatty ribbons of police tape were just visible from where they had marked out Joe's grave.

A near-empty bottle of vodka and an overflowing ashtray sat in front of Lyla at the kitchen table. She looked haggard; deep lines had grown around her eyes and mouth and her face seemed to have sunk, with soft jowls hanging from her jaw.

'Get what you came for then get out,' she slurred.

Seeing his mother like this distressed Riley; he went to go to her but Brendan grabbed his arm. 'Come on, do as she says,'

Brendan said, cajoling him towards the stairs. Lyla glared at Brendan, her fury chiselled across her face.

They found Riley's room just as he had left it. His duvet was in a rumpled heap at the bottom of the bed, his clothes were still on the floor and the curtains remained half drawn. He went over to his drawers and started to rummage through them.

'I had to get out in such a hurry that I couldn't take it with me. Cassie tried to get it but she couldn't either,' Riley explained as he pulled out a tightly wrapped bundle of bank notes and shoved it into his back pocket. He reached for a dog-eared cigar box with the edges of photographs sticking out of it. 'Some photos of us as kids – I didn't want to leave them behind,' he said. He breathed in sharply. 'I guess this is it then. Do you think we'll ever come back?'

'Who knows?' Brendan shrugged and they both stood for a moment, looking around. Then they made their way downstairs and back to the kitchen where Anne-Marie had joined their mother.

'You've got some nerve coming back here,' Anne-Marie announced viciously.

Brendan tapped Riley on the shoulder to keep moving.

'That little bitch with you?' she continued, stepping in front of them.

Brendan stopped. 'What little bitch is that Anne-Marie? Because the only one I can see is standing in front of me.'

'Oh, let me take my pick then. What about that pikey? You're a fool for letting her get her claws into you, Riley. She don't love you – she's just using you. You're just too stupid to see it.' She paused to inspect the intended damage her comment would cause Riley then turned to Brendan. 'Or your wife – that stuck-up little bitch. We were never good enough for her were we? Or, last but not least, there's our little bitch of a sister, running out on us at a time like this, when her mother needs her.'

'Shut up Anne-Marie. You're just as desperate to get out of this place as we were because you know full well that if you stay, you'll end up like her,' Brendan said pointing at his mother. 'And just look at it. D'you want to end up like that?' he sneered. 'Come on, let's get out of this shit hole,' he said to Riley. When he got to the utility room he stopped and picked up his dog's lead and whistled for him. Kaiser obediently came over to him, with his tail between his legs. Brendan grabbed a chunk of his fur and shook him gently. 'Come on boy, I'm not leaving you here,' he told him.

Cassie had started to get jumpy and, knowing she hated being confined, Jemima had climbed out of the truck and encouraged her to do the same. They were both staring towards the house, with snow falling heavily now, catching in their hair and eyelashes. Cassie spotted them first, and she stopped shuffling from foot to foot. They watched the figures walking towards them through the snow.

'He's got Kaiser!' exclaimed Cassie.

Brendan stopped in front of Jemima, the dog standing between them.

'I couldn't leave him Jem, not with her; she's not fit to look after anything,' he said and he watched, after weeks of waiting anxiously, as she finally broke into a smile.

Lyla's jagged scream sliced through the air, startling them, and as they turned to see what was going on, they saw her staggering towards them, swinging a shotgun haphazardly in her arms. She stared at them like a wild animal ready to fight for survival as she swung the gun, with great effort, up onto her shoulder and stopped.

'You're never going to have him! You will never take him from me!' she shouted hysterically. They stared back at her in horror, watching her take aim, sinking under the weight of the gun and too much vodka.

The gun fired with a solid, decisive boom, which echoed around them and rolled out into the distance before being swallowed up by the trees and the snow. They looked at each other, trying to figure out if Lyla's shot had made contact.

Riley's hands reached for his stomach before he concertinaed to the ground, as if his backbone had been yanked from him like a ripcord. As he dropped the cigar box, the flimsy lid fell open and the photographs of his childhood tumbled out; faded images of the precious memories he had returned for now scattered around him. An icy wind caught their edges, flipping them over in the snow like playing cards.

Cassie fell to her knees beside him, grabbing his head in her hands, trying to comfort him. Jemima, too, dropped to the ground beside Riley, the cold from the snow biting into her knees. She took one of his hands, stroking it with hers.

'Brendan, do something!' she screamed. But he just stared rigidly down at Riley, his face frozen with disbelief. Jemima turned back to Riley. She let go of his hand and wiped the hair from his brow as a thin line of blood escaped his mouth and started to creep its way down towards his jaw.

Cassie clawed at him. With great effort he turned his eyes to her as she took his hands; she clamped them against her stomach, pressing hard.

'I love you both,' he rasped and then Jemima saw the last of his life leave him, peeling away from him like film. His chest fell still and his limbs went limp, but his eyes kept their brilliant blue, their charge still electric.

'He's gone Cassie. I'm sorry, he's gone,' Jemima whispered to her, her voice squeezed high in her throat.

Cassie's body started to shake; a great tension inside her was being activated. She looked down at her hands, still clasping Riley's to her womb. Slowly, she let go of them to reveal her stomach protruding in a neat, small mound.

'You're carrying his baby,' Jemima gasped and Cassie nodded her head in short, stilted movements. Then she looked at her hands, turning them slowly over and seeing Riley's deep red blood shining brightly on her palms and along her fingers. The blood was still warm, but the cold air was cooling it quickly, draining the last signs of his life away from her.

She looked up at Jemima. 'She was right – Nora – she got it right. It was his blood,' she choked. Then the force of her pain escaped in a long high-pitched howl and the tears that she had kept locked away since she had first met Brendan, since she had first come to Lowlands, that she had repeatedly refused to let fall, broke free like a river bursting its banks.

Brendan turned abruptly, striding over to his mother who was swaying and pointing the gun towards him.

'You've killed him!' he bellowed.

She dropped the gun a couple of inches and looked puzzled by what he was telling her.

'Riley is dead! You've fucking killed him!' he shouted, snatching the gun away from her. She continued to look up at him, confused, like she had joined a conversation halfway through. Brendan turned the gun and jammed the handle into the side of her head, knocking her to the ground; then he turned it on her and stared down the barrel at his mother lying on the floor. Her head was split open just above the temple, but she was still conscious and now becoming very aware of what he was about to do.

Anne-Marie had run out of the kitchen, screaming at Brendan to stop. Jemima turned to see what was happening and she, too, saw what Brendan was about to do. She scrambled to her feet, losing her footing slightly as she threw her body into a sprint. She swung herself between him and Lyla, the shotgun jabbing sharply against her breastbone.

'No!' she cried, frantically searching his eyes, trying to pull him back from where his anger had dragged him. 'Brendan, no more! Please, no more,' she implored.

His mouth momentarily flinched and his eyes slowly focused on hers. The bright blue that had caught her attention just over a year ago was as vivid as ever. He blinked sluggishly. He felt exhausted and dropped the gun to his side. Jemima exhaled and wrapped her arms around him, holding her head tight against his chest, picking up his heartbeat and reconnecting with its steady thump. 'No more,' he said hollowly.

CHAPTER 47

Two years later

JEMIMA, BRENDAN AND Martha were sat in the downstairs study at Clouds Reach opposite Mr Harrington of Harrington, Finch and Bone Solicitors. Mr Harrington adjusted his tie, lightly touched the papers in front of him, and coughed nervously.

'I need to make absolutely sure this is what you all want; after all, Jemima, with your own family growing, I need to be sure you understand that this is a sizeable portion of the estate you are agreeing to be given away.'

Jemima smiled and reached for Brendan's hand while rubbing her stomach with the other; she was seven months' pregnant and could feel their baby moving gently inside her, responding to Mr Harrington's voice.

'We are sure. We have all discussed this. She has been such a huge help and we couldn't have managed without her. This is what we all want,' she replied and turned to Brendan who was gently rubbing her back and smiling at her.

Mr Harrington turned to Martha. 'Well then,' he smiled, 'we just need the signatures.'

They said their goodbyes and watched Mr Harrington climb into his shiny vintage car. Brendan shut the front door and Jemima turned excitedly to him.

'Come on, let's go and tell her,' she said, clutching Martha's left shoulder and smiling excitedly as Martha managed to squeeze her hand.

Brendan lapped up her enthusiasm, treasuring it. Two years ago he thought this side of her was lost forever. But gradually she had come back to him, piece by piece, and now they were expecting their first child; they were expanding beyond the two of them. They had both come a long way. He took the handles of Martha's wheelchair and they made their way out to the garden.

Cassie was standing on the lawn, the warm grass tickling the soles of her feet. She was trying to find him and knew he must be hiding, probably in the large rhododendron which was spilling with huge magenta blooms. As she called his name, her voice was light and content.

'Riley, come on, where are you?' she laughed.

The shrubs rustled, then he appeared; his white-blond hair was ruffled, his cheeks were round and rosy and, as he threw her a broad smile, there was the unmistakeable flash of his bright blue eyes – his father's legacy. The toddler waddled towards her and held his arms out for her to scoop him up. She intuitively pulled him tightly to her, his soft doughy arms encircling her, and he buried his head into her neck. The smell of him still overwhelmed her – sugar and soap, sweet and clean. He giggled as she squeezed him, a soft, tumbling laugh he only had for her, because he was hers – all hers – from the moment they had shared the same heartbeat. He was the child she was told she could never have. Her miracle – the only thing she had left of his father before he was so cruelly snatched from her. Her son was the most precious thing in her life and all that had been good in it was wrapped up in him.

She could feel someone watching her; her back prickled. She turned with Riley in her arms and looked over to the cherry blossom. She knew he was there watching her. She squinted against the early May sun and saw Brendan step forward, emerging from beneath the boughs heavy with plumes of sparkling white blossom. As he moved, some of the petals fell around him, like tiny stars floating to the ground.

'Cassie, we have something we need to tell you,' he said and she felt Riley squirm in her arms, pushing away so that he could join his uncle. She bent down and released him; he shrieked with exuberance at Brendan's arrival. Brendan lifted him up high so he was flying horizontally in the air, with Brendan's hands firmly clasping his sides. His legs wriggled and his hands reached for Brendan's face, and the two of them laughed together – as if only they got the joke.

Martha loved watching Cassie and Riley; they filled Clouds Reach with life. It reminded her of when she and Bridget had cared for Jemima when she was small and of her mother, Lilly, as an infant. But having a mother and child together in the house gave it substance, returning it to a home once more. She was also grateful to Cassie for moving in with her and becoming her carer; without her she knew that her last days would be spent in a residential home. Martha had become stubborn to the point of making herself ill by refusing Jemima's requests to find a home they could all share. She wanted them to have their own lives, their own home – to live the family life that she and Bridget never had. Now that Jemima was expecting her great, great nephew or niece, she knew her insistence had been the right choice.

Cassie sat on the veranda with the sun warming her back, staring at them and not really believing what they were telling her. She loved it here; the house made her feel safe and it was the first place she had ever really felt able to settle, to put down her roots. She loved looking after Martha. She admired the old lady's determination and loved listening to her stories about the old times. It filled the gaps she had in her own family, giving her a history she could now pass down to Riley.

'So you see, Cassie, we have all discussed this and when I finally pass away we would dearly like you to have Clouds Reach. There are some items Jemima will inherit from the house, certain heirlooms, but the remainder of it will be yours and, of course, you will inherit it furnished,' Martha informed her, some of her words from the stroke still sounding sluggish.

'What do you say, Cassie, do you want it?' Brendan asked her and she looked back at him dumbfounded.

'But it's yours,' she said to Jemima.

'We have my trust funds. We have more than enough,' Jemima said, smiling.

'It will secure your future – yours and Riley's,' Brendan continued. His eyes narrowed slightly, waiting for her response, appreciating her unpredictability. They all watched her as she looked around at the bright borders spilling with blooms and the bees hopping from flower to flower, intoxicated with the abundance of pollen contained in the well-established garden. She looked back at them and smiled.

'It's what I always dreamed of,' she told them.

More by Harri Atkins

If you've enjoyed "Inside the cuckoo's nest" I would love to hear your thoughts, please leave a review on Amazon or Good Reads.

You can also keep up to date with all the news regarding my writing by following me on:

Facebook: Harri Atkins Author

Twitter: @harriatkins

Made in the USA
Charleston, SC
07 December 2016